The Shepherd King
Dawidh, King of Yisrael:

Foundation
Stone

by

D. Avraham

The Shepherd King

Dawidh, King of Yisrael:

Foundation Stone

by

D. Avraham

Beith David Yeshiva Publications
Har Hebron

ISBN: 978-965-91360-1-8

For more information:
Beith David Yeshiva
US: 216-539-7344
Israel: 02-960-5526
e-mail: publications@beithdavid.org
web: www.beithdavid.org

Table of Contents

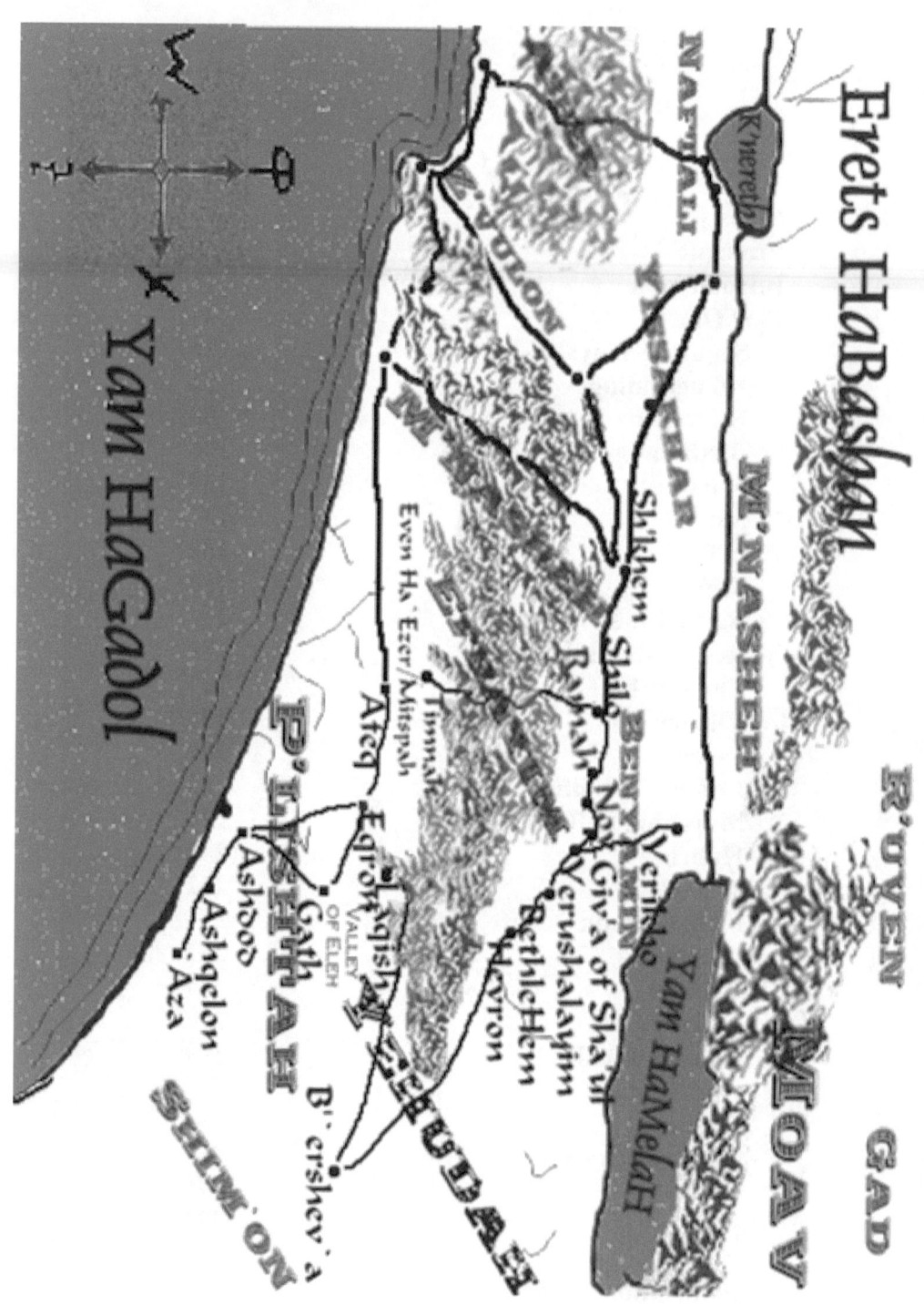

Erets HaBashan

Yam HaGadol

NAFTALI

K'nereth

ZVULON

YISASKHAR

M'NASHEH

Sh'khem

EFRAYIM

Even Ha'Ezer/Mitspah

Timnah

BENYAMIN

Afeq

Na'

Giv'a of Sha'ul

Yeriho

Yerushalayim

BethleHem

Hevron

Eqron

Lakhish

Gath

VALLEY
OF ELEH

B''ershev'a

Ashdod

Ashqelon

Aza

P'LISHTIM

Y'HUDAH

SHIM'ON

M'NASHEH

R'UVEN

GAD

MOAV

Yam HaMelaH

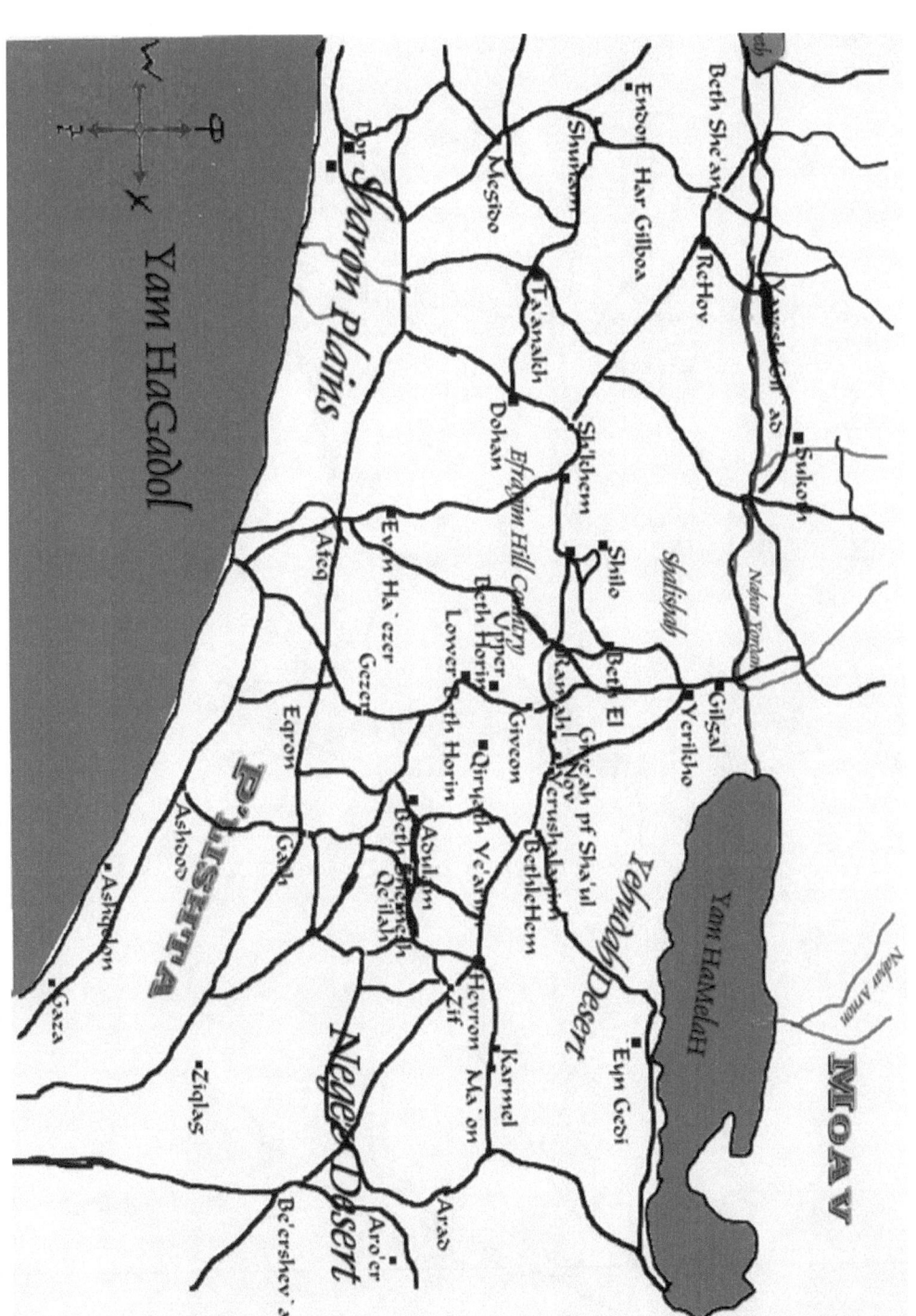

5

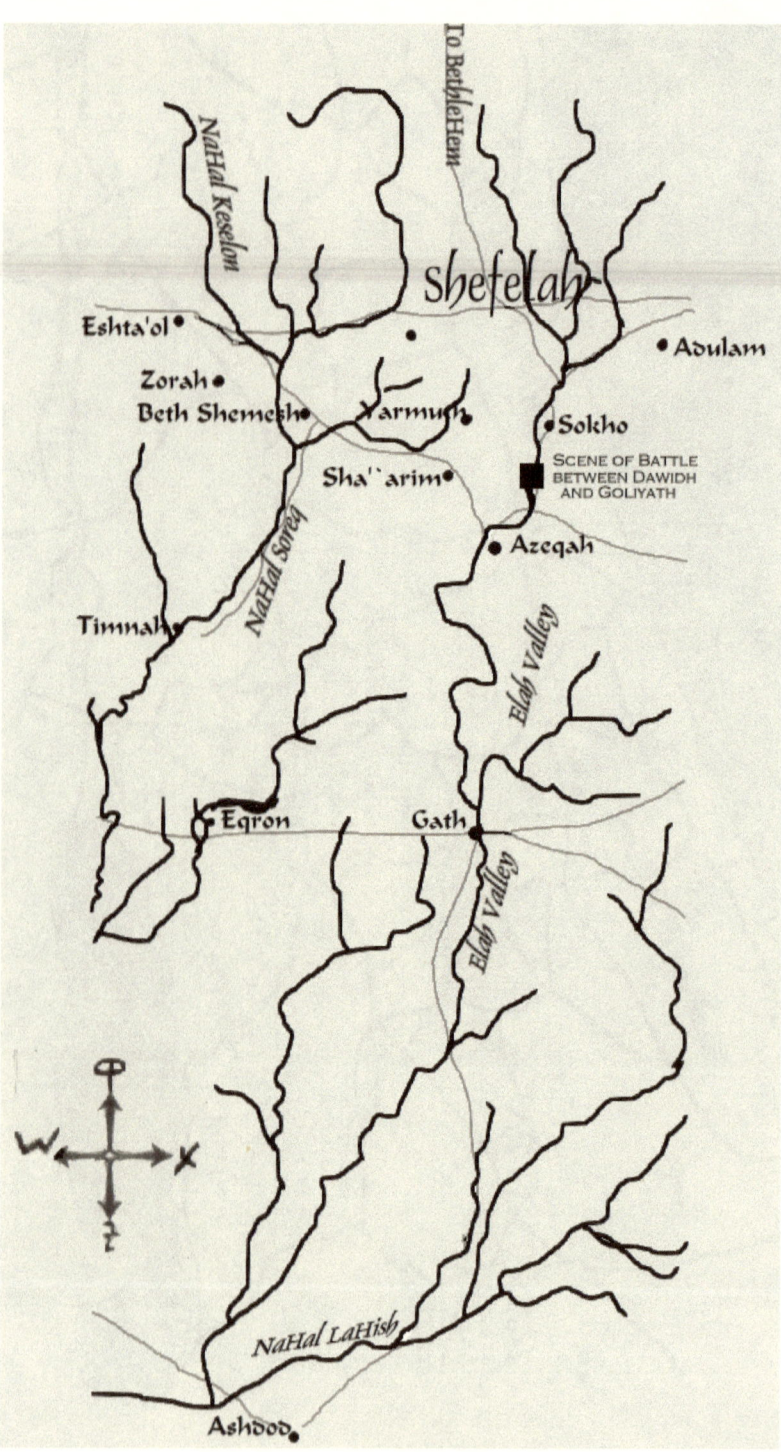

Eshta'ol

Zorah
Beth Shemesh

Adulam

Sokho

SCENE OF BATTLE
BETWEEN DAWIDH
AND GOLIYATH

Sha''arim

Yarmugh

Azeqah

Shefelah

NaHal Keselon

To BethleHem

Timnah

NaHal Soreq

Elah valley

Eqron

Gath

Elah valley

NaHal LaHish

Ashdod

W X

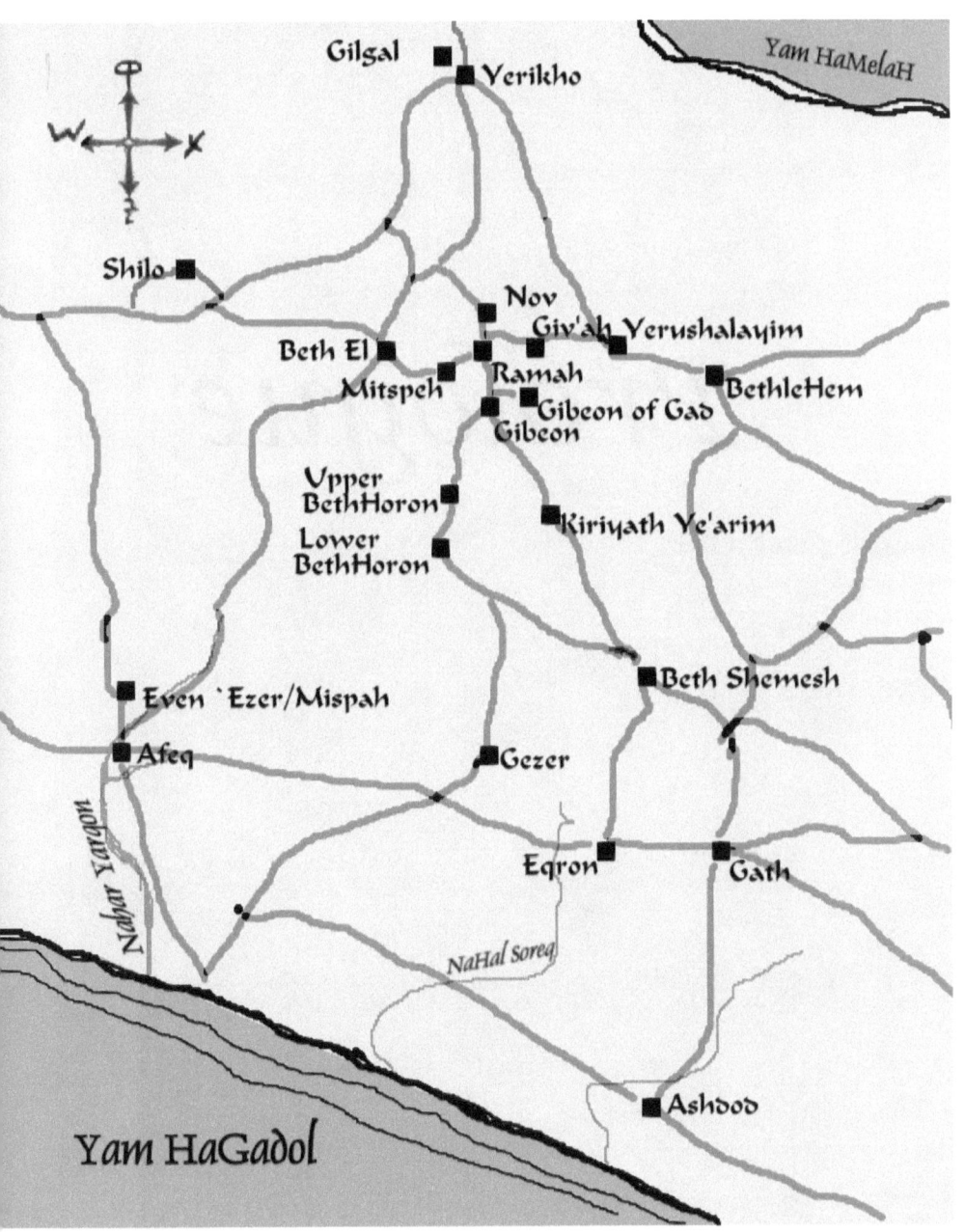

Yam HaMelaH

Gilgal
Yerikho

Shilo

Nov
Giv'ah Yerushalayim
Beth El
Mitspeh Ramah
Gibeon of Gad
Gibeon BethleHem

Upper
BethHoron
Lower Kiriyath Ye'arim
BethHoron

Even `Ezer/Mispah
Afeq Beth Shemesh

Nahar Yarqon
Gezer

Eqron Gath

NaHal Soreq

Yam HaGadol

Ashdod

Prologue

The Daughters of Lot

The Mountains near Tso`ar
500 years before the Exodus

Spotting the cave opening, Lot hesitantly entered, leaving his two daughters behind. He didn't hear anything, and there weren't any droppings on the ground, or any other markings, but he was far too harried today to try and evict some wild beast from his home. He blinked his eyes, trying to force them to adjust to the shift in light. He scanned the cave. It was large, at least three chambers, and blessedly empty. Exhaling a sigh of relief, he called to his daughters. They quickly materialized at his side.

Their clothes and their manner both spoke of wealth and position. But that was over now. Within less than a day, their entire world had been turned upside down. In fact, to their mind, the entire world had been turned upside down. In the minds of the two girls, the three of them might be the only people left in the world. That they had survived, was a miracle. It was only due only to their father's righteousness and the hospitality he extended to the two strangers from the night before.

Those two strangers turned out to be heavenly messengers, angels in disguise of men. At least that's what their father had told them. Their father had met them at the city gates and offered them hospitality. It was a custom forbidden by the city of S'dom, but their father often went against the grain. In gratitude for his hospitality, Lot was warned about the impending doom, and encouraged

9

to save himself and his family. No one had listend to him. With a heavy heart he was forced to leave his married children behind.

While the city was still visible behind them, brimstone and fire rained down on the city. It was awesome and horrible. The smell of smoke still hung in the air. They had been warned not to look back, but their mother couldn't resist. She was too connected to her home town. It was fatal. The girls were still too much in shock to feel the grief of their loss. They were still desperately scrambling to survive, to salvage their own lives. All of them seemed to be balancing on the edge of panic.

Lot sat on a boulder, hanging his head in his hands. He was confused and afraid, unsure what to do. His daughters watched him, themselves wondering about their future. *Was there a future?*

"Our father is old," commented the older daughter to her sister, "but I don't think there is any other man left in the earth." She had been expecting to marry in a few months, though her father hadn't yet arranged a husband.

The younger daughter shook her head. "What do you mean?" she asked.

The older daughter sighed. "I think we're the only people left in the world, and there isn't anyone to wed us, as is the custom of all beings in the world," she explained. "If we don't do something," she suggested, "then humanity will end. Maybe that's why were saved."

"What?" asked her younger sister, confused.

The older daughter gestured with her eyes towards their father.

"You don't mean?" asked the younger sister. She was on the verge of tears. Her mind was overloaded. She couldn't handle anything else.

"Is there any other way?" challenged the older sister.

The younger shook her head. "Father would never agree." Even though she had heard of things like that in S'dom, their father had been appaled by such behavior.

"We have wine," suggested the older daughter. We'll let him drink., and when he is drunk, well." She lowered her voice, even though she was already whispering. "We will preserve his seed."

"I don't know," the younger sister hesitated. She hadn't the strength to argue, but neither did she have the strength to agree to such an outrageous plan. "You go ahead and do what you want." She didn't need to take part in this, she thought.

"Oh no," argued the older sister, reading her thoughts. "You have to do it too. We both have to." "I will lay with him tonight, but tomorrow you have to do it," commanded the older sister.

"Ok," murmered the younger sister. She just wanted her sister to leave her alone.

Lot didn't need much encouragement to drink wine. The older sister presented him with a cup. Lot grunted his thanks. As the dark liquid touched his lips, he closed his eyes. He gulped down the rough wine. His face felt flush immediately. His daughter refilled the cup. Lot was struggling with his own emotions and fears. Silently, he successively emptied the stone cup nearly as fast as his daugter filled it. The numbing sensation that spread across his mind was welcoming.

Finally he stood. The world spun around him and he stumbled into the cave to lie down. The older daughter followed him in, and helped her father to lay down. She was gentle. Her touch was soothing. Caught between the strong wine and his own memories, he didn't really perceive who was with him, or what was taking place. She left long before he awoke.

The next evening, the older daughter said to her sister. "Ok, I laid with Father last night. It's your turn, now." The younger sister turned white. Had she agreed to this? She didn't know what to do. "Let's make him drink wine again tonight, so you can lay with him," prodded her sister.

The younger sister nodded, as afraid to refuse, as she was to agree.

Confusion had clouded Lot's mind all day. Now he had more memories to suppress. When his daughter handed him the cup of wine, he was all the more willing to accept it.

As Lot stumbled into the cave, after finishing his drink. The older daughter prodded her sister. Offering her some instruction, she pushed the younger daughter after their father. As he went to lie down, she entered his bed with him. His fortress of denial secure, Lot allowed his grief and fear to again conceal what was happening. He didn't perceive that his daughter lay with him.

Soon it became apparent that both of Lot's daughters were pregnant with child. The older daughter gave birth to a son, and she named him Mo'av, which means "from father," and he became the progenitor of the nation of Moav. The younger daughter also gave birth to a son, and she named him more discreetly, Ben-`Ami, which means, "son of my people. He was the progenitor of the nation of Ammon.

Introduction

From the first time I laid eyes upon him, I liked him. To this day, I still can't tell you why. But, there was something about this young man that caused my heart, which I had thought long frozen in a state of cynical decay, to soar. I later learned that his name was "Dawid." His name in the language of Yisrael means, "beloved." I would also learn, eventually, that for this young man; this name was at once the essence of truth and the bitterest of irony.

I had been standing in the Valley of Elah with my commander, waiting for one of the Children of Yisrael to answer his challenge. Neither of us really expected anyone to take up the gauntlet. Especially as the days turned into weeks until this morning of the fortieth day, it was clear that Sha'ul's camp was more than a little intimidated. Nevertheless we waited each and every day.

My master, Goliyath the P'lishti, had been steadily undermining the morale of Yisrael, coming out every morning and evening, shouting challenges to the camp of Yisrael that filled even my withered soul with zealous rage for our God. Yes, my God too. Despite my mercenary nature, serving as the shield bearer for the enemy, I suppose my soul was not entirely cut off from my people and my God, the Holy One of Yisrael.

We were just about to turn around and head back to our camp, when that young man, Dawid, made his appearance.

Goliyath stretched his body. "Let's go, Uri'yah, they aren't coming again," he said as he snapped his neck from side to side. My commander laughed, "Cowards. We've already won, Uri'yah." His comment strangely disturbed me. I scowled at my lapse into sentimentality.

Then he caught a glimpse of someone coming out into the valley. "What?" he was taken by surprise. I saw him too, and unexpectedly my heart filled with hope. Maybe today was the day that I had been waiting for. I laughed to myself. I didn't even know I was waiting for something. I had given up on hopes and dreams a long time ago.

Goliyath turned to meet the challenger, and his surprise increased. Anger and contempt soon followed as he went out to meet the fool.

"It's not their 'king,' that's for sure," Goliyath spat, but something told me differently. True, it wasn't King Sha'ul. Goliyath had met him on the battlefield many years ago, when this "king of Yisrael" was just another farmer playing soldier. I also had seen him on few occasions. No, it wasn't Sha'ul the son of Kish. Yet, some inner voice had awakened in me. I couldn't yet put words to the voice. The closest I could come to describe the feelings inside me was … anticipation, or maybe, a vague type of hope. But in what, I had no idea.

On the other hand, my master was clearly disappointed. I could read his thoughts. This young man didn't even have a decent weapon. Goliyath felt cheated. He felt as if he was being mocked.

16

Like some oversized child, he was always afraid that people were laughing at him from behind his back. Goliyath cocked his head to make sure he was seeing correctly. It looked like some shepherd searching for his lost sheep. I know what he was thinking, maybe even hoping: Maybe, this fool stumbled into the battlefield by accident?

"Lose you sheep, boy?" Goliyath's voice was dripping with disdain. He began to approach Dawid. I quickly followed

Finally, Goliyath accepted that this really was the challenger. He shook his head in disgust. He was a well-built, healthy young man. He was full of vigor, but clearly not a seasoned warrior. Goliyath was probably wondering if he had ever even seen a battle. He was muttering to himself. I could barely catch the words. "Why would the `Ivr'im send such a man?" It was beyond contempt. Goliyath was enraged. Someone had just spoiled his mood.

Goliyath released a shout. He noticed the staff, now, and mocked, "Am I a dog, that you come at me with sticks?" Goliyath laughed, but then something caused him to stop. I heard the laughter catch in his throat. Goliyath stared in wonder at the little man standing opposite him. He was calm. There wasn't any fear emanating from him. Goliyath must have concluded that this boy was insane.

Dawid smiled casually. Who was this young man that would tread with confidence in a place where most men would flee. In spite of myself, I liked him. I knew I would have to find out more about this boy. That is, if he managed to survive the next few moments of his life.

He looked so young standing there. Well, maybe not young, so much as fresh and alive. It had been some time actually, sixteen years, since the boy had reached the age of majority amongst his people. Thirteen was a special age for everyone in Yisrael. Yet, like most things for Dawid, that day was bittersweet. The morning of his thirteenth birthday was forever etched onto his soul, for good and for bad. For most, a day like that would have made someone an old man before his years. Dawid was just the opposite. His spirit shone bright, in spite of, or possibly because of, all the hammering his soul received. Like a well worked piece of leather, it would seem that this young man was being constantly stretched and softened by the Almighty Himself, but the light in his eyes never, or at least rarely ever, lost their shine.

***

Standing in the doorway, Dawid hesitated. Expectation, and fear that those hopes would be dashed, pierced his heart like a knife. *Maybe now*, he thought. *Please, Almighty, let it be different now.* Dawid was the seventh son, thus far the youngest, of Yishai of Bethle*H*em. Today was the day that Dawid turned thirteen. Thirteen, the age of majority for the People of Yisrael: It was a very special milestone in the life of a young man. It was the day that he became a man.

Dawid's six older brothers were all seated around the same low table, eating their morning meal. They were engaged in lively conversation, but the conversation came to a standstill as Dawid approached the table.

"What do you want?" Eli'av's acerbic tone bit into Dawid's heart. He was the eldest, and seemed to hold the most contempt for their youngest brother. All of their eyes seemed to bore into Dawid, Eli'av's most of all. Dawid felt their hate and scorn. They probably didn't even know that it was his birthday, today. They certainly didn't care. Dawid wanted more than anything for just one kind word from his older brother. Tears welled up in his eyes. He wanted to run, to hide, but the pain of having his soul torn asunder had welded his feet in place. Dawid's head spun as he waited for his brothers to finish the kill.

"He wants to sit with us," suggested Shim`a, the third son of Yishai.

"What?" Eliav scoffed. "He must have lost his mind. Why would we let *that* sit with us?"

Avinadav, Yishai's second son, looked at Dawid, and his heart cracked a little. He knew why Dawid was there. His eyes shifted from Dawid to his older brother, and sighed. He realized there would be no quarter in his older brother's war against Dawid, but he allowed himself to try. "It's his birthday today. He's thirteen today," offered Avinadav.

Dawid's eyes met Avinadav. Though they were swollen and moist, he tried to offer silent thanks with his glance. Amindav returned an uncomfortable half-smile. He felt sorry for Dawid, but he also felt like a traitor to his older brother. Eliav was not cruel by nature, most of the time. Avinadav didn't know what he had against Dawid, but he was sure that there be must be some justification for his hatred. Eliav didn't act that way with any of the other brothers, or even with the family servants. Avinadav had seen Eliav show kindness in some of the most unlikely places. His attitude towards Dawid was a mystery to him, but he, like the rest of the brothers, trusted his judgment and followed their older brother's lead.

"So what?!" attacked Eliav, "That's supposed to make a difference?" He shot a look of chastisement at his brother. "Don't you have chores to attend to?" Eliav challenged Dawid.

Dawid turned to leave, when their father entered. "What's this?" Yishai asked, looking from Dawid to the brothers seated at the table.

"It's his birthday. He's thirteen today," offered Netan'el.

Yishai shifted uncomfortable. "Ah, well, then." Yishai mechanically placed a hand on Dawid's shoulder. "Well, then ... eh, *Mazal tov*," he said flatly, his mouth almost curling into a smile.

Where his brothers were mean, his father was distant and reserved. He didn't seem to possess any fatherly warmth for Dawid. It might have been okay, except that Dawid was acutely aware of the love and warmth Yishai had, and regularly showed, for his brothers. It was as if he only had enough love for six sons, and by the time Dawid came he hadn't any left. His sterile politeness towards Dawid pierced his heart even deeper than his brother's cruelty.

It was true that Dawid did have a reputation for being a troublemaker, a big troublemaker. It had become a regular occurrence for Yishai to be accosted with accusations that his youngest son had either stolen or damaged something.

Dawid always maintained that the accusations against him were totally unfounded. He was the victim of a bad reputation, and people needed someone to blame. Anytime something bad happened in Bethle*H*em, Dawid was automatically blamed. His culpability was always assumed, evidence or not. How could his father believe all those lies about him?

But he did. Every time someone made even the most outrageous of claims, Yishai made restitution without so much as a protest. Dawid didn't understand it. His father was a judge in Yisrael, and an expert at getting to the truth of the matter. Yet, he didn't even ask Dawid for an explanation.

Dawid looked up, into his father's eyes, searching for something, some answer to all this suffering. Yishai returned a blank stare. "Thank you, *avi,* Father," said Dawid quickly, before turning and running out of the house. Tears were streaming down his eyes, as he ran. He just wanted to go, but he didn't know to where. As he ran he shouted to the gates of heavens, imploring his Father in Heaven to turn a kind eye towards him. Something. *Anything*. He ran till his lungs gasped for air. Then slowly, almost aimlessly, he turned back towards the family estate. Dawid headed for his great-grandmother's room. Mamma Ruth could always help soothe the pain.

"I know about being an outcast, my little lamb," Mamma Ruth's voice was soothing. She stroked his hair of his head as it lay on her lap. Dawid felt her voice blanket his soul and warm his heart, fanning the dying embers, so that the spark wouldn't die.

"The Holy One is preparing you for something grand," her voice was full of confidence, though Ruth herself wondered at the suffering of her great grandchild's soul. "Everything has a purpose," she soothed, assuring herself as much as the boy resting in her lap. "Even His chastisements are a kindness."

"But why? I didn't do anything. I don't deserve this," protested Dawid.

"I know, lamb, I know." Ruth sighed, and then offered, as much to herself, "Sometimes we just get placed into the middle of the story, without knowing its beginning or its ending. We simply have to have faith in the Holy One, that He knows the whole story, and in the end, everything will make sense." Ruth sighed again. "We should pray that we merit seeing the outcome; so that we can understand the good of all the difficult times."

Ruth was no stranger to difficult times. As she stroked the child in comfort, her mind drifted to the beginning of her story. Well, not the beginning, but a beginning, a time of choice and destiny, whose path still hasn't come to its conclusion.

Part One

Chapter 1

Separate Ways
The Month of Aviv, in the year 345 from the Exodus
The Fields of Moav

The winds came with the setting of the sun, bursting forth as if it had impacted against the horizon, sending the powerful gusts jetting across the desert plains. As the winds reached the village, their force seemed to increase with shrieks and wailing as they buffeted against the stone homes. When they arrived at what remained of a small estate, now in disrepair, their howl intermixed with the wail of the three women huddled on a goat's skin in one of the low stone structures on the hill. Ultimately, the women's wailing was no match for the winds, drowning their anguish in a torrent of heavenly fury. Even in the structure, the sound of their voices was almost lost.

"Oh daughters ... oh, my daughters," cried the elder of the women, her words breaking, a mix of anger and despair. "The world. The world. We're drowning in the attribute of strict justice." Her face and cry turned heavenward, stronger, but filled with bitterness and pain, "Where is your mercy, Holy One?" Her cry rose to a crescendo, "Have pity! Have pity!" The last syllables swallowed by her renewed weeping. "Dear God, have pity."

The old woman's cries broke against the cracked ceiling, sending the three women into another fit of wailing and tears. The two younger women, birth twins and twins of fate, had just buried their husbands, the sons of the elder woman, both struck down suddenly with an illness that broke their strong young bodies within a week, albeit taking another fifty to finish its task. Before they had retired of their bodies completely, what was left of the small estate had emaciated along with them.

During their illness there hadn't been time to reflect on the worsening of their lot, but now that their bodies had been buried and their souls departed, the women, the mother Naomi especially, gave release to the frustration and despair that had camped at their door. The death of her sons was only the latest chapter of a turn of fate that had brought her from being part of one of the most esteemed families in Yehudah to a poor childless widow adrift in a foreign land.

Tears choked the older woman. She felt as if it were the hands of the Almighty at her throat. Yet, though she would still deny it, a part of her bitterness was directed towards her own hands that helped mold this bitter fate. As tears welled anew, she tried to push the memories away, but they refused. Dancing at the edge of her mind, teasing, taunting her, reminding her; those memories stayed close enough to her consciousness to torment her. In her heart, she knew that she had taken those first steps that led her to this wilderness, to this oblivion.

It was over ten years ago, in their home in Beth-le*H*em. Now delirious, she laughed at the name, which means the House of Bread. What a terrible irony for it had been the seat of a famine, the second in less than ten years. The promise of the Almighty's bounty on His People seemed rescinded

Three hundred and forty-five years after the People of Yisrael escaped from slavery in Mitsrayim, the promise of a comfortable life in their own lands was kept just out of reach, like a carrot leading a donkey down the cart path. Their God's promise of peace and security always seemed close, but the nation was never able to grasp it. Invariably, the closer the people got to their goal, the more they succeeded, the more they backslided, turning their back on the their covenant with the Almighty. And He always seemed quick to remind them of their wayward ways. Most of Yisrael's neighbors were more than happy to be the agents of the Holy One's chastisement. War was a natural state of affairs in the region.

Yet, He also always sent a deliverer. No matter how far the Nation of Yisrael strayed, whoring after other gods, when they cried out in anguish from the weight of their oppressors, He would send a deliverer. The Holy One's presence would rest on some charismatic leader who would lead the people to victory against the foreign oppressor. They would throw off the yoke of tyranny, only to start the whole cycle anew; the same script, with different set of characters.

There were also other times, when instead of delivering them into the hands of a human enemy, the Holy One would turn nature against the people. Drought brought famine, and famine was hard on the people, and her leaders, the elders who would bear the responsibility for feeding a nation, bereft of food. When the Almighty rescinded His bounty, somehow the elders had to meet the demands of their people. And the people could be relentless in their demands...

The demands of the people – again, she chaffed at the memory of her thoughts then - they never stopped, the people nor the memories, and with such insolence. As if they deserved to be supported by her husband, Elimelekh. So what if that is the law? There were so many, too many. If they were to give out all they had to them, what would be left for her family? Her boys. Her precious jewels. The memories paused to let the bitter reality sink deeper. Her precious boys.

Given new strength, the memories returned to her thoughts and complaints: *She had two young boys to raise.*

Elimelekh was an elder, and he took his position as head of the tribe of Yehudah seriously. With his own resources, he sustained his people as best as he could. He would often go without himself, simply so his charges would be sustained. The weight of his tribe, and his nation wore heavy on his shoulders. Much of his personal wealth was diminished from the successive famines. For Elimelekh, it seemed only natural to use his patrimony, to fulfill the responsibility and duties of his position, which, likewise was an inheritance from his fathers.

But Naomi had cursed her husband's position as a leader of the community. What did it get them? Nothing. How could he feel responsible for them? What about her? What about her children? She had begged him to leave, to find respite from the constant demands of the people. She voiced her concerns, her fears, until they rang in her husband's ear more forcefully than the cries of hunger from his charges. They abandoned Beth-le*H*em for the plains of Moav.

Her voice rose in agony. Now she was the waif. Bitterness rose up at the Almighty's cruelty. "I stand convicted," she choked, "but I can not endure the judgment. Have mercy, have mercy." The tears broke forth, but the memories swirled to the dance of the howling winds outside.

In the beginning, after they had crossed the River Yarden at Yerikho it had been almost idyllic. Elimelekh had brought a camel train to the plains of Moav. There, the people had greeted them as dignitaries, welcoming them into their midst.

Moav was a distant cousin of Yisrael. Living on Yisrael's southeastern border, on the eastern banks of the Yarden and the Yam HaMelaH - the Salt Sea, the nation of Moav was descended from Lot, the nephew who had followed Avraham, Yisrael's patriarch, to the promised land from the banks of the Tigris and Euphrates. According to tradition, when the Almighty delivered judgment on the city of S'dom, he sent heavenly messengers to warn and rescue the nephew of His faithful servant, Avraham. Lot fled the city, as instructed, but losing his wife and all of his possessions in the process.

When the angels arrived in S'dom to rescue Lot, a mob of citizens besieged Lot's home, demanding that he turn over the strangers to them. Lot offered his two daughters to try and pacify the crowd, but the heavenly messengers robbed him of the opportunity to fulfill his offer, blinding the crowd with brilliant light. Yet, it would seem, they had already been lost to the wiles of S'dom. Those two daughters, corrupted by the influences of the decadent city, and despairing of any other survivors of the catastrophe, lay with their father in a perverted effort to preserve his seed. The nations of Moav and Children of Ammon were born from their unions.

While Yisrael languished for four hundred years, slaves to the global power of Mitsrayim - Egypt, Moav grew into a mighty nation, carving out a kingdom on the fertile eastern bank of the Yarden. Rejecting their father's loyalty to the Holy One, Lot's daughters, and their sons, served the gods they had come to know in S'dom. Moav became a patron of Khemosh, a terrible and vengeful god, and consort of Asherah, a goddess whose image graced nearly every home.

When the nation of Yisrael was liberated from Mitsrayim, and they returned home, Moav was far from welcoming. Camped on their border, the nation of Yisrael requested to pass through Moav, promising not to disturb its peace. However, Moav felt threatened by such a large nation, who had devastated the world power of Mitsrayim. Under the leadership of their king, Balaq, Moav attacked Yisrael. They learned quickly that they should have granted the liberated nation's request.

After Yisrael established herself within her borders, relations with Moav grew cordial, if not friendly. They shared a similar culture, their languages differing only in dialect, and trade benefited both nations. When Elimelekh journeyed eastward with his family to the Plains of Moav in order to escape the famine, the nation, this time, was more than welcoming.

Even when tragedy had taken Elimelekh from her, the blow was softened. The people of Moav had been supportive, even giving two of their royal daughters to her sons in marriage. Both Orpah and Ruth had agreed to accept the path of the 'Ivri God, and observe His ways. Naomi found comfort from her husband's death and companionship in her two new daughters-in-law. For a while, that first sign of impending tragedy, instead of serving as a warning, simply was accepted as a part of life.

Aside from the terrible cult worship of its gods, Naomi found the Moav culture similar to her own. Her ear soon became attuned to the different dialect, and after a time, her eyes no longer widened at the public play between men and women in the market. Her body was sated by the bounty of Moav's provisions, convincing her that all of her needs were being fulfilled.

A gust of bitter wind seemed to ignore the stones, enwrapping the women in a blanket of cold. They huddled closer together. Naomi's memory surged, choking up another bitter memory. This time, the first real signs of tragedy danced boldly in her mind.

MaHlon had burst into the common house looking for Khilyon. Naomi felt a surge of panic at seeing her son's agitation. A hollow seemed to form in the depth of her soul. She pushed herself away from it instantly, but a residue remained. "What's wrong?" She asked hesitantly. Her son calmed somewhat at the sight of his mother. "It's the sheep," his tone serious, but the alarm diminished. "Several died in the night, suddenly, and many of the others ..." His voice trailed off. "I don't know," he continued, "but they seem ... lifeless, and their wool is falling away."

Throughout the years of her marriage to Elimelekh, Naomi had become familiar with many of the trials of herding, but something in her son's tone, or some other unseen force, caused a lump of panic in her throat. She felt herself hurtling towards that abyss again. "It will be okay," she offered, trying to assure herself as much as her son. "It's not the first time we've lost a few sheep." Her son simply nodded and continued his search for his brother, Khilyon.

Within three days, the entire flock of over three hundred sheep died inexplicably. Two weeks later their flock of goats followed them to the ash pile. During the same fortnight, bandits managed to steal five of their camels and several horses. The brothers were forced to undersell another camel to buy a much needed milk goat and other supplies. As setback followed setback, their workers fled, accompanied by increasing speculative whispers of curses and encroaching darkness.

Rumors kept their neighbors at bay. Evil had come to roost amongst the strangers.

When the last of their workers finally fled, they liberally rewarded themselves with a generous severance. They took anything they could lay their hands upon. Within a month, the family seemed to descend as far as anyone thought possible. A cloud of doom hung over their lives. Each new day was met with dread and uncertainty.

Then, when failing to return from their fields, Khilyon went looking for his brother. He found him lying amongst the barley. He was conscious but incoherent. His body covered in a cold sweat. Two days later Khilyon was struck with the same malady. Though it took nearly a year of suffering, the two brothers never rose from their sickbeds. Yet, long before their last breath, the once proud estate was in ruins; nothing was left. The three surviving women were forced to dig their men's graves themselves.

The winds continued to howl, echoing the lamentations of Naomi's heart. She prayed for mercy from the Almighty. A bitter mercy – that He would be kind enough to end her suffering too and join her with her husband and sons. The winds seemed to laugh in response.

***

A thin line of light creased the eastern horizon heralding the imminent dawn. Naomi let out a small sigh as she noticed it. She sat outside facing the east, her back towards her home, consumed with thoughts and memories.

Sometime in the night the winds had stopped. And though she had been awake the entire night, she only noticed the storm's end long after it had settled. The storm of the last three days suddenly was no more and a calm now rested on the world. Naomi did not share the same calm. Today she would rise from her official mourning, but rise to what? Where would she go? The Almighty did not seem to leave her many options.

As her eyes focused on the horizon, she saw shadows. Against the backdrop of the rising sun, dark shapes seemed to grow before her. Blinking away the fog of her reverie, her consciousness gave voice to the visage: a trade caravan heading towards the west. Yet, it had been so long since she had seen such a vision; it felt more illusion than real.

As the caravan approached, Naomi recognized three men riding donkeys with another three or four walking along side. There were about a half a dozen camels, laden with various packs and sacks holding their wares. The men all wore light colored wools, which, with the rising sun at their backs, seemed to glow.

Then, the caravan seemed to stop in its tracks. Naomi watched in wonder, trying to decipher the travelers' actions, but it was too far. She watched the men dismount, and then the entire group froze in place. Her eyes winced to decipher details of the scene, but with the sun behind the group, their efforts were fruitless.

Almost as instantly as it had stopped, the caravan rejoined its trajectory, and now, with the sun firmly established in the heavenly sky above their heads, it was clear that the caravan's path was directed towards her estate. Though, she still couldn't decide if it was happenstance or by design.

Naomi rose from the ground, absentmindedly pulling her shawl tighter. Even though the morning air was cold, her chill seemed to emanate from within. She took a step or two towards their approach, but no more. Squinting into the sun, Naomi awaited their arrival.

As the members of the caravan became distinct entities, Naomi's eyes widened with her surprise. She saw the distinct fringe of her people hanging from the corners of the travelers' garments. Now searching, her eyes soon registered small black boxes peering out from beneath their head wraps. The boxes, a sign of the covenant with the Holy One and containing verses from their holy text, were mandated by the Almighty for the men of Yisrael to wear. The trade caravan was from the Land of Yisrael. And it was returning home.

Questions filled her mind. Considering the wares it seemed laden with, it had been a successful trade. Yet, how had Yehudah, beset by famine, anything to trade with anyone?

When the caravan was less than a hundred *amoth* (about fifty meters) away, one of the travelers, a short round man with a thick black beard, which seemed to grow away from his face, dismounted and approached Naomi. His hands folded across his chest, his steps were measured, his eyes directed towards a spot on the ground about a handbreadth before the widow.

"*TinaHmi min ha-Shamayim*. May you be comforted from the Heavens," the stranger proffered.

Naomi startled. The holy language, which her ears had longed to hear for over a year, combined with the unconventional greeting made her jolt. How? She questioned. Then her hand absently went to the tear in her dress over her heart, the ceremonial tear of a mourner. One is not suppose to offer the regular greeting to a mourner. She wondered at what point this stranger knew her status.

The tears fought to begin to flow anew.

"I," she paused to compose herself, "I rise from my mourning today." She paused before saying, "*Shalom Alekhem*. Peace unto you, sir." Then she added, as much to herself as to the visitor, "You're actually the first comforter we've received." The bitterness was not hidden from her voice.

The traveler shifted uncomfortably, not knowing how to respond. His bulbous nose seemed to twitch.

Almost as way of apology, Naomi explained, "I buried my two sons last week."

"*Barukh dayan ha-emith.* Blessed is the True Judge," the traveler intoned the traditional response for hearing bad news, but his words were hesitant, unsure as to how they would be received.

Suddenly, Naomi recognized him: It was Shimon, from the *H*etsron clan. She wondered if he had recognized her, though, in deference to modesty, it would be unlikely. She remembered him as one of the Elders, a pious man. Shimon wouldn't gaze at a married woman's face without cause. Despite the heaviness of her grief, her heart lifted, if ever so slightly, at the chance meeting of a fellow countryman. She wondered what this man thought of a daughter of Yisrael dwelling in the plains of Moav.

Naomi broke the awkward silence. "Forgive me, but I haven't any way of fulfilling the provisions of welcoming the stranger.

Her confession cued the traveler to action. Waving his hand, he offered, "We have plenty, allow us the merit of comforting the mourner, even if it is a little tardy." Without waiting for a reply. Shimon turned and quickly waddled towards his fellow travelers. His hands gesturing instructions even before his mouth voiced them. Within a short time, a small encampment sprung to life in the desolate courtyard of Naomi's home.

***

She watched the trade caravan diminish into the distance. Even though she had already decided that she too would return to BethleHem, she wouldn't have been able to travel with the caravan. Regardless, the news they brought was like a message from the Almighty Himself, a reprieve, if not a complete pardon, of her sentence. Yehudah was flourishing again; the Master of the World had rescinded His strict hand of Justice against her people. There was hope that her sentence would also be commuted.

Ruth and Orpah were busy bundling the few utensils that the family still owned as Naomi stood in the courtyard of her once majestic estate. Again, the memories berated her, yet, despite their sharpness, there was a point of light buried in their attack. Maybe, she would yet find solace with her people. Her people; the thought suddenly elicited pangs of fear. When she left them, she was a princess; she would now be returning as a waif. She would be at their mercy. She hoped they would show her more mercy than she had shown them.

Naomi turned to leave the courtyard; her two daughters-in-law were standing in the shadow of the afternoon sun. Tears stained their faces. Seemingly on cue, the three women embraced, sharing their silent memories. Yet, the hug was brief, for each realized that they should begin their journey. The three women silently left the courtyard and turned their steps towards the road that would lead them to the land of Yehudah.

The three women, holding hands began to walk together. They hadn't gone more than forty steps when Naomi stopped in her tracks.

Suddenly, she was hit with the realization that her daughters-in-law were leaving their home to become strangers in her country. Naomi wasn't even sure about her own survival; she surely couldn't bring these young women with her. She would have nothing to give them. Their future would be as bleak as hers was in Moav.

Naomi stopped in her track. "What are you doing, my daughters? Go back, both of you. Return to your mother's house. May the Almighty grant you peace and show you kindness in return for the kindness you have shown to the departed, and to me. Go. I have nothing to offer you."

The two women, the two sisters looked at each other, each wrestling with their own desires and expectations. Both had grown to love both Naomi and her God. How could they abandon them? For surely returning to their people, they would be cut off from both.

Silence seemed to hang in the air for an eternity.

It was finally broken by Naomi. "Go back, already. You've more than fulfilled your obligations to me. May the Almighty grant each of you rest in your own homes, in the home, and arms, of another husband."

Again, neither sister knew what to do. They stood there, shifting their feet, their eyes drifting from the ground to the other sister, waiting for some unknown cue.

Naomi pulled them into her arms and kissed them. The three broke into tears, weeping without restraint.

Ruth broke the silence this time. "We will stay with you, Mother. We will go back with you to your people."

Orpah immediately concurred, "Yes, Mother, we haven't anything really to return to. We will stay with you."

"No my daughters. I have nothing to offer you. I haven't even a home" Naomi tried to maintain her composure. In truth, she loved her daughters-in-law very much, and was afraid to face returning to Yehudah alone, but that would not be fair for them. That would not be good for them.

When her daughters-in-law remained silent, Naomi continued, "Return home, my daughters, my beautiful daughters. Why would you come with me? Am I going to have any more sons to take you for wives? You are free from your obligations, Return home."

Ruth shook her head slowly in silent protest. She couldn't articulate it, but she would not leave her mother-in-law. Abandoning her meant abandoning everything that had meaning in her life.

It would mean abandoning the holiness of her husband's people.

Orpah remained silent, but her thoughts were confused. She loved Naomi, but she did not want to remain alone. She felt abandoned, betrayed, by her husband and His God. There was a void inside her that was growing. He didn't even leave her with a child. Yet, returning to her mother's house would not be much of a future either; a childless widow was without very many good prospects. And then again, Naomi was the last vestige of any thing good she had had. She didn't want to turn her back on her.

Naomi persisted in her arguments to the silent responses of her daughters-in-law. "Return home to your people. I am too old to have another husband. Even if I thought that there still might be hope for me …" Her words trailed off. She hadn't anything to offer any man. She would spend the rest of her days alone. A pang of desire for the companionship of her daughters-in-law made her pause. But no, it was not right. She voiced her protest, "You are still young and beautiful. You have many children left in your womb. I am old. Even if I were to marry and conceive tonight." She laughed to herself at the thought. She was far from the merit of her ancestor, Sarah, who gave birth to a son in her old age. Yet she pressed her argument. She had to make the women see the futility of staying with her. "Even if I were to have a son, could you wait till he grew to manhood to take you in *yibum*, in levirate marriage? Would you remain alone and unmarried for them all those years? You

41

would be an old woman before he could build you a home and provide for you."

Ruth continued to shake her head in protest. Her tears flowed silently. The logic of her mother-in-law's words was sound, but she would not yield. She would not leave Naomi's side.

Orpah had ceased to weep. She stood frozen at the crossroads of indecision. She did not want to remain alone. The void in the hallow of her heart began to grow.

Naomi pushed harder. "No my daughters. It is terribly bitter for me, but you have hope; you have a future still." Finally, Naomi articulated her true thoughts, "The Hand of the Almighty has gone out against me. He has judged me, and I … "Naomi's eyes closed in resignation to her fate. She sighed, "I have to answer His decree, but you, my lovely daughters, return home. Begin anew."

Orpah was shaken, but she recognized the truth of her mother-in-law's words. She raised her head and looked into Naomi's eyes. Taking a step towards her mother-in-law, she took her hand and kissed it. They stared at each other for a long moment. Four tears, one after the other, disturbed the dust at their feet. Orpah wiped her eyes, and offered her mother-in-law a tight smile. They spoke no words, embraced again, and then Orpah turned to her sister, her twin.

Ruth hadn't moved. Orpah kissed her sister on the cheek; Ruth returned the embrace, but she didn't move with her sister's gentle nudge. Orpah didn't wait for Ruth. It was her own decision. Orpah turned and took a path towards her own destiny. This would be the first time their paths would part.

***

Orpah's feet turned onto the cart path, but her mind traveled a different route, drifting to the realm of possibilities. Voices danced into her head. She had been connected to holiness, and now there was this void, a deep chasm that needed filling. She longed for the touch of her husband, his embrace.

She reminded herself that he was no longer. Anger intermixed, and then replaced her sadness. Ten years, and the Holy One of Israel had denied them even one child. Ten years of divine judgment. Ten years of tense anticipation and disappointment. She had felt the holiness of the People Yisrael in the beginning; that is what caused her to cling to Khilyon, to choose his people, his God, but now, she was left with nothing. Bitter tears trailed down her cheeks. Nothing.

She wanted the touch of a man, any man. She needed to fill the empty spaces. She knew the space in her heart would remain empty, void, but there were other hollows that needed to be filled. It would not be the same. Being with Khilyon was as much a spiritual as a physical experience. When he made love to her, they were not alone; he had connected her to the infinite. Done in the modesty and purity of his people, he had made the coupling something more than human, something holy.

43

But, suggested the emboldened voices in her mind, there were other forces, other energies to be tapped. Her spirit could be satiated other ways. The Holy One of Yisrael had stolen her husband from her and left her a childless widow. She would flee from such demanding, exacting holiness and embrace its antithesis.

An audible sigh escaped her lips. Each step along the dusty trail-like road led her further and further away from her mother-in-law and all that was connected to her - her son, her people, and her God. When she broke from her internal reverie and became conscious of her surroundings, she realized she was a lifetime away from her former, though temporary, home. Night was beginning to fall.

Suddenly, Orpah noticed that she was not alone on the road. Seemingly out of nowhere, there was a donkey headed in her direction. It was already close. On his back sat a hunched rider. They would cross paths within moments. Had she seen him coming from a distance, she would have moved off the road into the fields, fearful of what might happen to a lone woman traveler. Now it was too late for such precautions, so she merely moved to the side of the road, to insure that the donkey would have plenty of room to pass.

However, instead of moving to the opposite side of the road, the donkey moved directly into her path. Her heart leapt, as anxiety crept up her spine. There was still some distance between them. Cautiously, Orpah moved to the opposite side of the road. Yet again, the donkey matched her move. Her breath caught, as she stopped in her tracks, waiting.

The donkey and rider reached her in moments, but each of those moments was impregnated with anxiety and fear. She noticed the rider was completely enwrapped in his dark cloak, the color of shadows. The cloak was draped over his head and shoulders creating a hood before folding back over itself covering his mouth and nose. His eyes seemed like distant glowing embers hidden in the recesses of those shadows. The donkey stopped within a handbreadth of her. Orpah felt the donkey's breath on her face. It was as if in a dream.

"*Shulmu*. Greetings," the low voice of the rider resonated in her head. She seemed to recognize the voice. It seemed to carry the same tone and measure as the voices of her soul. Her fear augmented, though surprisingly the anxiety diminished. She realized she had shut her eyes tightly, and now she slowly opened them looking up in the direction of the man's face.

"*Shulmu*," her voice was barely a whisper.

She felt as if the donkey rider smiled, though she couldn't have seen it. "The roads are treacherous for a woman traveling alone towards the dark. *Minna izimtu'a?* What could you possibly be seeking?"

Her heart leapt. She stared at the rider, but didn't answer. She knew she didn't need to.

"No, child," he chided. I'm merely an old traveler. However, if you continue on your path, and take the left fork at the crossing, you will find a band of P'lishti soldiers. There are about a hundred of them. I'm sure that they would offer comfort and hospitality to such a comely lost soul as yourself. Fare well."

Orpah's mind was swept away in reverie. It must have been the tension and anxiety, but when she regained her bearings, she was once again alone on the road. The rider and donkey seemed to have disappeared.

P'lisht'im: The very bane of Yisrael's existence, what greater nation to introduce her life's new course. From the time of Yisrael's ancestors' sojourn in their land, they had zealously fought against Yisrael's bringing the glory of the Almighty to the world. Lust: it was synonymous with the P'lisht'im. Descendent through wife swapping between Pathrusim and Kaslu*H*im, both offspring of Mitsrayim, they have come to represent the very essence of licentiousness. They lived on the Western coast of the land of K'na`an resolving to be a thorn in the side of the Nation of Yisrael, despoiling their plans for bringing light to the world.

Orpah recalled the geopolitical lessons of her youth she received in the royal residence of Moav. The very name for their nation, P'lisht'im, meaning open at both ends, defined their nature as being totally accessible to the spirit of lust. This is why they clung to the land of K'na`an, for the K'na`anim and the P'lishtim share a common bond to the forces of materialistic, egocentric desire, and the land of K'na`an, when it rebels against the forces of holiness, becomes the perfect focus for such forces. The battle for the Land of Kna`an or the Land of Yisrael is a battle between the very forces of Heaven and Earth.

Suddenly she recognized the rider and the voice in her heart. She had been given a mission, so it seemed, from the very "Accuser of Yisrael," the nation's Calumniator and Detractor, the Angel *Samu-el*, Israel's Denouncer before the Heavenly Court. Her head began to swim, her hear leapt with anticipation. She resolved to serve her new master well. She had trouble containing her excitement. The trace of holiness she had experienced was now gone but in its place, lust filled her heart.

***

Torchlight flickered in the distance.

She made her way to the camps edge. A dog's yapping reverberated incessantly against the dark night. As she approached she saw the large group of men in various positions of relaxation, conversing amongst themselves. Walking into the circle of light, her presence captured everyone's attention, all eyes turned, as if on command. Her dress was in the Moav style, road worn but quality, her stature, her presence, bespoke of her noble birth. She emphasized every nuance, every movement. Even the dog stopped his yelping.

"*Qarabu'in migru'in.* Noble warriors," she began, pausing for emphasis, "*Qarabu'in emmamu'in.* Heated warriors," she smirked. "*Ekhadat Orpah b'nt Aglon zeru Balaq Ma-alaku h'rabu.* I am Orpah, daughter of Aglon descendent

47

of the great King Balaq. Which of you thinks he can please such a rare flower in your camps?"

A pregnant silence permeated the camp. All eyes darted from the lovely princess to his comrade, each gauging her words, her intent, and his chances against his fellow. Suddenly, as if on cue, the dog sat up tall and yelped three short yelps. The silence was broken and all the men began their own clamoring. Offers from the exotic to the erotic, from the brass to the refined were thrown towards Orpah, and she reveled in their offerings. The men began rising to their feet, moving towards the woman, each wanting her for his own, but Orpah had other ideas.

"Wait," she called out, "with so many fine suitors, I suppose we'll all just need to learn to share." A devilish smile affixed itself to her face, as the crowd was thrown into silence for the third time. It was the last time the camp would know silence until the morning hours.

Orpah didn't wait for them but sauntered into their midst. Soon hands, some gentle, some rough, began to caress her form. She closed her eyes, trance-like; letting each sensation fill the crevices of her hollow soul.

***

Consciousness and feeling returned slowly. The air was warm and dry. The sun's morning light warmed her face. Sound seemed suspended. The sensations had been so overwhelming, that her mind, unable to process the events quickly enough, suspended itself somewhere between pain and pleasure. She was sore, but aches of pleasure mixed with the pain and the feeling of blood and sweat, and other fluids, along her sensitized skin. Even the air had a different sensation. She allowed her mind to drift, for what could have been moments or hours. Orpah felt a stirring within, and she knew. These forces had been more generous. She was with child, a very special child. A child with a hundred fathers and a ...

Orpah felt a wet sensation on her face and her eyes flutter opened to meet those of the dog. He was licking her cheek. She turned on her side, but let the beast continue its tongue bath. At least there was one gentleman, she chuckled. Then the chuckle turned to laughter, and as the laughter escaped the depth of her soul, Orpah felt the embrace of destiny. She remembered the donkey rider on the road, and offered him a prayer of thanks. Slowly she rose to her feet. She found her cloak, shook the dust from it and wrapped it loosely around her shoulders. She laboriously set off in search of a cistern or a spring to wash up. The dog quietly tagged along.

***

A few steps from her mother-in-law, Orpah hesitated and looked over her shoulder, waiting to see if her sister would join her but Ruth stood frozen, her mind processing the events. She fought to find expression for her desire. Her soul clung to her mother-in-law.

"Dearest daughter," Naomi's voice was soft but firm, "Your sister has chosen wisely. She is returning to her people and her gods. Go, child, join her, return with her."

Then something broke in Ruth. Her mother-in-law's encouragement gave voice to her struggle. She would not return to her former life, distant from the Truth, from the One True Master of the World. She couldn't bear to turn her back on the holiness of Yisrael, even if it meant a life of solitude. Ruth moved to face her mother-in-law; her voice was soft but resolute. Her voice resonated from the depth of her soul.

"Don't push me to abandon you, to "return" from following you. For where you go, I shall follow; where you rest, I shall rest as well. Your people are my people; you're God is my God. I'm not going back."

Ruth continued, her voice gaining strength. She would not let anyone steer her away from the Source of all living. "Where you die, will be my final resting place, and there I will be buried. Thus, may the Almighty do to me, and thus may He add to my suffering, but nothing, nothing," her voice rose in strength, but remained controlled, firm, "Nothing but death will separate me from you."

Naomi's jaw dropped. It all fell into place for her. She understood. Tears welled up, bitter tears. Naomi had spent so many years fighting her reality, and yet, she had missed the point. Her own struggle against her external situation and then her internal battle with the deeds of her past, her chaffing against the Almighty's judgment, had caused her to miss something - something essential: Even an adversarial relationship with the Master of the World was far greater than a life of emptiness and lies. Her arms searched for her daughter-in-law, but this time not for comfort, but for strength. It took a stranger to her people and her God to see what she had failed to recognize her entire life. Naomi was returning home; Praise the Almighty, she was returning home.

"Thank you my Lord," she whisper, "thank you," she directed her voice to her daughter. She could return home, no matter how hard the path might be.

Naomi and Ruth clung to each other and turned towards Bethle*H*em, and began their journey homeward.

Chapter Two

Homecoming

With the Mediterranean Sea on their western border, the P'lishti Empire was concentrated in a wide strip, originally known as the Land of Kaftor. The three thousand *amah* strip stretched nearly a twenty day march from the Mitsrayim River in the south to the Yarqon River in the north. Yet, their influence extended far beyond their 60000 square *amah* territory with garrisons, missions, and cultic centers throughout the Fertile Crescent.

Five city-states, each with their own sovereign lord, dominated the P'lishti Empire. The Lords of the P'lisht'im shared power, meeting regularly to decide common foreign and national policy. The seat of rule rotated between the five cities and their lord every few years. Every five years, a presiding lord was chosen amongst the five rulers. He was usually the most senior of the lords, and was accorded the honor of a sovereign, principally in the cultic and national ceremonies. While officially his voice was equal to the other lords, because of his seniority, his experience and position carried a tremendous amount of respect and influence. At the time that Orpah became a guest of the P'lishit'im, the crown of power centered in the city of Gath.

Orpah's breath caught as the wagon approached the city. It was magnificent. She practically giggled it was so pretty.

Her companion saw the delight register on her face and smiled. "Gath, *zanu klilulu aHa el*

Nish P'lish. Gath, one of the crown jewels of the P'lishti Empire." Resheg declared with pride. His eyes then slowly moved from the delight in Orpah's face to delight in the rest of her form. More beautiful and far more 'liberated' than any woman he had known, even the priestesses in the temples. She was a prize he would relish. *"u-att maalkatu'ai el uldu.* And you, my queen of pleasure," his voice thick with lust, "will certainly give that jewel a new luster."

Orpah was flattered. She offered a small, confidant smile, her lips slightly parted, her tongue brushing the edge of her front teeth. A rush of heat coursed through her body. My, how her fortunes had changed. She shifted her position coyly, allowing the white linen robe with red and black geometric designs to offer another tefa*H* of her flesh to show. The robe clung to her form, hiding as much as it revealed, suggesting more than showing, proving to be the perfect accompaniment to her new life.

The robe was just one of the presents her most noble suitors presented her that glorious morning. The gold and brass bracelets encircling her arms were also their gifts to her. It seems there were in fact more gentlemen amongst her paramours than she originally surmised.

After she had risen from her hedonistic night of liberation, she wandered to the other side of the clearing to the rim of olive trees that encircled it. Walking past the trees, she found the object of her search. There in the middle of an identical clearing was a cistern surrounded by a low wall, yet there were also several dozen P'lishti soldiers lingering nearby in idle conversation.

When she saw them, Orpah stopped short. They looked strange in the light of day; she was not accustomed to grown men with smooth, clean-shaven faces. It seemed ... unnatural. She had heard many stories about the P'lisht'im. How would these barbarians treat her in the light of day?

The moment of hesitation seemed uncomfortably impregnated. Then one of the soldiers, a tall thin man with a mop of light hair, noticed her and stopped his conversation short to turn towards Orpah. *"P'tny-ia.* My lady," he offered the bewildered widow from Moav, *"Ekhadu mtakalu kiasha l-ptny-ia sitta ni*Htu. I trust my lady had a restful sleep."

At the greeting, the other men turned their attention towards Orpah, and each offered a small bow. Another man, who seemed as broad as two men across the shoulders, took a step towards Orpah. "We didn't want to wake you, *p'tny-ia.* Can we help you with something? I assume you'd like to clean up. The facilities are not the highest standards ..." he demurred, "but we will at least give the lady her privacy." He gestured to the other men who passed out of the clearing, each offering a short greeting to the increasingly confused woman. She certainly didn't expect such civility. They were so nice and gentle.

While questions raced through her mind, Orpah was refined enough to maintain her composure and present an air of dignified, but

54

restrained, gratitude. The men had left her alone (with the dog) in the clearing. On the wall of the cistern, next to several clay bowls and pitchers full of water, they had left several other accouterments she had long forgotten about during her years of poverty by Naomi's side. There was a metal comb as well as oils and perfumes. As she approached the cistern, she noticed a beautiful robe of linen folded neatly on the wall. Her heart raced at the offerings, and when she lifted the robe, seeing the bracelets and other jewelry underneath, her head swam.

Slowly, in part to enjoy the refreshing water, but more to catch her breath, Orpah lingered in her bath. Surprise after surprise greeted her; she even discovered heated water within the clay pitchers. She did not know how to interpret all of this. Truth be told, she had been thankful that these P'lisht'im hadn't killed her when they had finished with her.

Discarding her old garments, she stood in the large clay basin and slowly poured the warm water over her head and shoulders, throwing her head back in sheer pleasure. She rubbed the perfumed oils, persimmon and pomegranate with a touch of balsam, into her sore muscles. She did not know what the future had in store for her, but at the moment she didn't care.

When she had finished bathing and dressing, the dress making her feel at once a queen and a seductress, she stood for a moment in repose. Fleetingly, she wondered where they had obtained such wares in the wilderness. Taking a deep breath, she returned to the clearing where the men had retreated. As she entered, all eyes turned. A smile came to her lips, memories of the night before.

"*P'tny-ia*," the broad man who had addressed her before spoke, "We, that is our company, thought that a lady of such caliber might do us the honor of returning with us to the city of Gath. We are sure that your virtues will be most welcome there, and we pledge to honor the lady with the finest accommodations, befitting the daughter of a king."

Orpah searched his tone for a trace of sarcasm, but found none. The whole situation was a riddle. Assuming a coy smile, one she anticipated using often, she bowed slightly, "*Kbdu-a kia li.* The honor is mine," "And," she added, "I hope the pleasures will be too."

"Here, Here," The company momentarily broke their guise of discipline and civility.

"Most welcome," added the broad man, whose name, she had later learned on the trip, was Resheg.

Resheg was the captain of the band of men, a company out of Gath, whose role was – Orpah wasn't too clear on how this worked – "to expand the influence of the P'lisht'im throughout the region."

According to Resheg, aside from the P'lisht'im and their parent culture, the Mitsr'im, no other nation possessed even a glimmer of culture. "And," declared Resheg his long straight dark hair bobbing off his shoulders as he talked, "the P'lisht'im have surpassed even the Mitsr'im."

While once considered the center of culture in the world, the Mitsr'im's reputation as connoisseurs and gourmets remained only out of a sense of a tradition that had once been, argued Resheg. Yet, today, there was a worldwide demand for P'lishti wine, and the delicacies of the empire were enjoyed in halls of Ammon, Moav and even as far as Qadem. P'lisht'im were also on the cutting edge of art and architecture.

Orpah enjoyed listening to his orations, full of pride of his people. His voice was soothing. Yet she was continually distracted by new discoveries she noticed in her host's appearance from the smoothness of his jaw line, to the touch of makeup around his eyes, from the oil in his hair or the ornamentation of his clothing. She had trouble reconciling the deep male voice with what she finally realized was an almost feminine visage.

"Oh!" She startled, when the contradiction materialized in her consciousness, causing her host to look quizzically at her in return. She wasn't even sure what subject she had interrupted.

"You don't agree?" Her companion asked. Fortunately for Orpah, he didn't wait for a reply, but offered a support for his argument. "These 'Ivrim," he nearly spat the word in disgust using the pejorative term for the nation of Yisrael, "are the single greatest impediment to the advancement of human civilization. They not only allow, but revel in the unfettered growth of their beards, like some kind of beast of the field, while at the same time cruelly blemish the most precious organ of their children before they are even old enough to protest."

"But that is a sign of their covenant with their god." Orpah was truly intrigued, by this new subject. She also noticed, with some surprise, that she referred to the 'Holy One of Yisrael,' as "their god." Her divorce from Him and His people, it seemed, was complete.

"What god worthy of the name would need a mortal to 'complete' his creation?" he asked incredulously, revealing a certain amount of knowledge about the customs of his adversaries. "Surely, the gods require their due, but have you heard of any other god asking his followers to disfigure themselves?" "I heard it renders these 'Ivrim incapable of enjoying that most beautiful of pleasures." His tone bordered on outrage.

"But," protested Orpah, "There are gods that demand child sacrifice. That's not more severe?"

"Is there a greater cruelty than making a creature live a lifetime disfigured and crippled? And not just one child or two, but a whole people?" Resheg asked incredulously. "Besides, the god of these 'Ivrim demands such austerity. How can one unite with the infinite without tapping into the forces that dwell within!?"

Orpah giggled in delight. This was such a different perspective as to how she had understood the world. She had once seen the Bnei Yisrael, these 'Ivrim, and their god as the pinnacle of existence, the fulfillment of a divine plan. She had admired their simplicity. Yet, maybe Resheg was correct. Maybe it wasn't simplicity, but a certain amount of backward primitiveness. Was it possible that the purpose of existence, of life, was to be found in the pleasures of this world? She had certainly enjoyed these 'uncircumcised' ones, she thought, referring to the 'Ivri epithet for the P'lisht'im. And she had connected to something, something powerful, as her pleasure centers exploded within. If only such forces could be harnessed and focused … is that what Resheg was suggesting? A smile of delight lit up Orpah's eyes.

Quite an adventure, these last few days have been, and such a riddle.

Somehow, they saw her as some type of sophisticated coquette, an avatar of prurience instead of a common tramp. She laughed to herself. She had already received far more reward than even the best prostitute's fee. A riddle indeed and she was sure that the donkey rider was the key. She thought she had caught a glimpse of him during her night of ecstasy, and then again on her ride to Gath. It didn't matter though, for she knew he was with her.

And now she had arrived. The gates of the city were magnificent. Four towering pillars with mushroom shaped capitals, two on either side, framed the expansive gate to the city. The pillars, as well as the mantle of the gate, were plastered white and adorned with images of serpents and birds in red and black relief, with a multitude of scarab images peppering the lintels.

A stele adorned the gate. Orpah recognized that it must be the dedication plaque of some important persona or a god, but the writing was completely foreign to her. In fact, it looked more like tiny pictures, than what she knew to be writing. She drew a long breath. It was all so beautiful. Pretty, she thought, might even be a better description. Then she thought that that might be an apt description for the new men in her life too.

Orpah giggled. She was excited. So far, she liked the entrance to her pretty new home. Now, she couldn't wait to get inside.

***

The journey to BethleHem passed much quicker than either woman expected. Hand in hand they walked, but each with her own thoughts, Naomi with her memories, and Ruth with her expectations. They soon arrived at the crossing of Yerikho, not far from the place where Yehoshu'ah and the children of Yisrael crossed into the Land of Yisrael on their return, their liberation, from Mitsray'im.

Yerikho, or rather its remains, stood as a constant reminder of the power of the Holy One of Yisrael. Yerikho had been the first conquest of the Children of Yisrael upon their return to the Holy Land. After forty years of wandering in the desert, Yehoshu'ah had led the triumphant nation over the Yarden and immediately attacked the city, circling it for seven days, with *shofars*, primitive ram horns, blaring. On the seventh day, Yehoshu'ah led the nation of Yisrael around the city seven full circuits. Upon completion of the seventh circuit, the walls simply sank into the ground and the Yisrael'im entered. No one was spared. The city was sacked and sent ablaze. A curse was declared for anyone who would dare rebuild it.

The story of Yerikho spread throughout the region, bringing panic to all the local inhabitants. They geared themselves for war, but it didn't help. In those days, the nation of Yisrael was unstoppable. Battle after battle brought the same results as the nation of Yisrael conquered most of the land on the western side of the Yarden. It was clear that the nation of Yisrael was marching with the Holy One Himself at their head.

Ruth envisioned herself as one of them, full of anticipation, tinged with an edge of trepidation. She remembered the stories, of both her youth and, later from the perspective of her husband, of the many miracles that the Holy One had performed for His People, and how the other nations, hers included, trembled in fear of His Might.

The crossing at Yerikho gave Naomi pause as well. Memories of her leaving the Land, and now, an opportunity to return, filled her with emotions: contrition and joy, tedium and excitement intermixed. World-weary sighs and gasps of anticipation periodically punctuated the women's silent journey.

So the two women went. Nearing summer, the waters of the Yarden were relatively calm. Placing their bundles on their heads, the two women waded into the cool waters at a point where the river widened a bit. Angling upstream towards the western bank, Ruth and her mother-in-law began the crossing in silence.

At its deepest point, the water tickled their chins. Naomi hesitated. It was much deeper than she remembered from when she had made the crossing in the other direction. She looked forward to gauge her distance to the shore. Had she made an error in choosing the spot for the crossing? A moment of fear seized her. Would she even be able to make it to the other side?

She looked over her shoulder, trying to judge if she had passed the halfway point. Her daughter-in-law offered a broad smile when their eyes met. Naomi drew a deep breath, pushing the pangs of panic way from her heart. The Almighty had split the Yarden for the nation of Yisrael, when they had crossed with Yehoshu`ah. If it was His Will, He would ensure that the nation's wayward daughter would reach the other side. She took several more hesitant steps, to discover the depth of the waters slowly receding. While the Holy One hadn't exactly split the sea for her, Naomi offered a prayer of thanks to the Almighty when her feet climbed the western banks of the Yarden. She wondered how long it had been since the last time she had offered Him such a prayer.

Turning north, Naomi led Ruth towards the main road into the heart of the territory of Yehudah, the largest of the twelve tribes of Yisrael. They found the road, a wide dusty trail crossing, a few hundred *amoth*. Nearing evening, the crossing was empty and silent. A litter of wagon tracks, hoof prints and footprints was the only evidence of the busy activity the spot must have seen during the day. The entire Yarden valley seemed suspended in silence as the sun sank below the horizon in front of them. A peacefulness settled on the land. They had made it. Both women looked at each other and smiled.

Ruth looked around with eyes of wonder. Suddenly she felt she found her self in a garden of beauty. Date palms seemed to stretch to the heavens. They formed square groves surrounding stone built pools. Networks of canals connected the pools to the Yarden, creating a panoramic patchwork of lush greens and deep browns. Naomi remembered the pools being empty when she had left the Land of Yisrael, but now they seemed overflowing. The sweet smell of fig trees and pomegranates permeated the air. Olive trees were everywhere, glowing in the red hue of the setting sun. The air was dry and sharp. The women's clothing, wet from the crossing, quickly dried in the evening heat of the Yarden valley.

The two women moved some distances from the crossroads, finding a small alcove of trees to rest for the night. After their long journey, sleep overtook them instantly, and the two women slept peacefully till the dawn.

Both women woke with anticipation before the rising of the sun. They watched the red globe peek over the horizon of their former home as they ate a quick breakfast fruit and grains. Filling their water skins, they quickly traveled west along the road, soon passing the site of Gilgal. All that was left of the first "capitol" of the Yisrael nation was a few stone buildings in disrepair. Gilgal had been the first resting place of the nation, after they had crossed the Yarden. It was where Yehoshu'ah had renewed the covenant between the people of Yisrael and their God. During the first campaign of the conquest, Yehoshu'ah had used Gilgal as his base.

Further west, the two women came to the ruins of Yerikho. By now, traders, farmers, and a variety of other travelers shared the road with the two women. Greetings were often exchanged, along with news between the travelers. While Yerikho remained in ruins, it environs seemed to thrive. Small communities dotted the landscape. West of the ruins, the road branched into three separate paths, albeit all three continued in a general westerly route. The most northern branch led to Bet El, the middle branch cut directly west towards Ramah and Giveon, while the remaining road bent southwards towards Nov, Yerushalayim, and BethleHem. Naomi and Ruth took the southern branch, though after a few hours, Naomi directed Ruth on a smaller road that cut more directly south, avoiding the roundabout through Nov and Yerushalayim. As they traveled south, the date groves soon disappeared, replaced by fields of grains, wheat and barley in the main, vineyards and olive groves.

The nation of Yisrael, for the most part, lived a simple agrarian and pastoral life. Small towns served as hubs for a plethora of small nameless communities, organized primarily on family, clan and tribal lines. The larger towns served as political, economic and educational centers for large regions. Rarely, when more national needs pressed, the elders of the various tribes gathered to decide issues and guide the nation. A charismatic leader, imbued with the spirit of the Holy One would serve as the nominal head of the nation, leading them in war, or serving as the chief justice of the pan-tribal court.

What united the tribes, the descendants of the twelve sons of Ya`aqov, was the *Mishqan*, the earthly seat of the Holy One's presence. At least, three times a year during the festivals, the entire nation made pilgrimage to the Almighty's Tent, to pay Him homage. The *Mishqan* currently rested in the city of Shilo, in the territory of Efrayim, nearly a day and a half's journey north of Bethle*H*em, Ruth and Naomi's destination, and the defacto capital city of the tribe of Yehudah.

So the two women went, until they arrived in the environs of Bethle*H*em. Bethle*H*em, like all other locales, comprised more than the town itself, but included the tens of small villages and farms that surrounded it. Twice a week, on the second and fifth day, everyone would converge on the main town. Large outdoor markets would be set up, and people would be able to barter for those items and foodstuffs, which they didn't produce themselves. News was exchanged and disputes were resolved, and all the necessities of public administration were attended to. Though the town of Bethle*H*em was large, most of the area's residents lived outside the city walls, and most of those who lived in the town had large holdings in the environs surrounding it. Ruth and Naomi passed several small nameless villages on their approach to the town of Bethle*H*em, as well as countless cultivated fields, vineyards and groves.

The fields of barley, some still green, others golden, but all tall and near their harvest, gently fluttered and waved in the gentle breeze like a sea of gold and green. The late morning sun made the fields glow with a warm light of their own. Periodically they were greeted by men and women making preparations for the upcoming harvest. It was the eve of the Pesa*H* festival and on the second day of the festival the `Omer, the first sheaves of the barley harvest, would be brought as an offering to the *Mishqan*.

Like the undulating waves of grain, the news fluttered before them: Naomi, the wife of Elimelekh, was returning home and with her was her daughter-in-law, a woman from Moav, who had clung to her mother-in-law and her God.

Soon a contingent of old friends and neighbors met the two on the road to greet them on their return, and welcome them home. As a group of a dozen or so women approached, Naomi heard one of the women whisper in surprise, "Can this be Naomi? What has happened to her?"

Another whispered in return, "This can't be Naomi. She always had such fine shoes, this one is barefoot."

The group paused, unsure how to approach their returning neighbor, who by all appearances was a shadow of her former self.

"Don't call me Naomi," Naomi called out to the women, trying to relieve the tension, "Call me Mara, for the Almighty has embittered me. I was full when I went away, yet The Holy One has brought me back empty. There is no reason to call me 'Naomi – Pleasantness,' for the Holy One has reprimanded me; He has revealed that my actions have not been pleasant. The Almighty impoverished me. Call me Mara."

Her words had the opposite of the intended effect. While they didn't actually move, it seemed as if the 'welcoming committee' shrunk several amoth away from Naomi. Daggers of silence hung in the air.

Naomi tried again. Extending her hands in supplication, she tried to remove the edge from her voice. "Sisters," she began, "the Holy One is wholly righteous. He has performed for me the _H_esed, the kindness, of bringing me this lovely righteous woman. Please come to know my daughter, Ruth."

The tension broke and the circle of women closed around Naomi and Ruth. Amidst an exchange of tears and hugs, Naomi, and Ruth, returned home.

***

67

Ruth paused from her labors. She had been grinding seeds from wild *shipon*, which seemed to sprout wherever the land wasn't cultivated. The grain was plentiful, but it was difficult to extract the seed from the wild grass. From its flour they would make crude cakes on the stones they heated from the animal dung that seemed to be as plentiful as the *shipon*. They had been living in a cave on the outskirts of Bethle*H*em for a few days, now.

Ruth now drew a breath and turned to her mother-in-law. "Let me go to the fields and pick up the leftover grain behind anyone in whose eyes I can find favor." Her mother-in-law had been teaching her the laws of *pe'ah* and *leqet*, laws of the Torah, the sacred text of the Yisrael nation, whose details required one to leave the corners of their field and the gleanings that fall during the harvest for the poor, the landless and dispossessed.

Even so, a lone woman would be putting her self at some risk to try and gather grain. While most, if not all, of the people would show her the requisite kindness, it would only take one ruffian to take advantage of Ruth's lack of protection. Yet they surely could not live on these *shipon* seeds for very long.

Naomi sighed. With a slight nod of her head, she consented, "Go ahead, my daughter. May the Guardian of Yisrael watch over you."

Ruth rose from her grinding and brushed off the front of her dress, a simple wool gabardine whose original color had now faded to a bleached cream. She checked her headscarf, tucking the stray locks of hair under coarse fabric. Recognizing the concern on her mother-in-law's face, Ruth walked over to her and hugged her mother-in-law's arm. With a kiss to her cheek, she whispered, "I'll be fine. The Almighty will guide my way."

As Ruth walked through the fields, her thoughts turned inward. She was happy. It was true that things were difficult, she couldn't remember when was the last time she wore a decent dress, but she knew that she was exactly where she needed to be. Ruth recalled an expression from her youth, 'nothing comes without its price.' The path to true happiness, wholeness, was fraught with difficulties. She hadn't any doubts. The Holy One of Yisrael was guiding her steps. She never felt more complete.

The early morning sun was warm; spring was transforming into summer. The fields of barley, which only weeks ago were still green, glowed golden in the morning light. Even the wheat had started to ripen. Ruth saw several fields full of harvesters. She also recognized in several places that there were poor following them, collecting what they could, but she continued on.

Finally she came to a large field. There were many harvesters, as well as a good contingent of needy, both men and women. She watched the harvesters and the foreman for a few pregnant moments, before deciding that this was the field where she would try her luck. Ruth walked over to the foreman, a young man close to Ruth's own age. As she approached, he turned to face her, but his eyes focused on the ground in front of her. Ruth

69

was touched by the gesture of modesty. It made her heart light that even poor women would be afforded such honor and respect.

"Please let me glean and gather the sheaves from behind the harvesters," she asked meekly. The foreman merely nodded and pointed to a place in the row of women who were already doing the same thing. Without another word, Ruth hurried to where he had indicated.

Ruth fell into line with the other women collecting the fallen sheaves. A few of the closer women acknowledged her with a friendly head gesture; they were too distant to exchange greetings respectably, and too busy to break from their work. Ruth found a rhythm and worked diligently the entire morning, collecting as much as her arms could carry.

As time passed, one of the harvesters noticed Ruth. He turned to his fellow worker. "Who's that?" he asked, with clear delight in his voice. She's beautiful."

"Keep your eyes in their sockets, N'muel. It's not proper to stare, and anyway, she's Naomi's daughter-in-law, and she's a Moavi convert. You can't marry her anyway."

"Ah, that's her. I heard about her," he said, half to himself. Then to his colleague he protested, "And I didn't mean it that way." There was an edge of embarrassment in his voice now. "It's just that she has a certain grace about her like ..." He searched for the words, "I don't know, like the elders, maybe." He paused, and then the question came to him, "Anyway, why not?"

"Why not what?"

"Why couldn't I marry her?" adding quickly, "if I wanted to, that is?"

"Don't you know your Law? It says clearly, 'An Amoni or a Moavi can not come into the congregation of the Almighty, even to the tenth generation, they can–not enter the congregation, | ever.'"

"Then how did Ma_H_lon marry her?" N'muel asked innocently.

His partner smiled ruefully. "I guess he thought she was pretty too." Then he added, "Maybe he didn't attend his lessons and forgot like you."

N'muel smiled, "Well, she's pretty enough to make someone forget."

"I thought you weren't looking at her *that* way."

"We should stop this," declared N'muel, "this isn't proper. Even if we can't marry her, she's still a convert and deserves our respect. Or did you forget that lesson?" he asked playfully.

"Therefore, you should love the proselyte," quoted his companion, from the Book of Law, known as the *Torah*.

The two men stopped their conversation and rejoined their task, though occasionally N'muel glanced over his shoulder at Ruth and shook his head woefully.

As midday approached, a small group of men approached the field, commanding the attention of everyone there. When they were within four amoth of the workers, the man at the center of the retinue shouted a greeting, "*Adn imakhem!* The Holy One be with you."

"*Yivarekh'kha Adn!* May the Holy One bless you," the workers returned, almost in unison.

"Who's that?" whispered Ruth to no one in particular.

One of the women nearby heard her and answered in surprise, "What? You don't recognize the elder, Boaz? Why he's the Father of the Great Court, and the owner of this field."

Ruth looked with awe. Boaz. She remembered the name. Someone had mentioned him to Naomi when they had returned. He was a cousin of Elimelekh. They also called him "Eb*ts*an," and he sat at the head of all of Yisrael. He has served as the *Shofe*t of Yisrael for seven years. Ruth gave a prayer of thanks that the Holy One had led her to his field.

Boaz was not very tall, but his stature commanded a certain presence. His white flowing beard and creased face bespoke of age, yet his body was far from bent. There was a spring in his every step and a light in his eyes that made them seem to dance with joy. All the men of his retinue, Ruth assumed them to be either his sons or his students, were transfixed on his every word.

Ruth understood why. She had never seen anyone like him before. Despite his simple outwards appearance, with only a staff and shawl marking his office, Boaz seemed to glow with an inner light. When Ruth's eyes met his, she recognized the same light of holiness that brought her to this people, only with Boaz its radiance was as intense as seventy suns. A gasp escaped from her lips.

The foreman had left his post to meet the retinue of the elder. After the initial exchange of greetings and the day's general report, Boaz asked the foreman about Ruth. "Whose young woman is that?" he inquired, for something about her resonated with him as if he recognized her soul.

"She is the Moavith that returned from Moav with Naomi, Elimelekh's wife."

"How did she end up here?" Boaz asked.

"I don't know," the foreman shrugged, "She showed up in the morning, came to me and asked, 'Please let me glean and gather among the sheaves behind the harvesters.' I sent her to work with the women and she has worked steadily from the early morning till now, with only one short rest in the field shelter."

"Call her over," requested Boaz. The foreman nodded to a young boy, who raced to where Ruth stood. When he reported his instructions, she was visibly shaken. Hesitantly, she came over to the group of men.

"*Ken, adoni.* Yes, my lord," she addressed Boaz.

Boaz offered a reassuring smile. "*Biti,* my daughter," he began, waiting for Ruth's anxiety to subside. "*Sh'ma''at.* Listen to me," he continued gently. "I request that you don't go and glean in another field; you can meet all your needs here. You should return here every day. Stay with the other women under my care. Watch the field where the men are harvesting and stay with the women. I have instructed the men that they should not harass or bother you in anyway. And when you are thirsty, don't hesitate to drink from the water jars which the men have filled."

Ruth shuddered and tears moistened her eyes as she listened to Boaz speak. When he finished she dropped to her knees and bowed until her face touched the ground. Upon rising to her knees, she exclaimed, "*Madu''a matsati Hen b''enkha?* Why have I found such favor in your eyes that you would give such notice to me, a *nakh'riyah,* a stranger and foreigner?"

Boaz offered another gentle smile. "I've been told about all that you have done for your mother-in-law since the death of your husband – of how you left your mother and your father, your homeland to come and live with a people you did

74

not know before." He paused and Ruth felt as if he had peered into the very depths of her soul. "May the Lord Almighty repay you for all you've done. May you be richly rewarded by the Holy One of Yisrael, under whose wings you have taken refuge."

Ruth's voice was barely a whisper. Her entire body seemed to shake with emotion. "May I continue to find favor in your eyes, my lord." She looked up towards the elder, "You have given me comfort and have spoken so kindly to your humble servant, though I don't even have the standing of your maidservants."

"*Barukh ha-ba-ah, biti.* Welcome, my daughter," Boaz offered, before returning his attention to the foreman. Ruth understood that the interview was over and returned to her work. Tears of happiness creased her face for the rest of the day.

When Boaz sat down under the field shelter to eat his mid-afternoon meal, his eyes scanned his companions. He had overheard several snippets of conversation concerning the Moavith, and of the prohibition in the Torah to bring them into the congregation of Yisrael. Was she fit to break bread with? Was it permitted to drink her wine? What did the prohibition involve, exactly? Could one be a proselyte from Moav at all? Did it apply equally to men and women from Moav? No one from Moav, to anyone's recollection, had ever accepted the Holy One and His Torah before.

Boaz refrained from engaging the topic. Despite the fact that he had a clear tradition from his fathers and teachers, he knew to broach the topic might open endless discussion and debate, which would spin in circles. Instead, when they sat down to eat, he sent a young boy to call to Ruth, "Come over here to break bread and dip it in wine vinegar."

At the sound of his invitation, all conversation stopped. Theory was theory, but no Father of the Court would invite her to eat if it wasn't an already decided ruling. They all understood the implications of his invitation.

Ruth meekly approached the diners. At the women's table, a large friendly woman gestured to her and moved over making a space for Ruth. She bowed politely and sat down. Boaz passed to her the dish of roasted grain and Ruth ate heartily, yet there was plenty left over when she had finished. She modestly placed the leftovers into her sack.

Ruth got up to glean, offering her gratitude as she did so. When she had returned to the field, Boaz instructed his men, "Even if she gathers among the sheaves, don't embarrass her, instead, without her seeing, pull out some stalks from the bundles, and leave them for her to pick up, and don't chastise her at all. We are taught not to oppress the proselyte, even with words."

As the sun began to set the harvesters retired from their labors. The remaining sheaves were removed to the threshing floor and the few remaining poor headed for home. Boaz had left the field shortly after the afternoon meal, but Ruth stayed till the last of the harvesters had gone home.

When she was alone she gathered her sheaves of barley in a large shawl and carried them to a small outcropping of flat rocks near the field. She spread them out in a row. Then taking a small log, she rolled it over her sheaves back and forth, until the majority of it was threshed. She then collected the seeds into the shawl. She lifted the sack onto her tired shoulders, she estimated that she had gathered a full efah, and began her return to the town of Behtle_H_em and her mother-in-law.

Ruth approached the glow of the fire pit outside the cave where she and Naomi were staying. Naomi was sitting outside the cave, with her back against the rock face. Her chin rested on her chest and Ruth heard the rhythmic breathing of sleep. It seemed that her mother-in-law had fallen asleep waiting for her daughter-in-law to return. Ruth placed the sack on the ground and gently stroked Naomi's arm. She awoke with a start. Ruth had pulled her from a distant dream. Naomi's eyes took a moment to focus on her daughter-in-law's face and the present.

"Where have you been?" she asked concern on her face, "I was beginning to get worried."

Ruth smiled at her mother-in-law's concern. "I'm sorry, Mother, but I found a good field and worked all day. I've brought you the sack as well as some leftover roasted grain." Ruth presented her mother-in-law with the remains of her lunch.

Naomi drew a breath. "Oh my," she said in wonder, her hands reaching for the roasted grain. She forced herself from wolfing down the food.

"Where did you glean today? Where did you work? Blessed be the man who took notice of you!" The grain seemed to bring color to her parched face. Her eyes then fell on the sack full of grain, and she shook her head in wonder. How had Ruth carried such a heavy burden?

"I worked in the fields of Boaz today," Ruth said while examining her mother-in-law's face, waiting for the reaction. She received one. Naomi's eyes lit up.

"May the Almighty bless him!" she practically shouted. The Holy One has not stopped showing kindness to the living nor the dead. Do you know that that man is our kinsman?"

"Yes, I heard one of the women tell you when we arrived."

"I think he's even one of our redeemers," Naomi added, referring to the kinsmen who are required to take the childless widow of their brethren in a levirate marriage, so that their name and their inheritance will continue.

Ruth shared in her mother-in-law's excitement, though she wasn't sure of the implications of what her mother-in-law suggested. There wasn't any such thing as a redeemer or levirate marriage in Moav. Yet, clearly her mother-in-law was excited about something. The tiredness of the day dissipated. Ruth sat beside Naomi and began to reveal the events of the entire day. She told her mother-in-law everything; from the way Boaz appeared, through his invitation, to the afternoon meal.

"He even said to me, 'Stay here, with my workers until they finish harvesting all my grain," Ruth said as she finished her story.

Naomi couldn't contain her excitement, "It will be good for you, daughter, to stay in his field and go with his young women, lest in someone else's field you might be harmed. The Almighty has clearly guided your steps. *Barukh ha-qadosh barukh hu.* Blessed is the Holy One of Yisrael."

Ruth went out every day to the fields of Boaz and stayed close to the young women throughout the barley and wheat harvests, and each night she returned to live with her mother-in-law. Each day she returned to a more and more rejuvenated Naomi. Slowly, both body and spirit were healed from the wounds of Moav.

As her spirit returned, and she worried less and less of her present circumstances, her mind turned towards the future, both hers and her daughter's-in-law's, and slowly, a plan began to develop.

***

The streets of Gath were as startling as the gates, but for different reasons. As the wagon navigated the broad streets, Orpah was struck by the dichotomy between its residents. Interspersed amongst the many soldiers in their plumed helmets and fine uniforms, were as many, if not more, poor rabble wearing filthy, dilapidated rags.

The wagon navigated the right-angled gate expertly. As it crossed the final turn and entered the city, several beggars thrust their hands towards Orpah, aggressively demanding charity. Resheg intervened and threw them a few coins, while signaling one of the escorts to push away, and prevent any further intrusions.

The contrast was so striking just inside the gates of the city, that Orpah actually felt a surge of relief as the convoy continued and she saw merchants and tradesmen. They seemed to form a bridge between the two other diverse groups of citizenry.

"*Kalmutin,* Parasites," Resheg spat in disgust when another beggar approached the wagon, "Why it's our lot to support such rabble, I'll never understand."

"But," began Orpah, "It's not their fault they're poor ..."

"Not their fault!?" Resheg returned incredulously, "There's plenty of opportunity to earn one's keep here. With a little hard work, no one should be hungry. Look at me, I worked hard and slowly I've risen in rank. The problem is that they get used to hand outs and then they forget how, or don't want to work."

This disturbed Orpah. She had only too recently suffered at the hands of poverty, and it wasn't because of her, nor her mother-in-law's, nor sister's, laziness. "Sometimes fortunes go awry; sometimes it's just the situation that causes one to be poor," she offered.

"Not usually," Resheg wasn't conceding his point, "and even in those cases, if it's because the gods choose to afflict or punish someone, why should I interfere?"

"Well, I don't know," Orpah was caught between voicing her objections, and revealing her past. She didn't want to say something that might upset Resheg's, or the other soldiers, impression of her. She desperately did not want to be one of the starving 'rabble' again.

Fortunately, her indecision was interrupted as the wagon came to a halt. Orpah broke from her own thoughts to take in her surroundings. The wagon and her retinue had stopped before what was clearly a temple of sorts. Two pillars with capitals similar to the capitals of the pillars of the city marked its gates, though the pillars resembled trees. Each was adorned on its face with three equilateral triangles, pointing downward, with a small circle in its center. Standing before each of the pillars, seemingly guarding the entranceway, was a statue of a matronly, large-breasted woman with her arms crossed underneath her breasts. Each of the woman statues held an object in their left hand; the left one was holding a bell, while the right one, a large three-sided tent peg.

Even without the geopolitical training of her youth, Orpah recognized the statue idol of Asherah or Asherali, the most popular goddess in the region. Almost every home, from the Nile to the Euphrates, had a representation of her in their home. Even some of the `Ivrim, she knew, much to the chagrin of their leaders and their god. This place, she concluded, must be a temple to the goddess.

That said, Orpah couldn't remember ever seeing a temple to the goddess. Shrines were commonplace on people's rooftops, near practically every green tree, and on roadways. Women, in particular, would frequently offer incense to the goddess as well as bake loaves of bread in the goddess' image. These loaves would be eaten at ritual meals in the hope of receiving a variety of blessings. Yet, in Moav anyway, Orpah wasn't aware of any formal cult involving priests and a temple for the goddess.

She knew her more as a folk goddess. Most of the common people had distant almost fearful respect of her. It was known that there were night creatures who wandered the earth collecting the souls of small children, boys in particular. People brought offerings to Asherah in hopes that she would offer protection. Yet, there was also the suspicion that it was she who stole the babies' souls. Contrary to deterring worship of the goddess, the stronger such suspicions were felt, the more it seemed to make people careful about bringing her offerings. No one wanted to affront a vengeful goddess.

Orpah returned her focus to the entrance of the temple and noticed that the statues were not quite like the many figurines that most people possessed. Aside from being of finer quality and detail, the lower genitalia of the woman were displayed on these statues in exaggerated detail. On the figurines she knew, the waist down was represented simply as a smooth cylindrical pedestal. Such an immodest sight would not be welcome in most homes. Orpah, herself, would have been shocked by it only days ago. She smiled; recognizing it merely surprised the evolving woman now.

Surprise after surprise competed for Orpah's attention until her focus fell upon a group of beautiful women exiting the temple. The woman in the center, at first glance a young woman of Orpah's age, was spectacularly dressed in a sheer gown that seemed almost transparent. The four women surrounding her wore similarly but slightly plainer apparel. Orpah guessed that the woman must be some type of ranking priestess. It was her companion's words that startled her the most. "Here comes the old whore now," declared Resheg.

As she approached the wagon, this beautiful priestess extended her arms in welcome. She wore a huge smile that drew Orpah in. "Resheg, I see you've accomplished your mission."

Resheg, in a mock sense of respect, leapt from the wagon, took the priestess' hand and kissed it with flourish. "I'm always at your service."

"You're in nobody's service but your own," returned the priestess lightly. "But I hold the keys to your desires, so you do me the occasional favor," she continued, tapping Resheg's groin boldly.

Turning to Orpah, she nodded her head, *"Shulmu, akhatu-ti.* Welcome, my sister. We have been awaiting your arrival."

Orpah should have been startled by the woman's words, but surprise had already gripped her when she saw the woman's face up close. She now understood her companion's statement better. The woman was far from the young woman Orpah had originally apprehended. As the woman neared, Orpah was able to detect the layers of caked cosmetics, which masked an aged face. Especially the eyes, thought Orpah, which were creased and dark. She wondered how old this priestess must truly be. She seemed ancient.

Finally, the woman's words registered, and Orpah startled from her reverie. "Excuse me. You've been waiting for me?" Two soldiers were now helping her down from the wagon. "I don't understand," confessed Orpah.

"All in good time," replied the woman cheerfully. Resheg remained standing next to the priestess now. She absently allowed him to continue to hold her hand, which he held in homage. It looked almost as if they were a couple. Her attention stayed focused on Orpah, "I sent Resheg to fetch you. He had explicit instructions. I see he followed them. *Roqeb-a Emeru-a,* The Donkey Rider came to me several months ago to tell me of your coming."

Orpah swooned. *"Roqeb-a Emeru-a* - The Donkey Rider." Her statement was as much a question as an acknowledgment. Then she

84

refocused on the woman, and the meaning of her words became clearer to her. "Are you a prophetess?" she asked.

The woman smiled. "I am privileged to serve the Goddess. I don't normally receive visions from her consort, but then you are a special case, my dear."

"I don't understand," repeated Orpah "am I to become a priestess?

"A priestess?" the woman almost laughed. "A priestess is but a weaver working on the loom of the world. You, my dear, are the skein and the shuttle. You are the weave."

Orpah was perplexed. Her face revealed her confusion.

The woman leaned into Orpah and lowered her voice, so only she could hear. "You have become an incarnation of the Goddess. You are the _Hirtu-a_, the consort of the _Roqeb-a Emeru-a_. You are to be the focal point, a periapt of our service."

Orpah's head began to spin. The consort?

The woman placed a hand on Orpah's stomach "You are carrying our champion in your womb. One of four whom you will bring into this world to fight and save us from the onslaught of the 'Ivri god who would have humanity deny this world and its pleasures. Who would keep humanity in darkness and separate him from the natural world, the world of the senses. Their god, in his jealousy, tries to prevent the world from experiencing the serpent fire and attaining enlightenment, the path for which humanity can become like gods themselves. His nation of slaves, the 'Ivrim, must not gain dominion here, or all will be lost. It is a battle between good and evil, a denial of this world versus its fulfillment."

For a fleeting moment Orpah wondered which side was which, but then memories of her night of liberation pushed all doubts aside. The donkey rider had saved her. He had given her the child she had so desperately wanted, and was denied from the god of the 'Ivrim. She remembered the power of her experience. The energy was too seductive to deny. She would serve him, and his consort Asherah, with all her heart.

The woman continued, "Their god has already prepared for them a redeemer, a champion of his cause. The child you carry will come to thwart him and their goal. He and his brothers will be a manifestation of all worldly power. He will humble the god who embarrassed the noble nation of Mitsrayim."

"But enough for now, my sister. You've had a long journey," the woman put her arm around Orpah's waist and began directing her inside. "Let's get you inside where you can refresh yourself. Welcome home."

Orpah was left speechless, her mind racing with a thousand thoughts. Everything she had known had been turned on its head. Momentarily, her thoughts turned to her sister, Ruth, and wondered on which path the fates had brought her. Pity transformed into anger at her sister's obstinacy. Her stubbornness to cling to some false ideal had almost convinced Orpah to follow her after the `Ivri god. A feeling of relief consumed her as she was led inside the temple, into a new world she couldn't wait to discover.

Chapter 3

Harvesting
Three months later

"I was thinking," began Naomi as she walked over to where her daughter was preparing pitas to place in their fire pit.

Ruth looked up and smiled. She was happy to see her mother-in-law returning to herself. She had color in her cheeks and light in her eyes.

Naomi returned the smile and began again. "I was thinking, daughter," she said tenderly, "shouldn't I be trying to find you a place to rest, a home, where you will be provided for."

Ruth laughed, as if her mother-in-law's desire was enough to find her a husband.

"No," rebuked Naomi, "it is not such a remote dream. Isn't it Boaz who has provided for you and whose young women you have been following in the fields? He is a relative of ours, and a redeemer. "

"I still don't know what that is really," answered Ruth.

Naomi paused and looked at her daughter-in-law. "Oh, of course not, how could you?"

"Well," she began, "according to our Torah - our Law, when a man dies childless." The memory still hurt, but less so. "When a man dies childless, his brother is obligated to marry his widow, and the son from their union, is considered to be the deceased heir. It is a kindness that has no equal for it allows for his brother's house to continue. On a more spiritual level, our tradition teaches that the soul of the deceased husband returns to this world in the body of the child, in order to fulfill his unfinished mission in this world. If there aren't any brothers, like inheritance, it falls to the nearest kinsman to redeem the widow, as well as claim the inheritance for their child."

Ruth was dumbstruck. She had never heard of anything like this before. Yet, like everything else she learned about these people, it confirmed her belief that they were divinely guided. "What man would take on such a responsibility for his deceased kinsman?"

"Well," began Naomi, "it is ordained from the Holy One, and that's good enough for many, however," she stopped.

"Yes?" Ruth urged.

"Well, there is a way out of it, actually. If a man doesn't want his brother's widow, or she refuses to marry him, then he must perform a special ceremony, called *halitsah*, which frees her to marry another. However, it is considered shameful for a man to refuse to establish his brother's house, and he must take a special name if he does so."

"What is it?"

"He is called, 'the house of the discarded sandal."

"That's an odd name," commented Ruth.

Naomi smiled, "That's because you don't know the ceremony he has to do, where after the elders try and convince him to marry his brother's widow, and he refuses, the widow removes a sandal from his foot and spits in his face before everyone who is sitting in the gates of the city. The name reminds him of his shame."

Ruth drew a breath. She couldn't imagine anyone wanting such shame. To be spit in the face in public: it would be embarrassing for everyone to know that one refused to keep his dead brother's name alive.

Naomi continued with her plan. "Tonight, he will be winnowing barley on the threshing floor. I am sure he will sleep there when he finishes. Wash and perfume yourself tonight, and put on your best clothes ..."

"What are you suggesting?" asked Ruth, suddenly apprehensive.

"In my merit, you should go down to the threshing floor, but don't let him know that you are there until he finishes his evening meal. Then, when he lies down, take note, and after he falls asleep uncover his feet and lie down by them."

"I don't understand." Ruth was confused. She wasn't sure what her mother-in-law was asking her to do.

"He's a sage. Revealing his feet will hint to him the commandment of *yibum*-levirate marriage and the *halitsah* ceremony. He'll recognize his obligation."

Ruth nodded, understanding her mother-in-law's plan, but she was terrified nonetheless. There were a myriad of things that could happen between here and the threshing floor, between now and the time Boaz would lay down to sleep. What if something went wrong? She took a deep breath; she would trust the Almighty, and her mother-in-law.

"I will do whatever you say," whispered Ruth.

***

Ruth crept down to the threshing floor. She had done everything as her mother-in-law had instructed. While her steps were silent, the beating of her heart was so deafening in her ears, she was sure that it would give her away. She snuck behind and between two towering mounds of grain, watching and waiting. Her lips silently beseeched the Holy One's providence.

She watched as Boaz ate his evening meal. Again, her heart soared at the sight of him. His face seemed to glow from some inner radiance. Ruth was sure that heavenly angels must not be much different. She watched him drink his wine at the conclusion of his meal, and then offer blessings of thanks. He seemed especially in good spirits as he laid out a sheepskin on the floor at the edge of the grain pile. He then lay down, covering himself with a large woolen shawl.

Soon, Ruth heard the steady rhythmic breathing of someone sleeping, yet she waited longer to be sure. Finally, her anxiety to act was outweighed by the tension of waiting and she silently moved towards the sleeping figure, and gingerly uncovered his feet, and lay down beside them.

Around midnight, something stirred and Boaz awoke with a start, his body shaking inexplicably; cold and fear gripped him. He reached down to recover his covering and by his feet lay a figure. He grabbed its shoulders and demanded, "Who are you?" His mind raced with possibilities. Fearing both the natural and the unnatural, he wondered if it was a robber or a night demon. As his hands groped toward the figure's head, they disrupted its head covering, and the unmistakable locks of a woman's hair caressed his hands.

Ruth was shocked into silence at first. She awoke to Boaz's tightening grip on her shoulders, and her tongue froze.

"Who are you?" Boaz repeated. He began to realize that the figure was human and further that it was a woman, and his tone softened, when he demanded a second time, "Who are you?"

"I'm Ruth," she stuttered out the words, "your maidservant." As her mind returned to her control, she repeated the expression that Naomi had rehearsed with her, "*ufarasta kh'nafekha 'al amath'kha ki gho-el ata.* Spread the corners of your garment over your maidservant, for you are my redeemer."

Boaz released Ruth as he leapt to his feet. His mind raced; did this young girl just request that an old man like himself take her as his bride?

"*Barukhah at l'adon biti.* May the Almighty bless you, my daughter," Boaz's voice was a whisper. He was deeply moved that this young woman, a stranger and even younger than any of his daughters, identified so strongly with the Holy One of Yisrael and His Law that she would give herself over to an old man like himself.

"This is a *Hesed*, a kindness, greater than that which you showed earlier," said Boaz, referring to Ruth's ministering of Naomi. "That you should turn to me, to establish the name of the deceased, may the Almighty bless you my child. You didn't run after the young men, rich or poor, despite the fact that your beauty has attracted attention. It is clear that you have come here for the sake of Heaven." Boaz's eyes welled with tears. He felt honored by the merit of seeing such devotion to the Almighty.

He saw in Ruth reparation and atonement of the sins of former generations. Ruth descended from Moav who began through a union between

93

father and daughter. Later, the nation of Moav tried, and almost succeeded in bringing Yisrael to ruin through promiscuity. Yet, here was a daughter of Moav who kept herself pure, offering herself to a man, not because of any selfish interest or physical desire, but to keep the name and seed of her deceased husband's family alive.

Again he repeated, "Bless you, *biti*." Ruth felt a surge from the blessing, as if it had been delivered from Heaven itself. "It's through the deeds of her righteous women, that Yisrael merits heavenly blessing," whispered Boaz, repeating a common aphorism of the sages.

Boaz took several breaths, reveling in the moment. He considered the situation. Ruth also seemed unable to move or to speak.

Finally Boaz broke the silence. "And now, *biti*, do not fear. I will do for you as you ask. Everyone who has passed through the gates of my people already knows you to be a noble woman."

Ruth's gasp was audible. She closed her eyes, her heart voicing her thanks to heaven in place of her lips, for she was overwhelmed by the moment. Boaz had just agreed to take her as a wife and establish Ma*H*lon's seed. She barely heard the rest of his words.

"Yet now," continued Boaz, "even though I am a potential redeemer for you, there is another who is a closer relation than me."

Ruth broke from her reverie. She didn't quite understand. She thought that she had just heard him agree to marry her, and now he was demurring? Her eyes betrayed her question.

Offering a gentle smile, though he wasn't sure if she could see it in the darkness, Boaz tried to reassure her. "Sleep here tonight. You'll be safe here, and in the morning I will talk with the redeemer of whom I spoke. If he is prepared to redeem you, well and good. But if not, then I will redeem you and take you as my wife. As surely as the Holy One lives, this will be the last night you will be forced to sleep alone. Lie here until the morning, *biti*, my daughter."

Ruth nodded, trusting in the sage's wisdom, and while she was willing to accept whatever Heaven would decree, a small part of her hoped for this angelic sage.

Hearing her name, Ruth awoke from her sleep, though she didn't remember dozing off. It was still dark, but the eastern horizon began to glow in anticipation of the morning lights. Boaz had awakened her, and now he beckoned her to leave, "So, it shouldn't become known that a woman came to the threshing floor," he said, fearing the misunderstanding that might ensue.

When Ruth was ready to leave, Boaz called her over. "Bring me one of your head scarves and hold it out."

Ruth removed one of the headscarves, and held it out while Boaz poured into it six measures of barley.   As he poured each measure, Boaz mentioned that each represented a different blessing that he now bestowed on Ruth's seed: "The spirit of wisdom and understanding, the spirit of counsel and restraint, the spirit of knowledge and awe of heaven."   He then placed the full scarf on her head, so she could carry it home.

Shortly after Ruth left, the elder made preparations to go to town and the gates of the city. He had business to attend to.

When Ruth returned to her mother-in-law, Naomi asked excitedly, "How did it go, daughter?"

The tension inside of Ruth broke and the entire episode came out in a rush, everything mixed together.   Naomi listened intently.   After she had finished her tale, the tension now dissipated, Ruth remembered herself and presented Naomi with the bundle of grain, "He gave me these six measures of barley, saying that I should not return to you empty handed."

Naomi had trouble containing herself as well.   She recognized the symbolism.   It was as much a bride's price.   Providence had certainly been good to them.   She gripped her daughter-in-law's shoulders as much to steady herself as Ruth.   The grip reminded Ruth of Boaz's only a few short hours ago.

With a smile that radiated her entire countenance, Naomi said gleefully, "Wait, daughter, for the results are soon to come to fruition.   That man will not rest until the matter is settled this very day." Naomi pulled her daughter-in-law into her arms hugging her tightly. "Blessed is the Holy One of Yisrael, who brought me to this moment."

"Amen," answered Ruth, her body alive with anticipation of the day's events.

***

The sweet smell of date honey and other spices permeated the air as thick columns of smoke rose from the incense altars in the corners of the temple courtyard. Above, overlooking the large open courtyard, there was an overflowing of onlookers on a roof supported by two ornate columns. Orpah struggled to keep from looking up. She focused her gaze forward, sitting on the southern side of the courtyard on a freshly constructed dais. She sat in the middle of a wide bench facing northward. Like a statue, as she had rehearsed for so many days beforehand, she sat erect on the edge of the bench, her hands cupped under her chest, her feet planted solidly, legs slightly parted. Her belly already exhibited signs of her pregnancy.

She was a vision of the small statuette that graced nearly everyone's home. Her hair had been styled in tight curls, which clung to her head beneath a coronet that wound around her brow in the shape of a brass serpent. Two more serpents entwined each of her forearms, their heads resting on the back of her hands, while two others spiraled up her calves, the head of each resting on the inside of her knees, their tongue outstretched towards her 'most sacred spot.' The rest of Orpah's body was

97

clean-shaven and perfumed. She was now accustomed to the frequent homage she now received from laity and priestesses alike over the last few months.

She had learned so much in such a short time about the power and energy hidden within her. When her senses were raised to their highest pitch, she had discovered how to focus them under the guidance of Shiv_Ha_'innana, the high priestess who had greeted her at the temple gates. Feelings and Pleasure were transformed into raw energy, which brought her special sight, visions and enlightenment. She could actually see the *nur'naHasha* - serpent fire, as it was called, coursing up and down the spine of others. When a votary paid her homage, she could tap into it, drawing its power into her, opening up channels to the spiritual. It was intoxicating.

The soft, steady drum beat returned Orpah to the present. The ritual was starting. This was the first time she would participate, let alone be the center, of a public community ritual. With the harvest long ended, the fields needed to be prepared and sanctified for the next season's yields. The Lord of Gath, Avimelekh by title as much as by name, would present himself before Orpah. Their union would create the spiritual energy, which Orpah would 'weave' into an offering. If received, the tapestry of energy could influence the gods to bestow their bounty on the earth. Their fertility rite would insure the fertility of their lands. All of Gath crowded along the rooftops to witness, and participate in this most important ritual.

Two rows of 'Asheritu,' the young virgin priestesses, none more than fifteen years old, marched into the courtyard to the beat of the drumming. They entered in regular intervals, clad and veiled in translucent colorful material, which hung down unbelted the full length of their fronts and backs, though remaining open at the sides. When they spanned the eastern and western edge of the courtyard, they turned as one unit, facing in. The line of young women on the western side each carried a small bell, which they held in both hands out in front of them; on the eastern side, the women similarly held a ceremonial three-sided tent peg.

The drumming increased in volume and rhythm, reaching a crescendo. On cue the Asheritu broke from their line, their bodies seeming to succumb to the force of the music. To the beat of the drumming, they gyrated and gesticulated in ritual dance. The energy of the entire temple reached a terrifying pitch. Orpah could smell the excitement, yet she remained focused. Allowing the energy to excite her, rouse her, she wove it into a tight pattern holding it deep inside her soul. She kept her physical body immobile. She felt the nur'naHasha racing up and down her spine, the tongue of its flame licking at every nerve center. Her sacred spot burned with hot fire. While her eyes were focused forward, she could see through her peripheral vision the rainbowed colors of energy dancing throughout the entire congregation as they began reciting the name of the goddess, "Asherah," in a low ecstatic mantra. The pulse of energy grew to a fevered pitch.

Then, almost without warning, the drumbeat stopped, and the Asheritu fell to their knees in three rows, bell and tent peg interspersed, all facing Orpah sitting on the dais. One beat of the drum and in unison, they all prostrated themselves, arms extended forward. Many of the people on the roof did so as well, and Orpah was overcome with a sensation of everyone's release. Their energy suffused with her own, brought her own fire to a crescendo, yet she held the serpent tight, weaving the energy together, saving and storing it, as she had been taught.

The Asheritu first returned to their knees, then their feet and formed two rows facing each other, five amoth apart. Another beat and they again returned to their knees, keeping their backs erect and eyes forward.

Two more beats of the drum, and from the north side, the Lord of Gath entered, escorted by four officers and four Qadishtu, the learned priestess of Asherah. Orpah recognized Resheg as one of the officers, wearing only a colorful plumed headband, the feathers beginning at his forehead and extending back down the spine. The other officers were similarly adorned.

Orpah suppressed a smile. Resheg had visited her often since her arrival. She liked him, though it seemed to her that he was less a devotee of the goddess than he was to the way she was worshiped. Suppressing an urge to giggle, she pushed the thought from her mind and returned to the ceremony.

The Qadishtu, walking on the outside of each of the corners of the retinue, wore bracelets on their arms and legs similar to Orpah's, but they didn't wear a coronet. They walked erect, with their hands folded under their chest, four more human replicas of the statuette. The Lord of Gath, in the center of the group, wore only a coronet, though instead of serpent, the symbol of an ox graced his forehead. When they were in the center of the courtyard, the entourage stopped quickly.

"A libation," Avimelekh called out, "to the Goddess Asherah." As his words rang through the temple, two soldiers, dressed in their military apparel came running out from the corners of the courtyard, each with a large clay jar. They ran and stood by the two large columns in front of the altar on the western edge of the courtyard. Another Qadishtu appeared on the altar. The entourage turned as one towards the altar.

"*Gir-ba-an-n Hamaru* An offering of wine," shouted Avimelekh, and the soldier by the left column brought the jar up to the priestess who poured the libation on the platform of the altar. "*usham'nu.* And oil," continued Avimelekh, signaling the second soldier to bring the jar to the priestess, who poured a second libation in the same manner as the first. The two soldiers left the jars by the pillars and ran out of the courtyard.

The entire entourage snapped towards Orpah and kneeled in supplication. Orpah rose from her seat and moved to the edge of the dais. The entourage rose.

Orpah spoke, her voice channeling the energy stored inside her, magnifying it, till it echoed throughout the temple, "*Shuptia elu-tia, garn-a, illip-a samam-a kia izima-atiu damiutau bubbul-a seheru-a. Arts-ia ezebu-ia m'ezebu sapatsu. Kia-iam Ashera, manna yipadan-ah shuptia elu-tia ramu-ia? Manna yipadan-ah arts-ia d'mu? Kia-iam, khirtu-a seheratu-a, manna yipadan-ah shuptia elu-tia? Manna ysamu-o turu-a samu? Manna yipadan-ah shuptia elu-tia? Manna yipadan-ah eglu-ia*, the horn, the boat of Heaven, is full of eagerness like the young moon. My untilled land lies fallow. As for me, Asherah, who will plow my high field? Who will plow my wet ground? Who will station the ox there?

Avimelekh replied, "*Ptnya rabutu, ekhadu sar Gath ypadan-ah shupt-ku elutku. Ekhadu, avimlekh d'sarin Hamsu ypadan-ah shupt-ku elutku.* Great Lady, the Lord of Gath will plow. I, Avimelekh of the Five Lords, will station the ox."

Orpah descended the steps of the dais, her skin hot, "*Kiam ypadan-ah shuptia elu-tia, Ha'iru d'libbi, ypadan-ah shuptia elu-tia.* Then plow the field, man of my heart, station the ox."

Avimelekh broke from the entourage and approached Orpah, stopping an *amah* from her.

Orpah continued, her voice the quality of a whisper, yet heard throughout the courtyard, as she continued reciting the ritual script. All the difficulties she had with mastering the P'lishti language were now gone. Her voice sang, as if it were a heavenly echo. Her excitement continued to grow.

Avimelekh fell to his knees. The Lord of Gath bowed forward to pay homage to his goddess.

Orpah called for the bed, "Let the bed that rejoices the heart be prepared. Let the bed that sweetens the loins be prepared. Let the bed of kingship be prepared! Let the bed of queenship be prepared! Let the royal bed be prepared!"

Avimelekh rose. He and Orpah walked towards the entourage who stepped back, each couple, officer and Qadishtu, forming the corners of a square five amoth wide. Two Asheritu approached from the north carrying a woven mat, which was spread in the center of the square.

Orpah continued speaking. "We shall rejoice together and the heavens shall join us in our rejoicing. The land will be blessed. Abundance will be showered upon the fields from the heavens."

Avimelekh stood in the center of the woven mat and then sat down. Orpah approached Avimelekh and joined him on the mat. The four couple on the edge of the square mirrored their positions. The drumbeat began again slowly, and the couples began the fertility rite. Orpah felt the energy, and drew it into her. She could see the fire serpent dancing from the crowds above, descending and twisting between the couples and spiraling around her and Avimelekh, permeating her very being. She held herself, focusing as she had been taught; weaving the energy until it was overwhelming, blanketing the entire courtyard in radiant light.

Finally, there was an explosive release of energy. The lights swirled and the colorful fires all entered into Orpah and her womb. Wrapped in the powerful energy, the world exploded in red light. As pleasure exploded through her body, she felt the fetus grow in power, and she saw the *Roqeb-a Emeru-a*, the Prince of Heaven, standing before her, smiling. She felt him join with her and soon the energy increased to an even higher plateau. The entire temple was soon bathed in a weave of rapturous heat and color, as the entire crowd experienced a taste of the spiritual fire.

As the fire returned to its source, the Qadishtu and officers rose and approached Orpah and Avimelekh, helping them to their feet and escorting them to a table that was being set up on the western side of the courtyard, facing the altar. Boars were already being slaughter by soldiers, their blood sprinkled on the corners of the altar by Qadishtu, while their meat was placed on the coals to be roasted.

Everyone stood as Orpah was seated. Her goblet was immediately filled with wine. Holding it aloft, she took a sip, its taste magnified by the power coursing through her, filling her body. As she lowered the goblet from her lips, it was quickly taken from her hand, its content first shared amongst the officers and Qadishitu, then poured back into the large clay jar of wine, to be dispersed amongst the crowd.

Then a large fish, six amoth long was placed in front of Orpah. She leaned in and took a bite straight from the fish, sampling its succulent taste before it was removed, again, to be divided and shared with the worshippers. In turn, several boars were place before Orpah, who sampled each, biting into its flesh as a beast attacks its prey, allowing its juices to run down her mouth, neck and chest. These too, in turn, were removed to be shared with the congregation of Gath.

Orpah was in a state of ecstasy. *Roqeb-a Emeru-a*, her Prince consort, stood by her side whispering secrets of the universe in her ear. Visions of past and future danced in front of her. She was one with all nature and all nature was one with her. Suddenly, she saw a vision of her sister at the feet of an old man. In her vision, they both radiated white light. Anger crept up Orpah's spine. Inexplicably, she felt revulsion and hatred for the sister she had once loved. Orpah pushed the vision from her mind, to return her attention to her sacred spot and bathed in its fire.

Chapter 4

Birth Pangs
Gath

Something was bothering Orpah. She sat at the loom in her room and furiously shuttled the warp and the weave. Usually she enjoyed weaving, it brought her clarity of thought. It helped her in training to focus her spiritual 'weaving' as well. But despite that, it was her soul that was restless now. The ritual with Avimelekh had been beyond her expectations. She had reached heights of ecstasy she never imagined. Every fiber of her being was alive with sensation. Yet the vision of her sister had shaken her, and awakened in her such dark emotions.

As she contemplated the events, she became more and more convinced that the *Roqeb-a Emeru-a* purposefully placed that vision before her. Further, his purpose, it was becoming clear, was specifically to induce such an emotional reaction. The emotions were powerful and clearly they augmented the spiritual energy, but she was still left perplexed. Was it only the darker emotions that contained such power? Aside from not understanding why he would want to induce such feelings, Orpah didn't understand their source. She had been unaware of such sentiments towards her sister and even now, while they still burned within her, she couldn't fathom why she felt them.

Orpah lost control of the shuttle and the weave failed. She leaned back, and abandoned the shuttle, rubbing her eyes. They ached. She knew her sister was now on a different spiritual path from her own, but should that cause so much resentment?

Then a thought struck her, and part of the riddle seemed answered. She knew that the *Roqeb-a Emeru-a*, sometimes called B`aal, the Prince, and countless other names, was also the Accuser of Yisrael. By inducing her hatred at that moment, when the energy of all of Gath was being infused into her womb, he was endowing her unborn child with a powerful instrument for that nation's destruction. Her thoughts turned to Resheg and his contempt for `Ivrim. She had been told that her child would be the champion of the P'lisht'im in the war with the `Ivrim. Hatred was a powerful weapon.

There was deep hatred between the P'lisht'im and the `Ivrim. Simply the fact that the `Ivrim embarrassed the Mitsr'im in their flight from the Nile paradise was enough to engender disdain for that nation of usurpers and runaway slaves. The P'lisht'im had always admired the Mitsr'im, the regional, if not world, powerhouse. They held them and their culture in high esteem, the standard towards which to strive. And to top it all off, when the `Ivrim began their conquest of the Fertile Crescent, they became the chief competitors for dominance and influence in the region.

Further, the `Ivrim were polar opposites from the advanced and sophisticated P'lisht'im. If they and their god had their way, the P'lisht'im were convinced that the region would fall into backwardness and darkness. The P'lisht'im's hatred for the `Ivrim was more than simple regional competition; it was existential.

Yes, hatred was an important ingredient in the war between the P'lisht'im and the `Ivrim.

Yet, the other questions still burned: Why and from where did she have such hatred for her sister?

Her months in the temple of Asherah convinced her of the righteousness of her path. She learned that the physical license of the worship of Asherah was needed for brutish mankind, especially in this time of confusion. The physical union gives the brutish man and woman an outlet and an idea of how intoxicating true communion with the divine could be. For this reason, worshippers were required to tap into their centers of physical pleasure in order for them to get a glimpse, through its physical reflection, of the true ecstasy, which comes with spiritual union with the gods.

Despite the vision of her sister, Ruth, bathed in pure light, she was sure that she couldn't get there through her following the `Ivri god. The vision must have been a false vision placed there by the *Roqeb-a Emeru-a* simply to elicit those deep emotions. Yes, she felt something, some inner light, when she was with Khilyon. Involuntarily, the memory brought a smile to her lip. A feeling of warmth touched her heart at the memory of her husband. Yes, there was something there, but it was like a candle compared to the thousand suns coursing through her now. No, their connection to the heavens was as backwards and primitive as their culture.

Yet, she wondered, even if it was true - and she was sure it wasn't - but even if it were, why would her sister's enlightenment cause such resentment? After all, even if her sister did attain enlightenment, why would Orpah care? She had found fulfillment herself. She couldn't be happier. She had everything that she had ever wanted. Didn't she?

Well, she sighed as she rubbed her weary eyes again, smearing the remains of the green paint that surrounded her eye wells. That was a question she would have to explore another time. If nothing else, such a powerful emotion was an energy source that could be tapped. She would try and use her new powers of meditation to discover its source.

But now wasn't the time for self-reflection. She wanted to bask in the after glow of the ceremony. She wanted to enjoy her pleasure for a while. Orpah removed the light robe, allowing it to fall from her shoulders to the floor. She took an ember from the fire and lit the incense altar, filling the room with the sweet smell of date honey. Her hands slid over her body, caressing her growing stomach and enlarged breasts. Dipping her fingers in the mortar bowl, she scooped out some of the freshly ground flower pods and licked the resin off her fingers. The compound would help her relax and transcend this world. She allowed her fingers to attend to her sacred spot, and stoke the fire that still smoldered there. She began her exercises, moving her body as a serpent, gyrating her shoulders and hips, twisting her waist, generating and exciting the *nur'naHasha* within. Her movements were choreographed to bring the divine deep into her center. Colors swirled around her and Orpah's soul leapt into the abyss.

***

BethleHem

Boaz watched Ruth leave. He stood in awe of the Holy One's ways. Drawing a breath, he walked to a small hollow a few *amoth* away from the threshing floor. There was a break in the earth, and below was a small pool of water. Boaz disrobed and immersed himself in the cold, clean water, refreshing his soul and purifying his body. He exited the pool and dressed.

Returning to the threshing floor, he went to where he had left his possession and removed a large woolen shawl. Its corners were adorned with the ritual fringe ordained for the Holy One's nation. He meditated on the commandment to fringe the cornered garment, and then wrapped his head and shoulders in the Almighty's embrace.

Boaz opened a leather pouch, and removed a small black leather box. A leather strap trailed. He placed the box on his left bicep, underneath the shawl, affixing it in place with the strap so that, pointing forward, though it leaned slightly towards his chest. He wrapped the strap down his arm and around his middle finger. Boaz took a second box from the pouch, and placed it between the crown of his head and his brow, its leather strap circling from either side around his head, to rest in a knot at the nape of his neck. It resembled, to some extent, a coronet.

The boxes, the *oth* and the *totafoth*, contained selected passages from the laws of the Holy One. The passages contained those requirements to wear these "reminders" of His covenant with the nation of Yisrael, a symbol that one's thoughts and actions should be bound to the Holy.

Boaz covered his eyes with his other hand, and recited the passages, meditating on each word, allowing its holiness to fill him, as he tried to elevate his soul towards the heavens.

Completing the passages, he turned and faced northwards, towards the city of Shiloh, where the Mishqan, the tabernacle of the Holy One, currently rested. He focused on the spot between the two *keruvim*, the figures that rested on top of the Aron HaBrith, the Ark of the Covenant. Boaz directed his thoughts and his soul to that spot, the gates of heaven, and began his ascent. He sank to his knees on the sheepskin rug, bowing forward till his face brushed the rug, his hands folded on his chest. Boaz then extended his arms and then his legs, prostrating himself before the Sovereign of the Universe.

Boaz's lips offered praise and gratitude to the Source of Life; the Holy One Who in His kindness had made a covenant with Boaz's ancestors, a covenant that bound their descendants, as much as it enriched them. The elder focused his being, ascending from chamber to chamber in the Holy Palace. By the time his soul had arrived in the innermost chamber, the sage had nullified his will, his self and his being, to a level where he could be filled with the presence of the Infinite Being.

Boaz's conversation with the Almighty extended nearly an hour before he brought himself up to his knees, and then to his feet, returning to the world of the physical, but carrying with him the abundance of the divine. He breathed deeply, rejoicing in the worship of the Holy One, a gift as much as an obligation. His face was moist from tears, his mind resonating with clarity of thought. He was refreshed. The Almighty had filled Boaz with understanding. Boaz felt His Light, the afterglow of being in His Presence, coursing through him.

He left the threshing floor, as the sky was clear and bright. The morning sun hung above the horizon. As he walked towards the gates of Bethle_H_em, he rejoiced in the ways of the Holy One. This woman, Ruth, was special. From the moment he first saw her collecting sheaves in his fields, he had sensed that her destiny and that of Yisrael were linked. Her fidelity to the Almighty was so straightforward and uncomplicated that it filled him with awe.

He shook his head and sighed. He, himself, yearned for such simple, complete faith, for surely nothing could be stronger. It was what he constantly strived for, but as a sage and an elder of Yisrael, he was often so entrenched in polemics that such wholeness sometimes seemed lost to him. He had trained himself too well to always see the other side. Being *tam,* simple, in his relationship with the Holy One took effort. Thanks to the Almighty he fortuned to meet this young woman. If nothing else, it had strengthened his own bond with his Father in Heaven.

Deep in thought, he almost didn't notice the man he was seeking pass by. "Friend," he called out to the redeemer of whom he had spoken to Ruth. "Come with me, my friend," he said taking the redeemer in his arm and leading him back towards the gates of the city.

Bethle*H*em's city entrance led straight through a large gate system, eight *amoth* in width and twenty *amoth* in length. The length was broken up into three piers, which constricted the width to four *amoth*, creating two bottlenecks. The middle chamber in this gate system had access points from either side, which led to guard rooms. Defenders would be able to attack any invaders from three sides. Each pier also had large wooden doors, re-enforced with bronze bracers that could be shut and bolted. A solitary large stone tower guarded the entrance to the city.

The gate opened up into a city square, a wide paved open pavilion, rectangular in shape with low stone benches along the walls. This open square served as town center. At varying times it was a courthouse, a public forum and a learning center for the area's residents. Forming the square were several community and public buildings that opened up into it: granaries, storehouses, pottery kilns, and a winery. A bathhouse, a simple stone building housing ritual bath was just inside the gate. There were also several public cisterns housed in low building with a wide circular stairway spiraling deep into inverted bells carved into the earth. The staircase along the plastered cavern was built wide to accommodate traffic in both directions. The storehouses abutted, and in essence, formed the lower half of Bethle*H*em's protective wall.

The walls of the city were built of massive bricks built on a wide stone foundation. In many places, the wall was eight *amoth* thick. A ring of buildings used the fortification as their back wall. A cobblestone ring road, six *amoth* wide, paralleled the entire length of the city walls beginning and ending on either end of the town square. Other smaller roads fanned off of the square and the main ring road. Most of them were paved with cobblestones as well.

The cobblestone street leading out of town was crowded, as many of the farmers and their workers were making their way to their fields. The redeemer, as well, had been on his way to his field, but when the Father of the Court called him over, he was happy to oblige. The redeemer liked Boaz and had pride in the fact that such a great man in Yisrael was his kinsman.

Boaz grabbed a young boy as he was jostling past. "You, you're Gedalyah's son, aren't you." After Boaz, Gedaliyah was Bethle*H*em's most senior justice.

"Yes, your honor," a mixture of fear and awe on the young boy's face, wondering what kind of trouble he might have gotten into now.

Calming the boy with an easy smile, "Can you do me a favor and fetch your father for me, and as many other elders as you see along the way?"

"Yes, your honor," the boy nearly shouted, full of joy that he was asked to be doing such a great man a favor instead of being taken to task for something he might have done. He quickly sped off into the town.

Boaz indicated a space on one of the stone benches. "Come over here and sit down," he said to the redeemer, Paloni, who readily accepted his kinsman's invitation. Curiosity gripped him, but he knew that if Boaz called the elders together, he wouldn't reveal anything until the court was seated. So, he resigned himself to wait.

Paloni didn't need to wait long. After a few brief moments, he saw Gedalyah's son leading his father and nine other elders towards the pavilion. All of them wore the large woolen shawl of their office over their head and shoulders. Like most of the men passing through the gates of the town that morning, each was also crowned with their *totafoth*, the small black boxes containing passages of the Holy Scriptures bound to the crown of the head with a leather strap. Hidden beneath the folds of the shawl was a matching black box, an '*oth*. It too was strapped into place on their weak arms with a leather strap, which in this case snaked down the arm to be wrapped around the middle finger.

Smiling, Boaz bowed slightly to the boy, "Thank you." Producing a dried date from the folds of his robe, he tossed it to the boy, who caught it with a smile. Boaz winked and added, "Now, run along and stay out of trouble."

The elders sat in a row along one side of the pavilion. Gedalyah, understanding from Boaz's posture that he was a petitioner and wouldn't be leading the session, sat in the middle of the row. The elders of every community came into their position through the merit of their knowledge of the law, and, more importantly, their awe of Heaven. The nation of Yisrael had a permanent sitting court of twenty-three elders in every major town, yet not every issue required that all the elders be present. Of course, being a justice wasn't anyone's profession, despite its burdensome responsibility. Most of the elders were farmers, though some of them were tradesman. A good number of them also served as kohan'im, priests, serving in the *Mishqan* two weeks every year. In addition, all of the elders were teachers, each attracting several students to whom they could pass the traditions and mores of their society to the next generation.

Boaz stood between the assembled court and his kinsman, the redeemer. Gedalyah nodded for Boaz to begin.

Addressing the redeemer, but clearly so the court could hear, Boaz began, "A plot of land which belongs to our brother, Elimelekh is being sold by Naomi, who has returned from the fields of Moav. I have said and reveal this in your hearing so that you might respond, for you have first right of acquisition, and request you declare your intent to acquire it before those that are seated here, before the elders of my people. *Im ti'gh-ol, g'al. w'im lo yigh-al hagi-da li w'edh''a, ki eyn zulath'kha ligh-ol w'anokhi aHarekha.* If you will redeem it, then redeem it. However, if you will not redeem it, declare it to me now, so that I may know. For no one holds the rights to redeem it save yourself, and I am next in line."

Paloni's eyes moved from Boaz to the elders and back to Boaz. If Boaz was interested in this plot of land, it must be a choice piece of property. He had forgotten about Elimelekh's land, but the prospect of adding to his own holdings was appealing. He had a good harvest this year, and he could afford to seed more fields next season. He looked up at Boaz. *"anokhi egh-al.* I shall redeem it," he declared.

Boaz nodded his acceptance, and then, shifting his body slightly away from the redeemer and towards the court. "On the day that you acquire the field from the hand of Naomi, and," Boaz paused dramatically, "and from Ruth the Moavith, you also acquire the wife of the deceased, so that the name of the deceased will be established along with his inheritance."

The redeemer was taken aback. Marry the Moavith? Yet, he thought, wasn't that forbidden? Didn't the Torah forbid it? He knew there was a dispute about it; he had heard the scholars arguing ever since Naomi's return, but fear gripped him. No field was worth risking sanctions from the Almighty. It might put his current holdings at risk.

Before Paloni could speak up, one of the elders raised a question, "Is the Father of the Court suggesting that it's permitted to marry a Moavith?"

Boaz smiled and turned towards the court. He had been waiting for this. Several passerbyers stopped upon hearing the challenge. It was a question circulating in Bethle_H_em since Naomi's return.

"I have a tradition from my father, and he from his father, until Moshe, our teacher, that while the scriptures forbids a Moavi and an Amoni from entering the congregation of Yisrael, the prohibition does not extend to its women," stated Boaz.

"Moavi (male Moabite) and not a Moavith (female Moabite), Amoni (male Ammonite), and not Amonith (female Ammonite)," stated another elder, repeating the tradition he too had received. More passerbyers stopped to see the proceedings. Soon, a crowd gathered. Boaz was pleased. He wanted this law to be public knowledge.

"Yet has it ever been done?" asked another elder.

"Not to my knowledge," offered Boaz. "No one from Moav or Ammon, male or female, sought to follow the Holy One of Yisrael and join His people, until Ruth."

An audible gasp escaped the lips of the elders and the crowd. Most of Yisrael's jurisprudence operated on precedent. A tradition of a teaching was important, even crucial, but without actual precedent, it would be a daring thing to actually do.

"How do the elders hold?" Gedaliyah presented the question.

The other elders, nodded their heads, some less confidant than others, but they all agreed that it was permitted.

Gedaliyah voiced their response, "It is a valid tradition. One may marry a woman from Moav or Ammon, who accepts upon herself the yoke of Torah."

Another gasp was heard from the onlookers. The redeemer though was not convinced. His thoughts turned to Ma*H*lon and Kilion. Fortune hadn't smiled upon them when they married women from Moav. He didn't want to be another test case.

Paloni, the redeemer spoke up hurriedly, "I cannot, therefore redeem it, lest I endanger my own estate. You, Boaz, go ahead and redeem it yourself. I, I cannot do it."

Gedaliyah spoke to the redeemer. "Paloni ben Almoni, before this court of elders, please state your position on this property for which you are the rightful redeemer. The court bears witness."

The redeemer repeated, "I cannot redeem it. I transfer my right of acquisition to Boaz." Paloni turned to Boaz, saying, "You now have the right of acquisition."

Gedaliyah prodded, "Remove your sandal."

The Redeemer startled, and then remembered himself. Property was transferred legally in Yisrael by the removal and transfer of one's shoe. Paloni removed his sandal and handed it to Boaz.

Boaz took to the shoe and turned towards the court. Addressing the elders he said, "The elders of the court and the entire nation are witness today that I have acquired from Naomi all the property of Elimelekh and his sons, Kilion and MaHlon. I have also acquired Ruth the Moavith, MaHlon's wife, as my wife to establish the name of the deceased along with his inheritance, and so that his name will not be cut off from his brothers or from the gates of his place. You are all witnesses today."

Gedaliyah stood and the other elders followed his lead. They repeated the formula three times, "We are witnesses, we are witnesses, we are witnesses." The people who had gathered to see the proceedings also repeated, "We are witnesses."

Gedaliyah continued in the name of the court, "May the Holy One of Yisrael grant the woman who is coming into your home that she be like RaHel and like Leah, who together built the House of Yisrael. May you have valor in Efrathah and renown in Beth Le*H*em. May your house be like the house of Perets whom Tamar bore to Yehudah; from the seed which the Almighty will give you from this young woman."

Everyone in the gates, including Paloni, felt the blessing penetrate their hearts, and everyone responded heartily, "Amen."

***

Boaz and Ruth slowly walked down the stone path, side by side underneath a large outstretched canopy. The entire town seemed to line the path of the central courtyard of Boaz's estate. The afternoon sun was already low in the western sky. Ruth shyly stole glances of her groom. His face seemed to glow even brighter than the time she first noticed. She felt as if it filled her with the light of the Almighty. All the spectators would have surely agreed that that light also spilled out from her soul, enveloping her countenance as well. Ruth felt warm and happy.

A small boy holding a rooster and a small girl holding a hen walked before them, a symbol for a fruitful marriage. Ruth caught a glimpse of Naomi, tears filling her eyes, walking behind the canopy. Ruth was proud to "share" her marriage with Naomi, for it was due to her merit. It was not lost on Ruth that a child from her union would be redemption for her mother-in-law, a vindication from Heaven. Momentarily, her thoughts turned to her sister. She missed her. Ruth wished Orpah could have been here with her. Ruth was so happy. She hoped her sister had also found her place in the

121

world. Yet, in that same moment, her joy became tinged at its edge with a pang of bittersweetness. Ruth knew that her happiness came from her connection to the Holy. How had her sister turned her back on it? Maybe, she thought, her own happiness would serve as a blessing, helping her sister to find her way.

Soon they reached the entrance to one of the low stone structure that surrounded the courtyard. This was to be Ruth's new home. Several members of the congregation shouted the blessing, "May the Almighty give you the dew of heaven and the fatness of the earth, abundance of grain and wine." The answer, "Amen," resounded amongst the crowd.

Boaz ushered his bride inside: the first official time that they would be alone together. They would spend several moments inside, talking and touching for the first time, the first few flushes of intimacy. Long enough for them to consummate the relationship, even though that would actually wait until the evening. They stayed in seclusion long enough to be considered officially wed. As they emerged the awaiting guests cheered, shouting blessings and escorting them to the courtyard of the estate, where tables and cushions were set up. The bride and groom were escorted as king and queen to the head table. A basin and pitcher were placed before them, where they both washed their hands.

Boaz, taking the flat bread in his hand, offered a benediction, "May the Almighty bless this meal, and this union. He has been so gracious, sustaining us with all our needs, providing us with the grains of the earth, and filling our storehouses with breads. May all of His blessings be acknowledged, and may we partake in them for His honor, sharing His bounty with all. May our every bite be for a blessing, for us, and for the entire nation of Yisrael."

"Amen," the crowd responded, sealing the blessing with their approval.

The elder then sat, tore a piece off of the flat bread and dipped it into wine vinegar, before eating it. He then tore another piece and offered it to his bride, smiling warmly at her as he did so. Then he quickly broke off pieces of bread, dipped them, and handed them to others nearby who spread them around to all the guests, till everyone had tasted a piece.

Wine was poured into Boaz's goblet and he stood. Looking out at the crowd, his eyes tried to connect with everyone there. Everyone returned a look of love and respect. He smiled. "I am so blessed," he offered. He looked down at his bride, "so blessed." Looking out at the crowd, he continued, "I am so blessed to be a part of such a people, whose very breath is a sanctification of the Holy One's Name. May He fulfill our father Ya'aqov's blessing, and may all our eyes be red with wine, and our teeth white with milk. Blessed is the Creator of All, may all our deeds be for His sake, and may this wine, which He, in His abundance, blessed us with, be for a blessing."

The congregation repeated the well-worn phrase indicating the acceptance of his blessing as

Boaz took a sip from the wine. He then held it to his bride's lips, giving her to drink. Its sweet taste mixed with her tears, which insisted on streaming down her face. Many of the guests shared the same mixture of tastes in their wine cups.

The festive meal continued well past the setting of the sun. Dishes of roasted lamb and goat were interrupted periodically with sages offering words of wisdom, or those same sages spontaneously dancing before the bride and groom. One sage, an elder, in a burst of joy, grabbed three flaming logs and juggled them in front of the Boaz and Ruth. Soon another sage joined him and the two offered a spectacular performance, both consciously fulfilling the precepts enjoining them to rejoice with bride and groom and bring them happiness.

Ruth was surprised that sages and elders would behave so, though she enjoyed the performance. When Boaz whispered in her ear, explaining the commandment to Ruth, she couldn't contain her wonder. He explained that it wasn't only for him that such sages would perform, but even the simple laborer would be treated like royalty on his wedding day. He himself, he confessed, had performed acrobatics at most of the community's weddings.

"The secret," Boaz confided, "is to elevate the everyday and imbue it with a sense of holiness. Simply by fulfilling even a simple command of the King creates a bond between Creator and creation."

***

Gath
Six months later

The rounded chamber seemed to spin for Orpah, the light of its hundred lamps spiraling around her like fireflies circling a flame, the tail of their lights like comets'. The brightly colored depictions on the lower third of the wall of ugly dwarves holding a leaf shaped sword seemed to be dancing around Orpah forming a circle of protection. Dancing with them, at the place on the wall where the door was, was the image of a large pregnant hippopotamus with a crocodile tail and limbs of a lion. The images stretched to the ceiling. The room was thick with the smell of incense and the perfume of the garlands that littered the floor.

Yet, it wasn't the room that was dancing, but Orpah's head, spinning from the compound she had ingested earlier. She squatted on the large horseshoe shaped stone in the center of the room. Asheritu, wearing only a veil to conceal their face, formed a ring around the outer rim of the circular room. They stood motionless, chanting incantations in a low voice. Their chorus swept Orpah through realms of altered consciousness.

Forming an inner ring, the Qadishtu, their bodies painted in ancient symbols, supported Orpah's body from all sides, while they silently channeled their serpent fire into their charge.

Shiv_H_a'innana stood in front of Orpah calling out to the child in her womb. "Come, child," she coaxed, "do not be strong in her womb. Come and fulfill your destiny."

Orpah felt the contractions, but the sensation was disconnected from her consciousness. She felt as if she was swimming in a thick sea of honey. Remotely, she felt ShivHa'innana reach up inside her and draw a large object out of her. Vaguely, she was aware of the navel cord being cut. She collapsed back into the arms of the Qadishtu who sat her on the small bed that was between them and the Asheritu.

The baby, a boy, was placed in her arms.

"Name him quickly," commanded ShivHa'innana.

Roqeb-a Emeru-a, hugging Orpah's shoulders, whispered in her ear. Orpah repeated his words to the women assembled.

"Goliyath," she cried, "Goliyath."

***

BethleHem
Three months later

The room seemed crowded with women. Ruth wondered if there was enough air in the room. She certainly was having trouble breathing. She was squatting, straddling two large squared stones. A loose gown, now drenched with sweat hung from her shoulders. Several women hugged her sides, supporting her. Naomi hugged her, supporting her

126

from behind, her face pressed against Ruth's, her lips close to Ruth's ears, offering instruction and words of encouragement.

"Breath out, daughter, short breaths, "Naomi whispered, "Don't resist the contraction. Don't fight it. Try and focus through it."

The pain was incredible. Ruth had never experienced anything like this before. And it didn't seem to end. Another contraction racked her body. She tried hard to listen to her mother-in-law's advice but it was just too much pain. Blessings do not come without a price, she reminded herself. She tried to focus on what this incredible pain would bring her, but it was too much. Her breath caught, and she shook her head. She didn't think she could do this. She wanted to stop. Her voice broke out into a scream.

"A little longer," shouted the midwife who was squatting before Ruth, her hands between her legs. "He's already crowned. Now, my daughter, push!"

Naomi echoed the midwife's instructions, "Push, daughter. Help the child come forth."

Another contraction. More pain washed over Ruth, but she tried to focus and push with the pain. He was too big. There was no way that it could possibly exit her body. She so desperately wanted a child, but the pain was overwhelming. She pushed with all her might. She felt this extremely large object pushing out of her. She wanted this to be over already. She couldn't do this. She needed to stop. It was too big. And then, the pain stopped. Ruth felt this object, her baby, slide out between her legs. She collapsed against her mother-in-law in exhaustion. The crying of a baby echoed throughout the room.

"It's a boy!" shouted the midwife, who was hurriedly cleaning the birthing fluids off the baby's mouth and nose. She then held the baby in one arm, while tying off the umbilical. She cut the cord with a small flint knife she pulled from her belt. Another woman took the baby and wrapped him in a linen blanket. The midwife returned her attention to Ruth to make sure that the afterbirth exited as well.

The baby was quickly handed to Naomi, who took it with one arm, her other continuing to support Ruth. "It's a boy, my daughter. You've given birth to a son. Blessed is the Holy One."

Relief and joy washed over Ruth as she struggled to get a glimpse of her son, "A son. Praise the Almighty. A son." Ruth remembered the words of her husband, Boaz, "True fulfillment and happiness only comes with effort." She was spent from hers, but she had never felt so much joy.

One of the women turned to Naomi, "Praised be the Almighty, Who has not left you without a redeemer. May his name be worthy in Yisrael. He will renew your life and sustain you in your old age. For your daughter-in-law, who gave birth to him and who loves you, is better to you than seven sons. "

"Amen," answered the other women.

Soon the news spread from the room, to the men outside. It then spread to all of Bethle*H*em. "A son was born to Naomi."

Chapter 5

Nursing
Gath

The baby lost the nipple and Orpah had to use her free hand and return her breast to her newborn's mouth. It had been a long time, nearly twelve years, since she had a newborn in her arms. Orpah enjoyed the feeling.

Seated on a stool, Orpah wore only a collar and a girdle around her hips. Her long thick hair was bound on top of her head, falling down her shoulders and back in thick heaps. Her face was lined and bore the fatigue of having given birth only two weeks prior. Five Asheritu, 'dressed' like Orpah shuffled around the brightly lit room attending to their mistress.

One of the Asheritu sat before her with a basin of cool water, washing and massaging her feet, while another massaged her temples. Orpah closed her eyes, allowing the soothing touch of the young girls to penetrate. Her eyes ached, but she was accustomed to their soreness. The compound that a third Asheritu was preparing would help relieve most of the soreness in her eyes and her body.

Orpah had gotten used to being the center of attention, and barely paid it any mind. She drifted to the sensation of the pampering and her baby's suckling.

"Mother!" cried the excited young man as he entered the room. Orpah's face broke into a wide smile upon seeing her eldest son, Goliyath. Already four amoth tall, he was the image of a strong, muscled adult. Yet, he bounded into the room, full of excitement like the twelve year old boy he was.

"Is that how you greet your mother?" asked Orpah.

Goliyath ran up to his mother. In an exaggerated gestured he took her hand and kissed it, and then like a lion attacking his prey, his mouth went to hers, kissing her. Orpah wanted the kiss to linger, but Goliyath was exploding with enthusiasm.

"Mother," they've accepted me to academy!" the boy shouted with enthusiasm, breaking away from her embrace to face her. He was referring to the military training program, which was usually only open to men twice his age. "I bested ten men today in the competition!"

Orpah's hand caressed her son's face and then slid across his sculptured chest and stomach. He wore only a short white skirt. "You make your mother so proud." She smiled again, "My 'little man' is growing up to be a great hero."

Goliyath returned a boyish grin. Then he saw the suckling baby at his mother's breast. "Hey," he chided, "why does he get all the fun."

Orpah recognized her boy's energy. The competition surely stimulated his vigor. She looked into his eyes and saw that his lust was practically ebullient. She would have to capture such fire.

When Orpah was first confronted with taking her son as a paramour, the idea had scandalized her. The High Priestess ShivHa'innana had first proposed it more than three years ago.

"Even as water entering water has the same flavor, so faults and virtues are accounted the same as there is no opposition between them." The priestess's voice was like a song that penetrated to the depths of Orpah's being.

"You already know this world to be an illusion. Don't be enslaved by the illusion. Only in enjoying the world of sensation, can one remain undefiled by it. The very fact that it shocks you, betrays that the world of illusion still has a hold on you. You are still enslaved. Liberate yourself. Your son is already ready. He has participated in the rites of the Goddess."

When Orpah confided her hesitancy to Resheg, his nonchalant response soothed her. ""It's only a convention," he said calmly.

Orpah missed Resheg. He had become a confidant and advisor to her. His story was incredible. Over the years, he would drop small morsels of it, whetting Orpah's appetite, only for him to later demur. Resheg was an 'Ivri who turned his back on his people and his god, coming to embrace the Pelishti culture and lifestyle. Now, he had nothing but scorn for his former life.

Yet, that was all she knew. What and how he had become enthralled by the Pelishti world, and how he had risen to be one of its leading citizens, he had kept a riddle.

It was almost as much of a riddle as his disappearance. She remembered the day clearly. It still brought her dismay. There had been a festival at the temple. Four hundred and eighty men had gathered for the celebration. After ingesting sacred herbs, the men began having ritual intercourse with Qadishtu on the floor of the courtyard, while Orpah watched from the dais. Two Asheritu knelt before her and attended to her sacred spot during the course of the ceremony. The men were enjoined from releasing their seed in order to augment their serpent fire. The object was to bring them to higher realms of consciousness, strength, and bliss.

In the middle of the ceremony, someone had entered, approached Resheg and whispered something in his ear. Resheg froze for a pregnant moment and then disengaged from underneath the Qadishtu. Orpah remembered thinking then that it was the first time she could recall Resheg not 'failing' to retain his seed.

Resheg stood up and left the courtyard and the temple never to be heard from again. Orpah still hadn't seen her sweet escort or even the messenger, both of whom she discreetly sought for many days afterwards.

The newborn had fallen asleep in Orpah's arms. "Here, now it's your turn," she said handing Goliyath the baby, "place him in the crib." Then noting his energy, she added, "and be gentle with your brother." And son, she added in her thoughts shamelessly.

* * *

BethleHem

Ruth watched her son approach from a distance, and a tear came to her eyes. `Oved had grown into such a fine young man. A man: in truth, he would reach the age of majority, thirteen, in only a few short months. A lump formed in her throat. She wished her husband, Boaz, could have lived to see him. Everyone saw the elder sage in the boy. He was as gifted in the tradition, as he was generous and kind. She missed Boaz, and the light that shone in his eyes. She missed Naomi too. Her mother-in-law had finally gone to join her husband and children. Yet, Naomi had died full of life, content and complete. Life was bittersweet, thought Ruth. Her own life was a glaring example. There had been many difficult times, but, in truth, they only helped to augment the blessings the Holy One bestowed. It was clear that without the hardship, those moments of grace wouldn't have come. They were worth every struggle, she decided, watching her son.

Yet, of late, she had been disturbed by several vision, dreams and glimpses that she could not interpret. In the hour before she awoke, they came: A dream about a boy being pursued by lions and bears. While it wasn't her son in the dream, she felt connected to him, but she was forced to stand by and watch, unable to help. The boy overcame the lion and the bear, but something, she was never able to perceive what it was, would seem to fall from her. Like a seed, it would grow into a huge dog-like beast, who sought to crush the boy. She always awoke before the dream ended. It disturbed her, and she sought its meaning. For the moment, though, it eluded her. She prayed to the Holy One to send her clarity.

`Oved rushed to his mother's side. *"Shalom alayikh, immi.* Peace unto you, Mother," he said excitedly. He gently kissed her hand, as his mother returned his greeting, *"Shalom Alekha."*

"Well," she said with a smile, "I see you have news. You can barely contain yourself."

He practically burst with joy. "The sage Gedaliyah has agreed to take me as a student," he nearly shouted. Gedaliyah succeeded Boaz as the Father of the Court, and to become his student was considered a singular honor.

Ruth teared with joy. "Blessed is the Holy One," she said, not being able to fathom a life more complete. Her thoughts again turned to her sister. She always missed her at moments like these, wondering if she had found what she had been searching for, too. She offered a silent prayer for her sister, as she pulled her son close in an embrace. The Holy One had given her so much.

***

While Gedaliyah succeeded Boaz in Bethle*H*em, the mantle of leadership for the entire nation of Yisrael passed to pious man from the north, Ilon the Zevuloni, from the tribe of Zevulon. The spirit of the Holy One rested upon him, but he wasn't the leader that Boaz had been, and the nation entered a period of decline. He led Yisrael for ten years.

The *Shofet*, `Avadon ben Hallel succeeded him. `Avadon struggled for eight years to keep the enemies of Yisrael at bay. Yet, Yisrael fell. More and more, they succumbed to the surrounding influence. More and more, they distanced themselves from the embrace of the Holy One.

Upon the death of `Avadon, the Holy One caused his spirit to rest on Shim'shon, ben Meno-a*H*. Shim'shon was anointed the *Shofet* of Yisrael on `Oved's wedding day, shortly after his eighteenth birthday. Within a year, Ruth became a grandmother, with the birth of Yishai. `Oved eventually became an elder, sitting on the court like his father. Shortly after the celebration of Yishai's wedding, `Oved succeeded Gedaliyah as the Father of Bethle*H*em court of elders, a few months before his thirty-eighth birthday.

Shim'shon was a powerful person, yet the nation of Yisrael refused to follow him. While he valiantly tried to fight the enemies of the Almighty, he was like a general without troops. Too often, he seemed to be fighting his own people as much as their enemies. Frustrated, the controversial *Shofet* tried some unconventional tactics to defeat the enemies of the Holy One of Yisrael. He served as *Shofet* for nearly twenty years.

Chapter 6

Shim'shon
`Aza
383 years from the Exodus of Mitsrayim

Goliyath drew in a deep breath of the sea air. It felt good in his lungs. This was his first time in the port city of `Aza. While similar in many ways to his hometown of Gath, it was the differences that fascinated him. He enjoyed walking along the port, the salt air in his face, and the cries of the sea birds in his ears. The sun glistened off the brass plates of his armor. It reminded him of a trip he had made with his mother once to Ashdod.

She should be here, Goliyath thought. This victory was hers by all rights, and she should be sharing in its celebration. Delaiy'lah was her protégé, and it was only through Orpah's devices that this `Ivri brigand was brought down. But, his mother didn't like to leave her chambers much these days. Her eyes were continually bothering her.

Goliyath understood. His eyesight too sometimes seemed to fail him, especially from the periphery. He wondered what its cause was. Before Goliyath could finish his thought, he stumbled over a bystander that was just outside his field of vision.

"*Addaniqa!*" the bystander, a burly man, began to complain, recovering and turning to teach the clumsy pedestrian a lesson. The bystander's demeanor immediately softened when his eyes fell on Goliyath. Nearly five *amoth* tall and more than a third as wide, the officer from Gath was rarely challenged on the street. Most people gave him a wide berth wherever he walked. And, despite his advanced years, Goliyath was still growing.

Goliyath looked down at the bystander and offered him a boyish grin. He was in a good mood. "Please excuse me sir, I was so entranced by the beautiful scenery, I didn't see you."

The burly bystander was confounded. Normally, he would teach such a clumsy oaf a thing or two; he himself stood at nearly four and a half *amoth*. But this one was so huge, and he did apologize. He felt the eyes of his fellows on his back. Finally, taking a defiant posture, he said sternly, "Well, don't let it happen again."

"Again, my apologies," returned Goliyath jovially. He didn't need to prove anything. He turned to continue on his way.

"Did you see how that one turned tail?" the burly man turned to his fellows. "What has our military come to, producing cowards like these, and an officer no less?" The man barely finished his sentence when he felt a tap on his shoulder. He turned around, agitated at someone stealing his moment of glory. Goliyath towered above him.

"What was that you were saying about our military?" asked Goliyath, his tone was even, but his expression was dark.

"Eh," the words caught in the burly man's throat. Goliyath seemed to be growing in front of

138

him. The man didn't know what to do. He had a reputation to maintain, but he didn't think he wanted to tangle with this one.

Goliyath didn't give him long to decide. The burly man felt a massive hand surround his throat. It began to tighten. He was fast too, decided the burly man, who was being lifted off the ground. His hands now struggled to remove the grip from his throat.

Goliyath lifted him up to eye level. The man's face colored from red to purple. "No one," Goliyath lectured sternly, "no one maligns the great army of the P'lisht'im. Understand?"

The burly man struggled to nod his head in agreement. He was unable to voice anything but a gurgle.

"Fine. Today is a glorious day for our people. We're celebrating the capture and defeat of that 'Ivri brigand," Goliyath's face lightened. "Therefore, I'll let you off with a warning," he smiled mockingly, repeating the burly man's words, "don't let it happen again."

With a toss of his hand, Goliyath sent the burly man flying into a nearby stall. He then turned to the other bystanders and offered the sheepish grin of a twelve year old. "Sorry about the mess," he shrugged.

Now Goliyath was bothered. Why did that man have to ruin his good mood? He had been too generous with that braggart. His determined pace caused passerbyers to quickly make way, afraid of being in the path of such a hulking figure.

By the time he reached the temple, the brisk pace had relaxed somewhat, and Goliyath's mood again lightened. He had some time; maybe he would find a nice Harimtu or two in the temple, which would help him to exercise his frustration.

"Ladies," Goliyath said as he bowed in mock greeting to the large breasted Asherah statues framing the wide fortified entrance. The entrance chamber was like the one at home, with a brick framed hearth at either end. There were two veiled Harimtu seated by the northern hearth. They stood up as Goliyath entered, but they reminded him of used rags, and he turned away, looking for something else.

An Asheritu passed through from the courtyard, and Goliyath considered her, but he knew she was off-limits. He had gotten chastised enough times in his mother's temple for despoiling the virgin attendants. Yet, he couldn't help himself sometimes. They reminded him of the young maidens he found in the village raids. They always had such bright lights in their eyes, at least until they became his prize.

An oil lamp affixed to the wall caught his attention. It was a ritual lamp, but Goliyath snuffed the light between his fingers, a mischievous vice from childhood. He enjoyed the sizzle of the extinguished flame. An Asheritu quickly came over and relit the lamp. All eyes were apprehensively affixed on the giant wandering aimlessly in the entrance chamber.

Suddenly Goliyath recognized a familiar face. "Delaiy'lah!" he exclaimed, calling out the name of his mother's protégé.

"Goliyath, *minna atta abatu akhana?* What are you doing here?" She clucked, "Bored with causing trouble in Gath?"

"Maybe I wanted to see what charms you used to subdue that brigand," his tone betrayed his growing excitement. Delaiy'lah was a beautiful young woman, with long dark hair and almond eyes. Her long neck was framed in a colorful collar above a bare chest that, though not large, was firm and inviting.

Goliyath placed his large hands firmly Delaiy'lah hips and pulled her closer to him.

"Not so fast, Goliyath," teased Delaiy'lah, "I'm not a Harimtu, you know. You can't simply come into a temple of Asherah and have your way with her priestesses."

Goliyath grimaced. He didn't like these games. "I'm not some average petitioner," his tone did not hide his annoyance, "I am *the* Pelishti."

Delaiy'lah took a step back. She was just playing, but now Goliyath attitude bothered her. "I'm the guest of honor at the *akitu*, the victory celebration, I don't know that I'd have time to attend to you properly, she demurred. Her tone was firm, but her eyes searched Goliyath wildly, anxious of his response.

With a grunt, Goliyath released his hold on Delaiy'lah. "Who'd want to be with someone that allowed an 'Ivri to enter her 'temple' anyway," he spat. Goliyath stormed away. Delaiy'lah breathed a sigh of relief.

Goliyath left the temple of Asherah, bothered and annoyed. Why do people keep ruining his mood? The walk to the temple of Dagon, where the festivities were to be taking place, was a short distance. He found some other Pelishti officers who had also arrived for the celebration and joined their conversation. Talking with fellow soldiers was a welcome distraction. Everyone was excited about the capture of the 'Ivri brigand. He had caused the people much trouble, but now that he was captured, his exploits were a source of entertaining conversation.

The Pelishti Empire had expanded eastward, controlling large areas of the Yehudah and Efrayim hillside. Many of the 'Ivri towns, and their 'Ivrim, were now under their control, and many more under their influence. Many of them had started to see the righteousness of the Pelishti way of life. Yet, one 'Ivri had threatened the entire enterprise. "Shim'shon," a renegade self-appointed 'savior' of the 'Ivrim soon became a household name. Seemingly overnight, his reckless exploits made his name and his strength legendary from Ashur to Mitsrayim.

In the beginning, the P'lishtim had accepted and even admired, this son of Mano-a*H*. Their society was open to anyone who wanted to join. Shim'shon was a paragon of strength, and seemed to fit in with their society. He even married a Pelishti woman from Timnah.

The trouble, so the story goes, all started with a wager. The P'lisht'im loved their riddles. It was an infective pastime throughout the empire. Shim'shon, trying to fit in, offered one at his wedding celebration, giving the guests several days to solve it. If they couldn't, the thirty participants would each have to give Shim'shon a garment and a shawl. If he lost, he would have to pay each of them a garment and a shawl. Eventually, the guests managed to decipher his riddle, but Shim'shon was unable to pay his wager. Therefore, in frustration and desperation, he turned the brigand, murdering thirty innocent citizens of Ashqelon, taking their garments to pay his debt. From then on, this brigand caused the P'lisht'im nothing but trouble, burning fields, robbing, murdering and terrorizing the countryside. Even his own people saw the danger in letting him run free. Acquiescing to the P'lishti demand, they turned him in. Yet he escaped, causing even more mayhem. Despite the P'lishti military's best efforts, he seemed impossible to bring to justice.

Finally, recognizing that the source of Shim'shon's strength and good fortune must be supernatural, the Lords of the P'lisht'im turned to Goliyath's mother. Over time, her symbolic role as head of the entire Asherah cult became a functional role as well. She was known as a woman with whom the gods spoke. Since the source of Shim'shon's strength was supernatural, they would need the help of the gods to contain it. Orpah would beseech the gods, and give the Lords of the P'lishtim instructions for defeating this troublesome foe.

Orpah was more than happy to help. She learned much about Shim'shon from both her worldly and other worldly contacts. Orpah discovered that Shim'shon had a reputation for visiting the women at the Asherah temple in `Aza. She also learned that there was a particular woman, a priestess of Asherah in Soreq, whom Shim'shon favored. A plan for his capture came to fruition. Orpah prepared a trap for the brigand using this woman from Soreq, Delaiy'lah, as both the bait and the snare. First, Orpah took Delaiy'lah on as a protégé. For months, she trained Delaiy'lah in the art of weaving *nur'naHasha*. Delaiy'lah became a vessel for the serpent fire of Lilith, Asherah's name amongst the heavenly host of angels.

Delaiy'lah captured Shim'shon's heart, but despite her best efforts was unable to use his strength against him. On advice from the angel Samu-el, *Roqeb-a Emeru-a*, they changed tactics. Manipulating the *nur'naHasha*, Delaiy'lah wove a net of intrigue around her paramour, slowly and gently, extracting his secret from his very own lips.

As soon as they shaved the brigand's head, his incredible strength vanished. The Lords of the P'lisht'im came themselves to oversee his capture. Once bound, they bored out his eyes, and paraded him through the streets of `Aza. This once feared brigand had become a mockery, as had his god. He was now chained and imprisoned in an inner chamber of the temple, sentenced to 'grind flour,' for the gods.

* * *

Shim'shon's breath was heavy. The searing pain of his eye sockets either subsided, or he simply had acclimated to it. They still ached, as did the rest of his body, but it was bearable. Yet, what bothered him the most at the moment was the constant itching of his scalp. The annoyance grew, for he was unable to relieve it, as his fettered arms bound him, spread eagle, on some type of grinding stone. Unbeknownst to him, his hair began to sprout anew.

He was alone in the brightly lit room. Shim'shon knew of the light through the heat of the lamps, but he hadn't any vessel left to receive their light. He wondered if they kept the room lit for their own needs, or as some type of cruel joke on their eyeless prisoner.

The solitude was welcome. Since his capture, he had been the victim of unseen women constantly manipulating him, extracting from him what strength he had left, along with his seed.

Shim'shon accepted his fate. It was his eyes that brought him to this shame. He had succumbed to the wiles of women, instead of being loyal to his duty to the Holy One of Yisrael. The punishment, he decided, fit the crime.

And, the crime, he decided, was simple hubris. He had decided, as a messenger of the Almighty, that he would repair the character flaw of the P'lisht'im. He, himself, would raise them out of their spiritual degradation. They were ruled by the zodiac of Capricorn, the goat kid, which was also the sign of the Angel Samu-el.

In order to break its influence, he brought his first wife's family a goat kid, and clothing made from goat's wool. He wanted to transform the evil influence into positive energy.

Unfortunately, in trying to pull them out of the mire, he seemed to have been sucked in. It was a bitter irony that he was now a captive in the city of `Azah, whose name, boldness, comes from the word for goat.

Shim'shon tried to lift his head to heaven, as he released a bitter cry. His empty eyes sockets, however, were unable to shed any tears.

***

The festival was underway, but Goliyath was bored and wandered the periphery. He found these ritual celebrations tiring. Especially, in the temple of Dagon, whose rituals were particularly mild for Goliyath. He was used to the more colorful rites of Asherah. He wanted some sport, and he said as much to the young soldiers that had attached themselves to him as he wandered about. They should bring out the brigand, he suggested, and torment him in public.

The Five Lords of the Pelishtim and their retinue, feasting in the courtyard before the giant image of Dagon, also seemed bored. The appointed ruling Lord, for they ruled in rotation, was giving a speech for the fifth time, accompanied by appropriate libations and sacrifices. *"Ala'ainu heviu Shim'shon nakharnu Harabu matanu anna iddanu. Taklimu l-ala'ainu rabu w' Dagon saru.* Our gods have delivered, Shim'shon, our enemy, the destroyer of our country, into our hand. Give thanks to the great gods, and to Dagon their Ruler. Dagon has defeated the 'Ivri and made a mockery of his god."

The overflowing crowd of three thousand men and women on the roof of the temple courtyard automatically cheered in response. It contained less enthusiasm than before. Boredom seemed to infect them as well, but they were being well fed, so they responded as they were expected.

Soon the suggestion, whispered from ear to ear reached the table of the Lords. Avimelekh, the named title of the ruling Lord, welcomed it when it reached his ear. He dreaded having to give the same speech a sixth time.

Instead he called out, *"Qer''a l-listi-a.* Call for this brigand. Call for Shim'shon that he make sport for us." He whispered an aside to the lord seated next to him, "I understand he's been having quite a bit of sport over with the priestesses of Asherah." His companion chuckled in response.

***

147

The sound of the door opening stirred Shim'shon from some semblance of sleep. He tried to open his eyes, but then the bitter memory of his portion returned to him. A cry escaped his lips. He felt hands on him, moving him. He heard the chains being opened, and then closed again. He was moved from the stone, and made to stand as the fetters were rearranged to allow him to walk. Shim'shon was resigned. He moved to the will of his captors. He felt the salt air on his face as they emerged from the temple, and knew he was outside. There was a rough guard on either side of him, and he heard the footsteps of several others. Vaguely he wondered what was happening. He considered the possibility that they were taking him to his execution. The thought was disturbingly comforting.

Shim'shon was led inside another building. He heard the chattering of a large crowd. It sounded like the squawking of geese. Occasionally, he caught a curse or insult thrown in his direction. His captors led him into the center of a large open roofed arena, and stood him there, chained and naked, as taunts rained down on him. He surmised he was in the courtyard of some temple, as garbage didn't accompany the curses.

A small hand, that of a youth's, grasped his, and began to lead him towards the center of the courtyard. The crowd quieted down, obviously at the signal of some authority. The boy led Shim'shon to the two central pillars of the courtyard. There, before the image and altar of some god, Shim'shon was forced to stand.

"*Aga gabru raba d' `ivr'iu!* This is the great hero of the `Ivri!" shouted a voice of authority, mockingly. The crowd responded with cheers and curses, interspersed with more mocking of Shim'shon and his god, by the authoritative voice.

"Leave me be," Shim'shon said to the boy guiding him. "Let me feel the pillars, so I can lean on them, and let me alone."

The boy didn't respond immediately.

"Let me lean on the pillars," Shim'shon repeated before adding, "They may begin to throw things soon, it would be a shame if you were injured."

"They aren't going to throw anything," the boy said, "we're inside the temple of Dagon." Then the boy lowered his voice, a conspirator. "Yet, I will leave you," he whispered, "I am an `Ivri slave here, and have no love of these uncircumcised. May the Almighty restore your strength."

Shim'shon's expression was a mixture of a smile and a grimace as the boy placed his hands, each on one of the two pillars. "Let me feel the pillars, upon which this house stands," said Shim'shon to the boy, "then you must leave. Leave this house, and may the Holy One be with you."

Shim'shon took hold of the two central pillars, and cried out to the Almighty. His voice was strained from the abuse to his body, but the cry, coming from the depth of his soul, soon filled the heavens.

"My Lord, the Almighty," cried Shim'shon, O Holy One of Yisrael, *zokhrani na!* Remember me, please! Take notice of me, please!" Shim'shon's voice fell to a whisper, "Please."

"*w'Haz'qeni na! akh hapa`am hazeh.* Strengthen me, if only this one time," Shim'shon poured out his prayer, "If only this one time, O' Holy One, *w'-inaqmah n'qam aHath mish'they `eynay mip'lisht'im.* Avenge me, allow me to wreak vengeance on these P'lisht'im for one of my two eyes." Shim'shon breathed deeply. He would save the vengeance for the other eye for another time, another lifetime. He sighed with resignation.

The mighty man of Yisrael took hold of the two pillars. *"tamoth nafshi `im p'lisht'im.* Let my soul expire with the P'lisht'im," Shim'shon breathed as he pushed with all his strength. He felt strength returning to his arms. The columns began to give.

Several officers in the courtyard noticed Shim'shon, yet they stood transfixed, unable to fully comprehend the scene. Goliyath was at the far end of the courtyard, but then it too caught his attention too. He understood immediately. He began to shout a warning, but it was too late. Shim'shon pushed the thick support columns to the roof outward. They were soon uprooted from the floor. In a matter of moments, the roof collapsed on top of Shim'shon, bringing the crowd above crashing down.

***

Mortar and stone filled the courtyard along with a thick cloud of smoke. The screaming was incessant. Goliyath wrestled himself free from under a piece of ceiling and ran to the center of the courtyard. Bodies were everywhere. His heart screamed in horror as he wrenched bodies from beneath the rubble.

Goliyath trembled with anger. He vowed to himself that he would have his revenge. He would avenge his people of this mockery. "These 'Ivrim and their god will pay!" he shouted to anyone that would hear. He would make sure of it.

***

Part Two

Chapter 1

Rebel

The Hills of Yehudah,
Summer, Year 422 from the Exodus

The young man sat on the gradual slope overlooking the na*H*al - a dry riverbed. Perched on the flats of his feet, his knees bent up to his chest, he played a gentle tune on the small reed flute he had finished making only moments before. His charge, the flock of sheep and goats, lazily grazed on the various vegetation interspersed throughout the na*H*al.

The shadows of night had already begun to intermix with the light of day creating an eerie admixture of shadows, which seemed to dance to the melody of the flute. The young shepherd had chosen to take his father's flock out in the evening hours to mitigate against the heat of the *H*amsin, the desert heat wave that had oppressed the area for the last few days. In the evening, with the heat dissipated somewhat, the flock would be much more comfortable grazing on the sparse summer vegetation.

Of course, there were other dangers that came with the night. The young man, entranced by the night air and giving expression to the melody of his soul, seemed completely unaware that three figures slowly crept up behind him. The flock below seemed equally oblivious.

The three figures moved silently, each step deliberate, testing the ground before its commitment. Slowly they encircled their target, and then, on signal from one of them, they leapt towards their prey.

Yet, their prey was no longer there. At the moment of their leap, the shepherd rolled onto his back under and away from his attackers who collided one with the other. The shepherd continued his backward somersault around to his feet, where he then sprang up facing his attackers.

His face broke into a wide genuine smile, but the laughter, almost a chuckle, sounded forced. "Sons of Zeru'yah, you couldn't sneak up on a lame turtle!" Dawid clucked.

His attackers disentangled themselves from each other and turned towards Dawid, crouching on their heels. "How could you have possibly detected us?" asked Yoav in exasperation, "You must have the Holy One whispering in your ear!"

Dawid offered another chuckle. "The next time you want to sneak up on someone, don't come from downwind." He paused and then added, "or at least bathe before you do."

They all shared a laugh.

Yoav let out another exasperated grunt, "You defy logic, Dawid." He rose from the ground and held out his arms. Dawid met the embrace.

"*Shalom Ale'khem!* Peace unto you all," Dawid offered.

"*Shalom Ale'khah!*" Yoav responded. His two brothers also rose to their feet and greeted Dawid in the same manner.

The three brothers, Yoav, Avishay and Asahel, despite being only a few years junior to Dawid, were his nephews, the sons of Zeruyah, Dawid's sister.

Yoav, the oldest of the brothers, was also the tallest, taller than his uncle Dawid by nearly a full tefa*H,* a handbreadth. He had dark eyes and a thin angular face shadowed by a sparse dark beard. His face was framed by dark brown peyoth, the side locks mandated for their people by the Almighty, hidden amongst a tangled mop of hair. All of the boys seemed to have let their hair grow wild.

"Have you heard any news?" Yoav asked, as the four young men, ranging in age from fourteen to seventeen, returned to their crouched sitting position, surveying the flock below, who seemed to have been singularly unaffected by the commotion above.

"No, have you?" Dawid asked in return. It was understood that the "news" of the day could only relate to one thing: the battle at 'Even Ha-'Ezer with the P'lisht'im. The Nation of Yisrael had assembled a large army there to challenge the army of the uncircumcised at Afeq.

"I heard we haven't moved yet, but I don't know the details," offered Avishay, "I wish I was there."

The words hung in the night sky. All four of the young men had heard scattered reports of a massive P'lisht'im army on the battlefield. Their thoughts turned to some of Dawid's older brothers. Along with their father - the others' grandfather, Yishai, who was an elder on the tribal council, the brothers went to join the battle against the 'uncircumcised.'

"You think Eli'av and the others are okay?" offered Asahel, the youngest, voicing the other's concern.

"Yeah, I'm sure they're fine," Dawid smiled, "They could probably take the whole army of the P'lisht'im themselves, they're so hard-headed."

The others laughed.

"The Holy One of Yisrael watches over his people," Dawid continued, "don't worry."

"But," started Avishay. The words caught in his throat. Finally, the thought found voice, "But what about the warning, the vision of Sh'mu'el. Everyone's talking about it. Maybe it's come to pass."

Yoav waved his hands dismissivly. "When was that prophesy made? Twenty years ago? Thirty? What makes you think it'll come to pass now? Every time there's a hint of trouble, everyone begins with whispers of that vision."

Many years ago, a vision, his first, had come to Sh'mu'el, now famous as a prophet of the Holy One of Yisrael. It occurred when he was a boy ministering the Chief Kohen-Priest Eli. It was the first of many visions. Soon, in a time when true visions were rare, Sh'mu'el gained a reputation as a true prophet. Yet, his first prophesy still remained unfulfilled.

Eli was more than the Kohen Gadol, the High Priest. A year after he inherited the role of Kohen Gadol, Shim'shon met his fate. By default, it seemed, Eli also became the *Shofet* of the Nation of Yisrael. That was nearly forty years ago. That same year, a pious woman, named Hanah dedicated her newborn son to the service of the Almighty. Eli raised the boy, Sh'mu'el, as a son at the Mishqan. While he was still a young boy, Sh'mu'el heard the voice of the Almighty calling him. Eli examined the boy, and discovered that Sh'mu'el was receiving true prophecy. Sh'mu'el's vision was a confirmation of an early missive that Eli had received.

That first vision was troubling. Word of it was often whispered amongst the nation when trouble seemed to be at the doorstep. The Almighty had warned that he would bring judgment on Yisrael, for Eli, and in particular his two sons, had been remiss in their role as leaders of the nation. The Holy One had promised that He would cause a deed that would "ring in the ears" of the nation. Everyone would know that He had judged Eli for not reproaching his sons. The warning was frighteningly horrible, but Eli seemed unable, or unwilling, to address its cause.

"The Holy One did promise that He would send something that would ring in all of Yisrael's ears," said Avishay. "When was the last time that all the tribes were assembled to fight against the P'lishtim?"

Avishay's words sent a chill through everyone. The four sat in silence, each with his own thoughts.

"Even a true vision of doom can be annulled," offered Dawid.

The four sat in silence, each with his own thoughts.

"What is good in His sight, the Almighty, will do, Dawid declared, "Our task is to continually pray for His compassion. May it be His Will that we receive it."

The others quickly responded, "Amen."

"Enough of this," Yoav jumped to his feet. "I'm hungry, let's make some dinner."

Dawid laughed again, his broad smile breaking though the reddish beard. "You never fail to amaze me, always thinking with your stomach, son of Zeru'yah.

"You know that's not very nice," offered Asahel.

"What's not?" asked Dawid.

"When everyone calls us 'sons of Zeruyah.' You know we have a father too."

"Had," spat Avishay bitterly. Their father had disappeared shortly after Asahel's weaning without a trace. No one knew if he was alive or dead. As such, his wife, Zeru'yah couldn't remarry, for she was neither widowed nor divorced. The three boys had sometimes heard other's whispering behind their back that they must have sprung up from the earth. Since the day it became clear that their father was missing forever, no one in the family mentioned his name again.

"Sorry Asahel," apologized Dawid, "I didn't mean anything by it."

"It's okay," Asahel breathed, the tension relaxing from his young face. His coloring was like his brother Yoav, as was Avishay's. But unlike his two older brothers, Asahel was much rounder, with a cherubic face that made him look younger than his years. Even with the first sprouting of black hairs on his face, he looked two or three years younger than his fourteen years.

"What about dinner?" asked Yoav with mock impatience.

"I caught a few turtledoves earlier," said Dawid. "Help me pen the flock in the cave down there, and we'll make a camp."

Avishay patted a sack on his belt, "Good, I have some flour. I helped Yoash with his grinding and got some flour for my time."

"Let's get them penned," said Dawid.

The four young men descended the slope of the wadi, spreading out to encircle the flock, leaving an opening in the direction of a small cave several amoth across and up the other side of the wadi. The sheep were the first to move obediently in the direction its shepherds indicated, snatching an extra bite of vegetation here and there along the way.

The goats, on the other hand, rebelled. They seemed intent on going in the opposite direction, just for spite. Yet, the boys were well-experienced shepherds and were able to anticipate and block the goats' flight. Eventually, the entire flock, numbering more than four hundred moved down the na*H*al and up the other side. The flock followed Dawid, while Zeru'yah's sons brought up the rear. Soon the entire flock entered a large cave, a breach in the hard rocky landscape that nature had carved in the hill country of Yehudah.

Even before all the goats and sheep had entered, Dawid began moving the boulders and logs he had prepared beforehand into the entranceway of the cave. Inside the cave, the flock crowded around a water pool that Dawid had carved into the rock floor years before. He also created a channel in which he could direct the water of a small natural spring inside the cave to the pool. He used this cave often when he brought the flock out to pasture. The other young men joined him in creating the makeshift wall in the entranceway, and within moments, the flock was secured for the night.

Brushing the dust from his tunic, a simple natural colored four-cornered wool garment belted at the waist and ending in the intricately tied fringes called tsitsith, Dawid allowed himself a moment to look up into the sky. The night sky always fascinated him, especially in the summer months when it was free from clouds. The bright stars set in a magical pattern made him feel at the same time small, yet part of something vast. The night sky inspired tremendous awe of the Creator of the World in Dawid, and he could ponder it and it's intricacies for hours.

"Dawid, what are you looking at. The Almighty isn't going to send us manna from heaven. I'm hungry," complained Yoav.

"Alright," chuckled Dawid as he broke his attention from the stars. "Let's build a fire pit." "Asahel," he instructed, "bring some of those large rocks over here and we'll build an oven."

Dawid began to organize his friends, "Yoav, you bring the kindling and the dried manure from the donkeys. I piled it up over there." He gestured to a pile a few amoth away from the camp with his head, for his hands were busy clearing away an area of ground in front of the cave.

"Avishay, go into the small cave over there," Dawid again gestured with his head, "You'll find a bowl and a pitcher. Get some water from the spring and begin to make the dough."

Avishay emerged from the cave holding up a large plain ceramic bowl. "This?" he asked. When

Dawid nodded agreement, Avishay added, "I didn't find the pitcher though."

"It's probably by the spring then," offered Dawid, "Look around."

After about fifteen minutes, a fire was burning in a small stone fire pit. Avishay had also finished kneading the dough for the bread.

"Okay," said Dawid as he climbed above the cave, and rolled away a small boulder that hid an indentation. He brought out six turtle doves, handing them down, one at a time to Yoav. They were each tied with a leather thong around the base of their wings and their legs. They cooed gently.

"Wow, they're nice healthy birds, a lot of meat on these." Yoav said, admiringly. "My stomach is becoming impatient."

"Woy," Dawid exclaimed as he descended to the ground. His expression was pained.

"What happened?" asked Yoav with concern.

"I don't have a knife." Dawid said, his hand going to his forehead remembering. "Shimon had come by, to ask to borrow one. He was supposed to bring it back. I guess he got involved in something and hasn't had the chance yet. Do any of you have one?"

Three blank faces stared back at Dawid. They needed a knife to slaughter the birds.

"What are we going to do?" pleaded Yoav, "I'm hungry."

"Do you know where we can get a knife?" offered Dawid.

"How about Shimon. I hear he has one," joked Avishay. Yoav scowled at him in return.

"I don't know where he is," confessed Dawid.

"Why don't we borrow one," offered Yoav.

"Not too many people around here would loan us a knife," Avishay suggested, hinting at their reputation as troublemakers.

"Look why don't we just take one and restore it later. They would assume Dawid took it anyway," tried Yoav.

Dawid rolled his eyes.

"You end up having to pay restitution on all those things you don't steal. What would it hurt to one time take something we need?" chided Yoav, half seriously.

"Because it's forbidden," Dawid said sternly. Yoav had hit a soft spot. Dawid had a legendary, but truly undeserved, reputation as a rebel and a troublemaker. It was that reputation that had drawn Yoav to Dawid, wanting a bit of adventure. He soon learned the truth: that Dawid was as God fearing, if not more so, than anyone in Yehudah.

Yet anytime something went missing or was damaged, Dawid was blamed, and he always paid the restitution or repaired the damage without protest. The young son of Yishai confided in Yoav that his account was with the Holy One, not with his countrymen. He was sure that the truth would, in the end, be revealed. Yoav wasn't so sure. He occasionally caught Dawid shedding a tear or two over the accusations.

"Hey," shouted Yoav as a new idea struck him, "There's that P'lisht'im garrison at Beth Tapua_H_ right now. I bet they have a knife.

"That's your stomach talking," Dawid retorted. "I don't think they'd loan a bunch of `Ivrim a knife, unless they were going to stick it into our belly."

"And that won't satisfy your stomach," joked Asahel.

"Besides, even if we were going to try and 'borrow' it ourselves, it would take us nearly an hour to get there and back," offered Avishay.

"Look, anyway it's going to take us some time and wouldn't it be fun to join in the war, even if it's only taking a knife," Yoav seemed to have forgotten his hunger for the moment, as his thirst for adventure grew.

Dawid smiled. He would love to cause a little damage to those uncircumcised. "Why not? But you better let me sneak up on them. You still haven't bathed and they're a little bit more adept than a lame turtle."

They all laughed.

"This is going to be great!" exclaimed Asahel at the prospect of joining the adventure.

"Whose going to stay with the flock," asked Dawid soberly. He already knew the answer.

Everyone looked at Asahel.

"Why is it always me?" he protested, but he knew he wouldn't win this argument. Another adventure he would miss out on. He decided he needed to find a younger friend to join their fellowship.

***

Chapter Two

Battle Lines
The foot of Hill Country of Efrayim
Summer, Year 422 from the Exodus

Y'ro*H*om shook his graying head as he surveyed the valley below. Where the Yarqon River emptied into the wide valley at the foot of the hills of Efrayim, a sea of feathered helmets had already assembled. There would not be any element of surprise on the battlefield this day. At least, he thought, as he rose from the ground, with the early morning sun behind them they still had a better position. The P'lisht'im were to the north and west of the assembled tribes of Yisrael. They would be fighting into the sun. Absentmindedly he brushed the dust from the leather corselet that was fastened over his four-cornered dark blue tunic.

"What's troubling you, Y'ro*H*om?" asked Ya*H*atsi-el as he straightened the black leather straps of his companion's *totafoth* that had gotten twisted in the strap of the corselet, "You look concerned."

Y'ro*H*om turned to his companion, the lanky, chieftain of the tribe of Binyamin, and gestured to the array below. "Have you seen what they've assemble? They outmatch us by at least four times."

Placing a hand on his companion's shoulder, Ya*H*atsi-el offered a gentle smile, "Yes, but we have the Holy One of Yisrael fighting on our side. Numbers and military might mean very little."

"If He chooses to do battle for us today," returned the chieftain of the tribe of Dan, absently played with the locks of his graying beard.

"May we so merit, replied YaHatsi-el softly.

"Amen," was the automatic reply, but both men's wondered if they indeed would merit such a battle leader. The last few years have suggested that their merit with the Almighty was on the wane. More and more, the P'lisht'im had encroached inland, terrorizing the western villages of Efrayim and Yehudah. They had conquered and held Afeq for several years now and controlled a good deal of the lower hills along the central spine of Erets Yisrael. The tribes of Yisrael had assembled at Even Ha`Ezer, about eight thousand amoth to the southeast of Afeq to try and turn the tide and push back the encroachment.

Yet the chieftains of the various tribes had spent so much time battling amongst each other, that the P'lisht'im had sufficient time to gather a powerful army at Afeq. The two men watched for several moments as the warriors of the P'lishtim organized into well-disciplined ranks. Y'roHom noted the positions of the archers and the infantry, trying to guess how they would field when the battle was joined. Nearing sixty, he was a seasoned warrior for the nation of Yisrael and had crossed spears many times with the P'lisht'im.

The two men quickly turned around at the sound of someone coming up behind them. YaHatsi-el recognized the tall handsome, solidly built warrior as one of the captains from the Matri clan of his tribe. The warrior stopped a respectable distance and waited to be recognized.

YaHatsi-el's gray eyes seemed to laugh as he smiled. "You see, Y'roHom, with men of such character, who have awe of Heaven and respect for elders, how can you worry?"

"Would that all of Yisrael have a fear of heaven, then we wouldn't even need to take the field in combat," returned Y'roHom, before adding under his breath so that only YaHatsi-el could hear, "Neither Eli ha-Kohen ha-Gadol, nor his sons have joined our battle camp."

YaHatsi-el grimaced before turning his attention to the captain, "Yes, Sha'ul."

The captain bowed slightly in response, "Your honor, the other chieftains are assembling in the main tent."

"Thank you, Sha'ul," replied YaHatsi-el as he and Y'roHom turned to walk with the captain back to the main camp.

As the three passed through the assembly of tribal warriors, some of Y'roHom confidence was restored. The men of Yisrael were a fiercely independent lot, which sometimes made it especially difficult for their tribal leaders to come to compromise, but it was that same tenaciousness that made them fierce fighters on the battlefield. If we only had a strong leader, even a king, the thought teased Y'roHom's soul.

As they assembled, Ya`aqov's children, the nation of Yisrael, were an inspiring sight. While not assembled in fine uniformed rows like the enemy, an inner order seemed to radiate from the assembly. Grouped in their various clans and tribes, most of the men, ranging in age from twenty to sixty, engaged in silent contemplation or quiet discussion in groups of two or three. All were adorned with the small black boxes, the *oth* bound to their weak arm and the *totafoth*, at the hairline in the middle of their forehead – a modest crown for the chosen sons of the King of Kings.

From every tribe, the men were clad in a simple four-cornered tunic of varying colors, fringed with the requisite tsitsith, though the style of the fringe differed slightly from tribe to tribe. This one was tied with twenty-six windings, this with thirty-nine, yet each tassel, no matter the clan or tribe, consisted of seven threads bound by a single thread of blue. The blue, the color and hue of the deepest heavens, was intended to remind them of where their first loyalties should lay, where their first and last thoughts should turn.

The men's professions, for none of them were professional soldiers, were easily identifiable by the weapons they carried. This one carried an axe, this one a sickle. Most had staves or crude spears. They were not assembled for glory or honor but these farmers, shepherds and craftsman were deeply connected to the Holy One of Yisrael and His nation. In a way, they came out of a sense of extended family responsibility. Fulfilling their duty to their brothers and their Father in Heaven.

Y'roHom felt a surge of almost paternal pride as he passed by them. They all rose out of respect for the elders, as the trio made their way to the large rectangular tent in the center of the camp.

Framed by a low, thick wall, no more than two and a half amoth high, the tent of dark goatskins added another two and a half amoth to the walls' height. The result was a type of large hall that peaked on its centerline at eight amoth.

As they neared the opening of the tent, Y'roHom's musings gained an edge of bitterness as he reflected on Yisrael's nonagerian leader and his two sons. Their place, Eli's place, as the *Shofet*, the charismatic leader and chief justice of the Nation, was there. He didn't expect the ninety-eight year old high priest to lead the warriors on the field, but he should at least be sitting at the head of this court, or at least one of his sons. The last thought gave him pause. Maybe it was better that they weren't here. Like most of the nation, he wondered about the prophecy of Sh'mu'el, and hoped that its hour had not come.

***

The Camp of the P'lishtim
East of Afeq

Paremheb removed his helmet and peered into the morning sun. He was visibly agitated. Goliyath noticed his commander's mood. "What's wrong, sir?" asked the towering officer.

"What are they waiting for?" Paremheb asked no one in particular. Then he turned to his officer. When he had to crane his neck to look up at Goliyath, he shook his head in wonderment at his size. He seemed larger every day. "They could have attacked days ago, when we were half the force we are today. I fear a trap"

Goliyath shook his head, "What do the `Ivrim know of strategy. They're farmers."

"Never under estimate your enemy, Goliyath." Paremheb lectured. "That's a sure recipe for defeat. It's said that even a mouse can bring down an elephant. "

"Bah," returned Goliyath. "The `Ivrim are just afraid to fight," he decided, "We haven't anything to fear."

Paremheb ignored Goliyath's confidence. "We have `Ivrim with us, today?" he asked.

""Yes, there are three thousand in the camp," Goliyath answered without enthusiasm.

"No, I don't mean locals who decided to join us today. Do we have any veteran `Ivrim that we can trust?" Paremheb asked.

Goliyath grimaced. He didn't like to admit what he was about to say. "My armor bearer *was* one of *them*," he spat his confession.

"Well, bring him to me," instructed Paremheb, "we need to know what they're planning."

***

Removing the large white woolen shawl from his leather pouch, Y'ro*H*om draped the fringed insignia of an elder over his head his shoulders. He grasped two of the fringed corners, bringing them forward, folding up the sides to form a hood and cape. His companion, Ya*H*atsi-el had done the same. Sha'ul held the tent flap open for the two leaders. With a look of resignation towards each other, the two entered. Sha'ul followed behind.

They were the last to arrive. In a large semi-circle on the east side, facing west, sat the other elders, sixty-eight men, most reflecting the title in visage as well as rank. Three cushions, one at the semi-circle's zenith, were vacant. While Y'ro*H*om and Ya*H*atsi-el hastened each to his place on the far side of the semi-circle, the cushion at the zenith remained vacant. It was the cushion reserved for Eli HaKohen.

When he received his charge as both the Kohen Godel and the *Shofet* of the nation, Eli was filled with enthusiasm. At fifty-eight, he had been confidant in his ability to lead. But over the next forty years, each year seemed to weigh heavier than the last. Events seemed to take on a life of their own, and Eli felt increasingly incapable and ineffective in his efforts to serve the Holy One and His nation. He became very weary. At ninety-eight, he wasn't old in body, as much as he was in spirit.

Sha'ul retreated to the other side of the tent, which was filled beyond capacity with various

172

captains, warriors, students, and simple spectators. The onlookers all stood silently, respectfully, the awe etched on their countenance, while the elders engaged in lively conversation with their neighbors, everyone waiting for the proceedings to begin.

"With your permission," began the elder close to the semi-circle's zenith. At the sound of his voice, even in its modulated tone, the tent became silent. All eyes fell on Yishai, son of `Oved from Bethle*H*em. "We have delayed long enough. We must make a decision." His eyes surveyed the semi-circle. "Are there any last comments, before we vote?"

Y'ro*H*om gestured slightly with his hand.

"Y'ro*H*om ben Avi*H*ayl," Yishai acknowledged him.

Choosing his words carefully, Y'ro*H*om began, "They have assembled an army four times our size …"

"Numbers don't decide a battle," an elder to his right broke in.

"True," continued Y'ro*H*om, "but they most certainly help."

"The Holy One of Yisrael fights our battles," the other shot back.

Y'ro*H*om closed his eyes and drew a breath. "When He chooses," returned Y'ro*H*om, each word drawn out. "Please, you can question my loyalty to the Holy One afterwards, but let me finish." He looked to Yishai, who nodded in return before shooting a stern glance at the elder who interrupted.

Drawing another breath, Y'ro*H*om continued, "I am not proposing that each one return to his tent. That would be a desecration of His Name."

"But, instead, a change of strategy," he scanned the semi-circle to make eye contact with each of the elders. "If we leave a small defensive force, making the P'lisht'im think we are arrayed for battle here, but march the rest of the warriors quickly to the south - undetected. We can reach Eqron before dawn. We can take it virtually unopposed catching the uncircumcised by complete surprise. If the Holy One wills it, we can deliver a mortal blow."

Y'ro*H*om registered the sudden contemplative expression on several of the elders. They were considering the possibilities. Their expressions were positive, but there were too few of them. Others were already shaking their head, rejecting the plan before considering it. He released a sigh. It's impossible to fight a war by committee, he decided. He waited for the objections.

"What do we need such strategies for?" an elder to Yishai's right asked after being recognized. "Shouldn't our faith in the Almighty be simple and straightforward?" He voiced a question that was on several of the elders' minds.

It was a serious theological question, but now was not the time for a theoretical debate on effort versus faith. Y'ro*H*om tried a simpler answer. "Yehoshu'ah bin Nun, in the original conquest," Y'ro*H*om offered, "used strategy. In the battle of Aiy, you all of course remember, he drew the enemy out of their city, having first sent a small force behind it. When the city was empty of defenders, they entered and set it aflame."

Y'ro*H*om's comments caused a stir, but he saw it wasn't enough. They lacked a leader, he thought.

"Yes, but he had the Urim and Tumim," another elder offered, referring to the special breastplate of the Kohen Gadol.

The elder's comment brought a silent response. Everyone was painfully aware that Eli, the Kohen Gadol was absent from the session. All eyes turned to the empty space at the head of the circle.

"Enough debate," announced Yishai. He actually agreed with Y'ro*H*om, but he saw that the initiative was only causing a delay. The assembly wouldn't come to agree to the proposal. "Do we need a vote?" He read the expressions on the faces of the elders. He looked at Y'ro*H*om who shook his head in resignation. He recognized how the council leaned. At least, thought Y'ro*H*om, his plan got everyone to agree to attack now.

"Fine. It's decided. Prepare your men. We take the field in one hour. Let us pray to the Almighty that He should lead us to victory."

The Elders rose, everyone turning to the east, the direction of the Mishqan, the Tabernacle, at Shiloh. Yishai nodded to the three of the elders who were kohan'im, from the priestly lineage, descended from Aharon the Kohen. They took their place in front, facing the congregation. They pulled their shawls over their face before extending their hands under the shawl. In unison they blessed the nation in accordance with the ancient formula.

"*Yivarekh'kha Adn w'yishmarekh'kha.* May the Holy One bless you and guard you. *Y'-ir Adn panaw elekha w'yHunekha.* May the Holy One cause His Presence to shine upon you and be gracious unto you. *Yisah Adn pana elekha w'yasem l'kha shalom.* May the Holy One place His Presence upon you, and give you wholeness."

At the conclusion of the blessing, the assembled nation, with folded hands across their chest, fell to their knees and bowed their heads to the ground in supplication. There they stayed in deep meditation, entering the holy chambers of Heaven, each through his own gate, to commune with the Holy One of Yisrael.

***

I was not pleased with my new task. Yes, I was the 'Ivri who served as Goliyath's shield bearer. My name is Uri'yah, though some call me "the Hiti" because along with others from my tribe, Dan, we wrestled a huge amount of territory from the Hitt'im. I made a name for myself in that battle. Yet, making a name for myself didn't help me to pay the bills. I ended up joining the P'lisht'im to pay off some debts, and have some adventure. They have a regular standing army, not like the militias of Yisrael. Like I said, I didn't like my new task. I didn't relish the idea of spying against my own people.

But, let's face it, the P'lisht'im are definitely the masters of the land today. And I'm not the only one of Yisrael that fought for the other side. One has to make the best of a bad situation. Besides, considering my condition … well, I know that I haven't any prospects of building a home amongst my own people. In his "infinite wisdom," the Holy One "blessed" me so that I can't have any children.

Besides, being an armor bearer for that giant, I really only have to just stand by and watch Goliyath tear people apart. That man is not of this world. He doesn't seem to age, and he just keeps getting taller and bigger. I'm glad I stand behind him. At least I'm not doing anything actively against Yisrael. I've never killed a fellow `Ivri. Not only that it's bad enough I have to hear Goliyath cursing them all the time. No one expected me to out fight him, so really I don't do anything except receive a salary from these uncircumcised ones. It's not that bad.

But now, they wanted me to spy on my own people. My stomach turned. Despite my less than stellar relationship with Him, I actually offered a quick plea to the Holy One of Yisrael to get me out of this mess as I crept down the mountainside, away from the P'lisht'im camp, trying to stay hidden from sight as much as possible. Then my eyes caught the movement. There, on the other side of the valley, I saw the Children of Yisrael moving, breaking camp to take the field in battle.

"Thank you," I said to the heavens, as I turned around and hurried back to camp to tell Paremheb the good news. The commander didn't need me though; he already had his answer. There would be a battle here today.

∗∗∗

Chapter 3

Responsibility
Beth TapuaH, Yehudah

Dawid practically fell onto the sentry before he saw him. As he sank back into the shadows of the night, he offered a small prayer of thanks to the Almighty that the guard hadn't seen him. In fact, the P'lishti soldier seemed bored as he paced aimlessly in from of the low stone structure, which served as some kind of gate to the P'lisht'im encampment.

Outrage filled Dawid. This garrison was the P'lisht'im's latest indignation against the House of Yisrael. Built to the west of the small Yehudah village of Beth Tapua*H*, less than ten thousand amoth from *H*ebron on the road to Lakhish, it was clear evidence that the P'lishtim were trying to exert their influence over the totality of Yisrael's inheritance. It was an affront to the Holy One of Yisrael.

Dawid's thoughts turned to his father, Yishai. It had bothered him going to Even Ha`Ezer when there was this wound in his very own neighborhood that needed mending. Yet, as an elder, Yishai had a responsibility to the entire nation of Yisrael. Besides his father had said that a major P'lishti defeat at Afeq would have a positive effect throughout the land.

The thought of his father carried with it a lot of ambiguity for Dawid. He was proud to have a father like Yishai, a sage and elder among his people. Yet, he didn't much act like a father to Dawid. He seemed to have more compassion for the servants and strangers that passed through their home, and there were many. His brothers, too, treated him with such disdain. All his life, Dawid was continually trying to win their approval, but to no avail.

He didn't understand it, and probably never would. Dawid closed his eyes and drew a deep breath. No matter how much he tried to make peace with the situation, it cut deeply into his soul. He choked back a tear and pushed his thoughts away.

Thank the Almighty, his mother tried to make up for Dawid's ostracism. Somehow, it seemed to Dawid that because of her efforts though, she too became estranged from the rest of the family. He was always messing things up. Only it was not the case with Mamma Ruth, Dawid's great grandmother. Dawid loved sitting at her feet and hearing her stories or getting pearls of wisdom and sound advice. She always had time for Dawid too. Yet, of course, no one in their family would shun Mamma Ruth. Even Dawid couldn't cause that much trouble.

There. Dawid finally saw what he had been waiting for: the other sentry. He had been inside the building, but now he was coming out with a large steaming ceramic bowl.

"*Akhana addu, ki pi ekhadu abatu tabu rabu atsmi addanu aga.* Here we go," said the guard with the bowl, "I think I out did myself this time."

180

"*Atta santa kia addanu kulu* "You say that every time," answered the other guard, as he leaned his spear against the building and sat down on a large rock.

"*Atta la magaru aga, atta bashalu akultu addanu aHarru.* Well, if you don't like it, you can make the stew next time."

"*Addaniqa! Ekhadu dababu aga?* Relax. Did I say I didn't like it?" The other guard put the bowl between himself and his companion, and sat down on a similar large rock. They both removed a large wooden spoon from their side pouches and began eating the stew.

" *eli rushani, aga tabu rabu.* "On my shoulders. Actually, it is quite good," offered the first guard. His companion smiled in response.

Dawid saw his opportunity. He leapt from his hiding spot to suddenly materialize before the two guards.

"*shulmu.* Good evening," Dawid offered, with mock respect. He had learned the P'lishti dialect from one of the house servants. It had many similarities to the language of Yisrael, though it had a lot of loan words from the Mitsr'im. Yet, even with its similarities, to the untrained ear it's pronunciation sounded quite foreign. The two guards were startled. Their eyes searched Dawid, questioning. The one guard's eyes darted from Dawid to his spear propped up just out of reach.

Smiling, Dawid continued, "*Ibrutu uekhadu ereshani elo qiapu patru.* My friends and I were wondering if we might borrow a knife."

181

The guards' eyes looked past Dawid wondering where his friends were, and how many there were. "*patru?*" "A knife?" asked the guard, "what would an 'Ivri need a knife for? He'd probably cut himself. *Atta laereshana teshu, illidu.* You don't want any trouble, boy. Go, run on home." The guards remained seated, but tension filled their bodies.

"*La, nukhadnu la ershani teshu, akh ershani patru*" "No, we don't want trouble," answered Dawid coolly, "We just want a knife."

"Whose this 'we,'" asked the guard, "*Ekhadu dagalu illidu kutal-lu balkhudaiu.* I only see one wiseacre kid."

"Oh, they're waiting to see how friendly you choose to be," replied Dawid.

His confidence bothered the guards. "How many of these 'friends' do you have?" asked the guard. He started to shift his position. His eyes darted again to his spear leaning against the wall.

Dawid's mood changed. "A*tta ti-taru-ni patru - Are* you going to give me a knife or not, <u>h</u>*anpu* - heathen?" he demanded.

"*La*," said the one guard.

"*Qerebu uti-zazu-to.* Come and get it," said the other as he made a move towards his spear, but Dawid anticipated him, and grabbed it first. Both guards were on their feet facing the point of the spear. Dawid held it confidently, swinging it slowly from one guard to the other. They each gripped the dagger in their belt but hesitated from drawing it.

Yoav and Avishay rushed out of the darkness from either side. They each grabbed a guard from behind, one hand grabbing the wrist that held the dagger the other wrapping around the guard's throat.

"*Anutee* ebaruttu-*inai*. These are some of my friends," said Dawid.

"*Illidu kutal-lu*," muttered the one guard. "Maybe I should shout for all of my friends in the camp."

"I wouldn't do that," said Dawid, menacingly, bring the spear a hair's breadth from the guard's throat. "Release the knives," he said evenly.

Both guards immediately released their weapon. Yoav and Avishay, taking care not to ease their grip on the guards, slipped the daggers from their sheaths. They each pressed the point against the guard's back.

"Thank you," said Dawid.

The guard whom Avishay was holding suddenly stepped out, trying to throw Avishay. Dawid quickly lunged his spear towards the guard. It hit its mark, sinking deep in the guard's stomach, which seemed to explode, blood and bile pouring out onto the ground. Dawid jerked the spear back, and the guard fell first to his knees, and then onto his face, dead. The smell was sickening. Dawid controlled an urge to retch.

Yoav acted quickly, jamming the knife deep in and out of the other guard's kidney. His scream was cut short by another swift stroke of the dagger across his throat. He joined his companion in a pool of blood on the ground. Yoav's face didn't hide his pleasure, as an adrenaline rush surged through his body.

"Shh," commanded Dawid, looking sternly at Yoav. The three young men stood still and listened to the noises of the night air.

After several moments, Dawid nodded his head. They hadn't raised an alarm. "Let's go," he whispered, and the three disappeared into the night.

***

"What is it?" asked Yoav.

Dawid had stopped in his tracks after several steps, a look of concern on his face. "What do you think will happen when the others find the guards?"

Both Yoav and Avishay looked blankly at Dawid.

"They'll probably take out their revenge on Beth TapuaH. We have to do something. We can't leave it like this," answered Dawid.

"What can we do?" asked Avishay, "We can't take on an entire garrison. There are at least a thousand soldiers there."

"And all we have is two knives and a spear," added Yoav with a grin.

Dawid grimaced. "Well, we have to do something."

"You have any ideas?" asked Yoav. He was excited about the prospect of more adventure. His energy was still soaring from the previous incident.

"You need to calm down a bit," cautioned Dawid.

Yoav's smile only widened. "So?" he asked.

"I'm thinking," offered Dawid.

"Maybe we could warn Beth Tapua*H*, so they'll be prepared for a raid," offered Avishay.

Yoav's face didn't hide his disappointment. "What good would that do?" he answered. Yoav had a taste for more action. "No one would believe us, anyway."

"Hmm," considered Dawid, "Yoav's right. Nearly everyone who could do anything is up at Even Ha`Ezer."

Dawid drew a breath, and allowed his mind to quiet. "Holy One of Yisrael, help us," he whispered.

The other two youth's watched Dawid with anticipation, half expecting a messenger from the Heavens to arrive.

Dawid's face suddenly lit up as he opened his eyes. "Come on," he whispered through his smile, before turning back to the P'lishti encampment. He had a plan.

Chapter Four

The Battle of Even Ha`Ezer-Afeq

The foot of the Hill Country of Efrayim
Summer, Year 422 from the Exodus

The warriors of Yisrael shuffled restlessly as the anointed kohen-priest standing on the makeshift platform repeated the prescribed instructions.

"Hearken Yisrael, you draw near today to do battle against your enemies: let not your hearts faint, fear not and do not tremble, nor be terrified because of them, for the Holy One, your God is He that goes with you to fight for you against your enemies, to save you."

The elder, Yishai then stepped forward, while the other tribal leaders stood behind him. His voice was steady and serious. "What man is there that has built a new house and not yet dedicated it? Let him go and return to his house, lest he die in battle and another man dedicate it." Yishai paused before continuing, waiting for a response. There was none from the assembled.

"What man has planted a vineyard, and has not eaten of it? Let him go and return to his house lest he die in battle and another man eat of it." Again, the crowd shuffled their feet, but no one responded.

"And what man has betrothed a wife, but has not secluded himself with her? Let him go and return to his house lest he die in battle and another man know her." Several of the men looked around

187

to their fellows to see if any would leave but no one moved. Everyone knew the law, and rarely did anyone come to battle, who hadn't already a family to carry on his name, should the unspeakable happen and he fall in battle.

Yishai lowered his voice to a whisper, but it resonated in the hearts of everyone assembled. "What man amongst us is fearful and faint hearted? Let him go and return to his house lest he cause his brothers' heart to melt like his, and bring disaster upon Yisrael. The assembled warriors shifted more nervously, everyone questioning his own resolve, and his neighbors. For many this would be their first battle, and the prospect of dying had been remote until a few moments ago. Still, everyone stood their ground, and looked up to Yishai with confidence.

"These are your officers, Yisrael," declared Yishai, as the tribal leaders stepped forward. "*Hazaq w'emats!*" "Be strong and of good courage, for you fight, not for your own name and your own honor, but for the great Name and Honor of the Holy One of Yisrael. "*Hazaq w'emats!*" "Be strong and of good courage."

The assembled warriors responded as one, "*Hazaq w'emats!*" "Be strong and of good courage!" A surge of energy flowed through the crowd reaching a crescendo as the expression was repeated three times in response to Yishai's call.

"To battle, sons of Yisrael. To battle, and may the Master of the Heavenly Hosts lead us to victory!"

***

Parhemeb's adrenaline was pumping. He loved a good battle and even more so, he loved being in command. He barely disguised his delight as he shouted instructions to his commanders, everyone responding with precision.

They wouldn't be using the ox drawn carts or the chariots today. The field was too hilly for them to be effective. He sent two units of archers to either flank, while his infantry, divided into five independent units, began to descend the hill towards the valley. Another unit of archers waited in reserves, on the chance that some of the 'Ivrim would break through the infantry line. If so, they would be greeted by an onslaught of arrows.

Paremheb signaled to his lieutenant, who in turned signaled the trumpeters and flag bearers. The trumpeters signaled the advance with a loud blast, as the flag bearers marched before Paremheb and his guard.

Another short blast from the long brass trumpets at Paremheb signal and the archers loosed their first volley. The 'Ivrim were still too far for the arrows to have much effect, but it might pause their advance a bit, and it was always good to be the one to strike the first blow. Maybe the more timid of those backward farmers would panic and bolt.

Paremheb looked to the center of the infantry to see that Goliyath and his troop had already almost reached the valley. That one always had an extra measure of enthusiasm when the battle was with the 'Ivrim, thought Paremheb. He was a good solider, maybe not the most innovative, but he took orders well, and his six amoth alone was an asset on the battlefield. Especially against peasants.

Paremheb sighed. If the gods were with him, he would crush this rabble on the first attack, and drink a victory toast to Dagon before the evening meal.

***

The volley of arrows rained down harmlessly several amoth before the Children of Yisrael. They had been prepared, and had held back waiting amongst the trees that lined the slope. As the last arrow hit the ground, three short blasts from the shofar, a hollowed out ram's horn, and several thousand warriors exited the tree line to collect the arrows, before returning to its cover. The P'lishtim had arrows to waste, but the weapon stores of Yisrael were not so blessed with surpluses.

Yishai walked with Y'roHom and YaHatsi-el above the center of the army. They had decided to hold back and let the P'lishtim take the field first to reduce the enemy's effectiveness with it archers. Even the P'lishtim didn't relish the risk of killing their own men. Once their infantry fielded, their archers firing from a distance were neutralized.

However, Yisrael used their missile weapons, arrows and slings, at short range, within two or three hundred amoth, usually even less.

190

Ya*H*atsi-el's tribe of Benyamin in particular was famous as marksmen with the sling.

A young warrior came running up to Yishai, "One of their infantry units have reached the valley, a small one in the center. Four others though, are several amoth away."

Yishai grimaced. As Father of the Court, and in the absence of Eli the Kohen Gadol, Yishai was the provisional leader. They had expected them to take the field in unison. He looked to Y'ro*H*om, questioning.

"A trap or trick?" suggested Y'ro*H*om, though the uncertainty was clear in his voice. The P'lishtim were usually well disciplined.

"Maybe they're just over enthusiastic," offered Ya*H*atsi-el.

"Maybe …" returned Y'ro*H*om, but he was clearly perplexed.

Yishai turned to the messenger. "Hold for now. Watch the flanks and let's see what happens."

The three leaders walked quickly towards the front of the formation. Several others of the tribal leaders joined them. The excitement was palpable throughout the army. The elders had all agreed to hold until the P'lishtim were in formation and focus their force in order to push through the line and disrupt it. The calculation was that Yisrael would fair better in a less structured melee. Yet, if the P'lishtim didn't comply, it would complicate their strategy.

A second messenger approached Yishai quickly. "Four other units of infantry, much large ones, have now reached the valley. They all are advancing in formation. Just that one middle one is still out in front."

Yishai breathed a sigh of relief. With so many generals, changing strategy would be more of a challenge than fighting the P'lishtim army.

"Just over enthusiastic," offered Ya*H*atsi-el.

"Just over enthusiastic," repeated Y'ro*H*om, visibly relieved.

Yishai turned to Ya*H*atsi-el, "When that unit is in range of your slinger, hit them from every side." Then he turned to Asher's tribal chief, *H*ets'yah. "And your archers, *H*ets'yah. Over - enthusiasm has a price. But, the rest of the warriors should continue to hold back. Let's pray that the Holy One guide's our hands and brings success to our endeavors. "

***

Eli'av, Yishai's eldest, grabbed the shoulders of his brothers Avinadav and Shim`a and hugged them tightly. "This is it, brothers," he declared with excitement. "Today we show those P'lisht'im who rules this land!"

"If the Holy One wills," replied Shim`a.

192

"Of course He wills it," answered Eli'av, "Why would He hide his face from us today?"

"When did you become a prophet, Eli'av?" asked Avinadav, "When are the ways of the Holy One so simple and clear."

"Now you sound like Mamma Ruth, Avinadav," chided Eli'av.

"I could do worse," Avinadav shot back through his smile.

"Did Mamma Ruth say anything about this battle?" asked Shim`a. Everyone knew that Mamma Ruth was connected to the Heavens, and sometimes she simply *knew* things. It wasn't prophecy, per se, but people from all over came to her for advice and guidance.

"Not that I'm aware of," answered Eli'av, "Father was with her for a long time before we left, but if she said something, he didn't share it with me."

"Didn't he seem concerned when we left?" asked Shim`a.

"Father is always serious," answered Avinadav, "especially when he has to travel."

"What are you two worried about?" boasted Eli'av, "I'll protect you."

Avinadav laughed, "If you're lucky, I'll leave a few P'lisht'im for you."

"Oh yeah?" returned Eli'av, "How about we make a wager? The one who kills the most uncircumcised; the other two have to do his chores for a full month."

"Deal," shouted Avinadav.

"Deal," agreed Shim`a, grudgingly. "I think I'd be happy to do chores if the Holy One sees me through this battle."

"Now you're the one that sounding like Mamma Ruth," offered Avinadav.

All three shared a good laugh, as the anticipation of the battle mounted.

***

Goliyath was upset with himself. He had allowed his enthusiasm for the battle to overtake him and now his unit was several amoth ahead of the other units. That wasn't good. While he liked to be first to battle, the tactic of fighting as a solid line, a wall of spears had been the P'lishtim's greatest asset. But he refused to stop. He didn't want to lose the momentum. The truth is, he said to himself, he wasn't to blame. Why were the other units so slow? What did they expect?

Now he was halfway across the valley, and he could already see the accursed `Ivrim ahead of him. He snarled and increased his pace. The others should catch up to his lead. What were they delaying for?

The hail of rocks took him, and the rest of his unit, by surprise. A rock crashed into the face of `Ovedba`al, his lieutenant. The sound of crushing bone intermixed with his scream as he fell. A hail of arrows rained on the unit. Screams of pain filled Goliyath ears as several more of his men fell.

"Shields," Goliyath shouted, frustration mixed with anger. Curse his fellows. He was upset that they had lagged behind and caused him to be in such a situation. Quickly his unit formed a line of shields, to try and create a barrier between themselves and the missiles. Yet, alone in the middle of the valley, it was a futile gesture.

A large rock slammed into Goliyath side, and a surge of pain filled his vision. His anger reached a crescendo. "Stones? You throw stones? It will take more than a few pebbles to bring down Goliyath," he roared.

In furry, Goliyath charged towards the `Ivrim. "Forward," he yelled. His unit, now halved, chased after their leader.

***

The shofar blast sent a rush of energy up Eli'av spine. With his two brothers by his side along with several hundred clansmen, the firstborn of Yishai rushed out into the valley, spear held high. Eli'av shouted as he ran. He felt as if he could destroy the entire P'lishti army himself.

The P'lishti turned and set their shields to the onslaught of the `Ivrim. The sound of metal clashing against metal rang throughout the valley as the two walls of warriors smashed into each other.

Eli'av, with his unit, charged the forward infantry unit of the P'lishtim. As his spear crashed into a shield, his whole being shook and vibrated from the shock. The momentum threw him off of his feet and he fell to his back, losing his spear along with his balance. Fear gripped him but he pushed it away, as he rolled to his side, scrambling to regain his footing. A compatriot fell beside him, awash in blood, the blank stare of death on his face. In a panic, Eli'av rolled to the other side to see the disembodied head of one of his enemies.

His mind clouded. He scrambled to his feet, but he was unable to comprehend the battlefield. Confusion was everywhere. He searched for his spear, wildly. Anger and frustration at his own fear, spun him in all directions. Seeing a large duckbill axe, he leapt for it, tripping over several bodies. He tried to get a grip on his emotions but didn't know where to turn.

Finally he got to his feet, and turned to see the P'lishti warrior, Goliyath, and all rational thought fled from the young man's mind. He was a giant, nearly twice the height of a normal man. His face was like a raging bull, as he swung a sword whose leaf shaped blade was larger than a man's leg. Men of Yisrael fell quickly before his onslaught. Eli'av froze in his tracks.

Suddenly, hands were upon him, and he turned. Avinadav, his face covered with splatters of blood, was pulling him. He was saying something, but Eli'av couldn't comprehend the words.

Slowly, comprehension returned. They were pulling back, forming a defensive line. He allowed his brother to guide him. He looked over his shoulder again, to see that monster smashing three men with one blow, and his heart melted.

***

Chapter 5

Victory
P'lishtim encampment
Near Beth TapuaH, Yehudah

It had been difficult, but the three young men finally dragged the two bodies of the P'lisht'im inside the small stone building. Dawid was upset with himself, because he hadn't thought through the consequences of his actions. Now, he would do his best to correct his mistake.

He ran his hand through his long thick curly brown hair as he looked around the room trying to catalog its inventory, searching for those items that would help him cover their tracks, and protect the town of Beth Tapua*H*.

A clay stove still burned brightly against the far wall. Next to it was a table with various roots and herbs, some partially chopped, strewn across it. A dog's carcass, skinned and gutted, hung from the ceiling by one of its hind legs. Chunks of meat had been cut away, scraps of which intermingled with the chopped roots and herbs.

In the corner, several bronze feathered helmets were piled haphazardly along with a collection of spears, knives and axes. On the opposite wall were stack of quartered logs, and a pile of kindling. A large ceramic jug also rested against the wall, which Dawid surmised to be olive oil.

In a small niche on the near wall, by the entrance, Dawid's eyes focused on a small figurine of a woman, her hands cupping her large breasts. Without hesitation, Dawid crossed the room, and smashed the idol to the ground, stomping on the shards, until nothing recognizable remained.

"It should be that easy to destroy the army of the P'lisht'im," commented Yoav.

"When the Holy One wills it," returned Dawid solemnly, "it will be."

"What are you looking for?" asked Avishay.

"This!" declared Dawid, as he crossed the room to the far corner. There were several large ceramic jugs grouped neatly there. One of them had a dark liquid stain down its side. "Tar."

As Dawid examined the jugs, Yoav was playing with the armor and the helmets. He turned around, donning one of the helmets. "How do I look," he joked.

"Excellent," declared Dawid, "put on the corselet, too, and go stand outside."

"What?" asked Yoav incredulously.

"If someone comes by, they shouldn't see the sentry post unmanned. It would raise an alarm," answered Dawid.

Yoav wasn't convinced. "And if he should talk to me? What then? Unlike you, I don't speak P'lishti."

"Pretend like you can't hear him," replied Dawid.

Yoav stared blankly at his uncle.

"It probably won't happen; it's just a precaution," answered Dawid.

Yoav shook his head, but he donned the breastplate, took a spear and went to his guard post. "I can believe I've been enlisted to guard a P'lishti encampment," he muttered as he left the building.

Dawid called to Avishay. "Take a piece of cloth and soak it in the tar," said Dawid, handing him one of the jugs, "then place it in the mouth of the jug."

Dawid began following his own instructions, until all the jugs were sporting a cloth wick. He called to Yoav, who came in, proffering a salute. "Yes, sir," he joked.

Yoav started to remove his helmet.

"No," instructed Dawid, "keep it on. Avishay and I need to put them on too."

"What, are we joining the P'lisht'im?" asked Avishay.

"Not yet," joked Dawid. "It's just a uniform. But, we need to place these jugs around the entrance to the camp. If someone sees us, they'll think that we're one of them."

"When did you get to be so tricky," asked Yoav.

"I thought you knew my reputation," joked Dawid, "isn't that why you started spending time with me?"

They all laughed.

"Let's go," commanded Dawid.

***

It took some time, but eventually the young men had made a solid perimeter of tar jugs arching in front of the building's entrance. When they finished, the three P'lishti clad youths returned to the structure. So far, it seems, they had been undetected.

Dawid pulled the dead body of one of the guards to the pile of remaining tar jugs. "Bring him here," he instructed, and his two nephews quickly complied, bringing the second guard. Dawid. He opened one of the jugs and poured tar on the two dead sentries.

Dawid then went over to the stack of wood and took three stout fagots and wrapped them with some cloth. He handed one to each of his two companions.

"Here we go," Dawid said with a sigh. "May the Holy One give us success."

"Be strong and of good courage," joked Yoav.

Dawid and Avishay both smiled. "Be strong and of good courage," they returned.

"You two go light the ones outside. Yoav to the north, Avishay to the south. Meet in the middle. I'll light these, and then we'll meet at that clearing," Dawid said, referring to the clearing where they started this adventure.

Yoav and Avishay nodded their agreement.

Dawid lit the three torches from the stove fire, and handed two to his nephews. "Go," instructed Dawid, and the two young men raced from the building.

Dawid stood and counted several beats. He wanted to give the others a head start. Then he lit the dead guards on fire, before lighting each of the wicks on the clay jars.

When he was satisfied, he grabbed a leather pouch and bolted for the door.

Avishay and Yoav had been equally successful. They lit their line of clay jars, meeting nearly simultaneously. The three quickly arrived at the clearing to watch the results of the endeavors.

Suddenly, explosions pierced the night as jar after jar burst into flames. Flaming tar splashed in all direction; much of the dry growth caught fire. A light breeze fanned the flame and soon the entire eastern edge of the encampment glowed red.

Alarms were sounded in the camp. Shouts of both panic and instruction could be heard. P'lishti soldiers raced in all directions. Some, in their panic bolted from the camp into the night. Dawid smiled, satisfied, and signaling his two companions, the three counterfeit soldiers fled the scene.

***

"W'ay," exclaimed Yoav, when they were approaching their encampment.

"What is it?" asked Avishay concerned.

"In all the excitement, we forgot the knife," Yoav declared in exasperation.

"W'ay" agreed Avishay.

Dawid simply chuckled, "What would you do without me?" He threw the leather sack in front of them. It fell open revealing two knives, along with an assortment of herbs and roots.

"Wow," Yoav said, "I'm hungry."

They shared a laugh as they gathered the pouch and went to join Asahel and prepare a late supper, a festival meal in honor of their victory.

Chapter Six

Defeat
The foot of the Hill Country of Efrayim

The mood was somber in the central tent. While they held the P'lisht'im from advancing, it was clear to everyone that they had nearly been over run. Casualties were high, and moral was low. The elders needed to decide what to do next.

Y'ro*H*om entered the tent, and Yishai turned his attention to him. "How many?" he asked.

"It seems," started Y'ro*H*om slowly, "about four thousand." He had been sent to take an accounting.

"Blessed is the True Judge," Yishai said soberly. All of the other elders could be heard uttering the same expression, with varying levels of inflection.

"And maybe twice the number of wounded," added Y'ro*H*om. "It seems that the enemy suffered about the same number, if not a little higher." He took his seat in the semi-circle. It was clear that the Children of Yisrael did not win the battle, and while from a strict military perspective they did not lose; no ground was lost, and both sides had pulled back to their camp, it was clear to everyone that the Holy One had dealt them a severe blow through the P'lisht'im. Even the loss of one member of the nation would be cause for grief and self-reflection. The loss of four thousand was a national tragedy.

"Suggestions," requested Yishai.

No one stirred for a moment. Finally, an elder to the right of Yishai, Uzi'el, spoke. "I have a suggestion," he offered.

Yishai acknowledged him with a nod.

Uzi'el continued, "Why has the Holy One struck us down today, before the P'lisht'im? We need to rededicate ourselves to Him. We were not led, not by His appointed nor by Him. Let us bring the Holy One's very own Aron HaBrith, the Ark of the Covenant, from Shiloh to us here. When it is amongst us, He will save us from the hand of the enemy."

Yishai sat back, the expression on his face revealed his discomfort. The Aron HaBrith was not some magic talisman that did one's bidding. It represented the Holy One's seat, His Presence, in this world, and rested in the Holy of Holies in the Mishqan at Shiloh. Even though he could see the logic of the suggestion - after all, in the initial conquest the Aron HaBrith was used - something else intuitively gave him pause. He couldn't articulate the source, but the idea filled him with trepidation.

However, many of the other elders were visibly receptive to the idea.

"We would need Kohen Gadol Eli's approval," suggested Y'roHom. He was also skeptical of the idea. The Aron HaBrith hadn't been taken into battle since the days of Yehoshu'ah, and the thought of bringing it here, worried him, especially considering all the foreboding omens. That Yishai seemed concerned augmented Y'roHom hesitance.

"If we want the Holy One to lead us in battle, we need to provide a proper channel for Him to so," encouraged an elder.

"Like in the days of Yehoshu'ah," suggested another, "the Holy One marched before Yisrael. We need to re-conquer what was lost to those uncircumcised. This is the perfect way."

"Then why hasn't it been brought out since?" asked another.

"We haven't fought as the entire nation, since," answered someone. "We haven't been truly unified till now."

"This must be why the Holy One has struck us," answered another, "to compel us to bring His Aron HaBrith, so that He will be glorified in the victory."

It was clear that the consensus was in favor of bringing the Aron HaBrith to the battle.

"We'd need to buy time with the P'lisht'im," YaHatsi-el commented. "I'd doubt they'd wait for us to go to Shiloh and bring the Aron HaBrith here. It will take at least two days."

His comment descended like a brick on the forum, as everyone recognized the significance of such a crucial point.

Yishai, though grudgingly, recognized that the elders would not be diswayed. He turned to Y'ro*H*om. "Do you have any ideas as to how to delay the uncircumcised?" he asked.

Y'ro*H*om considered for a moment. "I wonder if they'd be amenable to a parley and a temporary truce to bury the dead. That would take two days, at least."

A small rumble of conversation erupted in the tent. "Was such a truce permissible?" "Would they agree?" Again, the consensus seemed to be in favor.

"Then, it's decided," declared Uzi'el, though his declaration held the edge of a question to it.

Yishai gently raised his hand, bringing the elders to order. "Let's see if these uncircumcised will parley," he offered. "But, bringing the Aron HaBrith to here, raises many legal questions that need to be answered first. The Aron HaBrith hasn't left the Mishqan in over four hundred years. Do we bring the Aron HaBrith without the Mishqan? And if so, where are the daily offerings, the morning and evening *tamid*, brought?"

Again, a rumble of discussion rolled through the council.

"I have a tradition," offered Amram, one of the kohen-priests that sat in the council, "that offerings are brought to the Mishqan, even if the Aron HaBrith isn't there. Only the altar is absolutely necessary for the bringing of offerings."

Another kohen, `Ovad'yah added, "I have a similar tradition."

"I'd want to confirm that with Eli Ha-Kohen Ha-Gadol," suggested Yishai. Nearly everyone nodded in assent.

"We need a contingent to go to Shiloh," Yishai looked around the council. "It should be at least twenty-three elders, in case decisions need to be made."

"You should lead it," Uzi'el suggested, "Only you can talk to Eli."

Yishai sighed in resignation, "Who will parley."

"Again, as Father of the council, it's your responsibility," offered Y'ro*H*om.

"I want you at my side," returned Yishai, "you're the most seasoned in the ways of war amongst us."

Y'ro*H*om nodded and added, "YaHatsi-el should also come, and Maqal, the elder of Efrayim, considering we're in his tribal inheritance."

Both men nodded soberly.

"With the help of the Holy One," concluded Yishai, as he rose. The elders followed his lead. "Uzi'el, prepare a mission to go to Shiloh. There should be at least a hundred warriors, with representatives from all the tribes. However, it shouldn't be too big as to attract attention. If the parley is successful, we want to leave immediately."

"With your permission and the help of the Holy One," Uzi'el answered.

"May it be His Will," Yishai offered.

"Amen," the leaders of Yisrael answered.

***

Paremheb allowed the wave of nausea to pass. He hated riding in the back of these horse drawn chariots. The terrain made them impractical for battle, but if he were going to parley, he should have all the trappings of his office. It was important to show these 'Ivrim who were the rulers and who were the subjects of these lands.

He had kept the group of those so-called elders, along with their retinue, waiting the better part of the morning. The four elders waited in their woolen shawls under the bright morning sun, and only when it seemed that their patience had been exhausted did Paremheb begin to ride out to meet them in the center of the battlefield.

He had been satisfied with the first melee. Though it wasn't the overwhelming victory he had hoped for, he could accept a parity of losses. He had more troops and they were better disciplined. If things continued, it was clear the 'Ivrim would break. Clearly, they had come to the same conclusion and were ready to discuss terms. This surprised Paremheb somewhat, as the 'Ivrim were known for their intransigence. He was willing to be magnanimous, however, and accept their surrender.

Yet, these were delicate matters, which is why despite his insistence, Paremheb refused to allow Goliyath to accompany him. If terms were to be discussed, he didn't want to back these 'Ivrim into a corner. Desperate men are not good adversaries.

As they approached, Paremheb pushed himself erect and steadied his legs in the chariot. The driver quickened the horse's gait, so that Paremheb's chariot pulled ahead of the other two, which transported the flag bearers of the P'lishti Empire. The two flags, the black outline of a bird with outstretched wings, its head turned back, on dark red background, fluttered gently in the late morning breeze. Five soldiers with feathered helmets and gleaming brass breastplates escorted the three chariots on either side.

Paremheb descended from his chariot and strode with his lieutenant towards the 'Ivri contingent. His head erect and shoulders back, he directed his gaze at the elder in the middle before speaking. He tilted his head slightly towards his translator. "*Shemu-i Paremheb, Sar Qarabu el Nish P'lish, ekhadu akhana l'shamu izimtuattuni,*" he said to the translator, who repeated the introduction in the language of the `Ivrim. "I am Paremheb, the Minister of War for the great P'lishti Empire. I am prepared to hear your plea."

Yishai returned the gaze, and held it for a moment. Something in the simplicity of his stare startled Paremheb. The P'lishti officer fought the urge to look away.

"*shalamu*. Greetings," Yishai offered in perfect P'lisht. "*Ekhadu ashum kiam putu milku ishtu dayia-nutu ishtu benenashi yisrael.* I represent the Council of Elders of the Nation of Yisrael."

Paremheb stared at the elder in disbelief. Where did this peasant farmer learn to speak P'lishti like a native? He quickly recovered his composure, nodding his acknowledgement.

Yishai continued in P'lishti, "*Nekhadu ereshnu l'sadrinu riqsu addaru ashum kiam a-kabatu anutee mitte ba-qarabu.* We would like to arrange a temporary truce in order to give honor to those fallen."

Paremheb was caught off guard, again. His gaze quickly went from one elder to the other, searching for some sign of a ruse. A truce to bury the dead? He quickly collected himself.

"*La ereshu-ni riqsu.* We don't need a truce," Paremheb dispensed with the translator and addressed Yishai directly, "*Nawu.* Surrender. *Maqatu ezebu u-turru mushubu u-battibatti. Taru ba-napishtu shalmish.* Abandon this futile show and return to your homes and families. Return to

211

your livelihood and your lives peacefully. *Kimmu na-erushu taklimu qalalu, zuzu ilta esheru sht'uettiru, uattunu ushurru izimtu ishtu ukabirnatu mittu rabbu.* We only require a token tribute, a tax for the maintenance of order, and you can save yourselves the need to bury more dead." Paremheb tone hardened as he enunciated the threat.

Yishai smiled as a father might to an uncomprehending child. "*La izimtani nasaktu betabi-zazu el nish nash-nakar.* We have no intention of surrendering our patrimony to a foreign people. *Kiam qalalu ilutuna ushaltu ma-alku sammamu u-arts minnu mattati annuti kbetabi.* It would be an affront to our God, the Creator and Master of the Heavens and Earth Who has given us this land as an inheritance. We offer you a truce for two or three days, so that we can both give honor to our brethren who have fallen."

Paremheb shifted his feet. He distrusted these 'Ivrim, but what would a few days buy them. "*Minna uma minu?* What are a few days?" he said dismissively with a wave of his hand. "*Kia, urkhish.* So be it. Go, be on your way. *Qabaru-u pagru-ku.* Bury your dead." He then added, "and make preparations for the rest of your people to join them."

Without waiting for a response, Paremheb turned and boarded his chariot. "Think about it over the next two days, if you will," he shouted over his shoulder as his chariot began its return, "Surrender while you still have breath to do so."

***

212

Chapter Seven

Coming to Shiloh
The approach to Shiloh in the Hill Country of Efrayim

In the end, Uzi'el had to turn people away from joining the mission to Shiloh. One hundred and twenty warriors, ten from each tribe, escorted Yishai and another twenty-two elders to meet with the Kohen Gadol at the place of the Mishqan, the physical representation of the Holy One's Presence in the world.

With the elders riding on donkeys, the party's pace was quick through NaHal Shiloh. The majority of the small force wound its way through the base of the dry riverbed, while a small band of warriors ran above the naHal to scout ahead and insure the contingent's security. It was decided to travel through the naHal instead of the road, to reduce the group's profile, and prevent the P'lishtim from learning of the delegation.

Despite the immediate mood after the battle, many of the warriors were now full of optimism. Simply the thought of fighting alongside the Aron HaBrith imbued them with a renewed courage. Everyone was familiar with the stories of the tradition, where the Holy One, through the Aron HaBrith, laid waste to Yisrael's enemies.

When Yehoshu'ah conquered the Land, it was the Aron HaBrith at the head of the army, which seemed to cause city walls to collapse asunder and stones from heaven to rain on Yisrael's enemies. Fear and trepidation melted away with the

213

thought of fighting alongside the Holy Aron HaBrith.

However, Eli'av was having difficulty dispelling his own personal demons. He walked alongside his two brothers, but his thoughts remained on the battlefield. Both of his brothers recognized his dark mood. They were accustomed to such fits of melancholy, and gave him a wide berth.

Nathan, Eli'av's captain, tried to comfort his soldier on the way to Shiloh. "One's first battle can be overwhelming," he began.

Eli'av dismissed the suggestion angrily. "I was doing fine. I simply tripped and fell." Yet the image of Goliyath sprang into his mind and he shuddered involuntarily. As he felt another wave of fear, he lashed out angrily. "Leave me. I'm fine. I'm just upset that I couldn't take more P'lishti heads!" But his bravado rang hollow.

During the day, his thoughts were overwhelmed with the realities of war. At night his dreams were consumed with monstrous images of the giant P'lishti ripping off heads. He wanted anything but to return to the battlefield, but when that realization registered in his thoughts, it was countered by frustration and self-loathing. He felt like a caged animal, which hadn't any means of escape.

Nathan tried to put a comforting arm around his clansman, but Eli'av pushed him away. Nathan recognized a potentially dangerous situation. The captain reacted strongly and spun Eli'av around, grabbing him by both his arms, placing his face directly in front of his soldier's. "Listen. You had better get a grip on yourself, Eli'av," though the volume was low, his tone was a shout. "Either you work through this, or go run back home. I will not have your fear infect others."

"Fear!" shouted Eli'av. "You're the coward Nathan! I didn't see you fighting that giant!" As soon as the words left his mouth, he wanted to retrieve them. His yelling focused everyone's attention on him. Their stares only lasted a moment. They all turned away again, but Eli'av felt exposed.

"The giant?" asked Nathan. "Is that it?"

Eli'av didn't answer.

"He's just a man," continued Nathan, "a little bigger, but just a man. Get a grip on yourself. Giants like `Og and SiHon were felled by our teacher, Moshe. That giant will fall before the Aron HaBrith just like they did. The Holy One is the final arbitrator in all things."

"I hope so," whispered Eli'av. He managed to recover his face, but in his heart, he wasn't totally convinced. He knew, at least he knew that he should know, that Nathan's words were true, but all his life, there were these seeds of doubt in his heart, and yesterday, during the battle, he feared they had begun to take root.

***

Sh'mu'el helped Eli, the Kohen Gadol, along the path. Eli moved slowly and with difficulty. His girth and his age seemed to anchor him to the ground. It had always been that way, he reflected. Now, at ninety-eight, with his vision clouded over; he had even less motivation to move. He preferred to just sit, and let the world move around him.

As the veritable head of the Nation of Yisrael for more than forty years, he should have done more, he knew. Yet, it was difficult, and despite his wide frame, he didn't feel that he had the shoulders to carry the burden. This one, Sh'mu'el, would do better when the time was right.

Sh'mu'el was dedicated to the *Miqdash* by his mother the same year Eli became the Kohen Gadol. His mother, *H*annah had come with her husband and his other wife to celebrate the festival. She had been barren for ten years, but her co-wife had given her husband seven sons. In her pain and grief, she cried out to the Holy One, desperate for a child. When He had fulfilled her prayer, she dedicated her son to His service. From the moment he arrived, it was clear to Eli that the Holy One had not only blessed the mother, but the son as well. Sh'mu'el was a gifted child, and Eli knew that he had been sent to bless the nation. He would be the one who would elevate Yisrael out of the muck of its own foibles, when the time was right.

When the time was right. He sighed. The thought left him with a sense of comfort. Though it also carried with it a sense of loss. He had hoped his sons, or at least one of them, would take the mantle of leadership. He had tried, so very hard in the beginning, to bring them to the role. They had grown up too comfortable though. It would seem, as sons of the High Priest, it was hard for them to identify with the needs of the people.

_H_ofni and Pin_H_'as, Eli's two sons were not bad boys, thought their father. They had just, somehow, missed the importance of serving the Holy One. They were too consumed with their own desires to worry much about His Will. To be a kohen-priest of the Holy One was not like being a priest of the false gods. One could not bend the service to fulfill one's own needs. Eli had hoped that they would eventually grow out of their selfishness. He was still waiting.

Eli breathed a deep sigh. He was so tired. His body was so heavy. It was too late now. The die had been cast. Events had taken on a life of their own, and there was very little he could do anymore, except wait, and hope, and pray. His large frame shuddered with another sigh. May the Holy One forgive him, but there was nothing which he felt that he could do.

Sh'mu'el, wearing a simple white linen garment, gently guided his charge to his seat in the courtyard of the city gate. His piercing gaze searched the horizon. He knew what was coming. It had been whispered to him through the wind.

Since he was a little boy, Sh'mu'el had ministered Eli. He loved him dearly, but he never understood why he allowed events to overtake him so easily. It was within Eli's hands to alter the course of destiny, but he seemed fettered by those same hands. He was so different from his mother, thought Sh'mu'el. Sh'mu'el's mother didn't seem to let anything stop her, even though, like Eli, she was ready to accept the Holy One's decree.

"Does your honor," began Sh'mu'el gently, "know why the elders are coming here to Shiloh?"

They had both heard how the first battle had gone, when the messenger came to tell of the impending visit.

"We shall soon find out," answered Eli, his voice strained with age. "We shall soon find out."

"I feel that Yisrael will go through some difficult times soon," offered Sh'mu'el, "they need the guiding hand of my master's leadership."

Another heavy sigh escaped Eli's lips. His face stared blankly towards the horizon. "Dark times and horrible trials await the nation," he whispered ominously, "I hope the Master has sent worthy leadership."

"Amen," whispered Sh'mu'el.

Both of the men fell silent, waiting for the approach of the mission from the battlefield, and the moment of trial.

***

Paremheb waited patiently as Goliyath unleashed another volley of curses and rage. He had crossed the line of insubordination a while ago, and any other soldier would have probably been lucky to lose his head by this point. But, Goliyath was a special case, and there was very little danger that his insolence would spread to other soldiers.

"Are you finished?" asked Paremheb calmly when the fuming giant paused in his shouting. "You should be severely punished for talking to me that way, Goliyath."

Goliyath stared at the head of the army, his emotions seething. He came close to challenging his commander.

"But I won't," continued Paremheb. "For now," he added after a pause. "I understand your frustration, but your lack of faith offends me. You simply don't understand the situation."

"Let the crows and vultures feed off their dead," screamed Goliyath. "They don't deserve to be buried!"

"Goliyath," Paremheb tone was patronizing, "motivation is one of the keys to winning any battle. These `Ivrim are a stubborn lot, but when they are forced to bury several thousand of their brethren, these peasants will be shaken to the core. I expect them to beg us to let them surrender in two days."

Goliyath didn't like being chastised. Further, he believed his commander had been taken off guard and was simply trying to cover up his blunder. What did it matter? In two days, he would feast on the bones of 'Ivrim and humble their god. He wouldn't be upset if Paremheb was humbled a little either. With a dismissive grunt, he turned his back on Paremheb and sulked off.

***

The room was crowded with women when PinHas entered, but he paid them no mind as he boldly kissed his wife on the cheek. She blushed at his indiscretion, though her heart always leapt when he was so brash. She wouldn't have been so pleased, however, if she had seen the wink he gave one of the maidens afterwards. She assumed the attendant blushed at seeing the affection of a husband towards his wife. Even though such demonstrative behavior was frowned upon in Yisrael, it alleviated her feelings of unattractiveness. She was in her ninth month of pregnancy and felt bigger than a house.

"You're in a good mood," sang Tsiporah, still glowing from the kiss.

"Yes, I am," answered PinHas spiritedly. "The elders are coming to meet with Father, and he wants me to be there. I have a good feeling about it."

"How is Father?" Tsiporah asked about her father-in-law. "He seems more tired lately."

"He's at the gate waiting for the elders with Sh'mu'el," said PinHas mentioning the prophet's name with displeasure.

220

He never understood his father's fondness for Sh'mu'el. He felt that the man was an upstart, who didn't know his place. Every time he was in Sh'mu'el's presence he felt his eyes on him, judging him.

The reproachments and the rumors were well known in Yisrael. Yet PinHas thought they were exaggerated and unfair. Maybe, he and his brother took a few liberties, but they surely didn't take anything that wasn't their due as kohen. In fact, some of the accusations were so ridiculous, that they weren't even worthy of answering.

But Sh'mu'el - every one seemed to love him - had turned a few indiscretions into a national liability. Everyone was waiting for the fulfillment of Sh'mu'el's prophecy. PinHas knew it would never come, and that eventually the upstart 'holy man' would be found out for the fraud he was.

Maybe, today was the day. He knew it was harder for his father to perform his duties, more and more. He had discussed with PinHas the possibility of stepping down, abdicating his post, which would make PinHas the Kohen Gadol. Maybe that was the purpose of the meeting with the elders. He felt it was time for him to be in charge. His lips offered his wife an inviting smile but his eyes scanned the rest of the women in the room. They all turned away when his eyes met theirs, but only after they had met his glance. They were there to attend to his wife and unborn child, but he was sure they would perform other roles too, if requested. His eyes feasted on the scene. He decided he would find a way to enjoy the fruits of leadership, when it was bestowed upon him.

***

Sh'mu'el helped Eli to his feet as the delegation approached the gates of the city. The Kohen Gadol had asked Sh'mu'el to make sure that he was standing at the first sign of the mission's approach. He had a tremendous amount of respect for Yishai's wisdom. Yishai as the Father of the Court, Eli's second, made his own position as its head bearable. It was a small kindness of the Holy One that he appreciated deeply. Sh'mu'el led Eli several amoth outside the gate, and they waited for the group to approach.

When the delegation neared, Yishai dismounted to transverse the last few amoth on foot to greet Eli humbly. Despite everything, Yishai had a fondness for Eli, and sympathized with his plight. There was no doubt in Yishai's mind that Eli wanted to fulfill the will of the Holy One. It was just that events had overtaken him, and he had allowed himself to become, to some degree, impotent. Yishai's heart swelled with compassion for the aged leader.

Yishai approached the Kohen Gadol. He gently took his hand and kissed it. "Peace unto you, *avi.*"

"And upon you, my son," answered Eli. "I was grieved to hear of the losses at the battle. May it be for an atonement, and may the Holy One redeem their blood."

222

"Amen," answered Yishai.

"What brings you to Shiloh, my son?" asked Eli.

"I have been charged with asking the Kohen Gadol of Yisrael for something dear," responded Yishai.

Eli startled at the answer. His intuition understood the reference, but he collected himself. "Come," he said, "let's sit in the gate and discuss the matter."

Yishai took Eli's arm and began guiding him back towards the city gates.

Eli nodded his head in the direction of his attendant. "This is Sh'mu'el," he offered.

Yishai nodded a greeting, "Peace unto you."

"*Shalom alekha, avi.* Peace unto you, Father," returned Sh'mu'el.

Yishai had never met the man before, but his first impression was positive. He had heard much of this prophet of Yisrael. As a Nazir from birth, a razor had never touched his head; his hair, tied in one long braid, hung neatly down his back, the knot of his *totafoth* hidden beneath. Yishai was immediately impressed with his demeanor. He recognized the glowing countenance of one who dwelled in the Light of the Holy One.

Sh'mu'el too was impressed with the great sage. As their eyes met Sh'mu'el recognized in Yishai, a man who served the Holy One with the totality of his being. He immediately respected him.

The delegation of elders followed Yishai and Eli into courtyard of the gate, the customary place for public discourse. There, on low stone benches, the custodians of Yisrael sat to try and safeguard the nation's future.

**

"No!" Eli's voice reached a fevered pitch. "It can't be done." The thought of the Aron HaBrith leaving the Mishqan brought him close to panic.

"Now," began Yishai, as he placed a comforting hand on Eli's arm. "I understand your concern. I too, am not in favor of bringing the Aron to the battlefield, but I could not persuade the council."

"We're not worthy to take it into battle. It hasn't been done since the days of Yehoshu'ah." Eli calmed, but his expression was still strained.

"It's already been decided," repeated Yishai. The other elders sat silently, patiently allowing Yishai to discuss the matter with the Kohen Gadol.

Eli recognized that arguing would be futile. He should have been at the court's session, and then he might have been able to convince the others. He sighed with resignation.

"Who will bring it?" asked Eli.

"That's your decision," offered Yishai. "I wouldn't assume that you are fit to travel."

"No, it will have to be my boys. My boys …" Eli's words dropped off. Suddenly he had a horrible premonition, but he dare not give it expression. "I had already considered abdicating in favor of my son. I am getting too old to perform my duties as required." Eli's voice was distant, his thoughts preoccupied with vague amorphous fears.

Yishai grimaced. "Maybe the prophet Sh'mu'el could come as well, or come in their stead?" He was loath to make the suggestion, but he wasn't sure of Eli's sons' aptness for the task.

"They're good boys," began Eli, repeating the expression he had used too often. He paused, turning his face to Yishai's, "In any event, Sh'mu'el will not go."

"Why not?" asked Yishai, perplexed.

Eli's eyes became distant. He seemed to be speaking from another place. "The nation of Yisrael is about to undergo horrible trials. It will shake the very foundation of our people's faith." His eyes returned to Yishai's, locking on them and drawing him in. "The Holy One has sent the cure, before inflicting the wound. It should be saved until the appropriate time. Sh'mu'el will stay put, until the Aron HaBrith is returned."

Yishai drew a breath. He understood the Kohen Gadol's words, all too well. They shook him to the very foundation of his being.

"Very well, *avi*," Yishai acquiesced, "May our deeds be for the Holy One's honor."

"Amen," answered Eli, "amen."

Chapter Eight

Marching to Battle
The east-west highway from Shiloh to Afeq

Yishai's eyes began to tear. A feeling of awe permeated his being. He stood with the other elders in a semi-circle, outside the eastern end of the Courtyard of the Mishqan. Enwrapped in their white shawls and crowned in their *totafoth*, the torchbearers of Yisrael stood, patiently waiting. The air was thick with anticipation, as the yoke of responsibility weighed heavily on each of their shoulders.

All thoughts were focused inside. Inside, past the fine linen curtains, hanging from silver hooks; inside, past the golden jointed wooden pillars with brass sockets and golden capitals; inside, where Eli and the kohan'im were preparing the Aron HaBrith. Deep inside, past the ten amoth square screen for the courtyard gate, with its embroidered work of blue, purple and scarlet, and past a similar screen for the Sanctuary, and another veil for the innermost sanctuary, the Holy of Holies, where kohan'im were removing the Holy Aron HaBrith for the first time in nearly four hundred years. Each and every one of the elders stood in silence, examining his own inner sanctuary and listened to the beating of his own heart.

The kohan'im, too, moved with trepidation. No one had even seen the Aron HaBrith save the Kohen Gadol, and then only once a year, since it came to rest here in Shiloh. It was not a thing to be trifled with.

Fifty amoth from the gate of the Courtyard, past the bronze altar was the entrance to the Mishqan, the Sanctuary. The Tent of Testimony stood in simple elegance, a rectangular structure of embroidered curtains covered in a tent of goat and ta*H*ish skins.

Eli's two sons supported him on either side as he slowly moved through the first chamber, simply called the Holy. Dressed in the regal attire of office, his hesitation of step this time was not due to his corpulent body, but the heaviness of his soul. His hands repeatedly returned to his *mitsnefeth*, and the golden plate bearing the Holy One's holy name, checking to make sure that their position was correct. As he reached the center of the twenty amoth by ten amoth chamber, he paused by the incense altar. Its sweet smell permeated the air, mixing with the smell of freshly baked showbread. Eli breathed in the scent, allowing it to balance his nerves.

Eli turned his face towards the Menorah, the seven-branched candelabra which stood closer to the veil. It was lit with olive oil, bathing the room in bright warm light. Upon consideration, its seven candles didn't seem big enough to emit such light. Eli reflected on its glow, and sighed. Distantly, he reflected on the nation's progenitor, Avraham, and wondered how he was able to heed the commands of the Creator seemingly so effortlessly. Avraham had been commanded to sacrifice his own son, and the ancient servant of the Holy One practically ran to fulfill His will. Eli sighed again. With effort, he forced himself forward.

At the veil, which separated the Holy from the Holy of Holies, Eli ran his hands down the sides of his beard, and then pressed them against the uniform of his office. Eli turned to his sons. "Are you ready for this?" he asked simply. He wanted to say so much more.

"Yes, Father," they both answered automatically.

"No," replied Eli gently. "Do not answer, before you consider. This is not our normal service. If we err, even slightly it could spell disaster for the nation. Are you ready for this?" His hands touched the two shoulder pieces at the edges of his efodh, inscribed with each of the tribe's name, all sons of Ya`aqov, Yisrael.

Ḥofni and PinḤas both startled as the implication reached them. They each wore a similar uniform though without the efodh, the golden plate and breastplate.

"Are you sure you immersed properly," asked Eli, "You're sure you hadn't anything, even small, that might have prevented the purification waters from reaching the skin?"

The both paused. Their father's concern worried them. PinḤas especially was shaken. Had they taken too much for granted?

"Father," he began, but words failed him.

"This," said Eli, fingering the breastplate he bore, "will be yours soon. The breastplate bearing a precious stone representing each of the tribes was more than a symbol of office. When a particular tribe was to be chosen for a task, and its wearer worthy, its stone would glow, indicating Heaven's choice. "Do you understand what that means?" he asked.

PinHas had been thinking about all the benefits of being the Kohen Gadol, but maybe he had missed something. He stared at the breastplate hanging from his father's chest and suddenly it looked very heavy to him.

"I'll make you proud, Father," PinHas whispered. He so very much wanted to at that moment.

Eli's eyes welled up. He pulled his sons into his massive body, hugging them tightly. He kissed them on each of their cheek and wept on each of their shoulder. Something stirred in his sons and they too wept. The embrace lasted for a long time, before Eli finally broke away, wiping his eyes and theirs.

"Come, now, let us serve the Holy One of Yisrael," he said.

Together, the three took the last few steps to the veil, which was intricately woven with images of k'ruv'im, heavenly denizens, guarding the realm that lay beyond. Two golden poles protruded from the veil, the staves of the Holy Aron HaBrith, the Ark of the Covenant.

Neither _H_ofni nor PinHas had ever seen the Holy Aron, and both now trembled with anticipation. As his father moved the embroidered veil to the side and he gazed at the Aron for the first time, _H_ofni half feared that he would be struck dead where he stood. He breathed a sigh of relief that he hadn't been. The exhale he heard escape from his brother's lips, indicated that he too shared the same thought.

The Aron was magnificent. It was the most beautiful thing either of the two sons had ever seen. The golden poles that had extended past the veil ran through two golden rings on either side of a rectangular box. The box was two and one half amoth long, and an amah and a half wide of pure gold, that seemed to gleam of its own accord.

Two k'ruv'im of pure gold seemed to sprout from either end of the golden cover, their wings spreading towards each other. While made of the same gold as the Aron, something about the figure of the k'ruv'im seemed fluid, almost animate. Their wings seemed to flutter as the three approached. It was there, from between the k'ruv'im, that the Holy One of Yisrael had told Moshe that He would meet him and speak to him. This was the earthly throne of the Heavenly King, and it was indescribably awesome.

Both of the sons gaze was drawn into the Aron, and they felt a hollowness in their souls, an unworthiness. Suddenly, all of their deficiencies were exposed and laid bare before their eyes. Fear gripped them. Vertigo seized them. They both felt as if they were being drawn into a deep chasm. Their heads spun, as if on a mountain top and all of the air in the room had thinned to nothingness. They were standing on the thin edge of a cliff with nothing to grab hold of.

Eli grabbed his two son's forearms firmly, returning them to the present. Both of them were surprised at the strength of his grip. It was as if, in the presence of the Aron, he had been revitalized. Both _H_ofni and Pin_H_as recognized that the opposite had occurred to them, but they didn't have time to examine that observation. They both quickly backed away from the precipe, fearing what lay beyond.

"Quickly," commanded Eli, "take down the veil and cover the Aron HaBrith with it."

Eli's sons quickly complied, unhooking the veil from its hooks and gently covering the Aron. Afterwards, Eli instructed them to cover the Aron with two other coverings, one of Ta_H_ish skins, and finally, a covering of blue.

"He knows," whispered Eli ruefully, "He knows. We can cover the Aron, but we can't hide from ourselves, or our sins."

Both of his sons glanced at their father, and then the ground, wondering to whom their father's comments were directed. Only the golden poles remained exposed, extending from either end of the coverings, hinting at what lay hidden beneath.

232

Eli called to the four kohan'im that were waiting in the Sanctuary. Hurriedly, the four, dressed as Hofni and PinHas, entered. They each grabbed a corner and lifted the Aron from its resting place. They stumbled momentarily, as the Aron was far lighter than any had expected. When they lifted it, it felt as if it carried itself.

Hofni and PinHas each took a long silver horn that had also been resting in the Holy of Holies, and together blew a long blast. The call of the trumpet shook them as much as the people outside. It reminded them of the call to repentance on the Day of Atonement.

More contrite than when they had entered, they began walking out of the Holy of Holies, their father between them. They crossed the Mishqan. The kohan'im with the Aron followed. When they arrived at the screen, a waiting kohen moved it aside and the entourage exited the Mishqan into the courtyard.

There, four men waited. They were dressed in simple white linen tunics belted at the waist. The four were from the family of Q'hat, of the tribe of Lewi, whose special role was to bear the Aron HaBrith when it was transported. It was a role that the family hadn't needed to fulfill for nearly four hundred years.

It had been necessary for the kohan'im to remove the Aron from the Mishqan, and bring it to the Lewi'im in the courtyard. In earlier time, such as in the Desert when the Mishqan was transported

233

regularly, the kohan'im would have simply covered the vessels, and the Lewi'im would have removed them from their resting place. Even the Lewi'im, whose task was to care for the vessels of the Mishqan, were forbidden from viewing them uncovered. Yet, since, in this instance, only the Aron was being removed, a decision was made to let the kohan'im do so, bringing it to the courtyard, so that the other vessels: the Menorah, the Golden Showbread Table, and the Incense Altar, did not need to be disturbed.

The Lewi'im traded places with the kohan'im carefully, so that the Aron would not touch the ground. The entire assembly solemnly crossed the courtyard to the awaiting elders outside. Everyone felt a surge of excitement mixed with trepidation. The Aron HaBrith was marching into battle, and with it, everyone assumed, the Holy One Himself.

***

Unlike the journey to Shiloh, the return westward was not made sureptiously. Rather, like the processional of a king, the delegation left for Even Ha'Ezer with song and trumpets blaring. *H*ofni and Pin*H*as led the processional, periodically piercing the air with blasts from their horns. The mood was electric. Filled with a combination of awe and happiness, everyone was charged with renewed vigor and sense of purpose. Even Eli'av's mood lightened and his courage seemed restored.

As the processional journeyed westward, news of the Aron HaBrith's presence preceded it.

Villagers came out to see the spectacular sight. The legends of Y'hosh'uah's conquest filled their vision. While almost everyone had visited the Mishqan during the festivals, no one had ever glimpsed at even a covered Aron HaBrith. The sight was inspiring to even the most jaded.

By the time the processional reached TapuaH, only twelve thousand amoth from Shiloh, the delegation had more than tripled in size. Onlookers and new recruits continued to join the mission before arriving at the encampment of the Yisrael army, swelling its ranks. When they did arrive, the earlier tragedy had been completely forgotten. The Nation of Yisrael was already celebrating their complete victory over the P'lisht'im.

***

Echoes of the celebration and exuberance soon reached the camp of the P'lishtim. Curiosity and concern soon filled their ranks. When Paremheb hear the noise, shivers ran down his spine. What trickery had those `Ivrim devised? Dread filled him. How had he allowed himself to be deceived? He would have to learn the source for their renewed spirit, and extinguish it immediately.

As the news spread throughout the P'lishti camp, panic accompanied it. The Aron HaBrith, the god of the `Ivrim, himself, the one that had wrought destruction on Mitsrayim had joined their camp. Fear and dread overcame even the mightiest of warriors. Many of the `Ivri recruits quietly slipped away from the camp to join their brethren or flee the battle. They would not fight against their own God.

Soon the conversations grew from whispers to public discourse, and from the rank and file to the officers. "Woe is our lot," cried one officer, as they sat in council with Paremheb, "They have never done such a thing before. How will we fight against gods?"

His fear was infections. Another joined his lament, "Who shall deliver us out of the hands of these mighty gods?"

Paremheb was beside himself. He had been duped, and now he too wondered if it would be possible to war against the god of the 'Ivrim. The stories of their god's vengeance on Mitsrayim were legendary, even in the P'lishti Empire. Their god had turned the Red Sea into blood. He had delivered pestilence and plagues on the country. There were stories of fire and ice descending from the Heavens. And most disturbing, their god had crushed the entire Mitsri army at the Reed Sea, drowning them while allowing the 'Ivrim to cross as if on dry land. Paremheb knew should stop such talk, it alone was destructive, but his own doubts seized him.

Goliyath was stunned and outraged. For a while, he had waited for Paremheb to take command, but this was too much. When he saw that the commander failed to control his officers, Goliyath stood up defiantly. "Give them a few days and they'll melt," he shouted at Paremheb. "They don't look like they're surrendering," he continued, "we do."

"You were tricked," he added.

Paremheb stared arrogantly in return. There was nothing he could say. Goliyath was right, but he would make that giant pay for his insolence. He was tired of it.

Goliyath turned his attention to the men. *"tiHizqu letsmkhu w'sharaHu. tidubaraiu k'gebar'im, P'lishti!* Strengthen yourselves and act like men, P'lisht'im," he bellowed.

"Do you want to fall to those accursed 'Ivrim? Do you want to serve them like they serve us now?" Goliyath was animate. *"t'hiyu gebar'im, qarabu'in migru'in d'p'lisht'im. t'hiyu gebar'im!* Be men, noble warriors of P'lisht'im. Be men!"

"But what about the plagues that their god wrought on Mitsrayim?" one of the officers interjected. "How can we stand against that?"

"That god has no more power," returned Goliyath, "he used what he had to defeat the Mitsr'im. Ten blows on Mitsray'im, ten on the sea, and ten in the dessert. He hasn't any more power. It is spent. I know the ways of these gods. They have limits. Had he any power left, would the 'Ivrim have served us for all these years." He thought of Shim'shon and the destruction he saw there, but it only spurred his rant more.

"Stop acting like cowards," he shouted.

"Their god destroyed the giants Si*H*on and `Og, and all their armies," offered another.

"Maybe," suggested another, "we need to bring Dagon here to fight this god."

Goliyath wasn't a big fan of the gods, any of them. Again, the giant's thoughts returned the spectacle in `Aza. He remembered how that `Ivri brigand had defied Dagon in his own temple. "We haven't any need for gods!" shouted Goliyath. "No god can stand against P'lisht'im." He would defy the `Ivri god himself, and repay him for that insult.

"Is this the army that has conquered kings?" chided Goliyath, "We are P'lisht'im. *t'hiyu gebar'im w'tliHmu!* Act like men and fight."

His thoughts turned to the memory of finding Delaiy'lah's mangled body. Such a waste of good flesh. His anger was fueled to boiling.

"I swear," shouted Goliyath, "I, Goliyath, will bring the `Ivri god to his knees. I will take him and make him a slave of the P'lishti, just like his miserable nation."

"We'll bring him to Dagon's temple, so Dagon can make sport of this worthless god," Goliyath sneered.

Inspired by the image, Goliyath grabbed the nearest officer and pulled him to his feet. *"tihiyi geber! tihiyi p'lishti!* Be a man. Be a P'lishti," he yelled into his face. He repeated the act with every officer until they were all standing on their feet, charged for battle.

When he got to Paremheb, the head of the army stood himself. Goliyath snickered. He pressed his face close to the commander's, "Lead these men to victory, or face my wrath."

Paremheb felt it would be safer to battle a hundred gods than deal with Goliyath at that moment. Much to his chagrin, Goliyath was right. He had reversed the failing moral. The officers were now charged. Paremheb needed to take advantage of their mood, before they thought again of battling gods. Paremheb began to shout orders, organizing the troops for battle. He would deal with Goliyath later.

***

Chapter Nine

Hubris
The battlefield between Even Ha`Ezer and Afeq

Charged with a new sense of purpose, the P'lishti warriors took the field of battle. Goliyath had everyone enthused. This was a battle for the honor of their nation. The force, as it entered the valley, was awesome. They seemed to extend from one end to the other. They moved as a one, a line of shield and spear marching forward. Three hundred thousand infantry marched under the black and red banner of the P'lisht'im.

To Y'ro*H*om, the advancing line reminded him of a locust plague he once witnessed. A line of death devouring everything in its path. The metaphor was not lost on him. He was reminded of the same plague the Holy One had visited on Mitsrayim. He shuddered with an unanticipated wave of dread. He was as confident and enthused as the rest of the Nation of Yisrael. He couldn't fathom losing a battle with the Aron HaBrith amongst them. Suddenly that same thought gave him pause. Maybe he should fathom it. Maybe it was hubris to believe that the Holy One couldn't let the symbol of His Might fail.

Y'ro*H*om shook his head and pushed the thought away. This was not the time for pessimism. He signaled to the warrior nearby, and the shofar blast sounded. The Nation of Yisrael moved forward. They would meet their enemy head on, and fight for the glory and the honor of the Holy One. They were still only half the force that the

P'lishtim fielded, but Y'ro*H*om was confidant that one man of Yisrael was worth far more than two of any other nation.

When the two armies met, it was the like the crashing of two hammers. The P'lishti infantry pressed forward, a solid line of shields, the points of their sharpened spears jutting an arm's length before the shield wall.

The infantry of Yisrael charged into the wall of shields with an assortment of spears, hammers, axes and more ambiguous implements of destruction. The line heaved, wavered and then finally splintered.

All along the P'lishti shield line, sections buckled, and Yisrael infantry penetrated. For a moment, even before the Aron HaBrith entered the fray, it looked as if the P'lishti discipline would break and its soldiers would be routed.

Yet, as sections of the infantry cracked and warriors of Yisrael penetrated the line, the P'lishti archers opened fire, raking the intruders, transforming their successful incursion into a deadly pitfall.

The battle pitched like a leaf in a storm swirl. The lines soon dissolved, and the field of battle melted into a tangled mosaic of warriors. Clouds of dust choked the air. Shouts of victory became indistinguishable from cries of anguish. For a time, chaos seemed to be the only constant.

Yet, as the silver trumpets sounded and the Aron HaBrith reached the center of the cyclone of battle, everyone seemed to pause.

Like a flame piercing a mound of straw, the enemy seemed to fall away from the Aron, its effect rippling like waves throughout the P'lishti ranks. Everyone, Yisrael and P'lishti alike seemed transfixed as the holy object wrought its destruction.

A blood-curdling cry pierced the air as Goliyath regained himself. Rage burned in the six amoth of flesh and sinew as the behemoth charged the Aron HaBrith indiscriminately felling anyone and everything in his path.

PinHas's eyes widened in horror as Goliyath charged him and the Aron HaBrith. His mind swam. Though, instead of the terrible image of Goliyath, he saw an even more terrifying visage. In place of Goliyath, he saw a darkly cloaked demon with fiery eyes coming to devour him. Remotely, he recognized in the demon the Accuser of Yisrael, and he knew that he was the target.

Yet, the demon never reached him. PinHas felt an invisible flame from the Aron HaBrith pierce his innards. Incredible pain surged from within, as PinHas felt his insides incinerate long before Goliyath's spear bored through his stomach. The contents of PinHas's belly seemed to seethe and boil as they splattered on the ground. The expression of horror remained transfixed on the kohen's face as it rolled across the field. Hofni's body, devoured by the same beast, accompanied his brother's dismembered corpse.

Shock permeated the atmosphere at the spectacle the Holy One's designated servants eviscerated by the spear of the enemy.

Like a raging bull, Goliyath continued. He plowed into the Lewi'im, dislodging the Aron HaBrith from their grip through the force of his charge. Spellbound, the nation watched the impossible as Goliyath seized the Aron in his massive grip, tearing the cloth of blue, the taHish skin, and veil from the Aron in one motion.

The k'ruv'im seemed to writhe in anguish at their exposure. The sons of Yisrael reeled in panic at the blatant affront to the Holy One of Yisrael. The warriors quickly averted their eyes. They hid their gaze from the sight of the exposed Aron HaBrith, as they would for a woman stripped of her coverings in the marketplace.

Goliyath screamed in anguish as jolts of pain shot through his body as he manhandled the Aron. His blind anger numbed the agony. His entire being was focused on desecrating the sanctified totem of the 'Ivr'im.

Even his own nation was mesmerized by the giant's audacity, as he struggled to force open the Holy Aron. Bolts of pain shot through his body as Goliyath fought to pry the covering from the Aron, but he would not be stopped. He persisted as the two nations stood frozen, witnesses to the perverse.

Awakening from a nightmare, Sha'ul, the son of Kish, from the tribe of Binyamin, was jarred from his stupor. Seeing the Aron HaBrith in the hands of an uncircumcised, he rendered his garment, and threw dirt on his brow. He cried to the heavens in despair. Passion filled him. Enraged at the horrible crime taking place before his eyes, he leapt from his position and raced towards Goliyath and the Aron. Righteous indignation consumed him. As he reacted for the honor of the Holy One, all personal considerations melted away.

Sha'ul arrived within several amoth, but it was too late. The Holy Aron was breached; Goliyath's fingers pried the golden covering from its base. As he cracked the Aron open, an unearthly cry seemed to echo from the heavens. White fiery fingers of flame darted from the broken seal and snaked up Goliyath's fingers and hand enwrapping his arm in a skein of lightning flashes.

The giant threw back his head in a scream of agony, but he would not be deterred. The Aron became unbearably heavy. He began to totter from its weight. The Aron seemed to be trying to escape the grip of his arm, and Goliyath was forced to one knee to maintain his balance.

Finally, Sha'ul reached the giant and blindly leapt headlong into his back. The monstrous P'lishti fell forward, struggling to maintain his hold on the Aron. His hand reached inside the Holy relic and removed the square stone tablets that rested within.

Guided by some unseen force, Sha'ul reacted. He quickly grabbed the discarded veil and coverings, and leapt towards the giant. Enwrapping

244

the tablets in the coverings, Sha'ul ripped them from Goliyath's grip and tumbled to the ground.

The P'lishti released a primal scream, a reaction to the pain and the truculence of having a part of his prize stolen from him. The Aron slammed shut, biting at his fingers. He spun around to see the insolent 'Ivri racing off with the tablets. His strength was spent and knew he couldn't catch him. Goliyath struggled to his feet and retreated to the P'lishti camp, Aron in tow.

The spell was broken, and the armies awoke from their trance to a new reality. Emboldened, the P'lisht'im overpowered their distraught opponents. Those who were not quick enough to flee were cut down. The P'lishti warriors routed their enemy, dispersing Yisrael, each to their homes in utter defeat.

***

Sha'ul didn't stop running, possessed by a spirit of desperation to return the ancient relic of his people to the Mishqan. He kept his thoughts focused on his goal, fighting against the natural tendency to reflect on the recent events. He feared that their implications would derail his mission. He sprinted from the battlefield to Shiloh, imbued with supernatural stamina.

As he approached Shiloh, Sha'ul was seized with indecision. Where to go? He allowed the forces that had directed him thus far to continue to guide him. He distantly hoped that it was a holy source that pulled him towards the left. He ran to the north of the summit, directly to the Mishqan.

Several kohan'im startled at his approach. Breathing heavily from exertion, words failed him. He tried to explain. He hadn't realized that he had been sobbing. Finally, he despaired of communicating. Rather, like a mother seeking refuge for her baby, he handed one of the kohan'im his bundle. The priest trembled when he recognized its identity.

"Eli?" was the only word that managed to flee the young warrior's lips. The stunned kohan'im pointed Sha'ul in the direction of the city gates he had circumvented, and he plodded towards them, his body moving like an automaton.

Yet, before he even reached the courtyard of the city gates, the entire city heard of the defeat of Yisrael and capture of the Aron HaBrith. From the Mishqan the cry went out. Eli heard the cry, but couldn't understand it. A man, Sha'ul, approached him. Eli heard Sha'ul's weeping. Panic began to creep up his spine.

"What is that I hear?" asked Eli, though his heart knew the answer. "What is that horrible cry of so many people?"

Sha'ul, in a state of near shock, said flatly, "I have come from the camp of Yisrael. I fled the battlefield today."

"What has happened my son?" Eli's voice was on edge of terror.

Through his sobs, Sha'ul reported, "Yisrael has fled before the P'lisht'im. There was a great slaughter of our people. Your two sons also," Sha'ul choked at the memory, "_H_ofni and Pin_H_as are dead."

The messenger paused before finally admitting, both to himself and the Kohen Gadol, "The Aron of the Holy One is captured."

As the words reached his ears, Eli was seized with a terrible shaking. He clutched at his chest and fell backwards from his seat by the side of the gate. As his heavy body crashed to the ground, Sha'ul heard the sickening snap of Eli's neck. Sha'ul fell to his knees, from despair as well as exhaustion, and crawled to the side of his nation's leader. He found him dead. Sha'ul burst into renewed fits of sobbing. He collapsed onto Eli. He wept until all the tears in Yisrael were spent.

***

Pin_H_as's wife screamed in agony. The labor pains began as soon as she heard the news. She was in a state of hysterics. When she heard the maidens whispering about Eli's death, her mind snapped and she shrieked like a caged bird. The midwife tried to calm her, then restrain her, but Tsiporah was uncontrollable. She would squat on the birthstone one moment and then leap to her feet the next, dancing across the room, muttering incomprehensible statements. Her entire world had come crashing down around her, and she was unable to focus on the moment.

Finally she collapsed in a heap on the floor, writhing in pain, her legs spread as the baby crowned. "Do not fear, my lady," cried the midwife. "You've given birth to a son," she exclaimed as she tied off the cord and bundled the baby. She tried to put the newborn in its mother's arms, but Tsiporah disregarded it. Instead she mumbled another incomprehensible phrase.

"Honor has departed from Yisrael," Tsiporah suddenly screamed, "The child's name is 'Iy-khavodh,' without honor, for the Aron was taken, my father-in-law is dead, and my husband is dead. The crown of Yisrael's honor has fallen from his head, today! The Aron was captured!" She screamed and then was silent. Gingerly, one of the maidens knelt by her mistress's side only to discover that she was dead. A shriek of horror pierced her lips and the whole room erupted in tears.

***

Dawid was struck. He had been feeling elated after the incident near Beth Tapua*H*. When the news of the Aron reached him, a searing pain pierced his breasts. Violently, he ripped at the cloth over his heart and tore at it, exposing his chest. He sank to the ground, and fell onto his face, the tears creating a puddle of mud beneath his eyes.

"No, no," he repeated into the dirt, his hands clinging to the ground, searching for an anchor to prevent him from sinking into total oblivion.

"Why?" he asked the Holy One. "Why would you abandon Your people, like this?" he repeated.

Dawid had never questioned his own mistreatment at the hands of his family. Well, that wasn't totally true, but he had come to recognize, through the guidance of his mother and great-grandmother, Mamma Ruth, that the Holy One's ways were wholly just. Though His plan might not be incomprehensible to us, it was always for our good. But this? Dawid could accept his own seemingly unjustifiable abandonment, but how could the Holy One hide His face from His own people.

Drunk with grief Dawid stumbled to his feet and ran madly to his great-grandmother's chambers. He entered the dimly lit stone room, to find Mamma Ruth, herself, sobbing at the news. Like he had done so often as a child, he fell to his knees at her feet, his head falling into her lap. She stroked his tangle of hair, as his sobs burst forth anew.

"I know, my child, I know," Mamma Ruth whispered. "Yet, He only hides His Face from us, to goad us to seek Him." "Like when you were a baby and we would play a game of peek-a-boo," she added

Dawid noticed that though Mamma Ruth cried, her sadness was measured. That fact somehow brought him comfort. He allowed her soothing words, and soft hands to gently stroke away the pain.

***

Yishai sat on the floor of his home, his clothes rent, earth and ash covered his brow. Tears streamed down the elder's face and moans of grief escaped his lips. He rocked back and forth in a steady rhythm. He had known. Yet, he had felt powerless to stop the events from unfolding. Weeks before the battle, he had had dreams, nightmares, of the catastrophe. His grandmother, the saintly Mamma Ruth cryptically confirmed his suspicions before he left. Yet, she also left him with the impression that there was little he could do to mitigate the blow. The Holy One needed to steer His chosen nation away from a dangerous cliff. The Holy One was not an idol who could be manipulated. The nation, and each of its citizens, needs to bend its will towards His, not the other way around. Chosen-ness was a responsibility as much as it was privilege. The blow would be painful. Yet, ultimately, she added, it would only strengthen the nation. It was for their good.

The aftermath of the battle had been overpowering. It was complete chaos. Yishai was not sure how he had managed to find his three sons. He thanked the Holy One for that small kindness. Their physical wounds were superficial, but, like the rest of the nation, they were devastated by the battle and the capture of the Aron. He wondered if they would recover. How could anyone in the nation recover from such a blow? He had anticipated it and yet his own pain was unbearable.

He mourned for the entire nation. Could they ever recover from such a blow? Was it possible that the Holy One had miscalculated? That was an impossibility of course, but some of his other thoughts were even more disturbing. Was it possible that He had abandoned His nation completely?

No. The Holy One had hidden His face from Yisrael before. In Mitsray'im, the nation served as slaves for nearly four hundred years. And He sent the nation of Amaleq, who attacked the nation when they left Mitsrayim. The attack of Amaleq was most telling, for it came at a moment when the nation had lost their way, when they became filled with doubt. Yes, thought Yishai, the Holy One hides His face, but only so we are forced to seek it. All of these trials and tribulations were only for the purpose of bringing the nation closer to Him. Tragedy came to perfect the nation, a fire removing the dross as in the smelting of gold. He would not abandon Yisrael, Yishai convinced himself. The Holy One had promised as much, for the nation had a role to play in His plan. It was His tool for the perfection of the world.

He was reminded of the Kohen Gadol's words before they parted. They brought him a certain amount of comfort. Eli too seemed to have known what would transpire. Yet, he had also seen that the Holy One had already prepared for its healing. He prayed the remedy would be sufficient. Tears accompanied his prayers up to the gates of Heaven.

Chapter Ten

War Captive
The Camp of the P'lishtim
Shortly after the battle of Afeq

Goliyath slumped in the corner of the central tent. He sat rocking. A low moan, almost a growl, escaped from his lips. Tendrils of smoke and steam rose from his blackened, smoldering skin. His eyes, barely open, seemed focused on some distant plane. A burning hatred flickered from time to time behind their glaze.

The dead bodies of nearly a hundred P'lisht'im warriors littered the ground around the Aron that shared the tent with the mammoth mound of living flesh. Their bodies smoldered too, victims of a fire ignited from somewhere inside their bodies: The penalty for daring to touch, even incidentally, the holy relic. The rancid smell of cooked flesh filled the tent.

Paremheb was content, though he wished the giant would die already. He would have taken care of it himself, quietly, except that he feared to enter the tent in the presence of the Aron. He kept his knife tucked inside his belt, ready for the opportunity.

This relic of the `Ivri god was quite a prize, but it was also a cumbersome obstacle. He had sent for a priest from Ashdod to advise him. These toys of the gods were beyond his expertise.

Yet, it delayed him. He wanted to press the attack, to march to Shiloh and sack the cultic center of these upstart runaway slaves from Mitsrayim. It was time to put an end to their constant rebellion. However, being unable to remove the Aron, he was stuck here, keeping his force close by to prevent any type of counter attack, or attempt to liberate the captive relic.

Not that he seriously suspected one, but he was woe to take such a risk. For the time being, he had to be content with allowing his warriors to ransack the neighboring villages, collecting their 'war prizes' from the local environs. He had several young fresh ones waiting for his pleasure in his tent himself, but the responsibility of dispatching of this relic pressed upon him.

A runner quickly approached Paremheb as he stood outside the central tent. "The priests have arrived," announced the messenger.

Paremheb smiled. Finally. "Have them meet me in my tent," he instructed the runner, as he himself turned towards his quarters. The messenger quickly turned to forward the message.

The sentries saluted Paremheb as he approached the large goat skinned tent that served as his private quarters. He nodded in response, and one of them quickly folded away the flap for his commander to enter. "Let the priests enter as soon as they arrive," he instructed.

Inside the tent, another soldier offered Paremheb a quick salute. "Has the commander come to 'interrogate' the locals?" asked Parhemeb's aide with a smile, referring to the commander's favorite game with his battle trophies. Four young girls lay on their stomachs near the center of the tent, a rope binding their hands and feet tightly behind them. They lay motionless save for a constant shudder, a silent indicator of their incessant weeping. They always weep, thought Paremheb.

"No. We have visitors. Priests," said Paremheb flatly. "Warm the wine."

His aide smiled and crossed the tent to the large clay vessels. They were decorated in the P'lishti style, black geometric designs on a dark red background. "The good wine?" asked the aide.

Paremheb shrugged, then winced slightly, "Not the best. They're priests," he mocked, "we wouldn't want to spoil them with too much worldly delight."

His aide chuckled in response and poured wine from the center vessel into the decanter and mixed it with water. He brought the clay decanter over to a small hearth near the back of the tent and placed it on a nearby stand to warm.

In the meantime, Paremheb reclined on a low couch arranged with colorful pillows.

The aide returned his commander. "Anything else, sir?" he asked.

"Yes," replied Paremheb, "prepare some supper, if you don't mind. I'm famished."

254

"There's already some dog roasting in the fire pit," offered the aide.

"That will do fine," complimented Paremheb licking his lips.

His aide brought him a goblet of wine. "It will be ready soon," he said.

Another solider called from outside, "Sir."

"Yes?" invited Paremheb.

"The priests, sir," announced the soldier.

"Send them in," called the commander.

A moment later, four men with shaven heads filed into the tent. Four wore white linen tunics. A fifth sported a long red woolen robe. His linen tunic, of the same color as his robe, was embroidered with a pattern of interlacing golden wheat and grape clusters. They stopped in the entranceway waiting for Paremheb to acknowledge them.

He should have stood out of respect, but he wasn't in the mood, so Paremheb merely leaned forward, raising his goblet towards the priests. "Welcome, servants of Dagon. Come and join us in our victory celebration. We have captured the god of the 'Ivrim today."

The colorfully dressed priest, the chief of the group, grimaced. It was hard for him to discern

Parhemeb's tone. When it was clear that the commander wasn't going to stand, he bowed slightly. "I am Rasqadu, a humble servant of the god Dagon. Praised be Dagon on your victory. You requested my presence?"

"Yes, Father," answered Paremheb lightly, "please, join me. My aide will bring you a cup of wine, if you please." From his appearance, it seemed the priest liked his meat and wine.

"Thank you," answered Rasqadu as he entered the interior of the tent, "I would enjoy a toast to Dagon, and your victory."

Parhemeb's aide brought the priest a stool and placed it opposite his commander. As the priest went to sit, the bound girls attracted his attention.

"War trophies," commented Paremheb, but he watched with fascination at the interest of the priest. He probably enjoyed other things as well, decided Paremheb.

"I see," stuttered Rasqadu, as he pried his eyes from the captives to sit before Paremheb. The four other priests remained standing silently in the entranceway.

As he sat, the aide handed Rasqadu a cup of warm wine.

"To your victory," offered the priest as he held the cup aloft.

"Thank the gods, particularly Dagon, for granting it," returned Paremheb, who also hoisted his cup.

The priest visibly relaxed upon hearing Parhemeb's response, and tasted the dark red liquid. "Very nice," he commented.

"Thank you," answered Paremheb. "I invited you here because we have a difficult situation."

"Yes," the priest leaned forward.

"We captured a relic of the `Ivrim. Some representation of their god, I suppose," continued Paremheb, "but it's proving quite deadly. I have a tent full of corpses where it's stored. Anyone who comes near it dies."

"Oh my," exclaimed the priest.

"Yes, and from the sound of it," continued Paremheb, "it's quite an agonizing death. I don't know what to do with it now."

"How was it captured then?" asked Rasqadu.

"Goliyath."

"Oh," said the priest knowingly. "And where is he now."

"In the tent, suffering," answered Paremheb casually, "unless he's finally died."

"Oh my," Rasqadu exclaimed again. "And what do you want me to do?" he asked.

"You're a priest. You tell me," returned Paremheb. "What should we do?"

"Hmm," considered Rasqadu. His eyes stole a quick glance at the captives. Paremheb noted it but held his tongue for the moment.

After several moments of consideration, the priest shook his head. "I really know very little about the 'Ivri god. Maybe Orpah of Gath can help?"

"Goliyath's mother," Paremheb barely hid the edge of disgust in his tone.

"The gods seem to talk to her," answered Rasqadu apologetically.

"Fine, you can go there to inquire at first light," offered Paremheb.

"Me?" the priest hesitated. "I didn't mean..." he stuttered for a moment. Parhemeb's cold stare rattled him. He didn't have a good defense. "I suppose, I could, if it's necessary," he offered.

"It's necessary," stated the commander flatly.

The priest's eyes again stole a glance towards the bound girls. Paremheb smiled thinly. "I see the girls have captured the priest's attention."

He tilted his head sideways and leaned forward towards the priest. "Does his honor want to taste one for himself?" It was hard to tell if the tone was one of respect or mockery.

The priest coughed and brought his face back towards Paremheb. His smile had an edge of embarrassment to it. "No, no. We aren't priests of Asherah," he chided.

"Very well," began Paremheb but his eyes held the priest's as he leaned back.

"But maybe," offered the priest, a little too quickly at first. "Maybe, it would be good to take her and initiate her into the service of Dagon, for his honor, that is." "If you can spare her that is," he added, wanting to sound as if he wasn't too interested in the girl.

Parhemeb's smiled widened, "Consider her a gift." He paused. "For Dagon, of course," he added.

"Of course," confirmed the priest.

***

The Temple of Dagon, Ashdod
Before dawn, two days later

Rasqadu shuffled through the temple precinct. Normally full with priests, this morning it was overflowing. Nearly double the amount of priests were enlisted to insure that the `Ivri god was also properly taken care of. The priests were preparing offerings of every kind of food, and drink

259

for the special guest. Along with his host, Dagon, and the assortment of other manifestations of gods that were always in attendance in the temple, there would be a plethora of offerings this morning.

The last two days had been a whirlwind. Rasqadu had traveled from Afeq to Gath and back again, finally bringing the captured Aron to Ashdod before sunset the night before. It had been placed in the house of Dagon, alongside the chief god of the P'lisht'im in his *naos*, as a special guest of honor.

The journey to Gath and meeting the famous Orpah of Gath had been an experience Rasqadu would never forget, even though he would very much like to. Paremheb had reluctantly agreed to transport Goliyath to Gath as well. Acknowledging that arriving in Gath without the priestess' son would be improper. He wasn't so enthusiastic about the idea, though.

Extracting the behemoth from tent was not the simplest of operations. Fear of the 'Ivri relic prevented anyone from entering the tent. Instead they were forced to open the side where Goliyath sat slumped. Tendrils of smoke still wafted from his skin.

Four stout warriors were selected to extract him. As they reached for him, they immediately recoiled their hands in shock. Expecting heat to be emanating from his body, they're hands instead were bitten by bitter cold. They all looked at each other in utter surprise. They looked back at their commander and the priest for an explanation. Both shook their heads, unknowing. Paremheb gestured that they should try again. Shrugging, they extended their hands again.

As the hands of one of the soldiers brushed Goliyath's skin, the giant awoke with a roar. Lashing out he sent the soldier flying from the force of his blow.

Paremheb reeled. Fingering the dagger in his belt, he thanked the gods that he hadn't had an opportunity to use it. Collecting himself, he called out to his giant warrior.

"Goliyath," he shouted, "stand down. We want to help you; to take you to Gath."

Goliyath heaved and swayed. Then suddenly he was on his feet. His eyes, half opened, remained unfocused as he spun around to face Paremheb. He tottered, the low moan increased in volume from his throat. Like a man in a stupor, he stood, unsteady and unaware.

Two of his fellow warriors ran to him, and guided him the two steps to the ox cart. Then, like a felled tree, he slammed into the cart, causing the oxen to startle and leap forward. Only the mass of their passenger prevented them from bolting. His massive form filled the cart. It rocked with his heavy breathing, but the moan seemed to lessen. The memory was still vivid in Rasqadu's mind as he moved through the temple precinct. That Goliyath, he was not of this world.

Rasqadu anointed himself with natron, before immersing in the sacred pool. Two priestesses and another priest exited the pool as he entered. He caught the eye of one of the priestesses and smiled a quiet greeting. She was a 'sight for sore eyes,' as the expression went, especially after his experience in Gath with the priestess Orpah.

The trip to Gath had been difficult enough. Rasqadu was not accustomed to travel, and his small mission needed to make haste. The jolting of the ox cart had thrown his innards into disarray, causing him to disavow ever traveling again.

His only consolation was his traveling companion, the cart driver, who had the sense to limit his conversation to a minimum. Rasqadu assumed that the young warrior, who was also Goliyath's shield bearer, was too concerned about his master's condition to chat.

That "young warrior," was me, Uriyah, and I was far from concerned about Goliyath. The truth of the matter was that I had developed an immediate hatred for the priest of Dagon. Not only do I have a quasi-national distaste for idol worship, rebel tribesman from Dan or no, I also found the person of Rasqadu quite contemptible. He was the type of priest who gives service to the gods a bad name. Not that I knew that many who were a credit to their profession. Moreover, I was doing a good deal of cursing my own situation. How did I ever get myself into such a confusing mess?

Many of my fellow countrymen, upon hearing that the Aron HaBrith was in the Yisrael camp, bolted from their position in the P'lishti army. I can't say that the thought didn't cross my mind as well. Fighting with the enemy was one thing, but even I'm not so cynical as to consider fighting against the Almighty, Himself.

However upon consideration, I decided that maybe I could be of some service behind the lines, as it were. Oh, that's not true, I was just being my usual mercenary self and I decided to wait to see what developed. During my years of service with the P'lisht'im, I've perfected the art of looking like a hero, while actually doing nothing. It was a talent. You have to act all fired up and charge the enemy head on, ducking out of the way at the last minute to find a nice quiet place to contemplate the daisies. It had provided a good wage from the P'lishti coffers, and kept me out of too many moral dilemmas, thus far.

Yet, even my normal cold heart stirred when my commander, Goliyath, seized the Aron. My stoic façade fell, and suddenly I was seized with an overwhelming desire to redeem my God's honor. It seemed to over take me. I lost my head and in the same moment when that young Benyamin officer heroically confronted Goliyath and retrieved the tablets. In an instant, I slaughtered several tens of my fellow P'lishti soldiers. Fortunately, I recovered. When the smoke settled, I managed to regain my composure. After insuring that my 'insane crime' went unnoticed – I had to dispatch only two witnesses - I resumed my post. However, inside I was troubled, conflicted. The truth is my façade had become paper thin even to me. Where did such feelings of loyalty come from anyway, I kept asking myself. I always thought I was angry at the Holy One for giving me such a miserable life. I tried not to dwell on it too much.

During the entire journey to Gath, and back again, I debated as to whether or not to murder the priest and send the cart over a cliff. Fortunately for my purse strings, I was able to rationalize staying in my position, for now.

It was clear when we arrived at the temple of Asherah in Gath that we had been expected. A small group of beautiful priestesses exited the temple to greet them. Three very large men followed them. Rasqadu was immediately impressed with the women's beauty. Predictable for a priest. He voiced his thoughts to the cart driver.

"What a lovely welcoming committee," the priest mused, "I wonder if one of them is this Orpah."

I had been to Gath and the temple of my employer's mother many times. I figured I'd shake him up a bit. "Here comes the old whore now," I whispered indicating with my head the central figure of the welcoming committee.

Rasqadu was perplexed by his companion's condescending remark, until the group of women came closer. Then he recognized that the beauty of the woman, who had initially excited him so, was an illusion. Layers of cosmetics had deceived him. Revulsion now replaced his desire. Yet, he reflected, a sensation of allure still remained, and the recognition of that, disgusted him all the more.

When Orpah overheard Uriyah's comment, she was immediately struck. She was reminded of Resheg, and her spirits lifting momentarily, searched for his face. Apprehending that her memory was from another time, her spirits suddenly fell. Then the recognition that the comment was made about her caused her even more discomfort. Had she truly become that old ... priestess?

She didn't have time, nor desire, to dwell on such thoughts, so she pushed them away. "Welcome, Priest of Dagon," she said, addressing Rasqadu cheerily, "we've been expecting you." "If you'll excuse me," she continued, "let me first attend to my son." She hurried to the ox cart carrying Goliyath, leaving the priest in wonderment. How could she have been expecting them, or known about her son, he asked himself. Other thoughts intermixed with his questions, and he felt a perverse desire for the woman again. Again the thought repulsed him as much as it beckoned.

"Oh my," was all that past Rasqadu's lips.

After Orpah had been by her son for several moments, she summoned the three men, her other sons, each nearly as big as Goliyath, and had them carry Goliyath into the temple. Rasqadu was mesmerized by the men in their resemblance to Goliyath. They were practically twins. One of them though, particularly left him speechless. He unabashedly stared at the man's six fingered hands. Orpah returned to Rasqadu, promptly. "Such good boys," she said off-handedly, the image of a doting mother.

"My apologies, Priest of Dagon," she smiled. It was a pleasant smile, but a shiver ran the length of Rasqadu's spine. The image of a serpent smiling before devouring a mouse filled his thoughts. He tried to smile in return.

"Congratulations on the capture of the Aron of the `Ivri god," continued Orpah. "Our patrons in heaven are very pleased," Orpah paused, and Rasqadu was transfixed by her gaze. "I understand," continued the Avatar of Asherah, "that you wish to bring the Aron to your temple in Ashdod." Rasqadu didn't know that. Or, at least, he hadn't been fully aware of that desire till now. "Know, it is a powerful talisman, and treat it with care," she warned.

"I have already prepared all that you need," Orpah continued, as one of the Asheritu stepped forward and handed me a bundle, which I put into the cart. "There's a special blue cloth in this bundle that you must cover the Aron with. Yet you mustn't look at it, until it is concealed beneath," Orpah instructed. "I suggest you have several warriors approach the Aron backwards, with the cloth draped across their back. Then once it's covered, staves should be placed through the rings, so that it can be carried. Whatever you do, do not touch the Aron."

Rasqadu could only nod in response. He seemed hypnotized by this old women standing in front of him. Suddenly he realized that she was holding his hand, and leading him into the temple. "Come, let us reenact the union of Asherah with

Dagon. If we are successful, they will couple in the heavens and we will merit blessings,"

Orpah smiled seductively, "Uriyah will wait for you here." Rasqadu wanted to protest, but his words stuck in his throat. It was as if his own will had melted away. Obediently he followed Orpah into her lair.

Rasqadu shuddered at the memory, even though he had experienced untold pleasure. Yet, the pleasure seemed tainted. He knew that he had paid some type of price for that pleasure, even if he didn't know what it was yet. The entire way back, he kept trying to calculate Orpah's age, and was confounded every time. Goliyath was known to have supernatural senesce. He had lived far beyond the normal age of a warrior. How old did that make his mother?

The Priest of Dagon shuddered again and then pushed the thought away returning his mind to the present. In any event he had Parhemeb's "present" to make up for it. After the morning service, he planned a relaxing day of 'initiating' her. Maybe that would help him forget about Goliyath's mother.

It was almost daybreak. Rasqadu dismissed his reverie, and adjusted his priestly raiment. Twelve priests in simple white linen stood behind him in four rows, carrying the various offerings, of wine, oil, meat, and meal. Along the stone path towards the double door entrance to the sanctuary where Dagon spent the night, stood six priests and six priestesses, some with lyres, and tambourines, and others with baskets of fresh flowers.

At Rasqadu's signal, those along the path began chanting the morning hymn to musical accompaniment.

"*qumiu, qumiu, b'shulum, dagon qadashu `alyianu.* Awake, Awake, in Peace, Most Holy Dagon. *Qumiu b'shulmu w'tbarakhu inni panintu.* Awaken in Peace and Bless us with your Presence."

Rasqadu proceeded slowly with the processional to the double doors. He stood for a moment at the gateway to the sanctuary. The offerings were laid out and incense lit. The chamber was completely dark. Rasqadu was to open the doors, which faced east, as the sun crested the horizon, so as to awaken the god, and invite his presence, insuring the day's bounty.

The choir continued chanting:

"*dagalu panintu dagon rabu.* Reveal your presence, Oh great Dagon."

The sun crested the horizon and Rasqadu cracked the seal on the gate.

"*naklimu sharaHu w'khabu dagon d'gabru w'koHu.* Let us offer praise and adoration, Dagon of Might and Power."

The High Priest Rasqadu opened the gates of the sanctuary as the bright orb of the sun rose into the sky, filling the darkened chamber with light.

"*ukoltu ninni dagon hihodu.* Sustain and us in your steadfastness, Dagon of Glory."

Rasqadu looked into the chamber as it filled with light and his heart stuck in his throat. The huge statue of Dagon was lying on his face before the Aron of the `Ivrim.

"Oh my," exclaimed Rasqadu, who in a panic called to the other priests to come and set the statue aright.

Several hours later, with the effort of nearly a hundred acolytes, the massive idol of Dagon was restored to his place, and the morning rituals were finally completed.

Dagon was anointed with oils, and perfumed. His clothing was changed. Rasqadu made sure to cover the statue with a red cloak for protection. Throughout his work with Dagon, he kept eyeing the `Ivri relic with suspicion. But that was impossible, he kept telling himself without conviction.

The next morning, the rituals began as normal, but Rasqadu was full of trepidation until he cracked the seal on the gate.

As he opened the doors, flooding the sanctum with light, his eyes anxiously searched the room.

"Oh my," he exclaimed.

Again, the ten-amoth tall statue of Dagon had fallen on his face before the Aron HaBrith. His arms and head were lying severed on the threshold. Rasqadu stood agape. It looked as if Dagon was prostrating himself before the Aron of the 'Ivr'im. Fear seized him, and he dropped to his knees and bowed before the Aron. He then quickly rose and walked backwards out of the sanctum vowing never to walk on the threshold again. He closed the double doors and quickly left the Temple precincts to find the Lord of Ashdod. He was at a loss as what to do.

"Oh my," he kept repeating as he hurried through the streets of Ashdod. "Oh my."

***

Chapter Eleven

Fifth Column
`Eqron
Seven Months Later

"I will not risk my city or the P'lishti Empire for a war trophy!" shouted Helets'iqesh.

"But who can know for sure if this Aron is the real cause," offered Ma`akhah, "What if we return it and we still have this … plague upon us." After a pause, he added, "Maybe it's a plague from Dagon for not destroying the Aron of the `Ivri god."

Ma`akhah words rang hallow. It was clear, even to him, that he was clutching at straws. Over the last seven months, wherever the P'lisht'im have brought the Aron of the `Ivri god, a horrible plague broke out amongst the populace. Wherever the Aron rested, priapism and phimosis spread throughout the male population. Simple logic dictated that it was the cause.

In addition to the painful and persistent 'swellings' of their members, many men also suffered from fevers and cold sweats. Everyone suffered; some people even died. Where normal daily activities had previously been taken for granted, even normal bodily functions were painful. Soon, life came to a halt in the city that hosted the Aron of the `Ivri god. No one seemed to escape the condition. The entire populace of the P'lisht'im cried out against their rulers.

271

"In Ashdod, Ashqelon, `Aza, Gath and now `Eqron, the statues of Dagon have all been toppled," said Helets'iqesh coolly, "that doesn't seem to be a sign of Dagon's dominance."

"Don't insult the great Dagon," moaned Rasqadu, but he wasn't very convincing, even to himself. He was one of the first to suffer. Even though most of the populace eventually recovered when the Aron was moved to another city, Rasqadu along with other leaders of the society hadn't. He was in constant pain. It was compounded by frustration. Everyday, he got to see his 'war prize,' yet he was unable to experience her. Though he would have gladly given her up, if he could once again relieve himself without pain.

"It seems clear," offered Paremheb as he shifted uncomfortably. Like the other leaders in the council, he also suffered, "we have to return the relic."

"That would be a sign of defeat!" shouted Ma`akhah.

"Yes," returned Paremheb coolly, meeting Ma`akhah stare.

"How do we get rid of it," Helets'iqesh asked the forum, but all eyes turned to the priest, Rasqadu.

"If you send away the Aron of the god of the `Ivr'im," he started meekly, "it seems that it should be sent with a guilt offering, so that we can be healed."

"What type of guilt offering?"

Rasqadu thought for a moment, looking at some of the other priests and magicians that were there. "Well, five golden `ofal'im, one from each of the five Lords, to represent the 'swellings," he suggested.

"And five golden mice," offered a fellow priest, "to remove the rodent infestation that also seems to have started at the same time. It might also be from this god's hand." He remembered the story of the plagues that were delivered on Mitsray'im when the `Ivr'im fled from there.

One of the magicians now spoke up, concurring. "Yes, if you do this, and give honor to the god of the `Ivri, he will lighten his hand upon you. "And from your gods," he added, looking at the priests. They all lowered their eyes.

"We are being humiliated," spat Ma`akhah.

An older soothsayer spoke up, "Yes, but why should you harden your hearts, as the Par`oh of Mitsray'im once did. In the end, they succumbed and let this people of his go."

Ma`akhah couldn't sit still. "But what if you are all wrong, and it's not because of this Aron, what then?" he demanded.

"Do this," the soothsayer offered, "prepare a new cart and take two nursing cows that have never been yoked. Tie the cows to the cart, and leave their calves at home. Place the Aron of the god of the 'Ivrim on the cart; put the guilt offering in a box next to it and send the cart on its way. Watch it, and see. If it goes up by the way of the border, towards Beth Shemesh, then the 'Ivri god has wrought this great evil upon your land. If not, then it is merely coincidence, and something else is the cause of what has befallen us."

Helets'iqesh looked at Ma`akhah, "Does that satisfy you."

"No," he answered, "but it will have to do."

***

BethLeHem, Yehudah

"They say they keep catching a glimpse of a mountain lion," reported Eli'av, "So far, he's keeping his distance, but they're worried. What should we do?"

Yishai considered for a moment. That was some of the best pasture in the area, and lions tended to keep their distance, but it wasn't worth the risk. He was about to answer when Dawid appeared at the entrance to the room.

"*avi?*" Dawid asked for Yishai's attention.

"Don't you have any patience?" snapped Eli'av. "Can't you see we're in the middle of a conversation?"

274

"Relax, son," Yishai placed a reassuring hand on Eli'av's shoulder, before turning to Dawid. His tone remained civil, but it seemed to lose the warmth and tenderness, Yishai reserved with his firstborn. "What do you need, Dawid?" he asked.

"I," started Dawid, but then he looked at Eli'av, and the words stuck in his throat. He took a deep breath and began anew. "I'm at the age," he suggested, "when I should be looking for a bride."

Yishai grimaced but it was Eli'av that responded.

"What you?" asked Eli'av incredulously.

Dawid shot back. "You were married almost two years by my age," he shouted.

"Boys," Yishai quickly interceded. "Eli'av, Dawid has a point."

Eli'av began to protest, but Yishai quieted him with a gesture. "However, right now is not a good time," he said. "The Aron of the Holy One is in the hands of the enemy. We are pursued at every opportunity. The Nation of Yisrael is in mourning."

Dawid closed his eyes. He felt the loss of the Aron as much as anyone, if not more, but it had been seven months, and people still needed to get married. He needed to get married. "But," he began, before shaking his head, realizing nothing he could say would help. He prayed the Holy One would give him the patience he needed.

"Soon," offered Yishai. "In the meantime, I have need of you."

Dawid looked up, "Yes, *avi*."

Yishai offered a polite smile. "We are having a problem with some of the shepherds in the far pasture area. Could you take responsibility for that flock?"

Eli'av looked curiously at his father.

"Yes, *avi*," Dawid said dutifully. He was crestfallen. He had hoped his father wanted him for something other than shepherding. He had plenty of shepherds and workers. He didn't really need him.

"Thank you," said Yishai.

Dawid sighed as he left the room. Before he would join the flock, though, he wanted to sit with Mamma Ruth. Maybe she could help him understand why it was that the Holy One seemed to test him so much.

***

The Wilderness of Yehudah

Dawid was distracted. He didn't understand. All of his brother's were married. Why did his father seem resistant to the idea of him getting married? Maybe it was just his imagination. After all, he was still a year younger than when Shim'a got married.

It was difficult, thought Dawid. A part of it, he was sure, was the loneliness he felt within his family, but he also wanted to fulfill the precept of having children. He wanted to build a family in Yisrael. What could be a more worthwhile venture than that?

Suddenly, Dawid caught movement out of the corner of his eye. A blur of yellow flashed behind him, and Dawid spun, but whatever it was had disappeared before he could get a good look. Maybe it was just his imagination. His heart raced, as he stood, his eyes scanning the sparse landscape. Dawid's body was taut, every sense tingling.

Then he saw it. From behind an outcropping of gray boulders, a huge mountain lion leapt towards one of the lambs. The flock scattered, as the lion pounced on the lamb. Somehow, the lamb came out from under the lion's powerful frame. The lion coiled for another pounce, but before he could spring, Dawid's staff cracked over his head. The lion spun on his heels to face his attacker. It must have been desperate or hungry to attack when there was a man there. Dawid stood poised on his toes, his staff resting in loosely in his hands, fear filling his heart.

With a growl, the lion coiled and sprang toward his attacker. Dawid sprang forward at the same instant, moving to the side of the lion and swinging the staff with all of his might, smashing it into the lion's side. The lion fell with a yelp and a thud. He rolled several turns before turning again on Dawid. Dawid stood ready, waiting, his heart pumping.

The lion leapt quickly, straight for Dawid, his sharp fangs aimed at the young man's throat. Dawid was barely able to lift the staff fast enough. The lion clamped down on the staff, splintering it. His body crashed onto Dawid. The two fell to the ground, hard. Dawid rolled, trying to get on top of the beast, the foul smell of his breath in the young warrior's nostrils. They rolled several turns down the side of a ravine, before stopping hard against a boulder.

Disentangling himself from the lion, Dawid, breathing heavy, stumbled back, his eyes glued to the dangerous creature. The lion lay motionless. One end of a piece of broken staff protruded from the lion's chest, the other exiting out his neck.

Dawid closed his eyes, his breath labored. The panic he had held at bay now crept up his spine. He tried to calm himself. *"hodu l'qadosh barukh hu.* Thank you, Holy One," he whispered. His knees buckled and he sat down on the ground. "Thank you," he repeated. Sweat seeped from his pours, and his body shook. Unable to restrain it anymore, Dawid allowed the emotions to wash over him. Tears poured down his cheeks. He just needed a moment or two, he told himself. Then he would go and collect the flock.

***

The Aron of the god of the ʿIvri was loaded on a brand new cart, built especially for the occasion. The five Lords of the P'lisht'im, themselves, loaded the burdensome relic onto the cart, using long staves to insure that they wouldn't accidentally touch the dangerous talisman. Two heifers stood nearby, their calves gently nursing. Four people came and separated the calves from their mothers, amidst cries of protest from both calf and mother. The heifers, which had never been yoked before, resisted being tied to the cart. Once secured, they shifted restlessly. The box, with the golden mice and the golden images of their swellings was placed next to the Aron, and the cows were released.

For a moment they stood. Then, as if goaded by an unseen driver, the heifers began to walk. Despite the expectation that hung in the air, a gasp of astonishment escaped the crowd's lips when the cows took the straightest path possible to the road to Beth Shemesh. They plodded along the highway, lowing from time to time, but not pausing until they reached the environs of Beth Shemesh. The Lords and their retinue followed, each in his amazement.

The people of Beth Shemesh were in the fields, reaping wheat as the cows led the cart into the fields. All eyes turned at the strange sight. At some point, someone recognized that it was the Aron HaBrith of the Holy One of Yisrael. Whispers turned into shouts and tears of joy as the symbol of the Holy One's Presence returned to Yisrael.

"*az yashir moshe u'vnei yisrael eth hashir hazoth.* Then, Moshe and the Children of Yisrael will sing this song to the Holy One," someone spontaneously began singing. It was the victory song of the Holy One's destruction of Par'o's armies at the Reed Sea. Every schoolboy knew the verses.

Soon others joined, "I will sing to the Holy One for He has triumphed gloriously. The horse and the rider He has thrown into the sea. The Holy One is my strength and my song; He will be my salvation. He is my God and I will praise him; the God of my father and I will exalt him. The Holy One is a Man of War; the Holy One is His Name …"

The cows stopped in the field of Y'hosh'u`ah and stood by a large stone. A crowd gathered. At first everyone simple looked, reveling in the miracle that stood before them. Eventually, people started to ask their neighbor, "What do we do, now?"

Two brothers, from the clan of Q'hat of the tribe of Lewi stepped forward. "We should offer the cows as a thanksgiving offering before the Holy One," they suggested. A rumble of ascent passed through the crowd and two brothers moved towards the Aron. Each grabbed an end of the staves, and they effortlessly lifted it off of the cart and placed it on the large stone. They then put the box with the golden devices next to it.

Someone else came and began breaking up the cart. Others joined him and soon a fire pit was built, where the cows stood. Its embers soon burned a bright red.

Despite all the commotion, the heifers hadn't moved at all. Several people lowered the cows to the ground and held them as someone else slaughtered them. He sliced across the throat, severing the esophagus and trachea, killing the animal instantly, in accordance with the Holy One's ordinances. The animals were quickly skinned and eviscerated. They were then placed on the fire, as a burnt offering to the Holy One of Yisrael.

The Lords of the P'lishtim watched the proceedings from a hilltop. As people started bringing other offerings, and rejoicing before their god, the rulers of the P'lisht'im retired from viewing the spectacle. They had seen enough. Frustrated they returned to their homes, wondering how, after such a victory only little more than half a year earlier, they could feel so defeated.

Chapter Twelve

Return
Mitspah
One Month Later

Since the death of Eli, Sh'mu'el had become a man transformed. Shedding his deference, he stepped forward into the role of Yisrael's shepherd with bold determination. Immediately, the prophet of Yisrael began making a circuit, visiting village after village. He mediated even the most mundane disputes, taught the words of the Holy One, and fostered a revolution of spirit within the nation.

Gently but firmly, he chastised the children of Yisrael to return to the path of righteousness. Wherever he went, his words rang in the ears of Yisrael. "If you return to the Holy One with all of your hearts, wholly; if you remove the false gods and the `Ashtaroth, the idols of Asherah, from amongst you, and prepare your hearts for the Holy One's presence, so that you serve only Him, then He will save you from the hand of the P'lisht'im."

The loss of the Aron HaBrith was a mighty blow to the soul of Yisrael. People had become complacent, as if no matter their actions, the Holy One would do their bidding. The defeat at Even Ha`Ezer woke them up. Diligently, they removed the idols from their homes, and their hearts.

If the Holy One had distanced Himself from Yisrael, then Sh'mu'el would close the gap. He would goad his flock towards His clear refreshing waters. Like sheep under the hot sun, Yisrael drank greedily, even if to some, the water still had a bitter tinge. To those who struggled with their desires and habits, Sh'mu'el gave them support. The good and straight path, he would counsel, is not always the quickest or the easiest, but it is the only way to truly reach one's destination.

When the Aron HaBrith returned to Yisrael, the happiness was pervasive, as if a heavy yoke had been lifted from the nation. Despite the fact that the hand of the P'lishti Empire was still heavy, people felt that they could now manage the load. They had hope.

Even when tragedy struck Beth Shemesh, the people accepted it. Shortly after the Aron's return, seventy men, leaders of the community tragically died. Each, as the expression went, was worth the weight of fifty thousand men, but the community solemnly accepted it without complaint. Instead, they turned inward, seeking the cause for such a blow. They realized that they had not behaved properly with the Aron HaBrith, not given it the proper respect. Coming as it did, on the back of a cart, caused them to forget the deference it required. Instead of chaffing under the punishment, they recognized their mistake, and accepted responsibility. They should have known better. The people of Beth Shemesh took steps to correct their errors.

They sent to the city of Qir'yath Y''arim, which was a city of kohan'im. A large delegation from the city came to Beth Shemesh, and transferred the Aron HaBrith to the home of Avinadav of Giv''ah. The kohan'im designated and

283

sanctified Avinadav's son, El'azar, charging him with the proper care of the Aron. It was decided to leave the Aron under his care, until the Holy One would make known His Will. Despite that the Mishqan had been erected in Nov, the Aron stayed, for the time being, in Qir'yath Y''arim

After all these events, Sh'mu'el recognized that the nation was ready for an assembly. They were ready to beseech the Holy One of Yisrael as a nation, and ask for atonement. Now that his throne had returned to Yisrael, it was time to ask the King to return His Presence. The prophet of Yisrael sent messengers throughout the land, *"qivtsu eth kol yisrael hamitspathah, w'eth'palel ba`ad'khem.* Gather yourself, all of Yisrael, to Mitspah, and I will pray before you to the Holy One. We will, as one people, ask that He turn His face towards His nation, Yisrael."

When Yishai heard this, he breathed a heavy sigh of relief. The ways of the Holy One are just and true, he confirmed to himself. Just like Eli had said, He had sent the cure before the disease. The Holy One would never abandon His people. Like the rest of the nation, Yishai was renewed with hope.

Yishai gathered his three eldest sons, Eli'av, Avinadav, and Shim`a and headed north to the gathering at Mitspah. He left N'than'el, Raday, and Otsem, their three brothers in charge of the homestead. Dawid, as usual, was left to his own devices.

As they were leaving the homestead, Eli'av and Dawid passed each other. They were not in the habit of speaking to each other, though Dawid would have faced any challenge for a kind word from his older brother. Dawid was looking down, when suddenly, he felt his Eli'av's body slam into his. Dawid was thrown back a bit, off-balance.

"Watch it!" screamed Eli'av.

Dawid looked up at his older brother. His face was a blank. What does he want from me now, he thought. He wasn't sure, but he had the feeling that Eli'av had bumped into him on purpose.

Eli'av's face was full of anger. "Apologize," he demanded.

Dawid automatically opened his mouth. He habitually began to apologize, but then stopped. Not this time. He closed his mouth and simply stared at Eli'av. His face neither betrayed anger nor fear, but rather simple determination. Something in Dawid's expression shook the oldest son of Yishai, and he flinched. Dawid caught the hesitation, and noted it. Suddenly he saw his older brother very differently.

After several moments, Dawid said calmly, "You're holding up, Father;" a simple statement of fact.

Feigning indignation, Eli'av took the opportunity and quickly exited from the confrontation. His emotions churned as he caught up to Yishai, but he refused to examine them too closely.

Mitspah was beyond Yishai's expectations. The hill, near where Yisrael had suffered defeat less than a year ago, was swarming with people. Tens of thousand of men from Yisrael heeded Sh'mu'el's call. There, and throughout the borders of the Land of Yisrael, the people of Yisrael were fasting. The nation stood penitent.

An altar of unhewn stones had already been built in the center of the encampment. Kohan'im had drawn water and were pouring it as a libation on the altar.

"How can we have an altar outside the Mishqan?" Eli'av asked his father.

Yishai smiled proudly. That was the question of a scholar he thought. "When Shiloh was destroyed," Yishai explained, his smile fading at the memory of the Mishqan's destruction, "private altars became permissible again."

"Now the Mishqan is at Nov, but it isn't considered a permanent sanctuary like Shiloh was," he continued. "We have a tradition that there will be a new permanent home for the Mishqan, someday, but in the meantime ..." He gestured towards the altar. "Besides, a prophet can erect a temporary altar if he sees a need. Sh'mu'el has brought the people along. I have confidence in him."

"Why is the Mishqan in Nov and the Aron in Qir'yath Y''arim?" asked Avinadav.

Yishai shook his head. "Such is the state of the nation today," he said, almost to himself. He turned to his son, "When Shiloh fell, we set up the Mishqan in Nov, while the Aron was," he paused. Even though the Aron was returned, its capture was a deep wound for the sage. As a leader of the nation, he bore responsibility for its failures. "In captivity," the words came with difficulty. "When the Aron was returned, the Holy One caused it to be brought there, to Qir'yath Y''arim. That's the situation today. When our people become whole again, I'm sure the Mishqan will host the Aron, wherever that is." Yishai smiled, "Maybe this prophet will succeed in healing the nation, making it, and everyone of us, whole again."

Sh'mu'el stood on a makeshift platform near the altar. Yishai noted that not only had the prophet's demeanor changed, his appearance was different as well. Even at the young age of forty, his long flowing mane of hair was now white as snow, and it was no longer tied neatly behind his neck, but left loose, almost wild. His light eyes seemed to burn with an intense fire. His face was ageless. He still dressed in a simple white linen tunic, belted at the waist, but now he also wore the fringed shawl, the emblem of an elder. His visage was intense and powerful, a living column of white fire. Despite the overflowing crowd, his words not only reached everyone's ears, they penetrated their hearts.

"May the Holy One of Yisrael cleanse us of our sins, just as we pour a water libation on the altar," he began. "We need to pour out our hearts in prayer, like water, to the Holy One."

"We simply need to make an effort to turn toward Him, even the will to return to Him is enough, and He will bring us within His loving embrace. Return us, Holy One, towards You, and we will return, renew our days as in times past."

"Yisrael, you have strayed from the Holy One, relying on ceremony in place of service. The Holy One cannot be bribed. Even in the innermost chambers of our hearts, all is revealed before Him. Return Yisrael to the Holy One with a full heart. It is impossible to serve both the Holy One of Yisrael and the foreign gods of lust and desire, of power and self. The greatest deception is the one we desire. One can serve himself, or he can serve the Holy One of Yisrael; one can dwell in the small petty world of his own needs, or fulfill the purpose of his existence and accomplish his role in the establishment of His Kingdom."

Then the prophet turned his face towards heaven and spread his arms in supplication. *"ribono shel ha`olam.* Master of the World, You demand only that a person say before You, 'I sinned,' and Yisrael says before You, '<u>H</u>atanu. We have sinned.' How can you not forgive us?"

Sh'mu'el continued for nearly an hour, with words of both affirmation and reproachments. After his words of teaching, he sat for the rest of the afternoon before the nation, listening to requests, adjudicating disputes, and listening to the problems and complaints of the people. For three days, the nation of Yisrael stood before Sh'mu'el at Mitspah.

***

Soon the word spread to the P'lisht'im that the 'Ivr'im were gathered in force at Mitspah. Though most of the information Paremheb received suggested that the 'Ivrim were not preparing for war, he chose not to convey that to the council.

"It's time to teach them a lesson that they'll never forget," declared Paremheb before the Lords of the P'lisht'im.

"Let us gather in force and stop these rebellious 'Ivr'im, lest they think that our returning the Aron of the 'Ivri god was a sign of weakness, and they use it to throw off our rule," agreed Ma`akhah.

By the end of the day, the P'lisht'im had gathered an impressive force facing the camp of Yisrael at Mitspah. Their army did not go unnoticed by the nation of Yisrael.

"I didn't know we were assembling for battle," Avinadav breathed, as he looked at the massive formation across the valley. He still hadn't recovered fully from the last battle.

"We weren't," stated Eli'av distantly "but they didn't know that." "This is a mistake," there was an edge to his voice, "our prophet must not have thought about how they would react."

Shim`a looked askance at his older brother. It was hard to tell if his tone was mocking. "But," he began, but stopped mid-sentence. His brother couldn't have been doubting, let alone mocking, a prophet of the Holy One. "What do you think is going to happen?" he finally asked.

Eli'av shrugged. "Another slaughter," he suggested.

Avinadav began to laugh but then he realized his brother wasn't joking. "You're not serious are you?" he asked.

Again, Eli'av shrugged, but he didn't say anything. Both Shim`a and Avinadav looked at each other, wondering what had happened to their brother. Didn't he have confidence in the Holy One's Providence?

Others in the camp also shared their concerns. Everyone seemed to be looking across the valley nervously. Many people openly voiced their fears. The P'lisht'im were a powerful foe, and no one seemed sure of the Holy One's plans.

Yet, instead of allowing their fear to overwhelm them, the nation turned to their leader and encouraged him to beseech the Holy One. They gathered around the prophet of Yisrael.

"Don't stop crying out to the Holy One," someone shouted.

"Pray for us," another cried.

Several people pressed Sh'mu'el, "Will the Holy One save us from the P'lisht'im this time?"

Sh'mu'el was calm. His demeanor was soon infective. Without a word, but offering smiles to the many people he made eye contact with, he climbed down from the platform. He strode confidently across the clearing to a makeshift pen where sheep were being kept. He gently separated one of the suckling lambs from his mother, taking him in his arms. It frolicked playfully, suckling on the prophet's finger for a moment. Sh'mu'el brought the small animal near the altar. Removing a leather strap from his belt, Sh'mu'el quickly bound the lamb's legs together. The lamb squealed in protest. Sh'mu'el gestured to someone nearby to hold down the lamb.

Standing, Sh'mu'el removed a small object, about a span in length, wrapped in a swatch of red wool. Methodically he unwrapped it to reveal a bronze, single-edged knife. With utmost concentration, he ran its edge up and down the fingernail and flesh of his index finger, first on the right face of the edge, then the left face, before checking the point of the edge itself. Satisfied he looked up to see the Father of the Court standing only a few amoth from him. With a smile, Sh'mu'el approached Yishai, "*avi*," he invited, holding the knife before him.

Yishai nodded in response, and took the proffered knife. Scrutinizing the blade in the sun for a moment, he then ran its edge back and forth over his fingernail and flesh as the prophet had done, performing the twelve mandated tests to insure the blade's sharpness and smoothness. While the Holy One demanded offerings, He also circumscribed the causing of suffering for even the lowliest of His creatures. An animal never felt pain from the cut of smooth, sharp knife, his nerves severed before their signals reached the brain. Satisfied with the knife, Yishai handed it back to the prophet, "Your honor."

Shmu'el took the knife and knelt by the lamb, being careful to conceal the blade behind his back. He closed his eyes and focused his thoughts. His thoughts concentrated on the commandment of ritual slaughter, the manifestation of the Heavenly Will, elevating the mundane act to its supernal root.

With his left hand Sh'mu'el stretched the neck of the lamb, pushing his palm against his chin and grabbing its throat with his fingers. When he was satisfied that the esophagus and trachea were firmly in his grip, he slid the knife back and forth across the throat, careful not to press, but allowing the sharpness of the blade to slice through the flesh. The skin and flesh folded away from the blade as it sank into the lamb's throat. A kohen quickly knelt beside Sh'mu'el to collect the blood in a small silver vessel.

As the lamb's soul departed it twitched and jolted, the automatic reflexes of an animal whose soul was already gone. Sh'mu'el handed the knife to Yishai, who checked it again, nodding his satisfaction. While Yishai checked the knife, Sh'mu'el, with the help of two others, quickly skinned the lamb, opened its belly, and removed the innards and entrails, carefully checking the organs for defects. Someone else had already lit the pyre under the altar, and it burned brightly.

Sh'mu'el lifted the lamb onto the altar. The kohen then handed Sh'mu'el the vessel of blood and the prophet dipped his fingers and splayed the blood against the base of the altar seven times. He took the remaining blood and poured it into the fire. The flames leapt and danced around the altar. Within moments the lamb became a whole offering to the Holy One of Yisrael.

Turning his face heavenward, Sh'mu'el cried to the Holy One of Yisrael, beseeching Him to deliver His people from the hands of the P'lisht'im. As he prayed, the nation prepared for battle. Y'ro*H*om organized the various captains. They listened intently as he quickly discussed positioning and placement. The P'lisht'im had already descended to the valley and were moving quickly toward the Yisrael encampment. Time was of the essence.

Even before Y'ro*H*om finished his briefing, Ya*H*atsi-el hastily led a contingent of slingers from his tribe towards the battle lines. Soon, the other tribal leaders began moving into position, waiting for the signal to advance. The mood was somber, but confident. Nearly everyone seemed secure in their relationship with the Holy One, and recognized that He would do what was best. No matter what it was, they would accept His Will.

***

Paremheb was quite pleased with himself. His reputation had grown with each battle. Even after the entire debacle with the Aron, his reputation continued to be held in high esteem. No one had held him responsible for that mess. Now, all five Lords of the P'lisht'im had assembled together, and they were giving Paremheb complete reign. He smiled. This battle would be over quickly. His intelligence now assured him that the 'Ivrim were not prepared at all. They had gathered merely for a ritual celebration. The lords would be witness to their slaughter. His fortunes were assured.

In fact, Paremheb was doubly pleased, for he didn't have to deal with Goliyath, who was still recovering in Gath. It was unfortunate that he was still alive. Though he had his uses, thought the commander, he had become more of a nuisance than an asset. No matter. This battle should put an end to the rebelliousness of the 'Ivrim, at least. He would insure it. Goliyath's rebelliousness, he would save for another time.

Taking the field, Paremheb thought he heard thunder in the distance. Yet, that was impossible. It was the middle of summer. Yet, there it was again, and looking around, he saw that others seemed to hear something as well. What could that be?

As the nation of Yisrael began taking the field, the prophet, still dressed in white, but now carrying a large bonze sword strode to the front ranks. "For the Holy One," he shouted. Lifting the sword above his head, Sh'mu'el hollered a war cry and began running towards the field of battle. All of Yisrael followed him.

Then Paremheb saw it. The entire army saw it. It was fearful. A vision of white clad soldiers seemed to fill the valley. They did not seem real, or more precisely they did not seem natural. But that only intensified the fear. The thunder increased, yet no one could discern its direction. It was as if it originated from within their very being. The P'lisht'im trembled in fear. Each of them shuddered, as if the hosts of Heaven had descended to do battle on behalf of the nation of Yisrael.

It wasn't clear who broke ranks first, but like a skein of woven cloth, the whole P'lishti army soon began to unravel. Seemingly before they even engaged the enemy, the nation of Yisrael watched as the P'lisht'im were confounded. Weapons held high, throats filled with battle cries, the warriors of Yisrael struck hard, decimating the ranks of their enemy. They seemed to melt before them. No matter where they turned, the P'lisht'im were felled with vengeance.

Shofars sounded and trumpets blared as the warriors of Yisrael pursued the army of the P'lisht'im, now in full retreat. Yisrael chased the uncircumcised to the meadowlands of Beth Sharon, slaughtering thousands of their enemy on the way.

Returning to the camp of Yisrael, Sh'mu'el was the image of a butcher. Splatters of red freckled his white garments, hair and beard. The bronze sword, now dark red with blood hung loosely from his hand. The people swarmed around him as he strode purposefully towards a large stone. It soon became clear, as reports came in, that

Yisrael hadn't suffer any losses at all. A feeling of renewal rippled through the nation. That was what had happened in days of yore, under the leadership of Yehoshu'ah. Prayers of thanks were on everyone's lips.

Spotting a large boulder, Sh'mu'el took the stone and used it to make a marking. In a place roughly between Mitspah and Shen, he piled rock upon rock. "This place, shall be known as Even Ha`Ezer, The Stone of Help," he declared, "For from here the Holy One has come to our aid."

The battle was decisive. One by one, many of the towns that had come under the control of the P'lisht'im stopped paying tribute. The area between Eqron and Gath was restored to Yisrael sovereignty. For now, the P'lisht'im seemed contained; their expansion stunted.

***

Goliyath lay on a slab of stone, his breath heavy. The room was brightly lit, but cold permeated the air. He drifted between consciousness and unconsciousness, his mammoth body, a mass of pain. Hatred burned in his heart. He was convinced that it was this focus that kept him alive; his hatred, so pure, for the `Ivr'im and their god, and all that they stood for. He would heal. Goliyath was sure of that, and then he would set things right. He was the better man. He was *the* P'lishti, and no one, not even a god, would stand against him.

Part Three

Chapter One

Assignments
The Council of Lords
Gath, P'lishti Empire
Twelve years later

Goliyath rose from his resting place. His blackened skin crackled as he moved. The giant P'lishti was used to the sound and feel already. He barely paid it any mind, but it caused the others in the room to look askance. It caused shivers to run up my spine every time I heard it. Goliyath cracked his neck from side to side and stretched his muscles, causing even louder popping sounds. He felt like he had been asleep for ages. Something stirred in him now, and he knew. It was time. The hour for which he was created was at hand.

It had taken longer than he expected, but he had returned to, even excelled, his former condition. There wasn't a man, or several together for that matter, who could match him. I should know. I worked with him day and night, regretting every moment of it.

"Uriyah," he called to me, his armor bearer. Over this last period he seemed to have forgotten my nationality, and called me by given name. I quickly presented myself at his summons. It was clear that Goliyath, despite himself, liked the man who had served him for over a decade. He knew I was an 'Ivri, but I was at least quiet. I did my job without complaint, and did it well. Goliyath had no time for talkative assistants. He didn't particularly care about the man he worked with and his dealing outside his service.   Thankfully, I rarely ever indulged in idle chatter.

For my part, I hated Goliyath. Thus I rarely wanted to engage in conversation with him.   He paid well, and I was thankful for that, but I spent a lifetime waiting for the day when the giant would fall. I know it will happen, I had had a dream about it several times. In fact, I told myself, though it was only part true, that the only reason I continued to serve the P'lishti warrior was because I wanted to see the fulfillment of that vision with my own eyes. I didn't spend much and thus had already accumulated enough of a fortune to be comfortable well into my later days.

Dutifully, I brought Goliyath his uniform. The brass all gleamed brightly. I was good at my job.   Lifting up the body armor of brass scales, Goliyath took it and held it up to his torso. It was heavy, weighing in excess of five thousand sheqels of brass.   I buckled it from behind my master. I was forced to stand on a stool to reach the buckles, for even though I'm considered tall, Goliyath's six amoth and a span height was beyond my reach. Then I buckled the brass greaves on Goliyath's legs and arms, before handing him the large brass helmet.

"The vacation ends today, Uriyah," smiled Goliyath. "Bring me my spear and sword."

I left the room, before returning with the implements of war. The sword Goliyath placed in a sheath across his back, but the spear, whose staff was as thick as a weaver's beam, he held in his hand. Its head of iron weighed six hundred sheqels. Afterwards, I brought the shield that I would have the "honor" of carrying myself.

"We're going to impose ourselves on the council meeting today," said Goliyath.

"What?" I asked, both startled that Goliyath was taking me into his confidence and confused by the statement.

"The Lords are meeting in Gath this afternoon. King Akhish son of Ma`akhah, is hosting them. He wants to move aggressively against the `Ivrim. I'm going to impose my opinion," Goliyath smiled. He had the smile of a snake. "Can you guess what it is?"

I simply smiled like a crocodile. Within my mind, I blessed my master, "May it be your undoing."

***

The room was impressive. Akhish had spared no expense. Five grand thrones of dark stone were arranged in a wide semi-circle on a stone platform three amoth high at the north end of the large hall. Red tapestries hung behind each of the chairs, bearing the symbol of each city in black. Other tapestries of various designs hung along the western and southern walls. The eastern wall housed a large niche, which began three amoth from the floor, extending to the arched ceiling, eight amoth high. Filling the recess was a statue of

Dagon and Asherah. On either side, smaller idols of varying sizes and shapes filled the hallow.

The five lords of the P'lishti Empire sat inattentively in their chairs. An old man, dressed smartly in a purple robe, stood before the platform and droned incessantly, listing the smallest details of tribute and trade, both between the cities of the P'lisht'im and with her neighbors.

Suddenly, the wide double doors at the south end of the hall burst open. Several of the lords jumped from their seats, as if under attack. Akhish rose slowly from his seat in the center, "Who dares …"

His words trailed off as the frame of the doorway filled with the large figure of Goliyath.

"Goliyath," stated Akhish, his tone a mixture of resignation and accusation. "Can't you wait to be announced?"

The large warrior offered a smile. *"qerebu goliyath, qarabu migru dp'lisht'im ilu sharitu dsar'im.* Presenting Goliyath, warrior of the P'lisht'im, at the service of the Lords."

Behind Goliyath, the entrance hallway filled with the Lords' personal guard, responding to the intrusion. I turned to face them, but gave a shrug when the captain looked at me questioningly. The captain of the guard then looked towards Akhish, "Sir?" he inquired. His eyes darted from his king to Goliyath and back. No matter how many men he had, he wasn't looking forward to a confrontation with the giant.

"*shi lu kiam.* It's all right," dismissed Akhish. "*Goliyath, eheru,* please enter." Akhish returned to his seat, before addressing the older man. "Paqidh, you can finish the accounting later."

The older man bowed slightly, before exiting the hall. He skirted past Goliyath nervously as the giant strode towards the front of the hall with his armor bearer in tow. Even with the height of the platform, Goliyath nearly met the eyes of the lords.

"What do you want?" asked Akhish curtly.

"Redemption," Goliyath stated flatly, before continuing, "victory for the P'lisht'im, of course, and defeat of the `Ivr'im." Goliyath drew himself up to the full extent of his height. Among other things Goliyath wanted to teach that upstart `Ivri who stole the tablets from his hands, and total victory from his clutches. He understood that during his long recovery, the `Ivr'im had made that upstart their king. The king of the slaves. It would make his victory all the more complete when he delivered the crowned head of their insolent chief slave on a platter to the Five Lords. "Give me control of the army, and I'll conquer all the lands between here and the Yarden. Your power and wealth will increase tenfold."

Akhish sat back in his chair. No one would contest Goliyath's sincerity or his loyalty to the nation, but he was never known as a strategist. He

302

looked at the other lords. They seemed equally ambiguous.

"If you fail?" asked Helets'iqesh, the Lord of Eqron.

"I won't," returned Goliyath coolly. "And, he added as an after thought, "even if I did, I wouldn't be around to give excuses. I would give my life for this. It is my life."

"If you succeed?" asked another Lord.

"I ask for nothing but the glory of the Empire," answered Goliyath diplomatically. "The spoils of war will more than satisfy my hunger," he added.

"Well said," offered Akhish, "let's see if you can deliver. If the other Lords agree, I see no reason why not to give you a chance."

Helets'iqesh asked, "How long do you need to prepare the army?"

"One month," answered the new commander.

"*shi lu kiam*. Let it be so," offered Akhish.

"*shi lu kiam*," responded the other lords.

"May the gods be with you," Akhish said to Goliyath.

Goliyath was already leaving, but upon hearing his king's blessing, he looked over his shoulder. He smiled before responding, "as long as they don't get in my way."

Everyone in the entranceway moved aside as the giant lumbered out of the hall.

***

Giv`a of Binyamin

Sha'ul the son of Qish of the Matri clan of the tribe of Binyamin sat on a low stool. He was slumped forward, his elbow propped on the table in front of him, supporting his forehead. His other arm hung loosely in his lap. His eyes were closed, but his shallow breathing indicated that he was awake. Occasionally, he shook his head slowly. He was not the image of a king, but rather of a man with a troubled spirit.

Sha'ul was beside himself. He simply wanted to capture what he had lost. His mind drifted to a simpler time, when he was confidant of the Holy One's presence. The king remembered when he was a simple farmer and part-time warrior fighting for the Almighty's honor. He could almost remember the feeling of indignation when he saw that giant P'lishti soldier desecrate the Aron. Almost, but in the end, he only remembered having the feeling. He couldn't tap into that place anymore. That place where his own self was nullified before the Holy One seemed as distant as the Heavens themselves. He felt like a man who lost his arm, and was only left with the memory of

304

how he had once used it. He would do anything to get that feeling back.

"What are we going to do?" whispered Av'ner, Sha'ul's uncle. "We can't have our king in such a state. The people will lose hope."

"Things don't look good. I fear someone might already be preparing to challenge his rule," answered Do'eg the Edomi. He already had some suspicions. He heard that Sh'mu'el visited Bethle*H*em not long after the *incident*. Do'eg was a convert from Amaleq whose intelligence and loyalty had helped him rise to become one of Sha'ul's most trusted advisors. He didn't want anything to threaten his position.

Someone suggested, "Music might lighten his mood."

Av'ner thought for a moment. "That's a good idea," he confirmed. He immediately strode to the side of the king. The other advisors followed.

"Our lord," he began. "Sha'ul," he continued, placing a hand on his nephew's shoulder. Sha'ul looked up into his uncle's face. His eyes were red-rimmed, his face taught. Did his uncle understand his loss? He wished his father was still alive.

"Let our lord instruct his servants to seek a man who knows how to play the *kinor*, so that when this evil spirit fills you, he can play music and it will help you," suggested Av'ner.

Sha'ul stared at his uncle. The other advisors and servants crowded around. His eyes were distant, but he forced a small smile. "Provide me with such a man that can play well." Maybe there was a way, he thought. He sighed, before repeating, "*na wahavi_othem elay.* Please, bring him to me."

Do'eg spoke up, "*hineh,* Sir, I have seen one of the sons of Yishai from BethleHem, the sage. He knows how to play quite well. He is also brave, and experienced in battle, prudent in speech, attractive and," Do'eg paused, before adding with emphasis, "*wa'haqadosh barukh hu `imo.* The Holy One is with him."

Av'ner looked askance at Do'eg. They needed a man to play the kinor, not a replacement for the king. What is going on here? He Do'eg knew to be a learned man but his description was exaggerated. What was Do'eg suggesting? Sometimes, Av'ner felt that the convert from `Amaleq had his own agenda. He couldn't put his finger on it, but he felt that Do'eg was planting seeds that he intended to sow later.

However, Sha'ul either missed the hints, or didn't care. He latched onto the idea. With the help of the Holy One, this man might help him overcome his depression. It was known that schools of prophets used music to help them attain a meditative state. "What is his name?"

"Dawid," answered Do'eg. "I met him, while working for the sage Yishai son of `Oved, of

306

Bethle*H*em. He spends most of his time with the flock."

"Send for this young man, immediately," commanded Sha'ul. *"wayishlaH mal_akhim el yishay.* Send a messenger to the elder Yishai, asking him to please send me his son Dawid, who is with the sheep."

***

Efes Dam'im
Between Sokhoh and `Azaqah

Despite Goliyath's reputation as a loner, he had learned quite a lot about organizing an army during his extended years of service. The force he put together in his allotted month was impressive. They were well trained and ready for action. Even his critics grudgingly offered their compliments.

Goliyath was not a fan of complicated battle plans and involved strategies. His tactics were simple: attack the enemy with overwhelming force. Anything else was the refuge of the disadvantaged and weak. In the end, the stronger army always won.

During the preparation, Goliyath ate, slept and lived with the army. The men grew attached to him, learning to respect their gigantic commander. He worked as hard, if not harder, than he drove them. His directness and seriousness motivated

307

them towards excellence. They repaid Goliyath's leadership with loyalty.

When Goliyath determined that the troops were ready, he gave them a week's furlough. He took the opportunity to visit his mother at the temple. It had been a while since he had paid her his respects, and, just like when he was a little boy, he still had a need to share with her his accomplishment. Goliyath was sure she would be proud of him.

A month later, with little fanfare, Goliyath marched his army to Sokhoh, which was in Yehudah. He quickly raided the town. He was confidant that word would soon spread. Goliyath took his army and encamped in Efes Dam'im, and waited. That 'Ivri king, Sha'ul would come to him, and then they would settle an old score. Goliyath still replayed that scene in his memory and dreams when Sha'ul stole the tablets from his hand. Thief. He wanted to see how brave this "king," was now.

Chapter Two

The Anointed
The Wilderness of Yehudah

The young man, his body taut from a vigorous life, his skin tanned from many days under the hot desert sun, leapt onto the outcropping of brown stones. His bright brown eyes tracked the mixed flock of sheep and goats. His mind flashed to the story of his people's history, of their beginning, their liberation from slavery by the Almighty.

Deep in his reverie, he raised his shepherd's staff over his head, a black leather strap snaking up his arm to secure the *Oth*, the sign of the Almighty's Covenant with His People. The *totofoth* embossed with the letter *Shin* on either side, sat atop his brow, peeking out from under his *mitsnefeth*. The black straps fell from the nape of his neck forward, trailing down the front of his off-white wool tunic. His tunic, a simple four-cornered cloth with an opening for his head was adorned with intricately knotted fringe, *tsitsith*, at each of its corners. His entire being was surrounded by the instructions mandated by the Holy One of Yisrael. And today, he felt it. He felt embraced by the light of the Holy One.

In his mind's eye Dawid was "our teacher Moshe," the great leader and teacher of the people Yisrael. The flock below was the nation of Yisrael, and Dawid was leading them across the parted sea. It was kind of a game he played when alone with the flock, even though he was a little too old for such games. At least no one could see him. Dawid aspired to be as devoted to the Holy One as the nation's teacher, Moshe. What was the harm in a little fantasy?

Dawid's voice rang out in song, his lips repeating the words of the Torah. *"az yashir moshe uvney yisrael eth ha'shir hazoth la'dny.* Then Moshe and all the children of Yisrael will sing this song to the Holy One..." A natural smile spread across the young man's face. Full of joy and life, he threw his head back, his dark curly side-locks bouncing off his reddish beard. He allowed the laughter to escape and fill his soul.

The last few months had transformed him. In place of the mop of hair, he kept all but his side-locks and beard shaven. His soul too, was more balanced, focused. Many of the anxieties and concerns that had once filled his days were but a memory.

"Holy One," he called out to the Almighty, "I'm not Moshe, our teacher." He laughed at the suggestion, but continued, "I know You don't err, but ..." His voice trailed off. Ever since the prophet Sh'mu'el had visited their home, Dawid had been filled with both overwhelming joy and overbearing awe. Ah, how his fortunes had suddenly changed.

He sang, *"ev_en ma-asu habon'im haythah l'rosh pinah.* The stone that the builder's had rejected has become the keystone . . ." This was a verse that he had composed.

Tears came to his eyes, and his voice changed from verse to prose, "I will do my best, Holy One ... with Your help." His voice was a whisper.

Breaking from his reverie, Dawid took a loose corner of the cloth wrap from around his head, and wiped the moisture from his eyes. He noticed one of the small lambs was distant from the rest of the flock. He was crying for his mother, but not getting a response. He continued to wander further from the flock, his cries increasing.

With one hand Dawid unfurled the leather strap wrapped around his staff, while his eyes scanned the ground for a suitable stone. Bending his knees he scooped down picking up a small rounded stone. In what seemed like one fluid movement, practiced a thousand times, he placed the stone in the belly of the leather strap. Running his hand down the length of the straps to keep them from tangling, he raised the sling and began circling it over his head, his eyes never leaving the lamb. After a few revolutions he directed his sling towards the young lamb, though with only a fraction of his strength, sending the stone sailing in an arc to interrupt the lamb's path of flight.

Startled, the lamb leaped nearly vertical, and then, with change in pitch and fervor to his cries, bolted in the opposite direction. His new course brought him to rejoin his flock. He quickly located his mother, taking suckle from her teats as if he hadn't eaten in a week.

A smile of pleasure brightened Dawid's face. "Thank you, Holy One," he declared to the heavens, and a new tear moistened his deep eyes. For Dawid, the Hand that had smashed the Mitsri army at the Red Sea was the same one that had guided his small stone, saving him from having to chase after an errant lamb.

"Thank you Holy One," he repeated, "and," he continued, "Please, watch over my brothers who are now fighting for Your Great Name, with your anointed, King Sha'ul." Dawid missed his brothers, even though they rarely treated him well. Things were a bit better now, with everyone except Eli'av. With him, things might even be worse.

Taking the leather sling he began wrapping it around his staff. He remembered when Ittay had taught him how to use the sling. Now he could sling a rock as well as anyone from the tribe of Binyamin. He missed Ittay. The young man had come to his father's house as an indentured servant, but his father had treated him like one of his own sons, even better. He had become a companion to the lonely Dawid. Even after his seven years of service were over, Ittay found time to come and visit, and they always sought each other out at the festivals.

Thinking about Ittay, brought his thoughts back to the King. Ittay's tribesman, Sha'ul, the son of Kish was king now. Along with Sh'mu'el, Sha'ul had led the people to victory after victory, against Ammon and Amaleq. The P'lisht'im, after nearly ten years of quiet, had begun to flex their muscles again. Sha'ul had assembled an army and was facing them in Valley of Elah. Dawid's brothers were there with him now.

He was a bit jealous. His brothers had the honor of fighting the Holy One's enemies. Yet, unlike times past, he had not simply been shoved off to mind the flock. It was his turn now. He had just returned from several months at the King's side. Dawid shook his head. Even to him, the events of the past year seemed surreal. His life had been turned upside down.

Shortly after Sh'mu'el's visit, a messenger from the king came to Yishai's home, requesting his youngest son's presence. Someone had recommended him as singer and musician. The King's soul had become restless, and it was thought that music would dispel his melancholy. Dawid already had a reputation as an accomplished musician, especially with the *kinor*.

It had been fantastic at the king's court. Dawid, the perpetual outcast, became friend to the king, the anointed of the Holy One. It was magical, if not a bit overwhelming.

Not all of Dawid's challenges had been transformed by Sh'mu'el's visit though. He was still unmarried. His thoughts turned to that chance meeting with Mikhal, one of the king's daughters. He had nearly knocked her over when he was running to deliver a message to King Sha'ul. Accidentally, their eyes met. Dawid muttered a quick apology and continued on his errand, but his thoughts continually returned to those beautiful eyes. They were large and deep, reminding him of a calf's eyes. They were the most beautiful things he had ever seen.

He pushed the thought away. The king's daughter: that was beyond even his active imagination. Dawid needed to focus. It wasn't proper to think about a woman whom he could never marry. It would simply confuse him. Silently, the young man offered a prayer to the Holy One that He should find him a suitable wife.

A king, the Holy One's chosen one; it was a new experience for the nation of Yisrael. Not one that everyone accepted or appreciated. Dawid's father had originally been opposed, especially since the proposed king had been chosen from Binyamin. The tradition was clear, Yishai would tell whomever would listen, that the scepter should be in the hands of the Perets clan of Yehudah. That was the blessing, and inheritance, that Ya`aqov had given his son Yehudah, and there was a tradition that the merit and responsibility would remain with Yehudah's son, Perets. Unfortunately, to some people the argument rang hollow, considering Yishai was from Perets.

Yet, that wasn't Yishai's only objection. Rather, he questioned whether a hereditary king was the best thing for Yisrael. Even though it seemed that it was mandated in the Torah, Yisrael had yet to anoint a king. The concept was daunting.

Dawid remembered when the elder Y'roHom came to their home to see his father a few years ago. Dawid, his curiosity overwhelming, had crept close to a window of the door where they were talking. The news was already in the air, and Dawid was excited just at the thought of it all. He had been able to steal snippets of their conversation. Y'ro*H*om had been a long time proponent of a king.

"The P'lisht'im are gearing up for war again, and Na*H*ash of Ammon is making trouble in the east" he argued, "We need a strong military leader."

"Sh'mu'el has don a fine job of leading the nation," answered Yishai.

"But he's getting old," responded Y'ro*H*om.

"He's only fifty!" exclaimed Yishai, "You and I are older by half that."

Y'ro*H*om sighed, "Yes, but he is slowing down. May he live to a hundred and twenty. He's already delegating things to his sons, and, well, his sons aren't him. It's evoking memories of Eli and his sons."

"Silliness," Yishai grimaced. Then, looking exasperated, he said, "and you want a king? Who's to say a king would be any different? Can you guarantee his children will follow in his footsteps? All the more so, there's a chance for abuse ..." His voice trailed off.

"It's written in the Torah," proffered Y'ro*H*om gently. "*som tasim `alekha melekh asher yivHar hawayah elokekha bo.* You must surely appoint a king over you, whom the Holy One chooses," he quoted the verse.

"wa_amarta asi'mah `alay melekh k'khol hagoyim asher s'vi'votha. When you request to appoint a king over you, like all the other nations," Yishai reminded him of the beginning of the verse. "Why should we request?"

Y'roHom placed a hand on the other sage's shoulder, "Yishai, we need a king, someone to organize us and lead us into battle, someone with fear of Heaven, someone who will listen to the court. Nearly all the other elders are agreed. The people cry out for such a thing. Please, talk to Sh'mu'el. Ask him to beseech the Holy One, to request that He choose the man whom we should anoint."

Yishai sighed, nodding. "Let's see what the Holy One wants, and if it is His choosing, I will accept His Will. Gather the elders, and we'll go together to visit Sh'mu'el at Ramah."

The prophet was more opposed to the idea than Yishai, at first. He seemed to take it as personal criticism. Yet, the Holy One told Sh'mu'el to agree to the demand. In due course, Sh'mu'el anointed Sha'ul king of Yisrael at Gilgal, the place where Yehoshu`ah had camped when he conquered the Land of Yisrael. The location's choice carried tremendous significance. It was a vindication for those who initiated the idea.

Sha'ul was an unexpected selection. No one would argue that Sha'ul, in his person, was a fitting choice. Everyone remembered his heroism and self-sacrifice at Even Ha`Ezer. While everyone stood in shock, he alone acted for the honor of the Holy One. Now the Holy One brought him honor. However, everyone thought that the king would come from Yehudah. That seemed to be the meaning of the blessing that Ya'aqov gave to his sons. The choice of someone from Binyamin gave everyone pause. The Holy One's choice was cryptic.

In the beginning, Sha'ul had exceeded everyone's expectations. Even Yishai was impressed with him. At Mikhmash and Giv'a of Binyamin, the young king led the nation to overwhelming victory. Sh'mu'el himself was impressed and became very fond of the new king. Oftentimes when they would meet, their conversations extending long into the night.

Then something happened. A fatal flaw was exposed, as it were, and everything began to unravel. When he went to war against the nation of 'Amaleq, the Holy One commanded Sha'ul through the prophet Sh'mu'el, with very specific instructions. He told him that Amaleq should be completely destroyed. Nothing was to be left. Nothing.

Sha'ul assembled an awesome army, numbering more than two hundred thousand warriors. The nation of 'Amaleq quickly fell; their king, Agag, was captured. Yet, the Holy One's instructions were somehow forgotten. Agag wasn't killed. The people saved the best of the livestock from destruction. They were reluctant to destroy things of value. Wasn't there a commandment in the Torah against wanton waste and destruction?

Sha'ul listened to the people and was swayed. That was the problem. Instead of following the instructions of the Holy One, he allowed himself to be led by the people. He didn't want to confront them. He failed to lead. He failed to be the anointed emissary of the Holy One, at least, in that one moment of indecision. When Sh'mu'el was informed, through prophesy, he was terribly upset, both at the affront to the Holy One and at the failing of his beloved king. He felt a tremendous amount of compassion for Sha'ul. He had grown to love Sha'ul. Deciding to bring a remedy and repair the breach, Sh'mu'el quickly traveled to Sha'ul's encampment. He intended to confront the king about his trespass.

Yet, faced with his transgression, Sha'ul made things worse. First, he tried to justify the actions of the people, telling the prophet that the livestock had been preserved to bring as an offering to the Holy One. Then, he argued with Sh'mu'el, angling away his responsibility, when confronted with his error.

The scene that transpired before Yisrael was terrible. Sh'mu'el confronted Sha'ul with a vengeance. Sha'ul insisted that he had obeyed the commandment of the Holy One. The people, he argued, took the spoils. The more he justified and argued, the more Sha'ul demonstrated a flaw in his leadership. Sh'mu'el raised his voice. It penetrated to the very depth of Sha'ul's being.

"Does the Holy One get delight from burnt offerings?" he asked mockingly, "Behold, to obey, is better than to bring an offering; to take heed is better than the fat of the ram." The prophet pointed an accusing finger at the king, "*ki HaTath qesem meri w'awen uth'rafim haf'tsar.* Rebellion is like the sin of witchcraft; stubbornness is akin to idolatry!"

"*ya`an ma_s'ta eth d'var hawayah wayim'as'kha mimelekh!* Because you have rejected the word of the Holy One, he has rejected you as his anointed king!" Sh'mu'el's voice shook with emotion.

Sha'ul was struck. Suddenly, as if cold water was splashed on his face, he recognized the truth of the prophet's accusations. Repentant, he whispered, "I have sinned." Yet, then he immediately stumbled again. He quickly added, "I transgressed the word of the Holy One, and your instructions because I feared the people and obeyed their voice."

Sh'mu'el scowled. How could he fear the voice of the people more than the word of the Almighty?

"*na,* Please," continued Sha'ul, "*wa`atah sa na eth HaTathi w'shuv `imi w'eshtaHaweh la'hawayah.* Pardon my sin. Come with me, and be by my side while I prostrate myself before the Holy One."

Sh'mu'el turned away from the king, who, in desperation, grabbed his robe. The robe ripped. "The Holy One has torn the kingdom of Yisrael

319

from you this day," warned Sh'mu'el, "and given it to your neighbor, who is better than you."

Sha'ul had cried, truly regretting his actions. He asked the prophet to stay, "*HaTathi*. I have sinned," he said, simply, "Yet, please do me the honor of praying with me, as I bow before the Holy One."

Sh'mu'el grimaced. He loved Sha'ul. Silently he nodded. He would accompany the king. The two knelt, bowed and prostrated themselves before the Holy One, beseeching his mercy.

When they arose, Sh'mu'el requested that Agag, the king of `Amaleq be brought to him. They brought him out in chains, and Sh'mu'el strode over to Agag, taking a sword from one of the warriors as he passed by him.

"Surely the bitterness of death is past," said Agag.

Offering a wry smile, Sh'mu'el answered him, "Just as your sword has made women childless, so shall your mother be childless amongst women." Lifting the sword in his hand, Sh'mu'el struck Agag in the neck, and with all his strength hewed the king in two. As the split corpse fell, the prophet tossed the sword on the steaming flesh. Without a word, he left Gilgal, and went to his home in Ramah.

From that day, the spirit of the Holy One seemed to depart from Sha'ul. However, Sha'ul still strove to fulfill the Almighty's Will.

That was how Dawid came to become a part of the King's court, for when the spirit of the Holy One left the king, a dark mood descended to replace it. Nothing suffers a vacuum, and when the Holy Spirit no longer filled, the emptiness in his soul became a magnet for other forces. It was horrible to witness.

Dawid trembled at the thought. He could only imagine the terrible emptiness that his king must have felt. To be filled with the presence of the Holy One, and then have it vanish …

For Dawid could relate as how Sha'ul must have felt when he was first anointed. He had heard the stories about how Sha'ul suddenly began prophesizing, filled with the spirit of the Holy One.

Dawid sighed, his body swayed as if listening to a melody, emotions welled up. There were times when he felt consumed - enwrapped was a better word - with The Holy One's kindness. It was stronger now, almost palpable, since the holy prophet Sh'mu'el had visited him and …

To lose such a feeling... Tears welled up in Dawid's eyes. He couldn't image such pain.

***

The Valley of Elah
Near Sokhoh, Yehudah

Sha'ul did respond to Goliyath's challenge. As soon as the king heard that the P'lisht'im were camped at Efes Dam'im, he moved his army there. Av'ner sent out messengers to all of Yisrael, and the nation responded. Sha'ul assembled his forces on the northern ridge of the valley of Elah.

"What are they waiting for Av'ner?" asked Sha'ul, as they stood on the ridge overlooking the valley.

"They seemed to have learned from their folly at Mikhmash," suggested Av'ner, "They're consolidating their forces, hoping for a definitive victory." It was the P'lisht'im's overconfidence, among other things, which brought them defeat at Mikhmash. They divided their forces and engaged in punitive raids as a response to the killing of their governor at Giv`a. Sha'ul took advantage of their dispersal, and along with the brave fighting of his son, Y'honatan, brought victory to Yisrael.

While Yisrael was camped at Giv`a of Binyamin, Y'honatan and his lieutenant decided to try their luck themselves. Full of confidence in the Holy One, they approached the garrison of the P'lisht'im at Mikhmash. He went up between two sharp outcroppings of rocks, one named Botsets, and the other called Sene. The one point rose sharply from the north opposite Mikhmash while the other rose like a sharpened tooth from the south opposite Gav`a.

Spying the garrison, a holy spirit filled Y'honatan and said with a smile, "Come let's go over to the garrison of these uncircumcised ones. Maybe the Holy One will make things happen for us, for nothing is beyond the Holy One. He can save by the many or by the few as He wills."

The armor bearer returned Y'honatan's smile, his adrenaline pumping. He said to his commander, "I am with you, whatever you decide to do. Do whatever is in your heart."

So the two passed over and revealed themselves to the guards of the garrison. When the guards shouted down a challenge to them, Y'honatan was convinced that the Holy One had delivered the uncircumcised into their hands. The two climbed up the steep incline on their hands and feet to answer the challenge. As they got there, the guards immediately went to attack the two warriors of Yisrael but Y'honatan was quicker and he quickly slew his opponent. His lieutenant also dispatched his attacker. They were pressed hard, but the P'lisht'im couldn't surround Y'honatan and his companion. Their skill and fervor was no match for the P'lisht'im and twenty uncircumcised men soon littered the ground at their feet.

There was a trembling in the camp, as shouts from the garrison could be heard. When they discovered that Y'honatan was missing, they realized what was happening, and Sha'ul mustered the troops. When they arrived at the field of battle, they discovered a huge confusion. Y'honatan had caused the P'lisht'im, in their panic, to turn on one another. In addition, the `Ivr'im that had joined the P'lisht'im forces, turned on their masters and sided with Yisrael. Caught by surprise, the P'lisht'im melted away. The victory had been total for the men of Yisrael.

"We aren't going to be able to surprise them this time," agreed Y'honatan, Sha'ul's son.

Sha'ul smiled. He still had hopes that his son, Y'honatan would succeed him as king, regardless of Sh'mu'el's "predictions." He had proven himself to be a fine warrior. His exploits were famous now, especially in his attack on the garrison and his surprise attack on the P'lishti governor at Giv`a.

"Unless," continued Y'honatan enthusiastically, "we rush them now."

"No," answered Sha'ul, "we don't know what's waiting for us. It might be a trap."

"The Holy One will be with us," stated Y'honatan confidently.

Sha'ul shifted uncomfortably. "In any event, He has given us wisdom. We should use it prudently," he demurred.

The P'lisht'im were arrayed on the southern edge of the valley. They had been camped there for several days, and even though Yisrael had begun to assemble their forces, the P'lisht'im failed to initiate hostilities. Sha'ul was reminded of the battle at Afeq, when the Yisrael forces took too long to decide on a course of action, and had allowed their enemy to assemble a large force.

Suddenly Sha'ul remembered another aspect of those horrible days, as he saw a giant warrior leaving the P'lishti encampment. The warrior strode to the middle of the valley. He was horrible, large and fearsome. A lump of fear welled up in Sha'ul's throat. Memories of the giant that had captured the Aron HaBrith filled his head, yet the bravery he had then, failed to enter his heart. Panic seemed to fill his chest instead. He fought it back.

Goliyath felt good, full of his own power and prowess. With each step he took, he could almost feel the awe coming from the 'Ivri camp. He and his shield bearer, me, stood in the middle of the valley for several pregnant moments. It was telling that no arrow was fired, nor stone hurled towards him.

His eyes scanned the northern ridge of the valley. He couldn't see anything, but that mattered little. His eyesight had never been good. Fortunately, he rarely needed it. Goliyath focused his mind, as his mother had taught him, weaving all of his strength and energy, bringing it up from his lower abdomen to his throat. His voice echoed throughout the valley, magnified and focused to shatter the hearts of his enemy.

"Why do you come out in battle array?" he asked mockingly, speaking in the language of his enemy with perfect diction. *"Hallo, ani ha_p'lishti.* Hello, I am *the* P'lishti! And you are mere slaves to Sha'ul." He paused. It seemed that even the sounds of nature were silent before him. "Choose a *man* for yourselves," He smiled, for of course they had already chosen Sha'ul as their man, their king. Yet, Goliyath also knew that sometimes the 'Ivri'm referred to their god as a 'Man of War.' He remembered hearing them sing their victory song at the crossing of the Red Sea. He would be happy to take on both. "Choose a man for yourselves, and let him come down to me," he challenged. "If he would be able to fight with *me*, and kill me," Goliyath chuckled as if there were man or god who could challenge him, "then we will be your slaves."

"But," Goliyath continued his challenge, "if I prevail against him, and kill him, then you will be our slaves and serve us."

"You have nothing to lose really," added Goliyath, "you are slaves. What difference does it make who your master is?"

Silence filled the valley. Goliyath waited. When it was clear that no one was forthcoming, and Goliyath didn't really expect anyone to accept his challenge, he continued to mock the `Ivr'im. "I defy the ranks of Yisrael this very day," he made a point of calling them by the name they choose for themselves to further their humiliation, *"baru lakhem ish w'yeredh.* Give me a *man* and we will battle each other!"

"What does it mean, father?" asked Y'honatan.

Sha'ul shuddered. In vain, he tried to recall a hint of the emotion that filled him when he faced the giant over a decade earlier. The spirit escaped him. In its place, fear filled his heart, his and all of the nation's hearts.

***

Chapter Three

Anticipation
The Valley of Elah
A month later

The mood in the Yisrael encampment was somber. No one knew what to do, especially King Sha'ul.

When the giant first issued his challenge, it seemed most prudent for Sha'ul to ignore it. Y'honatan had wanted to teach the uncircumcised a lesson, but his father immediately dismissed such a possibility. He would not risk his son's life, any more than he would risk his own. Sh'mu'el's words rang in the king's head, and he was wont to do anything that might risk the continuation of his monarchy.

While it was clear that the challenge was more than a simple duel between champions, no one acknowledged that fact openly. Each time the P'lishti issued his call, it seemed as if a small piece of each of the men of Yisrael died. As if a part of their soul was extinguished. One more candle snuffed out between the fingers of the giant. The more they ignored it, the more they tried to rationalize their failure to answer the call, the decay spread.

By the third day, when it became clear that his king was unable to respond, Av'ner pulled his nephew aside.

"We can't allow this to continue," Sha'ul's military chief said gently, "it will destroy morale."

Sha'ul lifted his hands in resignation, "What would you have me do, Av'ner?" he asked, "Fight that thing?"

Av'ner didn't answer immediately. He simply looked at Sha'ul, his king, questioning.

Sha'ul pressed his argument, "Do you know who that is? Do you recognize him?"

"Yes," Av'ner answered simply. Then he added, "Does the king want me to answer the challenge in his name?"

Sha'ul turned to look at his uncle, shock and fear etched on his face. "No," he objected, "I need you by my side." His words trailed off. Sha'ul was having difficulty facing the emotions churning in his soul. He knew he had to do something. But what? He had trouble facing himself; he hadn't a chance against the giant.

Do'eg approached the pair, taking care to remain discreetly outside hearing range.

Sha'ul turned to acknowledge him, "Yes, Do'eg."

Approaching them, Do'eg began, "My lord, if I may?"

The king nodded, prompting him to continue. He had come to value Do'eg's counsel.

"What if the king offered an incentive, a reward of some sort, to the warrior that took up the challenge," Do'eg suggested. "It's possible that someone would be filled with the spirit of the Almighty and ..." he allowed his words to trail off, leaving the suggestion open-ended.

"What type of an incentive?" interjected Av'ner.

Do'eg shrugged, "Maybe, marriage to one of the king's daughters." Then he quickly added, "I mean, certainly someone that was filled with a holy spirit would be fit to be a son-in-law of the king."

Sha'ul's eyes lit up. "Yes," he answered. This is the answer he was looking for, the way out. Av'ner was skeptical, but upon seeing Sha'ul's reaction he held his tongue.

At first the news generated a tremendous amount of excitement. Yet, the days wore on without a response. Everyone was waiting for his neighbor to take on the challenge. Days became weeks, which turned into a full month, and no one stepped forward to accept the gauntlet. Soon, the prize become as much of a mockery as the challenge.

***

Goliyath strode back to the camp, a wide grin across his face. He was returning to the P'lisht'im camp after issuing his challenge to the 'Ivr'im, as he had every morning and evening for the past month. It was going well, very well, for him that is. It isn't at all what he had expected. It was a thousand times better than he could have imagined. I, on the other hand, seemed to be nursing a growing ulcer.

He had expected, of course, to instill fear amongst the `Ivr'im, but he also expected his challenge to have been met. Goliyath assumed that their 'king' would be too ashamed not to face him in single combat. He had been proven wrong. Now, demoralized, and shaking with fear, the `Ivr'im were defeated long before an arrow was fired. Such a defeat would keep them in line for two generations at least. There would be no turning back again.

"Sir," one of the officers approached Goliyath, hesitantly. The giant commander handed me his helmet. He cracked his neck from side to side, before looking down to acknowledge the man. The officer hesitated at the sound of the giant commander's neck. One of my cheap pleasures was watching people approach Goliyath.

"Sir," the officer finally continued, "if I may, how long do you intend to continue this? It seems clear that they aren't going to accept your challenge." His words trailed off. He didn't want to sound like he was questioning Goliyath's judgment. Then he added, "the men are a bit restless." I had to agree with him. I was getting tired of this game as well. It made me very uncomfortable. Fortunately, I had an active imagination, and I was able to dream up at least thirty different ways that Goliyath would meet his end during the past month. Unfortunately for my growing ulcer, none of them came to fruition. On the other hands, every day that Goliyath didn't descend into the pit of Sh'e'ol, I earned another day's wage.

Goliyath's grin widened, causing the officer to shrink back. He placed a hand on his soldier's shoulder. "Ur'ba''al," Goliyath said lightly, "do not be in such a hurry to die."

The officer, Ur'ba''al, didn't know how to take the statement. How had his commander meant those words? He feared it was a threat for questioning the giant's decision.

Goliyath released a laugh. "Victory is already ours. Learn to savor it," he said. "Soon, when the 'Ivr'im themselves begin to disband, when they realize that they have no king, and no master to protect them," Goliyath's face became serious, "When they realize they are nothing but walking corpses, we will deliver the death blow, and wipe them from the face of the earth."

Ur'ba''al caught his breath from the intensity of his commander's zeal. He was glad he was on Goliyath's side.

After several moments, Goliyath broke the silence. "Forty days," he said flatly, "Know your enemy." Goliyath's words were cryptic. He continued, "All their legends, all their beliefs. After forty days, they'll know in their heart of hearts that they are finished."

Ur'ba''al was taken aback. He had never seen this side of his commander before. Even I was surprised. How did he know that? I wondered.

Goliyath didn't let the impression remain. He turned to his officer and winked. "If you place your wager on that," he said playfully, referring to the betting pool he was sure the men had started, you better give me a cut."

"Yes sir," Ur'ba''al answered. Again, he thanked the gods that he was fighting behind Goliyath, and not opposite him. The man was unpredictable, and unsettling.

**

The Wilderness of Yehudah

Dawid reclined against the boulder as he tightened the sinews on his *kinor*. He had just finished constructing the shell-shaped instrument from a piece of olive wood. He strummed his fingers across the four strings. The chord had a nice resonance. The hardness of the olive wood created a deep echo. He liked the sound.

Dawid sat upright, and adjusted the *totafoth* on his forehead. Gently he strummed and picked at the strings of the *kinor*, allowing the music to fill him. He learned this technique from the prophet Sh'mu'el after the visit. The youngest son of Yishai accompanied the prophet back to his home in Ramah, staying and learning with him for a few months. It had opened up entire new worlds to Dawid.

As the music filled him, Dawid's consciousness seemed to expand. He became aware of the wind, and the scents it carried. The sun's warmth caressed his face. The sounds of nature danced with the music of the *kinor*. Dawid breathed steadily, deeply, entwining his senses with the harmony of the chords, the melody of the strings.

The music faded, as Dawid's consciousness entered a heavenly chamber. An image danced before him. Formless at first, it soon began to take shape. He saw a vicious dog, barking and howling at something beyond Dawid. He perceived it to be a flock of sheep.

The dog wanted to attack and devour the sheep. Anger and protectiveness welled up inside Dawid. He remembered the feelings he felt when he rescued his flock from the lion and the bear. A staff appeared in his hand, and he crouched, ready for the attack. The dog grew, filling his vision, and trepidation touched his heart. Suddenly the dog stood on its hind legs, its form transforming into that of a man. His beard was fire, and his eyes were dark as coals. The man held a fiery sword in his hand. For a moment, Dawid had a memory of Esaw, Ya`aqov's twin brother, and nemesis.

Dawid summoned his courage and attacked with all his might, but the man easily parried the blow. Laughter from the man filled Dawid's head, but the young man stood ready again. The man's sword flashed and danced. Dawid recognized that it wasn't a sword now, but a fiery serpent, its flames licking and hissing towards Dawid. A sheen of filth covered its body. The man too, now seemed to be a part of the snake, or it, an extension of him.

A hurricane of emotions swirled around Dawid as he looked at the serpent. The emotions battered him, spinning him in circles. He watched as the man and serpent grew. Fire arced and danced around the man, feeding him.

Somehow, as if it was whispered on the wind, Dawid realized that it was his anger and fear that were feeding the beast. The more he strove against it, the stronger it became.

Drawing a breath, Dawid stepped into the storm, towards the eye. The hurricane still swirled around him, but it no longer affected him.

From somewhere, he recalled the story of Moshe and Aharon in Par`o's court, where Yisrael's leaders' serpent devoured the serpent of Par`o's magicians. Dawid filled himself with heavenly spirit, and his staff transformed into a serpent. His had a golden glow, where the other had a sheen of pollution. The distinction was subtle. Dawid wondered at how he was able to perceive it, for only when he didn't focus on it was it apparent to him.

He extended his arm and his serpent swallowed the man's. The fire dancing around his body diminished. Soon the image flashed and the man became a vicious dog again, yet larger, and more fierce than before. It appeared twice the size of a lion.

Dawid didn't feel any fear, as the dog closed in on him. He now knew how to stop it, destroy it. Filling himself with heavenly spirit, Dawid nullified himself, making room for the light of the Holy One. The serpent in his hand transformed into pure light, which now flowed from him like a vessel, and then shot out like a bolt of lightning. It obliterated the dog, causing it to disintegrate, like a clay vessel smashed against stone.

From within his vision, Dawid recognized that someone was approaching from the north. He forcibly but carefully stepped out of the heavenly chambers, and slowly returned to reality. Taking a deep breath to steady himself and return his equilibrium, he stood to greet the approaching man.

"Master," it was one of his father's younger servants. He was running quickly towards Dawid. "Master Dawid."

Dawid offered the young men a genuine smile, as he unlatched his water skin from his belt. He held it up before the servant, as an offering. Like so many others upon contact with one of Dawid's smile, the servant was unable to resist smiling in return. He then extended his hands waiting for his master to fill them.

"Thank you, sir," proffered the servant, as he wiped the excess water from his mouth. "It's hot today."

"What brings you way out here," asked Dawid, though he could have guessed the answer.

"Your father, sir, requests that you come home. He would like to speak with you." Answered the servant, before adding, "I will watch the flock."

Dawid nodded, and handed the servant his water skin and staff. Pointing out a small lamb, Dawid instructed, "Yits*H*aq, right? That lamb's an orphan. Make sure he suckles from one of the other ewes at least three times a day, ok?"

"Don't worry, sir," returned Yits*H*aq, "I'll take good care of the flock, till you get back."

Dawid smiled. "Fare well," he offered as he hurried to report to his father. He wondered if he had news of the battle.

Chapter Four

Regret
BethleHem

Yishai's eyes welled up as the youth, but he was no longer a youth really, entered the brightly lit room. He stood in the doorway, respectfully waiting for his father's permission to enter. He was such a good boy. Why hadn't he been able to see that before? Yishai choked back a wellspring of emotion. Silently, for his mouth would have been unable to form the words, he gestured for his son. His son ... The elder's eyes closed, closing off the torrent within. Again, he gestured for his son to enter and take a seat by his side.

His son, yet, for the nearly twenty-nine years of the boy's existence, Yishai didn't, couldn't, have known. All those years of suspicion and hurt, of degradation... And the damage to the relationship with the boy's mother – his wife ... Why didn't she say anything? Yet, Yishai knew the answer already, and the ones to all the other questions surrounding this boy ... this young man. He knew the answers but he had trouble reconciling them in his heart. So, he continued to ask them.

So many years lost. The responsibility, of course, fell directly on Yishai's own shoulders. He knew that it was because of his own foolishness. His wife, his dear righteous, saintly wife, bore such a heavy burden, such heavy, unjustified shame. And she did so, simply so that Yishai would not suffer that which was due him. It's through the deeds of her righteous women that Yisrael merits heavenly blessing, remembered Yishai.

The elder statesman of his people allowed a heavy sigh to escape his lips, keeping the rest locked in the depth of his soul. Now was not the time for unburdening. "Dawid, *beni*, my son," he allowed himself to use the reference, though it was still awkward on his lips, "How is the flock faring? Can they be left with the boys for a few days?" He wanted ask so much more. He wanted to know how he, his son was faring, how he had survived a lifetime of degradation, and always with a smile on his face …

Dawid startled for a moment. His father had never acknowledged him as his son, let alone called him such. He had waited a lifetime to hear such sweet words. Of course, now, he too knew the reasons why it was so. At least he knew in general, but there were still so many questions. He realized that they would remain unanswered for now. "Yes, father. There's one lamb that's orphaned …" he paused, wanting to add, "like me." He continued instead saying, "but I'm sure Yits*H*aq, the one from Efrayim, can care for him. He's been with us for a while."

"Yes, he's a good man. His past mistakes are behind him now." Yishai recalled the image of Yits*H*aq when he arrived, sentenced by the court to pay off his debt, incurred as a fine for his theft, through six years of service. Yishai's thoughts drifted to his own past mistakes and wondered if, like Yits*H*aq, he would have a chance at a new beginning. He looked at his son … his son. He was a good man. He would have been happy to have known him.

Only a few months previously, when news that the prophet and sage Sh'mu'el was coming to Bethle*H*em did the issue begin to take on any relevance. His imminent and unexpected arrival to the central town of Yehudah was outside his normal circuit. It brought with him conjecture, suspicions and rumors. Before his entourage approached the stone gates of the town, the seat of its court, the elders of the city gathered to greet the Prophet of Yisrael.

Noticing the calf amongst his train, the elders grew reticent. Is it possible that a "*H*allal," a murder victim, was found in the vicinity of their town? Such thoughts shook the hearts of the elders, of which Yishai was their leader. As the elders of the town they would bear the bloodguilt for such a tragedy. Each of them began to examine his heart and his deeds, probing where his service of the Almighty had fallen short, allowing for such a travesty to occur under their watch.

Yishai knew Sh'mu'el. He had been impressed with him, but his visit was unexpected. Suddenly, Yishai was shaken by a thought of his own past. He was suddenly reminded of a long buried secret of his own, of his wife and her son, Dawid. His heart leapt to his throat. Had he failed to mete out justice, as he should have?

Yishai, the father of the court, led the twenty-three sages to greet the venerable prophet, each one wrestling with his own private accounting of the soul.

"*Shalom alekha avi.* Peace unto you, Father," Yishai greeted the prophet. Yet, while his mouth completed the formal greeting, he couldn't keep the question from the tone of his voice, "Your arrival is in *Shalom*, in wholeness and peace?"

"*Shalom alekha, avi.*" was the prophet's simple response, his eyes locking on Yishai's. He knew what troubled the sage. The Holy One had revealed it to him.

The other elders relaxed. Sh'mu'el's response seemed to assure them that there wasn't any blood on their hands. However, the prophet's penetrating gaze merely intensified the court father's disposition, penetrating, as it did, to the very depth of Yishai's soul. Yishai felt the secret he had buried there nearly thirty years ago begin to stir. He feared it would soon be exposed.

"In Peace," he offered again, this time with a smile. Then the prophet raised his voice to the growing crowd that had gathered, "And to make an offering to the Almighty. Sanctify yourselves, and come with me to the offering!"

Sh'mu'el offered a private smile to Yishai and the two embraced. "It has been along time, Father," began Sh'mu'el, "I hope you are faring well."

Sh'mu'el turned Yishai around and taking his arm, began to walk with him in the direction of

Yishai's homestead. The gesture gave Yishai pause, for the prophet had never been to Bethle*H*em before. As if reading his mind, Sh'mu'el, "Is knowing one's way around such a great task for someone who hears the whispers of the Holy One on the wind?"

Yishai startled. Even though he knew, intellectually, that almost all was revealed before the prophet, to be confronted with it was a little unsettling. Yishai was often blessed with insight, glimpses of the divine, but to be in constant contact … It was too awesome to fathom.

"We will build a temporary altar in your courtyard," Sh'mu'el began, before adding, almost as an afterthought, "with your permission, of course." Yishai noted the tone. Again, he wondered why the prophet would come here, now. The last time he had seen Sh'mu'el was at the anointment of Sha'ul as king. He had heard that there was an incident between Sha'ul and Sh'mu'el. Yishai had been the one, as a representative of the court that had pressed Sh'mu'el to anoint a king. But Sha'ul was the Holy One's choice, not his. Was this somehow related? What was the prophet planning? He was being very circumspect.

As they neared Yishai's home, Sh'mu'el turned to the elder and said, "Sanctify and bring all of your sons, Yishai, for today is a special day." He squeezed the sage's hands.

Yishai startled, again. Did the prophet emphasize the word "all," or was it his own trepidation? Eli'av, Yishai's oldest, had pressed close to see the venerable sage, and heard the private invitation to his father and his heart leapt with joy. Taking the initiative, he offered, "I'll tell the others, Father."

Yishai nodded his agreement and Eli'av quickly ran to assemble his brothers. He would remind them to immerse in the miqweh, the ritual bath, and sanctify themselves for the feast. Eli'av's feet were light with anticipation, for he too detected something in the prophet's words, and the almost casual glance Sh'mu'el directed in his direction. Maybe, Eli'av thought, he would be designated for some special role.

Yishai's steps were leaden. He tried to control the flood of thoughts and emotions in his mind, and in his heart. It had been his foolishness, his insecurity, that brought his wife, his family … this shame … this mistake. The father of the court led the prophet to his home, while his thoughts raced. As nearly the entire town accompanied them, Yishai's heart was filled with foreboding; theirs, with exuberant anticipation.

When they arrived at the entrance of Yishai's estate, a servant met them with a silver bowl and pitcher. Recovering from himself, Yishai offered the servant, Mikha a smile, and took the vessels from him. Eli'av and his brother, Avinadav, brought the prophet a wooden stool. Gently they encouraged Sh'mu'el to sit. Their father turned to face the prophet.

"With your permission," started Yishai, "this is the custom of my home when we have the honor of receiving a guest." "Welcome to my home. Peace unto you." The elder statesman knelt before the prophet of Yisrael and began to remove his sandals. Sh'mu'el started to protest, but Yishai insisted.

"It is my honor and privilege. You have journeyed long; allow me to wash your feet in the tradition of our father, Avraham. The prophet of Yisrael wouldn't begrudge me the fulfillment of a family tradition." Sh'mu'el grimaced, but he grudgingly allowed the elder to remove his sandal.

Yishai finished removing the sandals and began to pour the cool water over the sage's feet, first the right and then the left, alternating three times. When he had finished, his son offered him a wool towel in which he gently dried the prophet's feet and returned them to their sandals. *"Barukh haqadosh barukh hu shenathan li zkhuth l'rHots riglei hanavi.* Blessed is the Holy One Who has given me the merit of washing his prophet's feet."

The throng of townspeople, who had been transfixed in silence, responded fervently, "Amen." In that one word, Sh'mu'el heard the respect and admiration the city had for its Court Father. His heart was lifted, and some of the heaviness and his own trepidation of his mission dissipated.

***

Yishai and Sh'mu'el sat next to each other on large cushions at the head of the banquet. Nearly the entire town of BethleHem was present. The smell of roasting meat permeated the air. Delicacies

343

of all kinds lined the courtyard for the impromptu feast in honor of the Holy One. For several hours previously, Sh'mu'el had made himself available to hear petitions, and offer advise to those that needed. Now, however, everyone waited for the prophet to begin the meal, but he delayed.

"First," Sh'mu'el leaned towards Yishai so that only he could hear, "we need to take care of some other matter."

Yishai's heart leapt to his throat. Again, anxiety and trepidation filled his soul. He turned to the prophet but Sh'mu'el interrupted him.

"I have been sent to anoint one of your sons in place of Sha'ul," Sh'mu'el whispered.

Feelings of relief intermingled with unexpected joy left Yishai speechless. He was completely taken by surprised.

"Please present them to me," asked Sh'mu'el.

Yishai turned towards his eldest, pride filling his heart. "This is Eli'av, my firstborn," Yishai offered.

Eli'av stood before the prophet. He was a handsome man, with a bright face, and quick eyes. Sh'mu'el immediately was taken with him. The prophet thought that surely, this must be the Holy One's anointed.

Yet, the Holy One answered Sh'mu'el differently. The prophet heard the Almighty's Will resonate in his heart and head. "Do not look at his appearance," was the message from Heaven, "nor his stature, for I have rejected him." The Heavenly voice continued to resonate, "It is not as a man sees, for men rely on outward appearance, but the Holy One sees what is in his heart." "He can not be my anointed," the Holy One said to Sh'mu'el. The prophet felt a sting. Was the Holy One accusing him of being superficial!?

Sh'mu'el whispered to Yishai, simply, "Not him." Eli'av caught the words, and was crestfallen. Though he didn't know for what he was rejected, it upset him. The prophet should give him a chance to prove himself, he thought. Somehow, Eli'av managed to hide his feelings.

Yishai grimaced slightly, before presenting Avinadav. Sh'mu'el received the same heavenly answer. When Yishai's sixth son passed before Sh'mu'el and was rejected, the elder began to feel indignant. Was all of this a plan to embarrass him?

Sh'mu'el said calmly in a low voice, "The Holy One has not chosen these. Are there any other children?"

Something in the prophet's tone broke Yishai's heart. Indignation melted into shock. A truth that had been before his eyes all this time was suddenly revealed. A tear escaped his eye, though Yishai didn't yet know exactly why.

"There remains the youngest," Yishai said quietly, his voice distant. "He is tending to the flock."

"Send for him, *avi*," Sh'mu'el said gently, "we cannot begin the festival until he comes here."

As if in a trance, Yishai called to Eli'av, telling him to bring Dawid.

"But," began Eli'av. He stopped mid-sentence upon receiving a stern look from his father. "*ken, avi*," he answered before running off to find someone to fetch Dawid from the pasture.

When at last Dawid arrived, even Sh'mu'el was taken aback by the sight of the unkempt ruddy youth. Looking the ruffian, with long brown hair and a scraggly red beard, Sh'mu'el immediately had an image of `Esaw, the murderous twin of Ya`aqov. At that same moment, his heart was filled with a rebuke from the Holy One, "Do not judge this one by appearances. Yes, he resembles `Esaw," confirmed the Holy One, "but whereas `Esaw killed for himself, this one will only kill upon the instructions of the elders. Arise and anoint him, for this is him."

Sh'mu'el stood and approached the young man. Dawid, awkward and uncomfortable, offered him a smile, not knowing what else to do. Sh'mu'el couldn't help but smile in return. "*beni*, My child," whispered the prophet, "do you know how beloved you are in heaven?"

346

Dawid opened his mouth to speak, but then closed it again, not knowing what to say. Finally, after a long pause, he tried, "Father, I." His words trailed off.

"I know," answered Sh'mu'el, "I know." The prophet took the horn of oil, and dipped his finger inside. He placed a drop of oil on Dawid's earlobe, on his forehead, and on the back of his neck. He placed a drop on his right thumb and the large toe of his right foot before pouring a measure of oil over his head. The oil ran down Dawid's side-locks and cheeks. It dripped down his beard, some of it running into his mouth. Dawid smiled, unsure of what was happening. Tears welled up in his eyes. All of his brothers watched along with their father, unsure themselves as to how to interpret the scene. Dawid felt a rush of clarity as the oil penetrates his skin, as if it washed away some invisible barrier. He felt as if the Heavens were embracing him, and the Holy One Himself had kissed him on his cheek.

***

Shortly after the prophet Sh'mu'el had left, allowing enough time that his departure wouldn't be too inappropriate, Yishai quickly retreated from the main house. He made his way quickly through the grounds. It was all he could do to stop himself from running. The Prophet's anointing of this "son of Yishai" opened up many old wounds and created many new questions.

As he approached the chamber's door, his heart caught in his throat again. Yishai knocked lightly on the door, and waited.

"Enter, *beni*," called the voice of an aged woman.

Yishai, restraining the urgency of each movement, slowly entered. Yet, as he entered and his eyes focused on the elderly woman sitting at the weaver's loom, all restrained was lost. Without proffering a greeting, the community elder blurted out like a child, "You knew. Didn't you?"

An angelic smile creased the wizened face. "*shalom alekha, beni*," she returned the greeting that should have been, and then said calmly, "Yes, I knew."

"Why?" Yishai started, but the words choked in his throat. "All those years ..." His eyes filled with tears. "Mamma Ruth, why?" He now entered the dimly lit chamber. He wanted to run to his grandmother, to place his head in her lap as he had done so many times as a child, yet his feet refused to yield more than a few steps.

"Do you remember when you came to me nearly thirty years ago? Do you remember the battle within your soul then?" Ruth placed the loom on the table beside her chair. "Do you remember?"

He remembered.

He remembered the day he had overheard those two men in the market. They were fools and

348

gossips, but they had struck a sensitive nerve. It was an old wound, a generational wound. A controversy that even the great sage Boaz hadn't put to rest. In fact, the circumstances surrounding Boaz's marriage and subsequent passing only added fuel to the critics and gossips.

The debate amongst the sages was ancient: While the Torah clearly forbids the marriage of a convert from Moav to a daughter of Yisrael, it was not clear from the text itself, if the prohibition extended to the women of Moav, a Moavith, as well. Many sages interpreted the ruling, "Moavi, and not Moavith, Amoni, and not Amonith. Elimelekh's court ruled that the prohibition did not apply, and in fact his two sons married daughters of Moav. Yet they died childless.

Of course, the gossips pointed to their death as divine proof that it was forbidden. When one of those women, the saintly Ruth, came back to BethleHem with her mother-in-law Naomi, the debate raged anew. Boaz and his court established conclusively that there wasn't any prohibition to marry a daughter of Moav who converted, accepting the Holy One of Yisrael as her own. To demonstrate this, Boaz married Ruth himself, at the age of ninety. Despite the fact that no one challenged his ruling, his death after their wedding night certainly emboldened his critics.

Ruth was Yishai's grandmother, and if her status was questionable, then so was his. In the sage's effort to serve his Creator, he allowed the skepticism to engender self-doubt. After six boys and a daughter, he began to question his own bloodline. In an act of piety, which he would later regret, Yishai separated from his wife. He did not divorce her formally, for he would not leave her adrift and unsupported. However, with her consent, he abstained from any physical contact with her. How could she refuse her husband? His sons were also informed. Their lives continued uneventful for three years.

Yishai grew in wisdom and in time became the father of the court like his grandfather Boaz. Everyone saw in him, a true continuation of his ancestor's sagacity and merit.

Yet there was still a void in his life, the burning question of his lineage. Yishai decided to take an extreme step. He wanted a child that did not have the stain of doubt surrounding him.

He had recently acquired a young Kenani maidservant. She had adapted well to their household and demonstrated an inclination towards the service of the Almighty. On a clear summer evening, he called the young women to the courtyard. The young girl approached him, hesitantly. He appreciated her natural modesty.

She was attractive, with dark almond eyes and high cheekbones. She was very different in appearance from his wife. A bitter smile crossed his lips. He remembered the night he married Nitseveth. At sixteen, he had barely been able to control his passion, his desire. He still truly loved her. He prayed for her constantly. May she find comfort in the Almighty. Now though, even though the elder sage was able to note this girl's physical beauty, it only affected him marginally. He had long ago conquered his passions. Not that he didn't have them. He was human, of course, but he learned how to keep them outside of his being. He would use his urges to accomplish his goal, but his interests in this girl were solely for the sake of Heaven.

Yishai would free and marry this girl, conditionally. He would create a legal reality, wherein his child, through this woman would be free from any suspicious legal status. The formula was legalistic, but sound. If it was not forbidden for a woman convert from Moav to marry into the congregation of Yisrael, then this girl would be freed from her service, making her a full-fledge convert to Yisrael, and Yishai would be married to her as such. However, if it was forbidden for a woman convert from Moav to marry a Yisrael, meaning Yishai was a *mamzer*, a product of a forbidden union, then this girl would not be freed, and he would marry her as a maidservant. The child of a *mamzer* and a maidservant would have the status of a servant, which Yishai would subsequently free, making him a full citizen of Yisrael. It was this conditional declaration that Yishai would make to her, sealing their union. The truth, no matter what it was, would be covered by both sides of the legal condition, creating an offspring free of any suspicions taint.

Yet, unbeknownst to Yishai, the young woman was overwhelmed by the entire experience. He later learned that immediately after he had bound her with his conditional wedding vows, she ran to her mistress, Nitseveth. The maidservant didn't feel comfortable with the situation, but Nitseveth calmed her. She understood her husband, and knew his motives. Even if she thought they were misguided, she knew they were pure. Nitseveth knew in her heart of hearts that her sons were not *mamzers*. She knew that Boaz hadn't erred, and that her husband was chasing after ghosts. "Don't worry," Nitseveth calmed the Kenani girl. "I'll take care of everything." She remembered the story of her ancestors, Le'ah and RaHel, and how they had switched places on their wedding night.

That night, when Yishai entered the young woman's chambers, to consummate the marriage, Nitseveth was waiting instead. In the darkened room, and in the modesty of his coupling, Yishai did not discern that it wasn't the maidservant but his wife. He didn't learn the truth until thirty years later.

When the maidservant failed to become pregnant, Yishai, already uncomfortable with the entire incident, abandoned his plan. However, Nitseveth's pregnancy soon became noticeable. Yishai failed to connect the incidents. The Holy One closed his eyes to the coincidence. Instead, he assumed that his wife had faltered, unable to maintain the celibate life that Yishai had imposed. He blamed himself for her failure. Yet, the sin still needed to be addressed. What had been a plan to remove the suspicion of *mamzer* status on his family lineage brought an actual *mamzer* to his doorstep.

Yishai wasn't the only one to notice Nitseveth's condition. He still shuddered at the memory of Eli'av coming to his father's chamber.

"*avi*," began Eli'av.

Yishai acknowledged his son, who began to voice suspicions of his mother. The anger in Eli'av's voice was troubling, but his son's solution was even more disturbing.

"We should kill her and the child, to remove the stain of shame from the family," Eli'av suggested.

Yishai was aghast. While he immediately understood that his son's reaction was coming from a place of pain. He needed to move quickly to mitigate it. "Everyone errs, Eli'av," he began. "It is true that an adulteress is liable to death, but not without witnesses, even," he paused, "when there is 'circumstantial' evidence." Yishai then added, "And a *mamzer* does not deserve punishment, though we will have to keep him from marrying in Yisrael."

"We'll keep things quiet for now," offered Yishai, "there's no reason to bring shame onto the family, but the boy ..." he trailed off, "he needs to be kept at arm's length, and, with the help of the Holy One, we won't have to worry about who he marries."

Eli'av left his father's chambers unsatisfied, but he fulfilled his father's words. He was particularly scrupulous about keeping the boy at arm's length and not making him feel like a member of the family.

Yes, he remembered. The memories chaffed at Yishai's soul.

"Our tradition teaches," offered Ruth bringing her grandson back to the present, "that when Yosef was sold into slavery, and his father, our father Ya`aqov, thought him torn to pieces by a wild animal, he mourned him as such." Ruth continued, emphasizing each word, "Yits_H_aq, his father, knew the truth through prophecy. But he didn't reveal it. If the Almighty wanted Ya`aqov, to know the truth then, Yits_H_aq reasoned, He would have revealed it to Ya`aqov."

Ruth offered a comforting smile to Yishai, "Everything is for a reason, and everything has its time. You, my child, are gifted with spiritual insight. Why didn't you see the soul of your child? What was blocking your vision? It would seem it was necessary for him to grow up an outcast."

"That doesn't relieve me of my responsibility, my accountability," whispered Yishai.

"No," Ruth acquiesced, "but regret is the domain of evil, don't let him take residence." She stood, and approached her grandson. When she reached him, she caressed his face. "What was - is no more. One cannot alter the past." "But," she added, "one always has the present." She paused, "and the future. Dawid is a wonderful young man. You should get to know him."

***

Yishai looked at Dawid. There wasn't any time now. Time he so much wanted. "Dawid," he began again.

"Yes, Father," answered Dawid.

"Your brothers have been encamped with King Sha'ul a long time. Please take to your brothers, an efah of this parched grain," he indicated the sack on the table next to him, "and ten loaves of bread to their camp. Also, bring these ten measures of goat cheese to their captain and inquire after their welfare, please. I'd like you to leave first thing in the morning."

"*ken, avi*," Dawid answered. He too had so much he wanted to say. Most of all, that he understood, and that he accepted what was. Yet, he didn't know how to begin.

"Dawid," Yishai began again, but paused.

Dawid leaned forward, waiting in anticipation.

Finally Yishai continued. "I have a feeling that your destiny awaits you, there, in the valley of Elah." Yishai paused again, looking for the right words. He needed to give his son instruction, but he himself was unclear as to what he sensed. He simply knew that Dawid would face a challenge in the valley of Elah. He didn't know what, but he wanted him to be prepared.

355

Finally he offered, "Make sure, whatever you do, that it will be for the sake of Heaven."

"*ken, avi,*" answered Dawid, anticipation dancing in his soul.

Chapter Five

Towards Destiny
BethLeHem, Yehudah

It was still dark when Dawid awoke. In fact it would be several hours before the sun would peak over the horizon. Yet, this was a very special time for Dawid. In the quiet of the pre-dawn morning, Dawid was able to feel the presence of the Holy One the strongest.

He kept his eyes closed as he drew a deep breath, allowing the crisp moisture of the late night air to fill his lungs. The sensation of awakening filled his every pour; his lips whispered his thanks to his Creator for the restoration of his soul. A quiet happiness filled his heart.

Heaven's song filled him, while the night sounds danced in his ears. He rolled from his side to his back and allowed himself a smile before opening his eyes. While offering his thanks to the One who gives sight to the blind, thoughts drifted to his father. His father; he knew that Yishai had tried, had wanted, to tell him something yesterday, but didn't know how. There was a gulf between the two of them of memory and habit. Dawid resolved that he would double his own efforts to bridge that gap. Sympathy flooded Dawid for his father. How horrible he must feel to realize after twenty-nine years of living with a betrayal, that it never happened.

Sitting up on the straw mattress, Dawid reflected that it is the Almighty Who makes the bent erect and clothes the naked. Dawid had been so alone and naked only a short time a go. The Holy One had brought him from being a veritable pariah in the eyes of everyone to an anointed servant of the Most High. He released a sigh, reveling in the miracles of the Holy One.

Taking the pitcher of water resting near his bed, Dawid washed his hands and his face, removing the dust of sleep from his eyes.

As his feet met the ground, Dawid focused his mind on the miracle of creation, on the creation of land, firm and stable, resting on a sea of water. Gratitude welled up, as Dawid recognized that the Almighty prepares the steps of all men, and provides for all our needs.

He adjusted the simple tunic, belting it with a cord. Dawid knew what awaited him. His father confirmed it. He didn't know what form it would take, but today, he would meet his destiny. "Holy One," whispered Dawid, "just as I tie this belt, please gird me with your strength."

Dawid removed a black square box with a long leather strap from its leather pouch, the *oth*, the sign of the covenant between the Holy One and His People. The young man strapped it to his bicep wrapping the strap seven times down his arm, then three times around his finger before tying it off around his hand. As the anointed, Dawid now had his own special covenant with the Holy One. He would make every effort to fulfill it.

Taking the second black box, Dawid strapped the *totafoth* on his head, a simple crown for the children of the King of Kings. Dawid wrapped his *mitsnefeth* around his head. He smiled. "Holy One, please help me, so that my head rules my actions today."

Dawid's gratitude magnified as he focused on the gift of being born in Yisrael. What a privilege to serve the Holy One as a free man. Dawid knew that he was privileged to serve only one master, the Almighty, and not be, as so many others were, a slave to every whim and desire that caught one's attention. By being bound to the Torah, Dawid was free to realize his true self.

So many people, thought Dawid, went through life, asleep to its beauty and depth. He thanked the Holy One of Blessings, for removing the slumber from his own eyes, allowing him to truly be alive.

The sound escaping from David's lips was barely audible in the night air, but his meditations resonated loudly within his heart, and its echo reverberated in the heavenly chambers. Dawid focused his thoughts so as to enter those chambers. He spent the remaining hours of the night in prayer and meditation.

As the sun rose on the horizon, Dawid rose from his meditations. Gently nudging YitsHaq awake, he waited patiently as the young man became fully conscious. He had returned to the pasture and the flock after meeting with is father, before setting out on his journey. He wanted to make sure that YitsHaq had everything he needed during his absence. Smiling through his sleepy eyes, YitsHaq, nodded. He was awake, he gestured, "Go, have a good journey. May the Almighty be with you," he managed to voice.

Dawid smiled and wished the man well. Taking the parched grain, the breads, the cheese, and other wares as his father had instructed him, he placed them on a grayish-white donkey that stood in the courtyard. Dawid turned westward towards Beth Shemesh, leading the donkey by foot at first. It felt good to stretch his legs with a brisk pace. Anticipation filled him. Dawid was anxious to see what kind of day the Holy One had prepared for him.

Dawid was also excited about meeting King Sha'ul again. He had enjoyed being in the king's service. Dawid admired Sha'ul very much. He was in awe at the responsibility resting on the king's shoulders. The fate of the nation, both in this world and in the heavens, was dependent upon the anointed king of Yisrael.

Then it struck him. He was also anointed. How was that possible? When Sh'mu'el had anointed him with the holy oil, Dawid, at the time, had assumed that it was for serving the Holy One as a student of the prophet. Dawid drew a breath.

It had never been mentioned directly, but he now seemed to understand. He had been anointed to replace Sha'ul. Not immediately, that was clear. Sha'ul was still in the role of king, and that role must be honored. Everything was starting to make sense now. He knew what the prophet had told Sha'ul at the incident with 'Amaleq. All of Yisrael knew. It seemed that the spirit of the Holy One had left Sha'ul. And now it rested on Dawid. When Sha'ul retired from this world, it seemed that Dawid would be his replacement. The young man's feet stumbled on the path. The weight of his realization was overwhelming.

"Master of the World," began Dawid, "You know what is in every man's heart. You know that my only desire is to want to serve You, to do Your Will, but You created in me all these other desires and distractions. Please, help me to overcome them, and guide me in this role You chose for me. I'll try not to let You down."

Dawid continued the rest of his journey in silence, but his thoughts were far from quiet. He was honored and humbled that he would have been chosen, yet, he didn't understand the choice. He had always been a loner, not necessarily by choice, but he had never been a leader, really. Others were always striving to be at the forefront of events. How would he be able to become a leader of men? In the end, his thoughts always came to the same conclusion. He would rely on the Holy One. At least, he could be confidant that He knew what He was doing.

***

As the sun rose on the morning of the fortieth day since the two armies had encamped in the valley of Elah, the warriors of Yisrael, again, formed their battle lines. No one seemed to take their position with any enthusiasm. Yet, with no other choice before them, they went through the motions. No one really expected the battle to begin. The thought of which filled them with dread. They wanted it to be over already. Almost everyone on the battle line felt trapped, a victim of circumstances beyond his control. They all seemed to be waiting for something, or someone to release them from their destiny.

Dawid arrived at the encampment shortly after sunrise. He left his donkey and other equipment with the equipment officer and ran towards the battle line looking for his brothers. He knew that they were serving under Y'honatan's command. He had met the king's eldest son when he had been at Sha'ul's court, and the two had formed an immediate affinity for the other. Dawid was looking forward to seeing him again, too. In fact, Dawid thought with chagrin, he would prefer to be seeing him than his brothers.

"Avinadav!" Dawid shouted when he recognized his brother. Avinadav was standing in a small circle of four other men.

When Avinadav turned and saw Dawid, he smiled. "Dawid, what brings you here?" he shouted, opening his arms for an embrace. Avinadav was glad that Dawid was able to put the past behind him. He wasn't sure he would have been able to do so, so easily. In any event, he was growing to love his youngest brother.

The two embraced. "Father sent me," Dawid offered. "He sends greetings and some fresh food. It's been forty days since you came here. He wants to know how you are faring."

Avinadav began to answer, when Goliyath's daily challenge interrupted him.

"Hallo!" came the mocking shout, "Are you still here, slaves of Sha'ul? Why do you come out in battle array?"

Dawid, and all of Yisrael, turned towards the shout. Dawid saw the giant for first time. He was horrible.

"*mah zeh!?* What is this?" asked Dawid. No one answered. As he looked around, everyone avoided eye contact.

Goliyath continued with his challenge. "Hello, I am *the* P'lishti! And you are all mere slaves to Sha'ul," he shouted. "Choose a *man* for yourselves, and let him come down to me," he challenged. "If he would be able to fight with *me*, and kill me." Goliyath's laugh roared like thunder before he added, his voice dripping with mockery, "then we will be your slaves."

Dawid was incredulous. How come no one had removed this cur's head already? He looked around, but was amazed that no one seemed to share his anger. How could they let this uncircumcised speak like this?

"But," Goliyath continued his challenge, "if I prevail against him, and kill him, then you will be our slaves and serve us."

"Who do you think will get the honor to teach that uncircumcised P'lishti a lesson and remove the insult of his presence from before Yisrael?" Dawid asked to no one in particular.

Goliyath's voice rose to echo across the valley, "I defy the ranks of Yisrael this very day. Give me a *man* and we will battle each other!"

What gall. Dawid scoffed. Who did this heathen think he was? He was sure that one of the men of Yisrael would rush out to meet him any minute. Someone had to remove the tongue of this insolent dog. Dawid wondered who would have the honor of being the hand of the Almighty that would cut him down. A tinge a jealousy filled him for the man who would get the honor.

But no one moved. In fact as Dawid looked around, he realized it wasn't only the men near him, but everyone in the camp seemed to hide their face from his fellow. Fear seemed permeated the air.

Then, like men rehearsing lines from a play, every warrior, standing in his own fear, tried, meekly, to convince their fellow to engage this giant. One said to his friend, "Have you seen this man that has come up to cajole Yisrael, why don't you go out to meet him?"

"Don't you want the prize?"

"Surely the one that kills him will be rewarded beyond his dreams by the king."

"Who wouldn't want to marry his daughter and make his father's house free from the obligations of the state?"

Dawid was amazed. He couldn't understand the chatter. It was clear to him that everyone was waiting for his neighbor to do something. Why weren't these warriors fighting for the opportunity to kill this dog?

Finally he spoke up. Addressing the men who stood by him, he asked, "What was that? What did you say would done for the man who kills that uncircumcised P'lishti and removes the insult from before Yisrael?" Dawid's anger flared, *"ki Heref ma`ar'khoth elok'im Ḥayy'im?* Who does that uncircumcised think he is, insulting the army of the Living Holy One of Yisrael?"

All eyes turned towards Dawid. Everyone recognized that he alone seemed unafraid of the giant in the valley.

Dawid had trouble containing his passion, now that he had voiced his indignation. He repeated, *"ki mi hap'lish'ti he`arel hazeh ki Heref ma`ar'khoth elok'im Ḥayy'im?* Who does that uncircumcised dog think he is that he can insult the armies of the living God!?"

Dawid noticed wonder as it replaced the fear in the eyes of the men around him. He had drawn a crowd, yet still no one was able to maintain eye contact with him. Dawid's heart fell. How could the men of Yisrael be afraid of one uncircumcised heathen?

He had trouble controlling the wellspring of passion. How can they sit there while this dog mocks the Holy One of Yisrael? How is it possible that there isn't a mad rush to take this living insult's head? He is a living God! *Elok'im Hayy'im hu!* He is THE living God! How can His children suffer such insults to their Father?

"*mah*?" Dawid cried out. "How come you're not rushing to remove his head? How can you suffer him to take another breath?"

One of the men turned to the excited youth, "*na`ar*, Child, look at him. He's an armored giant. His sword is taller than you!"

Another one mused, "The man that could take his head ... the king would give him his daughter, and riches and ... "

The young man's mind flashed to Mikhal's eyes. Dawid was distracted for a moment at his memory of the king's daughter, but he pushed the thoughts away. This wasn't the time. "The Holy One gives victory to whom He pleases, *ki ayn la'hawayah ma``'tsor l'hoshi''a b'rav o vim`aT,* " shouted Dawid, "size doesn't matter!"

Eli'av now rushed over. He saw the crowd gathering and when he realized it was around Dawid, anger welled up inside him.

Again! Eli'av had had enough of his younger brother's distorted view of the world. He barked at him, "Who asked you? What are you

366

doing here anyway? Eli'av felt his emotions churning inside of him. Where were these coming from, he asked himself. Why would he be jealous of Dawid? But he knew. He had never had any thoughts of grandeur, but when Sh'mu'el the prophet had come to their home to anoint someone, a new deliverer …

This is silly, he thought to himself. He pushed his thoughts aside. How could he be jealous of that!? Yet when he looked at Dawid and how he inspired the other men, how his very being seemed to bring the others beyond their own petty little worlds, he felt …hatred. He spat in disgust. The boy had been considered a *mamzer* not more than a few months ago, and now ...How could he be the "anointed of the Holy One of Yisrael?"

"Where have you abandoned our too few sheep?" he shouted at his younger brother, "To wander in the wilderness?" Eli'av's intellect told him that these emotional outbursts were unwarranted, but he found himself unable to reign in his bitter feelings. "I know your obstinacy and insolence. Your mischievous heart brought you down here to see the battle? Go home and mind your own business."

Eli'av's jaw tightened. He knew that in his heart he was lacking such simple and strong faith, and he hated his brother for having it. Moreover he hated himself for being lacking, and Dawid over and again for making him aware of its absence and eliciting such horrible emotions. It was Dawid's fault that he had been estranged from his mother all those years. If he had never been born …

367

"*mah?* What?" Dawid was thrown back by his older brother's onslaught. "What have I done now?" he implored. Why was Eli'av always so angry with him? What did he ever do to him?

Dawid turned away from Eli'av and addressed the others. He would not let his brother stifle him this time. It wasn't about him or his relationship with his brother. It was about the insult to the honor of the Holy One.

Dawid's voice was steady. He felt a clarity of purpose. Dawid felt enwrapped in the presence of the Holy One. He said, "This uncircumcised brute curses the Almighty and calls us out to challenge. And we just sit here and tremble at his size, and talk about the earthly reward one will receive if one takes his head?"

Dawid paused, looking, even moving, from warrior to warrior. Then he offered a gentle smile, "Removing this accursed uncircumcised dog from the world and avenging the offense against the Holy One and His Chosen King is more than sufficient reward." He shook his head in disbelief, "How do my brothers restrain themselves from tearing this affront down?"

The crowd was now silent. All eyes were on Dawid, "He says it is of little consequence – whether we are slaves to the P'lisht'im or to King Sha'ul - claiming that the P'lisht'im with their five lords and lack of a king are the bearers of freedom and liberty. We have nothing to lose, he claims."

A chuckle escaped his lips. "Yet, this uncircumcised lout is the slave-dog," Dawid shouted. "He laps at the feet of his ever changing masters. Any desire or urge he greedily devours like a dog on the street."

"The only freedom they have is the freedom from responsibility and purpose. The freedom to indulge their base and animal nature. There is no meaning to their lives, these masters of freedom, freedom from self-restraint, morality and all that is good in the world."

Dawid continued, opening himself, nullifying himself so that the truth of the Holy One could flow through him. "Their liberty is the liberty of vice and decadence, of licentiousness and self-indulgence. They are slaves to their every evil whim; bondsmen to the darkest desires of their soul."

Fear seemed to melt away from the men of Yisrael as Dawid continued, "This giant is no man, but a giant beast. He is not a mountain of flesh, but a molehill of spirit. He who would defy the Living God and would have you cast off the yoke of all that is good and holy, is no more free than a dog leashed to his own petty desires."

Dawid drew a breath, and the crowd seemed to draw it with him, "We... we are the children of Ya`aqov, the offspring of Yisrael. We are not slaves to King Sha'ul, but servants of *his* Master. Our king is not some earthly tyrant who is above the law, but the Almighty's earthly anointed guardian of the law. King Sha'ul is not a despot who makes caprices ordinances and fleeting ephemeral whimsical laws, but rather a faithful servant of the King of Kings Whose laws are eternal, Whose ordinances are the pillars of Truth upon which this world was formed."

"We are Yisrael, the chosen of the Holy One, the bearers of His Light in this confusing world. Those that hate us, that curse and defy us, do so because we are a reminder to the world that there is right and wrong, Good and Evil, and that our choices do bear consequences." Dawid paced before the crowd, "We remind them that they will pay a price for their indulgences, for their insolence. For every man was created in the image of Holiness, and when he profanes that image, when he debases it by acting like this two-legged dog," Dawid spat out the words gesturing towards the valley, "or worse, then he will have to answer to his Maker. Our existence is a testimony to that truth, and it makes him very uncomfortable. Our existence fills him with a blinding rage, for since he cannot destroy the Truth, he turns his anger on its messenger."

"We are Yisrael, the bearers of Truth. When we fulfill our role faithfully, no man, no people, not even the entire world can oppose us, for our king is none other than the Holy One of Blessing Who fights our battles and vanquishes our foes. Our enemies, those who would oppose us are quite simply His enemies."

Dawid paused before adding, "we are Yisrael. Never forget that."

There was uproar in the camp, as Dawid's message was repeated from warrior to warrior. Soon, word reached Sha'ul that there was a man in Yisrael who was ready to face the challenge of the giant.

Escorted, it seemed, by half the army, Dawid was brought before Sha'ul. The King of Yisrael sat on a low stool. A flock of officers and advisors crowded around him. Dawid noticed that their eyes betrayed the same fear that was in most of the other warriors. He was disappointed. Av'ner stood by the king's right side. His angular face was lined with concern and weariness, but Dawid did not detect any fear in his eyes. His hair and beard, speckled with gray, was somewhat unkempt, but his chiseled face spoke of duty and responsibility.

As he approached the king, Dawid noticed Sha'ul's son, Y'honatan. Their eyes met. Y'honatan's face broke into a warm welcoming smile. It lifted Dawid's heart to see him, and he smiled in return. There wasn't any fear in Y'honatan's eyes either.

Dawid bowed before Sha'ul, but his mouth stuck. He didn't know what to say. He had seen Sha'ul in some of his more troubling moments. That was why he had been called to his side originally, to play for him and placate his restless spirit. The king's face was drawn, and his eyes were red-rimmed. It looked as if he hadn't slept in a month. Dawid had seen that before. Yet, now there was something else. It was difficult for Dawid to discern, but it seemed as if the light behind his eyes had dimmed, like a candle struggling to stay lit in the wind.

"*avi*," Dawid said, as much a question, as a greeting of respect.

Sha'ul forced a smile. "*beni*," he began, his voice reflecting the same weariness that was etched on his face, "I understand that you want to answer the challenge of this P'lishti?"

"*ken*, " Dawid said, his enthusiasm returning. He then added more calmly, "*ken, hamelekh,* Yes, sire. Let no one be crestfallen over him. Your servant will go and battle with this P'lishti."

Sha'ul smiled again, but he shook his head. "You aren't able to go out against this P'lishti, to fight with him *beni*," said Sha'ul, "you are still a *na`ar,* a youth. You haven't even married yet." His words trailed off. "They will soon tire of their game and we will battle as an army," he justified, though he didn't believe his statement anymore than his men.

"This one," there was an edge of bitterness to Sha'ul's words, "he's been a man of war since his youth." "He knows how to fight," Sha'ul continued. "Do you know when I first saw him?" he asked Dawid. The memory was bitter now, for Sha'ul couldn't recall his former fortitude. His eyes seemed to almost tear. "He was the one who captured the Aron. He was the one," he repeated, "he was the one."

"Your servant kept his father's sheep," Dawid began to answer the king. His voice was a whisper but it was filled with strength. "When the flock was in my charge, there once came a lion and a bear, and he took a lamb out of the flock." Dawid's eyes locked on the king's drawing the king into his gaze. "I went after it, attacked it and rescued the lamb from out of his mouth."

Sha'ul was transfixed. Behind the story of the lion and the bear, there was something else, something he once knew, some higher meaning, but it escaped him, now.

Dawid continued, his voice almost a hypnotic, "When it turned on me, and rose to attack me, I caught it by the beard, and hit him hard, killing him."

The words hung in the air for a while, before Dawid repeated, "Your servant killed both the lion and the bear, and this uncircumcised P'lishti will suffer the same fate. For he has defied the armies of the living God."

A realization came to Dawid, something that he had never fully comprehended before, though it had always been there in the background. This is what his father had been trying to tell him. Dawid understood that his whole life had been leading to this one moment, and he was in awe. "The Holy One of Yisrael, Who delivered me from the paw of the lion and out of the clutches of the bear will deliver me out of the hand of the P'lishti."

Sha'ul had been drawn into Dawid's narrative. He knew. He was sure that though the story was also factual, it somehow also signified something deeper. Dawid had awakened something his own soul. For a moment, that elusive emotion was re-ignited.

"*lekh*, Go," agreed Sha'ul, caught up in Dawid's own enthusiasm, "*wahawayah yihiyeh `imakh*, and may the Holy One be with you." Sha'ul stood up, and placed his hands on Dawid's shoulders. "Go, and fight for the Holy One's honor."

"Av'ner," Sha'ul turned to his military chief, "Av'ner, have you seen this young man?"

"Yes, your honor," answered Av'ner, "quite impressive." Av'ner noted the renewed fire in his king's eyes. He gave Dawid a nod.

"Bring my armor," commanded the king, "if this young man is going to be our champion, then he should be properly attired."

Dawid was taken aback for a moment, as events carried him away. Several men hurriedly brought the king's armor. One man held the mail breastplate against Dawid's chest while another strap it to the back of the young champion.

Someone then handed Sha'ul his helmet and Sha'ul brought it to Dawid. "Allow me," Sha'ul said to Dawid before placing the helmet on his head. A warrior handed Dawid the king's sword in it its sheath and he girded it around his waist.

Dawid drew the sword and made several passes with it. It was a fine bronze double-edged blade, the shape of an elongated leaf. It gleamed in the late morning sun as Dawid tested it. The young champion noted its balance. It felt good in his hand. He would enjoy removing the P'lishti's head with it.

Dawid took a few steps and stopped. No. He had gotten caught up in this, but something wasn't right. If he battled the P'lishti like this, then he couldn't accomplish his goal. He needed to demonstrate to Yisrael that it wasn't swords and strength that determined the victor. Even if he bested the giant P'lishti, everyone would simply assume that Dawid was the better warrior.

No, there had to be another way. Dawid turned towards Sha'ul and said, "*avi, lo ukhal lalekheth ba_eleeh,* I cannot go in these, for it." Dawid's words stuck in his throat. Would Sha'ul understand? He should. He would've, before the spirit of the Holy One left him, but what about now?

"*ki lo nisithi.* I haven't tested them," Dawid finally said, using the word *nes,* which could be taken to mean either to raise a banner or to try.

Sha'ul's brow furrowed. Something bothered him. Was this young man mocking him, or … the thought was just outside his grasp. Sha'ul opened his mouth to protest, but Av'ner placed a hand on the king's arm. "Let him do it his way," suggested Av'ner. The king looked at his uncle and nodded. Dawid had already begun removing the armor.

Chapter Six

Battle
Valley of Elah

Picking up his staff, Dawid smiled. He looked at Av'ner. Their eyes met and Dawid felt his strength and loyalty. *"yihiyeh hawayah `imakh.* May the Holy One be with you," offered Av'ner. Dawid nodded. Absently, he adjusted his *totafoth*, making sure the helmet hadn't moved them from their place. He turned.

Dawid's eyes caught Y'honatan's and they smiled at each other. It was clear that the son of Sha'ul was filled with love for the son of Yishai. They would meet again.

Dawid turned to the men of Yisrael. His eyes burned with passion. "For the honor of the Holy One," he said. "We are Yisrael. His voice was full of confidence and love of the Almighty. He felt a surge of enthusiasm from the other warriors. Dawid had restored their spirits, though he recognized that it was only momentarily. A lot depended upon the upcoming event of the valley.

A smile creased his lips. Offering a confidant shrug and nod Dawid began his journey towards the valley. The crowd parted as he approached, closing after him when he passed. All of Yisrael followed him. All of Yisrael was with him.

A shudder ran up Sha'ul's spine. Several things began to fall into place: He suddenly remembered Do'eg's recommendation when they sought out a musician ... the references Dawid made. Was he the one that Sh'mu'el had mentioned to him on that day? Is he ...? The king turned to Av'ner, his military chief. "Whose son is that, Av'ner?" he asked, "What's his lineage?"

"_Haiy nafshekha hamelekh_. On the life of your soul, my king if I know," answered Av'ner.

"_If_ he returns," responded Sha'ul, "Inquire as to whose son the young man is." Sha'ul knew that he was from Yehudah, but if he was from the clan of Perets, then that would answer a lot of questions. He trembled at the thought.

Do'eg was standing next to Sha'ul, "You're trying to determine if he's appropriate for kingship, aren't you sire?" He paused, "First determine if he's fit to marry into the congregation of Yisrael."

"What do you mean?" asked Sha'ul.

"His father is Yishai," answered Do'eg, "whose grandmother is Ruth. She comes from Moav. Moav is forbidden from marrying in Yisrael."

"It's taught 'Amoni, not Amonith, Moavi, not Moavith," interjected Av'ner.

"So why isn't it _Mamzer_, and not _mamzereth_ (a female _mamzer_)?" argued Do'eg.

"Because, for *Mamzer*, it's written 'mum – zar,' meaning an outside defects, which also applies to women," answered Av'ner.

Do'eg, persisting in his argument, referred to another verse, "Then why not *Mitsri* and not *Mitsrith* (a female Egyptian)?"

Av'ner considered for a moment. Then he remembered, "Because with Moav, the Scriptures cites a reason why they aren't permitted to enter the congregation: Since they didn't welcome Yisrael with bread and water when we came out of Mitsray'im. It's the custom of men to come out to welcome, not women."

"The men should have come out to greet the men, and the women to greet the women," suggested Do'eg.

The others were confounded by Do'eg's arguments. Av'ner shrugged, for he couldn't answer Do'eg's challenge.

Sha'ul was also puzzled and dazzled by Do'eg's arguments. "Then, we need to make a public declaration concerning him and his family," suggested Sha'ul

"One moment," interrupted `Amasa, who had been listening to the argument. He was Dawid's brother-in-law. "Thus, I received from the court of Sh'mu'el the prophet: Amoni and not Amonith, Moavi and not Moavith. It's a received tradition from Moshe our teacher. There doesn't need to be a reason," he stated with confidence.

"Of course," remembered Av'ner, "how could I forget such a thing?"

Sha'ul also looked both relieved and frustrated. He wasn't sure what he wanted the answer to be. "Then it's settled," answered the king. "He looked at Do'eg, "Excellent dialectic, my son, however. You have a sharp mind."

Do'eg smiled, though he felt chastised all the same.

Turning to Av'ner again, Do'eg repeated the instructions of the king, "If he returns, find out whose son he is." Av'ner scowled. It wasn't Do'eg's place to command him, but he let it go.

The young man, Dawid, the son of Yishai, briskly made his way down the north ridge of the valley. A light breeze caressed his face. A feeling of deep joy filled him. A melody escaped his lips as he went, verses forming from his soul. "Then you spoke in a vision to your loyal one, and you said, 'I have placed my help upon the mighty; I have raised a young man from amongst the nation. I have found My servant Dawid, and with My holy oil I have anointed him. My hand shall support him; even My arm will strengthen him. The enemy shall not deceive him, nor the sons of the injustice afflict him. I will beat down his adversaries before him, and those who hate him, I will strike. My loyalty and kindness is with him, and in My Name, his horn shall be exalted.'"

As Dawid reached a small brook, he bent down. Meticulously he selected five flat stones with a sharp edge. Five, thought Dawid, one for the Name of Holy One of Yisrael, three for the fathers of the people, Abraham, YitsHaq, and Ya`aqov, and one for Aharon the kohen, Moshe's brother who stopped the plague in the camps of Yisrael when they were in the desert. Five stones, one for each of the five books of Moshe, whom this P'lishti cursed. Five, for the aspects of might, restraint, transcending oneself, discipline and fidelity.

Dawid took them, one at a time; one, he placed in his shepherd's bag, the small pouch at his waist, and the other four in the sack that hung across his chest and under his arm. Dawid removed the sling from his knapsack, unwound it, straightening the straps, before rewinding it around his hand. Dawid took a deep breath. "Holy One of Yisrael, this is for Your honor, alone. Please guide my steps, and don't let me fail to exalt Your great Name."

The young champion of the Almighty strengthened himself, and strode out into the valley. That's when I saw him for the first time.

Goliyath and I were both standing there, casually. The P'lishti commander made a point of waiting several hours to give them a chance to meet the challenge. He knew they were watching him, full of fear and self-doubt. Goliyath stretched his body, "Let's go, Uri'yah, they aren't coming again." He laughed, as he had for the last forty days. Then he caught a glimpse of someone coming out into the valley. I saw him too. "What?" he was taken by surprise.

Goliyath turned to meet the challenger, and his surprise increased. Anger and contempt soon followed as he went out to meet the fool.

It wasn't their 'king,' that was for sure. Goliyath remembered his face. The giant was disappointed. He looked at the young man again. They could have at least given him a decent weapon. Goliyath cocked his head to make sure he was seeing correctly, but it looked like some shepherd with his staff searching for his lost sheep. Maybe, this fool stumbled into the battlefield by accident?

"Lose your sheep, boy?" mocked Goliyath, his voice dripping with disdain. He began to approach Dawid. I was a few steps in front of him already. My curiosity was also peaked.

Something told Goliyath that this was really the challenger. I smiled. Goliyath shook his head in disgust. He was a well-built, healthy young man. He was full of vigor, but clearly not a seasoned warrior. Goliyath wondered if he had ever even seen a battle. Why would the `Ivr'im send such a man? It was beyond contempt.

Goliyath released a shout. He noticed the staff, now, and mocked, "Am I a dog, that you come at me with sticks?" Goliyath laughed, but then something caused him to stop. The man standing opposite him was calm. There wasn't any fear emanating from him. Was he insane?

Dawid smiled casually. A dog: not a bad description. Dawid remembered his vision, and steadied himself. He kept himself inside the eye of the hurricane.

I couldn't stop from smiling. I took an immediate liking to this young man. I could barely contain my excitement. Maybe today was the day I had been waiting for.

Goliyath became incensed. The little man's confidence upset him. He should be shaking in his skin, thought Goliyath. The giant commander released a roar. "May all the gods curse you, shepherd," he shouted. May your god become a laughingstock amongst the gods." Goliyath remembered the fate of the Aron he had taken. Disgust filled him as he shouted, "May he be forced to prostrate himself before Dagon and Asherah and all the other gods. May he be a laughingstock in the heavens, and may you be brought to the lowest depths of hell."

Dawid didn't break his stride. He was about two hundred amoth from the giant, but even from that distance, Goliyath saw his smile mocking him. "My God," shouted Dawid in return, "could care less about your curses. Why should anyone pay any heed to the howling of a dog?"

Goliyath was enraged. "Come to me, fool," he shouted, "and I will give your flesh to the birds of the sky and the beasts of the field."

"You come at me with a sword and spear," Dawid raised his voice, filled with the spirit of the Holy One, "but I come to meet you in the name of the Lord of Hosts, the Holy One of the armies of Yisrael who you dare taunt."

Goliyath was amazed at the boldness of this fool. Anger filled him, but a shadow of doubt also began to grow in the corner of his soul.

"Today, the Holy One will deliver you into my hand, and I will kill you, and take your head from you," continued Dawid. He returned the curse back to the P'lishti, "your entire army, the camp of the P'lishti, I will give today to birds of the sky, and to the wild beasts of the field. They will be satiated for a long time, so that the entire world will know that there is a God in Yisrael."

Goliyath stopped. Were his eyes deceiving him? He looked at this *shepherd* who spoke like a man, and for the first time in his life he felt a new sensation. Fear infected his soul.

Dawid continued to close the gap between himself and the giant. "All those assembled here today," he shouted, his voice even carrying to the camp of Yisrael, "will know that the Holy One saves not with sword or spear, for the battle is the Holy One's, and He will give you into my hands today."

Goliyath used his rage to push away the creeping sensation of fear. What had he seen? He was being ridiculous. Goliyath began charging this foolhardy man. He would silence him and the whispers of doubt in his soul with one blow.

When they were about a hundred amoth apart, Dawid quickly unfurled his sling, picking up his stride. He reached into his bag and took out one of the stones he had collected and placed it into the launcher. Drawing his hand down the strap, he began circling his arm over his head. Dawid pushed all of his emotions and thoughts away. He focused on the sling, becoming one with the weapon. He nullified his will before the Will of the Holy One. He became the Almighty's weapon, His tool.

The stone flew from the sling towards Goliyath, who continued to charge the man in blind rage. In the back of his mind, he registered that the missile was directed at him, but he dismissed it, a mere stone.

Even as the stone hit its mark, Goliyath scorned it. As it sank into his brow at the bridge of his nose, he was surprised to find that his legs had stopped moving him forward.

Goliyath sank to his knees with a thud, a look of horror and shock frozen on his face. The stone sank deep into his brain. The last thought Goliyath had, the last emotion, was of total disbelief. The spear fell from the giant's hand as he looked into the eyes of Dawid, who had now reached him, but his vision was clouded over. His mouth opened as if to question, and then he died. Goliyath fell forward at Dawid's feet. Dawid felt the ground tremble under the giant's weight. Goliyath died with barely a gasp.

Dawid whispered a prayer of thanks to the Holy One, *"hodu lahawayah ki tov."* Then he hesitated. He needed a sword to remove the uncircumcised's head. He looked around him for a moment, before spotting Goliyath's sword strapped to his back. He leapt onto the giant to release it from its hilt.

"You'll never get it out of there," I stated. I kept my cool; even though the truth was that I was jumping out of my skin. I knew he hadn't noticed me this entire time.

Dawid pivoted, ready for an attack from me, the shield bearer of the P'lishti. He recognized that I was from Yisrael immediately. I saw it in his eyes. "You're from the tribe of Dan, aren't you?" Dawid's question was as much an accusation.

I simply smiled, and nodded, adding, *"barukh haqadosh barukh hu,* Blessed be the Holy One of Yisrael Who gave you this victory. I've been waiting for years for someone to take his head."

"But," Dawid's question hung in the air.

"A man needs to make a living," I offered half-heartedly, and then added, "it's a long story, but first you need that sword."

"Why can't I get it out of the sheath?" Dawid asked as he struggled to figure out how to liberate the weapon.

I smiled at Dawid. I couldn't help but like him. "It has a special type of lock, to prevent someone like you from stealing it." I waited a beat and then added, "I can open it for you."

"So?"

"For a price," I completed my statement. My voice was calm, but I was worried about how this young man would receive such a statement.

Dawid didn't like this game. "What do you want?" he asked, but something whispered to him, through the holy spirit, and he saw a vision, somehow, of the soul of Shim'shon, the great warrior, superimposed on Uriyah's face. One eye was missing.

"I can't marry in Yisrael," I began, "again, a long story."

"Not so long." commented Dawid. "You're a eunuch," he finished, not even realizing himself that he knew that, until the statement had left his mouth.

"You do have the Holy One whispering in your ear," I mused in amazement. I quickly returned my businesslike demeanor. "I had a dream once, about you removing his head, though I didn't know it was you until today. Several years from now, there will be a woman, who's designated to be your wife. I want to marry her, while she's still a girl, to raise her as a daughter. Then, when she's mature, I'll divorce her and you can take her as is your due."

"Why?" asked Dawid.

"Let's say, I just want a taste of a normal life: of a home and a wife," I confessed. I surprised myself that I revealed so much to him.

Dawid considered for a moment. He didn't have much of a choice, and it didn't seem like such a horrible desire. He wasn't even sure what this man was talking about. Dawid knew what it was like to be an outsider. "Fine," he finally answered.

I rushed over and within moments released the sword. "It's a very special blade," I commented.

"It will be," offered the shepherd. Dawid drew the sword and in one blow severed the head of Goliyath. Well, the lad knows how to use a sword, I surmised. It rolled for a few amoth. Dawid grabbed it by the hair. He lifted it high, raising it towards the heavens. Dawid faced the P'lishti camp. The look of horror frozen on Goliyath's face stared at his countrymen.

The uproar in the P'lishti camp was deafening. "Goliyath is dead!" they screamed in shock, fearing for their own heads. The shock only lasted a moment. From there, it quickly turned into panic. Every one of them began to flee westward. They tried to make their escape along the winding course of the valley.

Dawid turned to face his own people, again lifting the head for them to see. The object of their fear was only flesh and blood. And now, it was dead.

A shout went out from the encampment. Shofars and trumpets sounded. Av'ner gave the command, and all of Yisrael pursued the fleeing P'lisht'im. Like a charging herd of bulls, they descended into the valley, and chased the uncircumcised like a lion after his prey.

The P'lisht'im turned northward to go around `Azaqah, bringing them up onto the road to Sha'ar'im and Beth Shemesh. There, Y'honatan and his forces were waiting for them. Now cut off, the P'lisht'im tried to turn and fight, but were slaughtered wholesale. The remnants again tried to flee, turning westward again, again following the course of the valley, towards the gates of Gath and Eqron. Only a few hundred made it inside the city gates.

When the warriors of Yisrael finished with the slaughter, they returned to their camp. On the way, they plundered the P'lishti encampment.

The celebration was incredible. It was clear to everyone that it was something much more profound than a simple military victory.

Smiling, Dawid entered the encampment, the head of Goliyath in one hand, his bloody sword in the other. Blood was splattered across his tunic. As he entered the fray, many warriors had followed him, including me. I decided to stick close to this *na`ar* from Yehudah. I know when its time to switch sides. Dawid had made good on his threat to

Goliyath's army would become food for the beasts of the field.

As we entered the camp, I heard someone come up behind us. "Dawid!" came a shout, an edge of challenge in its tone.

Dawid turned to see his brother, Eli'av standing defiantly. For a moment, Dawid was dumbfounded.

In the flash of a moment, Eli'av's face broke into a smile, and tears filled his eyes. *"kol hakavod l'kha, aHi haqatan.* To you belongs the honor, little brother," his voice broke with emotion.

Dawid's confusion deepened, but now it was coupled with joy. The two embraced. Dawid realized it was the first time in his life that he hugged his brother. When they parted, their eyes met.

"*aHi.* My brother," Eli'av whispered, "*aHi.*"

Dawid's eyes filled with tears. He was unable to respond.

Av'ner noticed Dawid and went over to him. "Come on, son, let's present you to the king." The two walked to Sha'ul's tent, the head of Goliyath still hanging from Dawid's hand. Sha'ul rose to meet them.

"Dawid," began Av'ner for the king, "whose son are you?"

Smiling, Dawid answered proudly, *"ben 'avdekha yishay beth halaHmi.* I am the son of your servant Yishai, of BethleHem." His heart soared when he declared Yishai his father.

"Which clan?" asked Av'ner.

"Perets," answered Dawid.

"Your father will quite proud of you, son," said Sha'ul, "you sanctified the Name of the Holy One today."

"Thank you, *avi*," Dawid responded, "May your servant continue to merit serving the Holy One and his king."

Sha'ul smiled, "Of course, my son. I plan on keeping you close by my side."

Av'ner placed a hand on Dawid's back. "Let's find a place for your trophies, son," he offered with a smile, taking the head from Dawid and handing it to a warrior nearby. "When we return to Nov, we'll put it near the Mishqan, along with the sword, as a reminder of the miracle the Holy One performed here today."

Dawid nodded, releasing the head and sword to the hands of one of the warriors. For a moment, it felt strange to give them, as if by surrendering the tangible proof, he might not believe what he had just experienced. It had been so overwhelming.

Y'honatan had been standing by his father, waiting patiently, but now his patience ended. He caught Dawid's eye and the two smiled. The two felt a kindred of spirit. Y'honatan interrupted his father, "*avi*, let the man be for a moment. Let's celebrate our victory, Dawid's victory. We can discuss politics and genealogies later."

Y'honatan close the gap between him and Dawid, and the two embraced. Separating, Y'honatan held Dawid at arm's length, measuring him. "We are going to celebrate. And, the guest of honor should be properly attired," he said, removing his robe and placing it around Dawid's shoulders. The king's son then removed his girdle, sword and bow and dressed Dawid in them. "There, our champion." He smiled. Dawid shared in his happiness. I found the scene strange, as if Y'honatan was surrendering more than garments to the son of Yishai. I also caught one of the king's advisors eyeing the scene suspiciously. I think it was Do'eg. I took note but chose to keep my thoughts to myself for now.

Y'honatan took Dawid by the arm and the two went to join the celebration. Sha'ul watched them as they went, admiration in his eyes, but suspicion filling his heart. He had to be very careful with Dawid, he decided. Do'eg caught the king's mood and whispered in his ear. The king's shoulder's relaxed. They had time. This story was far from over.

Appendix

Glossary

Places/Peoples

`Aza – Gaza
B'nei Yisrael – The Children of Israel
Bethle*H*em - Bethlehem
Erets Yisrael/Yisrael – The Land of Israel/Israel
Kna`an – Canaan
Mitsrayim/Mitsri(m) – Egypt/Egyptian(s)
P'lishtim/P'lishti - Philistines
Yehudah – Judah/Judean
Yarden – Jordan
Yerikho – Jericho
Yisrael - Israel

Personalities (selected) and Roles

Avimelekh- the title of the sitting head of the P'lishti Empire, it means, "my father-king."
Dawid – David
Goliyath - Goliath
Kohen – Priest
Kohen Gadol – High Priest
Lewi - Levi
Moshe – Moses
Par`oh – Pharaoh, the title of the king of Egypt
Samu'el – Samael, Satan
Shim'shon – Samson
Sh'mu'el - Samuel
Ya`aqov - Jacob
Yishai - Jesse
Y'hosh'u`ah – Joshua

Measurements

Amah/Amoth – Cubit(s), approximately the distance from the elbow to the tip of the middle finger; also the name of the middle finger. It's modern equivalent range from 43 to 55 centimeters.

A Day's Walk/March – The distance an average man can walk from sunup till sunset. Approximately 48 km.

Beqa – weight measurement. One half of a sheqel

Efah – a measure of capacity, which is equal to three se'ah. There are several difference opinions as to its modern equivalent, which range from 14.5 liters to approximately 25 liters.

Kaneh - Reed. It equals 6 amoth.

Kihar – Weight equivalent to 27 kilograms. 1500 Sheqel is equal to one Kikar.

Tefa_H_/Tefa_H_im – a hand's width, measured on the hand's back. Four tefa_H_oth equal an amah

Sheqel – weight, equal to twenty Gerah, approximately 18 grams.

Zereth – literally the little finger, but translated as a span. It is the distance between the thumb and the little finger. There are differing opinions if it is equivalent to two or three tefa_H_.

Other

Aron HaBrith – Ark of the Covenant

_H_allal – a person found dead, outside municipal boundaries. According to the Torah, the elders of the nearest town must offer an atonement offering if one is found outside their city.

Oth and Totafoth – tefillin, phylacteries

PesaH - Passover

Kinor – a small four stringed musical instrument, played like a harp.

Mamzer – a child of a forbidden union, such as an adulterous or incestuous union.

Miqweh – a ritual bath that removes spiritual impurities.

Mishqan - Tabernacle, the Desert Sanctuary

Mitsnefeth – a headscarf, wrapped around the head, similar to a turban.

Na*H***al** – Desert River bed which fills on occasion with flood waters

Ta*H***ish** – one of the skins used in the construction of the Mishqan. Its translation is disputed.

Tsitsith – ritual fringes tied on the corners of garments with four or more corners.

Yibum – Levirate marriage

` - representing the letter `Ayin, a glottal stop.

dh – representing the aspirated dhaleth. Sound is similar to "th" in "this."

<u>H</u> / H – representing the letter "*H*et," an aspirated "h" originating in the back of the throat.

Kh – representing the letter khaf, similar to "ch" as in the Scottish, "loch."

th - representing the aspirated thaw. Sound is similar to "th" in "both."

Ts – representing the letter tsadi, a dental